Praise for Anne Emery

Praise for *The Keening*
"The intricately developed story may appeal to fans of Cora Harrison's 'Burren' mysteries."   — *Library Journal*

"A rich and rewarding book, it arouses our sympathies for the long, painful history of the Irish within an engrossing mystery."   — Historical Novel Society

"Halifax author Anne Emery has superbly blended two fascinating storylines in *The Keening*, a splendid murder mystery with characters you wish you knew."
— *Winnipeg Free Press*

Praise for *Postmark Berlin*
"Emery has twice won the Arthur Ellis Award (both for earlier installments in this series), and readers who have not yet sampled her tough-edged crime fiction are advised to rectify that immediately. A fine entry in a consistently strong series."
— *Booklist*

"As in the earlier novels, this one relies on two particular strengths — immaculate research and moral worthiness — and along the way, it slides expertly around a whole slew of narrative conundrums."   — *Toronto Star*

Praise for *Though the Heavens Fall*
"Emery populates 1995 Belfast so conscientiously and evokes its atmosphere so faithfully . . ."   — *Kirkus Reviews*

"Anyone looking for a mystery series to read would be well advised to consider the Collins-Burke mystery series by Anne Emery . . . Filled with lots of suspense, a good plot and some history, *Though the Heavens Fall* is another excellent novel in this entertaining series!"   — *Hamilton Spectator*

"*Though the Heavens Fall* keeps us on our toes until the bitter end. And based on that ending, the sequel will be a must-read too."   — *Atlantic Books Today*

Praise for *Lament for Bonnie*

"The author's ability to say more with less invites readers along for the dark ride, and the island's Celtic culture serves as a stage to both the story's soaring narrative arc and a quirky cast of characters, providing a glimpse into the Atlantic Canadian communities settled by Scots over two hundred years ago." — *Celtic Life*

"The novel is ingeniously plotted." — Reviewing the Evidence

Praise for *Ruined Abbey*

"True to the Irish tradition of great storytelling, this is a mesmerizing tale full of twists that will keep readers riveted from the first page to the last." — *Publishers Weekly*, starred review

"This is a really tightly plotted historical with solid characters and the elegant style we expect from Emery." — *Globe and Mail*

"Suspenseful to the final page." — *Winnipeg Free Press*

Praise for *Blood on a Saint*

"As intelligent as it is entertaining . . . The writing bustles with energy, and with smart, wry dialogue and astute observations about crime and religion." — *Ellery Queen*

"Emery skilfully blends homicide with wit, music, theology, and quirky characters." — *Kirkus Reviews*

Praise for *Death at Christy Burke's*

"Emery's sixth mystery (after 2010's *Children in the Morning*) makes excellent use of its early 1990s Dublin setting and the period's endemic violence between Protestants and Catholics." — *Publishers Weekly*, starred review

"Halifax lawyer Anne Emery's terrific series featuring lawyer Monty Collins and priest Brennan Burke gets better with every book." — *Globe and Mail*

Praise for *Children in the Morning*

"This [fifth] Monty Collins book by Halifax lawyer Emery is the best of the series. It has a solid plot, good characters, and a very strange child who has visions." — *Globe and Mail*

"Not since Robert K. Tanenbaum's Lucy Karp, a young woman who talks with saints, have we seen a more poignant rendering of a female child with unusual powers."
— *Library Journal*

Praise for *Cecilian Vespers*
"Slick, smart, and populated with lively characters." — *Globe and Mail*

"This remarkable mystery is flawlessly composed, intricately plotted, and will have readers hooked to the very last page." — *The Chronicle Herald*

Praise for *Barrington Street Blues*
"Anne Emery has given readers so much to feast upon . . . The core of characters, common to all three of her novels, has become almost as important to the reader as the plots. She is becoming known for her complexity and subtlety in her story construction." — *The Chronicle Herald*

Praise for *Obit*
"Emery tops her vivid story of past political intrigue that could destroy the present with a surprising conclusion." — *Publishers Weekly*

"Strong characters and a vivid depiction of Irish American family life make Emery's second mystery as outstanding as her first." — *Library Journal*, starred review

Praise for *Sign of the Cross*
"A complex, multilayered mystery that goes far beyond what you'd expect from a first-time novelist." — *Quill & Quire*

"Snappy dialogue, a terrific feel for Halifax, characters you really do care about, and a great plot make this one a keeper." — *Waterloo Region Record*

"Anne Emery has produced a stunning first novel that is at once a mystery, a thriller, and a love story. *Sign of the Cross* is well written, exciting, and unforgettable." — *The Chronicle Herald*

FENIAN STREET

The Collins-Burke Mystery Series

FENIAN STREET

A Mystery

ANNE EMERY

Copyright © Anne Emery, 2022

Published by ECW Press
665 Gerrard Street East, Toronto, ON M4M 1Y2
416-694-3348 / info@ecwpress.com

All rights reserved. No part of this publication may be
reproduced, stored in a retrieval system, or transmitted
in any form by any process — electronic, mechanical,
photocopying, recording, or otherwise — without the prior
written permission of the copyright owners and ECW Press.
The scanning, uploading, and distribution of this book via
the Internet or via any other means without the permission of
the publisher is illegal and punishable by law. Please purchase
only authorized electronic editions, and do not participate in
or encourage electronic piracy of copyrighted materials. Your
support of the author's rights is appreciated.

This is a work of fiction. Names, characters, places, and
incidents either are the product of the author's imagination or
are used fictitiously, and any resemblance to actual persons,
living or dead, business establishments, events, or locales is
entirely coincidental.

Cover and text design: Tania Craan
Author photo: Mick Quinn / mqphoto.com

LIBRARY AND ARCHIVES CANADA CATALOGUING IN
PUBLICATION

Title: Fenian Street : a mystery / Anne Emery.

Names: Emery, Anne, author.

Series: Emery, Anne. Collins-Burke mystery
series ; 12.

Description: Series statement: Collins-Burke
mystery series ; 12

Identifiers: Canadiana (print) 20220227705 |
Canadiana (ebook) 20220227721

ISBN 978-1-77041-388-7 (softcover)
ISBN 978-1-77305-981-5 (ePub)
ISBN 978-1-77305-982-2 (PDF)
ISBN 978-1-77305-983-9 (Kindle)

Classification: LCC PS8609.M47 F46 2022 |
DDC C813/.6—dc23

We acknowledge the support of the Canada Council for the Arts. *Nous remercions le Conseil des arts du Canada
de son soutien.* This book is funded in part by the Government of Canada. *Ce livre est financé en partie par le
gouvernement du Canada.* We acknowledge the support of the Ontario Arts Council (OAC), an agency of the
Government of Ontario, which last year funded 1,965 individual artists and 1,152 organizations in 197 communities
across Ontario for a total of $51.9 million. We also acknowledge the support of the Government of Ontario
through the Ontario Book Publishing Tax Credit, and through Ontario Creates.

PRINTED AND BOUND IN CANADA

PRINTING: MARQUIS   5   4   3   2   1

MIX
Paper from
responsible sources
FSC® C103567

MICK QUINN / MQPHOTO.COM

Corporation Flats, Fenian Street, Dublin.

PROLOGUE

Shay Rynne

I had two godfathers when I was growing up: one who put people in prisons and one who had spent time in them. Maybe that explains where I've been and where I am today. One of my godfathers was Garda Detective Sergeant Colm Griffith, from County Clare. He is class. He is everything a policeman should be. My own father was Thomas "Talkie" Rynne, who got his nickname because, as a little lad, he never shut his gob. His da used to say, "Would you ever be giving our ears a rest? If I wanted to hear somebody talking world without end, I'd take myself off to the talkies." The pictures, he meant. When my grandda first started going to the films, they were silent. Then they got sound and were the talkies. So anyway, my father, Talkie Rynne, got into trouble with the law, when he lost the head and caused injury to a fella who had slandered him while a crowd of them were in their local, skulling pints. The man had been blackguarding Talkie about being out of work and on the dole — again — and maybe he'd soon be putting the wife out on the street to earn a few quid for the

Leabharlanna Poiblí Chathair Baile Átha Cliath
Dublin City Public Libraries

children's breakfast. Detective Sergeant Griffith made the arrest. He took Da's rambling, disjointed statement, and when the case went to court, Griffith went easy on the evidence. He knew he couldn't get up on the witness stand and tell the entire story. These are the things a Garda sergeant could not say in court:

> Your Lordship, this man, Talkie Rynne, served time in a prison camp — internment camp — during the Emergency of 1939 to 1945 and came out a different man from the man he was when he went in. He was never the same again. And that's because he was subjected to a level of brutality that a man does not easily — does not ever — get over. He was flogged by the prison authorities, Your Lordship. Whipped! Had he fallen into the hands of the Nazis? Or some other violent faction in a distant land? No, he suffered this torture one county over from us, in a prison camp in County Kildare. In the Curragh internment camp, Mr. Rynne was known as something of a comical card, a teller of tale tales, which you might guess from his nickname. A grand fella to have at the table of an evening. After the flogging, it was a rare occasion indeed that Talkie Rynne was a grand fella at the table.

DS Griffith could not be a member of the Garda Síochána and get up and say that stuff in court, as if he was a social worker. Or a defence barrister. Even though all of it was true about my father. Even though, like so many of the other IRA men who were kept in the Curragh camp — the lads called it Tin Town — he could barely function when he was released, could barely function in the everyday life the rest of us take for granted. Applying for work, signing on for the dole, even crossing the street in all the traffic, those things were overwhelming. So the detective did the next best thing for a man who had suffered badly and who was still bearing the consequences, a man with five children in a tenement flat. I was the first of those children, born a couple of years after the Emergency, known beyond the borders of neutral Ireland as the Second World War.

Colm Griffith gave his evidence truthfully: yes, Mr. Rynne had given a few digs to his opponent that night in the pub, after much provocation. But Colm made no mention of some other scrapes Talkie had got himself into in those years. So instead of being sent away for up to three years, he was sentenced to six months. And while Da was away from us, Colm came up with a little job for the oldest of the Rynne boys — that being myself — to work at after school and so bring some much-needed punts and shillings into the house. I was a messenger boy for some of the local businesses. Colm found me a second-hand bicycle and had a nephew of his fix it up and paint it. Colm checked in every so often to see how we were doing. How many coppers would do that? And there was no side to him, no angle, nothing for him in return. Just a good, conscientious man.

He stayed with me, in my mind, even on those occasions when I ran wild with the other lads from Fenian Street and engaged in the sort of behaviour that could have got me arrested. And nearly did. That happened when there was a crowd in from Galway for the All-Ireland final. The Gaelic football. Galway were playing Meath at Croke Park. Me and my pals didn't go to Croker for the match, but we made the rounds of the northside bars, having a few pints and enjoying the craic. Well, Galway won the match, and the spectators spilled out from Croker in the thousands. And a crowd of them came into the bar we were in and they had drink on them and they were cheering and boasting about their win. Fair play to them, who wouldn't? But soon it became "Sure, we've won it loads of times since the last time *Dublin* did." And my crowd argued back, and the Galway lads started black-guarding Dublin, laughing and mimicking our speech.

And I says to them, "Oh, are we sayin' this right then? Baa, baa, ye shower of sheep-shaggers!" And it was the fellas from Galway that threw the first punches. But when the guards arrived, every one of the guards a culchie — a country lad — they blamed us Dublin fellas. And the guards dragged me and three of my pals over to the Garda cars, and we thought they were going to arrest us and throw us in the nick.

But they meted out our punishment there in the street: gave us all a thumping. One of them belted me in the face and broke a back tooth and I was spitting up blood. "Yeh broke my fuckin' tooth, yeh savage!" And he says to me, "How about I break yer bollocks!" And he tried to kick me between the legs, but I dropped to my knees and he got me in the stomach, and it was such a vicious kick that I heaved my guts out there on the pavement. And I never forgot the pain of it.

Now, after an experience like that, I could have gone one of two ways: become a typical corner boy with a hate-on for the guards, or try to put some manners on the guards by becoming one myself and encouraging other lads from the Dublin slums to join up and have our city fairly represented on the police force. That's when the idea took hold in me. And the notion wouldn't go away, the image in my mind of Seamus "Shay" Rynne from Dublin city in the uniform of a Guardian of the Peace!

☙

My other godfather was a man who was interned in the Curragh with my father when the flogging was done on him. Finn Burke was renowned as a publican and a republican. He was strong in his belief that it was long past time that the British got out of Ireland after nearly eight hundred years of occupation. Sure, the War of Independence had got them out of the twenty-six counties of southern Ireland, but the treaty of 1921 left six northern counties in British hands. And there was no sign of them letting go their grip. So a number of republicans, my da included, stepped up their activities against England during the Emergency of 1939 to 1945. The campaign was carried out in England, but the weapons training and other preparations were done in Ireland. The members of the Irish government turned on their old comrades. They brought in internment without trial and harsh punishments for those who committed the same kind of offences the members of government themselves used to do. And there was a double standard at play: when Irish republicans were sentenced to hang in the North or in England, our government here called for clemency. But at home in Ireland, the press was heavily censored in any attempts to protest the death sentences handed down by the Irish government itself. The newspapers were ordered to use the word "murder" for the crime if it was committed here, while the offences elsewhere were to be called "killings."

Finn Burke was in the Curragh when my father was put under the whip. Finn never told me what punishments he himself was subjected to in there. Whatever the case, Finn came out with his republican credentials intact. Strengthened, in fact. After all, how much sense did it make that the forces of law and order were at times more brutal than the criminals or internees they had to deal with? Lock a man up, sure. But flogging him? Beating, torturing, or hanging him? Let's not give in to our worst, most barbaric instincts and subject him to torture. Finn Burke, like Colm Griffith, made a point of assisting the Rynne family when the father of the family was unable to provide for us, either because he was rendered incapable by drink or was in the nick.

Now, when I say I am strongly sympathetic to the republican ideal of a united Ireland without the Brits in control anywhere, and that I was inspired by Detective Sergeant Griffith to think about becoming a guard — and when I speak so highly of the two men who were so important in my life — that might create the impression that I am a man readily influenced by others, easily led. But that leaves out of account the lads I grew up with in the tenements in Fenian Street. Sure, I engaged in some "anti-social" activity in my early teen years — and not only in those early years — and made a show of myself with too much drink on board, got into scraps, robbed a few items from the shops. But then I abandoned that life of petty crime and made my application to join the police force. An Garda Síochána. That showed some independent thinking on my part, and it wasn't an easy matter to maintain my independence in the face of all the slagging and hostility I faced from my old mates in the tenement flats. Worst thing you could be, next to a tout — an informer — was a peeler. A cop.

PART ONE

CHAPTER I

Shay Rynne was determined to join the Garda, and what happened to Rosaleen McGinn had a lot to do with it. Rosaleen was a girl from the Corpo flats, built by the Dublin Corporation for the likes of the Rynnes and other families that wouldn't ever be able to buy a place of their own. The McGinns lived just a few doors down from the Rynnes. Rosaleen was four years older than Shay, and he'd had a crush on her from the time he was eleven years old. She had black curls and dark freckles and bright blue eyes. The same colouring as Shay himself, except the blue of his eyes was a bit darker and he didn't have the freckles. But they looked smashing on her. The only one who ever called her Rosaleen was her old gran; everybody else called her Rosie.

Even despite the age difference, she would come out and watch while the boys played football on a patch of waste ground near the flats. Some of those times, Alice Cotter would come with her. The Cotter family lived next door to the McGinns. Alice was in the girls' school, same year as Shay. Everybody called her Allie. She was at the top of her class, but there was mischief in her as well. She once showed him a set of lock picks she'd taken from one of her cousins, and she demonstrated for Shay how to pick a lock. But, she assured him, she only ever broke into the flats of people who tried to act superior. Like oul Mrs. Bolger, who got a parcel of fine new clothes for her daughter, a parcel from a niece in America, and hung the clothes out at the edge of her balcony, not to dry them but to display them for all to see. Allie picked her lock one night when the family was out, put one of the dresses on Mrs. Bolger's little statue of the Virgin Mary, and painted the Virgin's face with gaudy makeup. That was one of the many times she had the Fenian Street kids laughing.

The funniest thing was when her and Rosie would come to watch the football and they'd put on an act like the cheerleaders Rosie had seen in American films. Rosie and Allie would jump up and down and wave bunches of leaves like the things the American girls waved at the players. And Allie would shout out foolish rhymes like, "Go, Shay Rynne! Almost got it in! Stuff it in the net, lad, not the feckin' bin!" That was because one time Shay, well, he stole a ball from some of the boys at another school, and he thought they were coming for him and he stuffed the ball in the nearest rubbish bin. Even when he was the butt of their jokes, it was great gas when Rosie and Allie came to the matches.

Rosie worked part-time after school in Dixon's shop. Sometimes she'd come with a couple of bags of Tayto crisps and a bottle or two of ginger ale to pass around to the young fellas in the neighbourhood. Her working in Dixon's earned Shay his first beating upon arrest. He didn't know Rosie was working that day, honest to God; he thought it was old Dixon himself alone in the shop, and him half-deaf in his old age. So Shay was out doing messages for his mam and da, and stopped in at Dixon's to get them their copy of the *Irish Press*. And he saw the old man bent over behind the counter. Dixon couldn't see Shay, and he could hardly hear, so Shay grabbed a bag of iced caramels and then a bag of liquorice allsorts and stuffed them inside his gansey, and went up and paid for the newspaper. And didn't Rosie come out from the little storeroom behind the counter and stare the thief down with those sharp blue eyes. Was she a mind reader? Or had she heard the bags rattling as he shoved them out of sight? He started backing himself out of the shop, and she came for him. He got outside and turned to run, and she shouted, "Stop right there, you little gurrier, or you'll never set heel nor toe in this shop again!" He knew she meant it.

He stopped and knew he was in for it. She grabbed the edge of his gansey and the bags fell out. Then she snatched the newspaper out of his hand, rolled it up, and belted him across the arse with it. "Next time you see me coming, you'll not have your hand out for a bag of crisps. Nothing for you for a month, do you hear me?"

He was caught; he was guilty. There were no excuses he could make. All he could say was "Yes, Rosie. I'm sorry, Rosie. I won't do it again."

"You're feckin' right you won't." She handed the paper back to him and said, "Now be off with you."

By this time, oul Dixon was coming towards the door, saying, "Who's that? Who's that?"

And Rosie, bless her, said, "I don't know, Mr. Dixon, but he'll not be bothering us again." She didn't give Shay up.

Neither of them mentioned the incident again, and he never reoffended. At least, not at Dixon's.

Her generosity was on display in later years when Shay was well into his teens. Rosie had a part-time job that was even better than working in Dixon's. Shay couldn't believe his ears when one of the lads in the flats gave him and the other boys the news. "Did yis hear where Rosie's workin' now?"

"No, where?"

"Goss's Hotel."

"Oh, good on her, then. What's she doing at the hotel, cleaning the rooms and like that?"

"Better. She works on the desk at night. Have yis ever been in there?"

Shay set him straight. "I only stay in hotels when I travel to Paris and Spain, you eejit."

"Oh, right. Well, the way the place is set up — it's small, like — the desk is near to the lobby or the parlour or whatever they call it.

And fellas drink there, as well as in the bar itself. Waiters bring them their drinks while they're sitting around gabbing or having meetings."

"Right."

"So anyway, Danny" — that was Rosie's brother — "said she brought home half a bottle of wine the other night. Red stuff. It was brilliant, after you got a taste for it. What happens is these fellas in the lobby, they order a whole bottle for themselves, or more than one, and sometimes they don't finish it all. So Rosie sees that, and if the coast is clear, she cleans the bottles and glasses off the table. Being helpful, like. And if there's wine left in any of the bottles, she stuffs the cork back in and sneaks it out home at the end of her shift. That's how she handed it over to me and Danny the other night."

"Deadly!"

"Yeah, stay tuned, and yeh might get in on it."

A few weeks went by after that before Shay got in on it. He was messing around with Danny and a couple of the other lads out in the street after tea, and Rosie walked by and greeted them and listened to their blather for a while. Shay was able to look at her now without his face flushing a bright red. By that time, she was walking out with a fella from the Moss Street flats. Shay didn't begrudge him. He knew there was no hope for himself, him being not yet eighteen years old and in his last year of school, and her being a grown-up of nearly twenty-two. In fact, Shay had walked out with a few girls himself by then. Anyway, on this day she said, "May I take your orders, gentlemen?" And Shay would not like to repeat what some of the boys said to her, thinking they were Oscar Wilde or the other fella who was such a wit. Who was it? The man in the church over in the Liberties. Jonathan Swift, that was it. Shay had him in school. But Rosie let all that run off her back, and she went home and came out again with two bottles of wine she'd smuggled out of the hotel the night before. One of them was white and nearly full. The other was red, half-full. "Oh, where are my manners?" she said. "I've no crystal glasses for yis."

"Sure, you're grand, Rosie," one of the boys said. "We've loads of crystal at home, me ma has. Tired of it, yeh know?"

All were agreed that they'd be fine without the crystal glasses. And they were. They passed the bottles around and it worked on them like laughing gas. They had a grand couple of hours being half-locked and foolish.

But it wasn't all mischief and breaches of the Intoxicating Liquor Act. One time there was a series of hurling matches for young fellas, to be held on the pitch of one of the, well, snootier boys' schools. The ones that were more posh than the one Shay attended. And the organizers were meeting in Goss's Hotel, and Rosie got herself into the conversation, no doubt charming some of the men in charge of the event, and got them to invite a raggle-taggle crowd of lads from Fenian Street and the neighbourhood to have some time on the pitch between organized matches. The sliotar and hurleys would be provided. "And yis better not be acting the maggot out there," she warned, "or yer days as back-garden wine snobs will be over and done."

The boys didn't act the maggot, but they didn't distinguish themselves as hurlers, either. Some of them had never held a hurley in their hands before, let alone become familiar with the skills and rules of the game. And, of course, they had to put up with slagging from their "betters," some of the boys from the good schools — you know, the types with all the good manners who wouldn't behave like that. Except they did. But the managers of the tournament did their best to settle them down, and to keep the Fenian Street boys from running at them and putting the frighteners on them. It was a good day out.

So that was Rosie. The boys from the flats would have ripped the face off anybody who so much as looked at her the wrong way. Except none of them were present at Goss's Hotel the night of March 8, 1969.

တ

The first Shay heard about the night at Goss's, he was having a cup of tea and a smoke in Mamie's Tea Room, just around the corner from his family's flat. Mamie had been catering for local tea drinkers for years; her family ran the grocer's next door. Her regular customers were tea drinkers, coffee drinkers, and alco drinkers who had to be content with tea laced with as much sugar as could fit into a cup and still leave the appearance of a liquid. A regular crop of oul fellas patronized Mamie's every morning until the pubs opened. Shay had always liked the place. So there he was, and the talk was all about the snow, or the few little flakes of it falling from the Dublin sky. Somebody said they should all go out and make snowballs, and that brought up a story somebody had read in the news around Christmastime. The story was a look back to the visit by the Taoiseach — the prime minister of the Republic of Ireland — to Belfast in 1967 to meet the prime minister of Northern Ireland. The Taoiseach, Jack Lynch, was in his car when a preacher by the name of Ian Paisley and a crowd of his pals began throwing snowballs at Jack's car. And they were shouting, "No Pope here!" Jack — bless him for his humour — said to a man accompanying him, "Which one of us does he think is the Pope?"

So that was the talk in Mamie's until Tina Moore came flying in with her news.

Tina was an old classmate of Shay's little sister Francie. They were together in high babies and all the way up the school years. She shouted to the room at large. "Did yis hear that the peelers are all over Goss's Hotel?"

"What are they doing there?" Shay asked.

But Tina was going to tell the story her way. "Yer man was playing there, Mackey Walsh — him and his band! I was on my way home from Jeanie's place and I passed by Goss's and I heard them playing. Liberties Taken were invited to play for a hooley at the hotel for some political fellas, politicians, from here and in from the country."

It should be obvious from their name that the members of the band were from the Liberties, another working-class area of Dublin.

"And they were rocking the place down! Louder and a heavier, you know, beat than they usually have."

The choice of music was a departure from what you might have expected at a gathering of political types, especially if they weren't from the city. You'd have expected a harp, a fiddle, a bodhran, a session of traditional music. Or maybe a show band kitted out in suits and ties. But the politicians were obviously in tune with the times, or wanted to look it, if they were rocking to the sounds of Liberties Taken.

"So," Shay said, wanting to find out what she meant about the peelers. But an interruption came from behind him. A girl called Tracy.

"Have they not just returned from playing in London? The band, I mean?"

Somebody else piped up. "They have! And somebody said George Harrison was there to hear them!"

"Ah, go on with yeh," somebody said.

"Sure, he's only gorgeous, is Mackey," Tracy exclaimed. "You have all the luck, you being there, Tina!"

"Somebody was havin' luck, the way I heard it, or at least havin' a few cans on the house. It was party time up in the rooms after the lads were finished playing downstairs. The political fellas and Mackey and the others in the band, I don't know who all else was there. But I did hear they brought in a couple of the girls from the canal."

"Jaysus," said Tracy, "I should have gone to work on the canal after all! And if I got to be between the sheets with any of the boys in the band, I wouldn't even charge them for my time and skills! And you right there, you lucky cow!"

"But I wasn't really there, just peering in through the window while the band was playing in the big room on the main floor. But the sound came through. Mackey sang that song he has about Stephen's Green, the one that was on the charts last summer. I had to get home. I told my ma I wouldn't be late. But I knew if I got the chance I'd walk over again and watch some more." She leaned towards her listeners. "But come here to me! By the time Ma fell asleep and I could sneak out and back to Goss's, it was all hell broke loose. The guards were all over the back garden of the hotel, and they had the place roped off. There were fellas standing around, like, and somebody said there was a dead body in there!"

First thing next morning, word was out. Shay was leaving the flat when one of the neighbours gave him the news: it was Rosie McGinn lying at the foot of the back staircase of Goss's Hotel. And the rumour was that somebody had thrown her down the stairs. A terrible image formed in Shay's mind, of Rosie's lovely face smashed and bloody, the lips that so often formed a playful smile now gaping in her last instant of horror. Shay turned and ran back into his flat, into the jacks, where he bent over and heaved up the contents of his stomach. He heard his mother knocking on the door, asking what was wrong. When he came out, he told her, and had to help her to her chair. She didn't speak but kept shaking her head as if to deny what she wished she had never heard.

And if this tore the hearts out of Shay and the other lads and girls that had known Rosie, it was impossible to imagine what it was like for her mam and da, her sisters and brothers, at the funeral in Saint Andrew's church. It was a big church near the Pearse train station, and Shay and his family could hardly find a place to sit, it was so jammed. The funeral had to be delayed for several days because of the investigation. The investigation that went nowhere. You know your parents love you. Even a little child knows that. And you know it when you're bigger, even when you're having a row with your oul fella or the ma, and you're telling them to go to the divil. You know *parents love their children, no matter what.* But it takes being a parent to really understand it. Or it takes seeing a mother walking in to the funeral for her child. Shay had never seen anyone of any age so entirely devastated. Mrs. McGinn's eyes were red and puffy, her face streaked with tears. Ravaged with grief. She was a woman absolutely destroyed. Rosie's father tried to hold up, keep his wife going, and you knew that without his arm, she could not stand. But you could tell it was just as terrible for him, and him determined to look strong for the rest of them. Rosie's sisters were weeping, and her oldest brother, Danny, turned around; you could see the fury in his eyes. The crowd of younger fellas who were her pals felt the same fucking way.

Shay's mother, Deirdre, was beside him and she leaned towards him and said, sounding like one of the old Druids, "Life is short. Do not be taking it for granted." How true that was. When the funeral was done, Shay made a vow to Rosie's father that when he got into the Garda — which he was now set on doing, and he made a silent apology to Detective Sergeant Griffith for the years of delay — he would find the killer and have him in chains.

ↄ

One thing Shay knew well before he applied to the Garda Síochána: if they let him in at all, he would stick out like a Proddy who'd got on the wrong bus and ended up at the Knock Shrine, for the simple reason that he, Shay, was a Dub. Why would a Dublin man stand out as an oddball in his own city, a city of more than seven hundred thousand Dubliners? Because nearly all the guards were fellas in from the country. And a few women as well. The police working right here in Dublin regarded the local lads as a bunch of criminals. It wouldn't help in Shay's case that members of his own family — one of his brothers, a couple of uncles, and, most notable of all, his father — had form for criminal activity. All this information, on file with the Gardaí, would not make for a promising start to his career.

He knew there would be nothing gained by trying to prove to them what a bright spark he was, what a good student he had been in spite of the poverty of his upbringing. He had completed his schooling, hadn't dropped out like so many of the other lads. And he hadn't done badly at all; he'd done well enough to be admitted to University College Dublin for a year. But that came later; for the first couple of years after leaving school, he went out to work. You can't earn a wage packet if you're in classes all day and studying at night. And he needed the money. His ma needed the money for the younger kids. He thought about joining up with the Garda, but instead he pissed around and did a lot of underage drinking and chased girls and did odd jobs that never lasted for more than a few months at a time. But he always had a few punts and pence for the ma and the younger kids. Then he got a job that gave him a new interest in life: books. And the kind of girls that read them.

ↄ

You wouldn't think that a job as a night watchman on building sites would have anything to do with books or girls. But this was how it went. There was a lot of building going on in Dublin city, particularly new housing estates, after the collapse of some of the tenements on Shay's own street in 1963. Two houses crumbled on Fenian Street, and two little girls died as a result. That was only days after an old couple were killed by a house falling down on Bolton Street. So the drive was on for safe housing. Much of the new stuff that was built, it had to be said, could never be called beautiful housing. Big high slabs, many of them were. Shay was hired as one of the watchmen for a succession of building sites on the north side of the city.

Usually he travelled to work on his bicycle from his family's flat. But when the weather was bad, or he was tired or hungover, he took the bus. And depending on which bus he hopped onto in the mornings to return home, he sometimes struck it lucky. There would be a crowd of students on their way to classes at Trinity College in the city centre. And some of the students were girls. One particular day, he saw a foolish-looking young fella who had two smashing birds — lovely girls — enthralled with him, not because of his looks but because of his comical conversation. From what Shay could make out, one of the girls had to write a paper for a course at the uni, and her subject was humour. Irish humour. Could be a long fecking paper, that! So this fella on the bus was in his glory, saying, "You *must* read Wilde. And, of course, James Joyce. Some of Joyce's lines will have you wetting yourselves laughing." And there were other names, but Shay didn't remember them. Then it was "Flann O'Brien." He thought he heard "Gobble-een" but figured he must have had that wrong. "And don't forget old Swift; you'll find him entombed in Saint Patrick's, but his wit lives on." Or something like that, he said. There was a screech of laughter and Shay turned around, and those two girls were enjoying whatever comedy that little gossoon was giving them. And Shay said to himself, There's something in that for me.

When he got home that night, he wrote down the names he remembered and decided to make his first — first as a grown-up — visit to a library. But would they just let you in if you arrived by yourself? Did you need a — he didn't know — a mother or a chaperone or a teacher? Well, he'd brazen it out. The next day he got up, gave himself a thorough wash from head to heel, put on trousers and a shirt that were clean and pressed, and made the short walk from Fenian Street to the Pearse Street Library. It was a big lordly looking place made of stone with rows of round-topped windows. He'd been walking past it all his life but had only been inside on a couple of school visits. Well, here he was again.

He went in and walked up to one of the librarians sitting at a desk and asked her where he could find books by Flann O'Brien.

She said, "Of course, of course. Brian O'Nolan. Myles na gCopaleen!"

What? But he didn't say anything. She got up and led him to shelves full of books by Irish writers, and told him that if he needed any help, he had only to ask. He thanked her and began pulling out books and looking them over. And he had a laugh, at nobody but himself, when he saw that Flann O'Brien, Brian O'Nolan, and Myles na gCopaleen were all names for the same man. Obviously a larger-than-life character, if he needed all those different names. Shay memorized what shelf they were on and then wandered through some of the other collections. And it was when he ended up by the history shelves that he was well and truly gobsmacked. There were hundreds of fecking books on history. On Irish history alone, and some were about when the English took over the country hundreds of years ago, and all the efforts the Irish had made to be rid of them. The Rising of 1916, the Troubles of 1919 to 1921, and all the bother after that, especially up above. In the North.

He figured it would take some neck to ask for a borrowing card after wandering in off the street, but he decided to chance it. And it was no trouble at all. So that was the beginning for Shay Rynne the bookworm. In the beginning, it was just that if he ever worked up the nerve to chat up any of those girls on the bus, and they knew all this stuff, he didn't want to sound like a thick, an eejit who'd never cracked the spine of a book in his life. But once he got into it, especially the history, he loved it. For its own sake. And the history of other countries, too. Like France and Germany. And there were books about the class system. Higher classes lording it over and looking down their pointy noses at the lower ones. Shay trailed his hand along the spines of some of these and then let it fall. He already knew all about that.

He never told his mates, never let on when they were having a few scoops in Moroney's, or kicking a ball around on the football pitch, but he continued making trips to Pearse Street when he wasn't too shattered during the daytime after working nights on the building sites. Books that were about history or that had great writing in them, like Frank O'Connor's short stories — his favourite was "First Confession" — gave him a whole new outlook on the world. And he had some limited successes when he finally got up the nerve to chat up the girls on the bus, though he brought laughter upon himself when he tried out his new vocabulary on one of them — he wanted to get the impressive-sounding word "salubrious" into the conversation, and the girl and her pals went into gales of laughter and insisted that it meant scuttered with drink (that's not what it means, and Shay figured they knew it). They claimed that it comes from the Latin "he's well lubricated" (no, it doesn't) and that Shay was being "lubricious" to mention it in polite company (he was not). Even he had to laugh about it all. Anyway, it went well otherwise. His efforts won him a Trinity girl, for a while, until she threw him over for a fella studying to be a doctor.

But Shay was not the only one with ambitions. That was something he had in common with Allie Cotter. They had that in common, but they also shared many of the same interests. Books, music, sport, and — very important to him — a sense of humour, a sense of the absurd. Allie was the only one to whom he'd confessed his growing interest in literature. He hadn't confessed his hopes that this would give him a leg up, so to speak, with the girls on the bus. He didn't like to think of how she'd laugh at his pretensions in that respect. But somebody else had a laugh over his Trinity girl phase, and that somebody was Rosie McGinn, this being a few years before she was killed.

"Have yeh had enough of ridin' the bus and the girls you meet on it?"

"Wha'? How do yeh know . . . what are yeh on about?"

"I know, Shay." And her talk turned more serious then. "Do you really think you can carry on a secret life, nobody in the flats knowing about it? Cop on to yourself, will you? Now, the Pearse Street Library, that's a different matter altogether."

Oh, fuck. "What are yeh saying now, Rosie?"

"I mean it's good. You're a lad that likes reading, likes learning. Good on you, is what I say. The more we learn, the better. Harder for the powers-that-be and the *quality* to fool us and keep us down. And, well, it's enjoyable in itself, isn't it? Reading good books, good poetry, all that. But Trinity girls aren't the only ones who know how to open a book! I get books from Pearse Street, too. And so does somebody else we both know." She raised her eyebrows at him, but he didn't let on he knew exactly who she meant.

When that phase of Shay's life ended — the pursuit of the bus-riding Trinity students, but never his interest in the books — he and Allie Cotter began walking out together. It was Allie that Rosie had meant in her hint about the books, but he'd been in no need of a hint by then. He'd already begun to see Allie as more than just a pal. He remembered the very day. He had always loved seeing her with her little brothers and sisters, playing games with them, codding them with jokes, pouring them a cup of cocoa before they went to bed. But on one particular day, he was visiting her flat, lying on the floor in one of the two bedrooms, nursing a hangover. He heard a ruckus outside the building, a crowd of young boys shouting and laughing. And the target of their laughter was Allie's little brother Matty. He was around eleven at the time, and he was no match for the tough lads from the neighbouring flats. They were tormenting him for the way he talked; he had a stammer. Shay heard Allie march out onto the balcony, and she yelled down, "Matty, you get in here right now. We've had enough of yer fighting and all yer carry-on. Get in here!" What was this? Why was she giving out to him? Poor Matty was never a fighter; he was a timid little fella. In he came, and Allie said, "Come here, yeh." Shay peered out of the room and saw Allie rocking a crying Matty in her arms.

"Men don't cry!" the little boy wailed.

"Of course they do. Always have done. If they weren't meant to cry, would God have given them the parts of the eye that make the tears? We all cry; there's no harm in it."

And then Shay copped on to what Allie had done. She hadn't called down to him, "Oh, come in, poor little Matty," which would have set off another bout of taunting. No, she called him out for fighting, as if this was a habit of his, and so she let him save face in front of the gang outside. She offered her comfort in the privacy of their home. That's when Shay knew: it struck him like a punch to the heart when he realized how much he loved her.

The pair of them were a little self-conscious with each other; after all, they had shared many a laugh over the pratfalls each of them had endured while dating, or attempting to date, other people. But they soon got over that. He hoped she meant it when she said she felt the same way about him. And that's when he got into University College Dublin; they both signed up, her in archaeology and Shay in history and literature. He knew he'd only have one year at it; he'd have to go back to earning a weekly wage for himself and the family. So he'd make the best of that year. He and Allie had a great time, and Shay managed to cram in all the lectures and reading that he could.

Speaking again of ambitions, Allie was convinced that she was of Viking heritage. Her father's family had researched their history, and it seemed there was something to it. And why not? The Vikings had begun invading and looting in Ireland at the end of the eighth century. They had produced a number of settlements on the island, including Dublin itself. Many Irish were of Viking stock, descended from the Norsemen. She was keenly interested in this heritage, wanted to know more, and where better to study it — not in the Viking towns of Ireland like Dublin, Wexford, or Waterford — but at the University of Bergen in Norway? She had always said that ginger hair like hers was not unusual in Norway, so it seemed she would fit right in. And that's where she went. She even got a scholarship to go there. It was fine at first. She stayed in touch with Shay with letters that were full of love and humour, and she made the occasional visit home. He was saving his money and making plans to go over there, but it hadn't happened yet.

And then it wasn't going to happen. She rang him at home one night, and it was obvious she was half-gilled. She told him she had decided to stay over there for another year, maybe longer, so it wouldn't be fair to Shay to have to wait for her. Looking back on the conversation, Shay wished he had handled it like a grown-up, like a person with dignity, rather than saying to her, "Is tha' righ'? And who's ridin' yeh these days, Thor the god of thunder?" Or something like that; he couldn't remember because he was so rattled by her giving him the heave. No, that wasn't the way to show her that he was above her faithless ways, that he could cope quite well without her, thank you very much. But, well, that was that. He was heart-scalded, if the truth be told, and he had been missing her ever since. One thing he was grateful for, thank Christ in heaven, was that he hadn't proposed marriage to her, which he had intended to do. He'd had it all planned out. He'd save the money and go over to Norway and buy her a ring there, something Viking-ish, and, well, that wasn't going to happen now. His plan for a home and a houseful of little Shay-Allies was not going to happen. He missed her still. And that was brought home to him in a most painful way when he got a letter from her a couple of weeks after Rosie died.

Dear Shay,

I only just heard about Rosie. My heart is breaking here. And I'm heartsick about missing the funeral. I didn't know! By the time I got the news from my ma, it was too late for me to get home for it. I loved Rosie so much. We all did. What the f--- happened? Mam said somebody threw her down the stairs, or that's the talk at least. I hope you really do join the Garda and find out how she ended up dead! Because the other guards are as thick as pig shite if they think she slipped and slid all the

23

way down those stairs and there's no other explanation for her death.

— Allie

What could he do but write back to her in Norway, and tell her what he knew about Rosie's death, and promise he would write again whenever he learned more about the night at Goss's Hotel.

Shay had walked out with a few girls, of course, since the breakup and had a rollicking good time with some of them. But he hadn't found anything yet like the bond he had felt with Allie. And all too often the picture formed in his mind of Allie walking side by side with a tall, fair-haired Norse god. How could Shay Rynne compete with that? Well, obviously, he couldn't, him a dark curly-haired Irishman who only just met the height requirement for admission to the Garda Síochána.

CHAPTER II

Shay had never forgotten about wanting to join the Garda, and he sure as hell hadn't forgotten about the death of Rosie McGinn, but he'd heard stories about lads who'd tried to get into the Garda Síochána and hadn't been accepted. They were fellas like him, from Corpo flats around the city, boys who had grown up poor and wanted something better. But they couldn't get a foot in the door. Shay was sure he'd be sent away, and the shame of it would be written all over his face, shame over the fact that he was not good enough for An Garda Síochána — the Guardians of the Peace for Ireland.

But he had been good enough for Rosie McGinn. Oh, not good enough or old enough to take her to a dance or to the pictures. But good enough that she had treated him, and all the lads, as people worthy of her good humour, the occasional supply of candy, the leftover bottles of wine from the hotel. And kindness. He thought back to the time when he'd been chosen to play striker in a football match against the boys of another school. He'd been boasting to Rosie about this, and she promised she'd come and watch. But she didn't turn up till the second half and had missed his goal. Why?

Because when she'd started for the match, she met Talkie, who was also on his way to watch and cheer his son. Talkie was absolutely stocious with the drink and was loud and singing ballads. So Rosie intercepted him, lured him to Moroney's where, sure, he'd get even drunker, but he wouldn't cause his son to die of shame out there on the pitch in front of all the other lads. That was Rosie's kindness. Sure, she gave Shay a belt across the arse that time, but that was to teach him a lesson. And the more he thought about her, and thought about other girls and men, too, who had been victims of poverty and lack of opportunities in life, the more he got his courage up to apply to the Garda. And if they let him in, no matter what other duties he'd have to perform, he was going to track down the bastard who killed Rosie McGinn.

It was the first week in October 1970 when he put on his uniform and started his career as a guard, after completing his training at the Garda College in Templemore, County Tipperary. They didn't give him an easy time of it, the other trainees. And he wasn't welcomed with beaming smiles when he graduated and started work as Garda Seamus Rynne at Store Street Garda Station. Everything he had heard was true: they just assumed that any Jackeen — Dubliner — was a ruffian, a maggot, a blaggard.

But Shay knew he could always count on Detective Sergeant Colm Griffith as a friend and mentor at Store Street. One thing Colm did right away was ease things at home. The face on Talkie when Shay told him and Ma he'd been accepted for training! His ma, Deirdre, was delighted, but Da looked like any of the other fellas in the flats when the word "garda" or "guard" came up. As if Shay was being disloyal to his friends and to Talkie himself. It didn't help matters that Shay had burst in and made his announcement at a time when his father was on the batter. But since that was most nights, Shay might never have made his announcement if he'd waited for some time when the oul fella was dry and sober. But Colm was over a couple of days after that for a visit, and Da hadn't yet started on the drink that day. And Da always thought the world of Colm, and Colm was saying how brilliant it would be when there would be more lads like Shay, Dublin fellas, becoming guards, so they'd have a better understanding of the poorer people. They'd understand better than the men in from the bogs would, as Colm put it. And him in from the country himself, a farm in County Clare. Why should all the Garda jobs go to fellas from outside Dublin? So he got Talkie into the spirit of things, and Talkie laughed along with Colm and walked over and stood in front of his son and saluted. And it wasn't a sarcastic salute; Shay knew his father well enough to see it as a sign of acceptance, maybe even respect.

And there was one particular member of the family whose support Shay greatly appreciated. His little nephew Kevin was four years old by this time, son of Shay's sister Francie. There was a father, as there always was, but he had fucked off to parts unknown and left it to Francie to raise the boy on her own. And she was doing a brilliant job of it; he was a lovely little lad. The two of them lived in the flat with Shay, Talkie, and Deirdre, and Deirdre looked after Kevin when Francie was out working at the grocer's shop. Kevin's eyes lit up like stars whenever Garda Seamus Rynne came home in his uniform. Kevin had seen uniformed guards, sometimes roaring up to the flats with their sirens wailing; he knew their cars, and he had a couple of children's books featuring English bobbies or sheriffs in the USA. "You're a guard now, Shay? Where's your hat? I'm coming with you in the car!" Shay had taken out a bank loan and bought a blue second-hand Mini Cooper; he and Kevin pretended it was a Garda patrol car. So Shay would take Kevin for a spin in the Mini. He knew he'd always have a warm welcome from Kevin. And his mam and Francie. And usually from Talkie himself.

Whenever DS Griffith had an opportunity, he shared his wisdom and experience with the new recruit. There was one evening when they went out for a few jars together at Madigan's in Earl Street. With his newfound interest in books, Shay was gratified to know that James Joyce, Brendan Behan, and Patrick Kavanagh had lifted a jar or two there. Well, many of the pubs in Dublin could make that claim, and rightly so. But he kept that bit of enthusiasm to himself because Colm was filling him in on the city's criminal history.

"Now, Shay," he said, "if you'd only come to us sooner, if you'd been of age in the early 1960s, you'd have spent your days tracking down bicycle thieves, and investigating road traffic accidents fueled as much by drink as by petrol. You should take a look at the report prepared by our former commissioner in 1964. You'd almost wonder why we needed guards at all, there was so little crime. A few burglaries around the city here, but in the year going into September 1963, there were only four murders in this entire state."

"Not the situation these days," Shay said.

"Yerra, do you tell me so? We still have those minor offences. But serious crime is on the rise. We had to set up the Drugs Squad. You'll have heard about the raids in recent times, raids on people's houses. The detectives found marijuana and something they call LSD. Makes you hallucinate. They even found heroin! In this city! And then there's the guns. Fellas are getting hold of guns and robbing post office vans, and cash transfers going to businesses on payday. It's going to get worse, Shay, mark my words. And things are heating up in the North. Heating up! People being burnt out of their houses! We're already seeing the fallout from that, especially along the border. The refugee camps."

People were streaming across the border from the North to escape the attacks: loyalists — loyal to Britain, not to Ireland — were shooting Catholics and setting fire to their homes. So the Republic of Ireland had set up camps for those refugees. The television and the papers were filled with pictures of people with terrible injuries after being attacked. Shay remembered lying awake all night after seeing reports of university students being beaten and stoned for holding a march for civil rights. Rights as basic as "one man, one vote," which they didn't have in the North. It was a peaceful march. Yet the protesters, young lads and girls Shay's own age, were pelted with stones, beaten with iron bars, left bleeding and in agony. The men doing the beating were loyalists, and some of the attackers were members of the B-Specials, a reserve police force! And the police who were on duty? Some of them did absolutely nothing, just walked away.

All of this had inspired in Shay a determination to be a conscientious policeman who would never cause harm to innocent people, who would keep the Rosie McGinns of this world safe from harm. It also reinforced something he had learned at the knees of his father and his godfather Finn Burke: that the republican cause — the Brits out and the thirty-two counties united — was a just cause. But he knew he was in for a measure of conflict between those two guiding principles, because the republican cause was often pursued by means that were anything but just. Now, in Madigan's pub, he returned to his conversation with Colm Griffith.

"I've been wanting to go up to the border," Shay said, "to the camps. Maybe help the people out somehow."

"That would be good of you, Shay. I'm sure they could use the company, the support, supplies of all kinds. So maybe you'll do that. But here we are in Dublin, and you'll have trouble enough to keep you busy here in the city!"

And busy he was, with some of those traffic accidents Colm mentioned, these ones being on the city streets, and he also found himself between flying fists outside the bars at closing time, the usual things you'd expect. Store Street Garda Station was on the city's north side. That suited Shay, being on the other side of the River Liffey from the place he'd been raised, the flats where his old mates still lived and carried on their less-than-Garda-friendly activities. Of course, to hear his fellow guards tell it — tell it to his face or in stagy whispers as he passed by — Shay himself was nothing but a corner boy, a scut from the flats. And it was only a matter of time before he would reveal his true colours, disgrace himself and his uniform, and be booted back across the river to Fenian Street. There was one big gom, a rough-faced bully boy from County Cavan, who would put up his arm and look at his watch every time Shay crossed his path, as if to be saying, *It's only a matter of time.* Only a matter of time before the young Dublin Jackeen would knock some poor oul pensioner over the head and make off with her takings from the bingo. And there were a couple more of that type, slagging Shay for his "accent," him from the very city where they were working, the capital of the state, and them from way beyond in the west of Ireland with their bogger accents you could barely make out a word of. Them, slagging

Shay! But Shay knew there would be ignorant fuckers like this at every station.

Colm Griffith had taken Shay under his wing at Store Street. He made it clear to Shay that he would be looking out for him, watching his back. In return, he expected Shay to live up to the high standards Colm himself had always lived by. "I know you'll not be letting me down." And Shay assured him he would not. Letting down Colm Griffith was unthinkable. And he didn't want to let himself down, either. Once he had made his decision to join the Garda, Shay knew this was the future he wanted. He would prove himself to all those begrudgers. And he would do his best to show a new side of the Gardaí to the people of the Dublin tenements: no prejudice against them, and no special treatment for the people with money, with the fine houses and cars. Garda Rynne's justice would be blind to all that.

.୧৩

Shay had a bit of luck early on. The most obnoxious of the pricks he'd been stuck with for the first few weeks on the job was moved up and assigned to other duties, so Shay no longer had to overhear his loud references to *Fenian* Street and see his hands flying apart to mimic a bomb going off. Shay had felt like telling him that if it hadn't been for men like the Fenians — the name was first used by Irish revolutionaries in the 1850s — and their successors, this Garda Gobshite would be doffing his cap to the Brits in Dublin Castle. This country would still be a Brit colony, like the North. But that arsehole was out of the way now, and Shay was teamed up with a new partner, Vince Foley. He was a fair-haired lad from County Waterford and he didn't slag Shay about his speech, so Shay never let on that during their first few days together there were big chunks of Vince's conversation that Shay couldn't understand at all. They went out on patrol together in their unmarked car, or sometimes on foot, hunting down pickpockets and bicycle thieves and other small-time offenders.

And Vince knew of a great opportunity for Shay. There was a place available for renting, and the price was reasonable. The owner was a cousin of his mother, who had offered it to Vince, but Vince liked where he was living. So, it was available if Shay was interested. They went to look at it, and Shay said, "It's brilliant, Vince!" It was a little one-storey terraced brick house in Emmet Street, just off the North Circular Road. A place of his own. Shay could move into Emmet Street at the end of the month.

Vince had close to a year on Shay in seniority and was familiar with the investigations that had been carried out during his time and before. So one day while they were driving along Gardiner Street, Shay brought up the subject of Rosie's death. He told Vince he had known her all through his childhood. Vince understood his distress over the fact that her death — Shay had thought of it from day one as her *murder* — had never been solved. Had never actually been classified as a murder. Vince had not worked on the case, but he said he was on fairly good terms with the officer who had headed the investigation, a man with the unlikely name of Larracy McCreevy.

"That's a mouthful."

"His mam's surname, I guess it was. Of course, fellas couldn't help but call him Larceny when he became a guard. But he answers to just plain Lar. Anyway, I say I'm on fairly good terms with him. That just means he never gave me a bollocking for anything I ever did or failed to do; it's not everybody who can make that claim!"

"A hard oul streak of misery, is he?"

"He is. As I say, I've never been caught on the wrong side of him, not yet at least. But, Shay, you'll want to be careful about why you want to speak to him. Don't want to get his back up against you."

"If some bastard killed Rosie, any member of the Garda would want the man found and charged . . . What?" Vince was laughing. "What is it?"

"Shay, if some bastard killed her and we missed it — the guards missed it — and closed the investigation, and some young turk comes along and shows that the murder inquiry was a failure or there was no murder inquiry at all, that might be the last thing Detective Sergeant McCreevy would want! You know Detective Inspector Hennessy here is on track for promotion."

"Yeah, they say Hennessy will be a superintendent someday."

"It may happen someday; it may happen some year down the road. But McCreevy is fierce determined to move up, take his place as detective inspector whenever he goes. DS Griffith is after the same spot. Well, they're not the only ones angling for promotion, but . . ."

"What am I supposed to do then, Vince, let Rosie's murder go unsolved in order to spare the delicate feelings of the original investigators?"

"'Delicate' is the word to keep in mind as you head into this, Shay. Tread lightly."

"I'll do that. But how in the fuck did they come to the conclusion that . . ."

"That she fell. The body was found early on the morning of March the ninth, 1969, at the bottom of the back staircase in Goss's Hotel. The state pathologist concluded that she died of head injuries consistent with a fall. There were marks on her neck —"

"What kind of marks?"

"Marks which appeared to have been made by someone's hands —"

"So somebody had his hands around her neck? Is that what you're telling me?"

"Made by someone's hands but were not the cause of death."

"When can we meet DS McCreevy?"

"I'll see what I can do."

*

Two days later Vince and Shay walked into the detectives' room. Each detective had a desk, and lockers lined the dull green walls. Vince and Shay approached the desk where Detective Sergeant Larracy McCreevy was shuffling through some papers and making notes. McCreevy was a big lump of a man with narrow grey eyes and a dark moustache. Shay didn't like the cut of him at all. But he would play this by the rules set out by Vince Foley: tread carefully and don't get the man's back up. Vince told McCreevy that Shay had something he'd like to ask about, and Shay said it was about the death of Rosaleen McGinn.

"What is it you want to know, Rynne?" McCreevy said in his bogger accent from wherever he was reared at the arse end of the country.

"Well, the thing is, sir, I knew Rosie all my life, until she was . . . found dead."

"And?"

Don't tell him you want to see the case reopened, Shay thought. You've not the rank or the bottle to ask for that. "I'd just like to hear what you found during your investigation. It's been on my mind, like."

"Well, your mind won't be put to rest by hearing about your pal Rosie's last night on earth, Garda Rynne."

Shay cautioned himself that patience must not only be done but be seen to be done.

McCreevy sighed as if it was *his* patience being tested. "There was a hooley that night upstairs in the hotel, in a couple of the rooms. The big rooms, suites. And it turned into exactly the sort of racket you'd expect from a bunch of drugged-up rock 'n' rollers and their camp followers, or whatever they call them these days. The little slappers who follow around after the hippies and rock music bands, and hop into the crib with them without so much as the wink of an eye directed to them. The kind of thing we've come to expect in *Dublin*."

Shay didn't know whether to laugh at this oul culchie's take on the modern world, or to take him on for his insult to the city of Dublin. But all he said was, "Whose party was it, sir?"

"Whose party it was, starting out, was two of our county councillors, local fellas, who rented the two rooms so they could host a crowd from out of town. County councillors and a couple of TDs." TD meant Teachta Dála, a member of the Irish parliament, called the Dáil. "They got together to talk things over, enjoy a few drinks. But one of them, I don't know who, remembered what an enthusiastic reception that band had received from the crowd in the lobby, the birds in particular, so they decided to haul the lot of them off their stools in the hotel bar and invite them up to one of the councillors' rooms. And once the party moved upstairs, your friend Rosaleen and one of her fellow employees brought a week's worth of bottles and cans up to the room. Everyone we spoke to gave the same account. Up to that point. Then a couple of the witnesses revealed that wine and whiskey and porter weren't sufficient to satisfy the tastes of some in attendance. So then, as they say, drugs were involved."

DS McCreevy glared into Shay's eyes as if he, by the mere fact of being a Dub and an acquaintance of Rosie McGinn, had appeared at the party with a backpack filled with hashish and cocaine and heroin for the boys in the band, the girls hanging off them, and their elected representatives who make but apparently ignore the laws.

"And I'm sorry to say" — McCreevy's sorrow was well hidden behind the obvious satisfaction in his big fat face — "Rosaleen McGinn was one of the brassers who settled in for the party and partook of the booze and whatever else they were ingesting that night."

Shay couldn't fucking let that go. "Rosaleen McGinn was not a brasser, and she never did drugs."

"Well, it was either drugs or cheap French wine that made her lose her footing on those stairs. A witness told us she was seen drinking with one of the *ladies* from the canal."

The Grand Canal was one of the areas of the city where a man could find paid female company any night of the week.

"What *lady* from the canal?"

McCreevy gave him the evil eye. "Would you like to ask that question again, guard?"

"What lady, *sir*?"

"Garda Rynne, we were satisfied with the statements we got from our witnesses. Satisfied that the girl's death was the result of a fall. An unfortunate accident, which resulted from her being drunk, or high on drugs, and losing her balance. And she tripped on the stairs and went flying down."

Shay took a deep breath and warned himself not to lose the rag with this arsehole. "I heard there were marks on her neck."

"There's nothing particularly significant about that; her death resulted from head injuries caused by a fall."

"But what did the pathologist say about the marks? What did they look like? Sir?"

McCreevy shrugged. "Said they could have been caused by some-one's hands."

"Well then! That tells us —"

"It tells us nothing, except that she may have had contact with somebody at the party. There was a lot of, let us call it, physical con-tact going on that night. Not surprising, with those brassers on the scene. And as you might expect, they were less than cooperative with our investigation. Stonewalled us completely. Wouldn't even admit they were there."

"So how do you know they were?"

It was clear that he didn't like Shay's tone, but he answered, "Their faces were recognized."

"Yeah, because some of your witnesses — some of these fine cit-izens, our elected representatives — are amongst the kerb crawlers who go down the canal looking for the girls at night."

"Don't get above yourself here, Rynne. I've been very patient with you; not everybody would be. We were satisfied with our witnesses' statements."

"Kind of embarrassing for the political men, being caught out at a hooley like this. I'm thinking they may not have told the whole story. Sir."

"What you're thinking, Garda Rynne, has no bearing on the inves-tigation that concluded that the girl's death was an accident. Now, if you don't mind, I have *crimes* to deal with. I suggest you do the same." He glared at them until they turned and left.

As the two young guards walked away after their fruitless meeting, Shay said to Vince, "He couldn't be arsed to look into the case again, no matter what I might have told him, the oul culchie fuck." He caught himself then. "Ah, sorry, Vince."

But Vince hadn't taken offence. "Ah but sure, I know he gets on your wick, Shay. You're not alone in that!"

"So," Shay continued, "it falls to me to get the killers off the street."

"How are you going to do that? If you're still here, I mean, after talking back to McCreevy like that! He's not one to forget."

"Good. Maybe he'll remember some more important details about Rosie's case. But until he does, it's up to us to view the scene, question witnesses, bring in a suspect, put the frighteners on him, clatter him a bit if necessary."

"Ha, ha. You've some neck, Shay. You're having me on, aren't you?"

Shay looked him in the eye and didn't give voice to a reply.

℘

An hour or so later, Colm Griffith came striding into the large crowded room where the uniformed guards received their assignments and did their paperwork. He summoned Shay with the crook of his finger and led him into a small, airless interview room. He shut the door. This was not Shay's guardian angel standing over him now, but more like an avenging angel. Shay had never seen Colm giving him an unblinking stare, fists clenched at his side. Then it began: Shay got a bollocking.

"What in the hell were you doing, Shay, giving out to DS McCreevy as if you'd come down on him from the commissioner himself? Between you and me, Shay, McCreevy is a man with ambitions and a high opinion of himself. And he does not want that opinion questioned. Ever. You're not helping yourself going at a man like him."

"I know."

"So, what were you thinking, giving out to him like that? I can tell you he gave out to me about you, my — well, I'll spare you what he called you. So? Explain yourself."

"I . . . I . . . well, you know about Rosie."

"I know about Rosie."

"It's just that the Gardaí —"

"We are the Gardaí, Seamus."

Shay could only stand there, lost for the words that had flowed so freely towards McCreevy. The man facing him now was the man who had supported his family, his father, had smoothed the way for Shay to join the Garda. Shay was seeing a side of Colm Griffith he had never seen before. But he had never worked with Colm until now, so he'd not have seen it. Then Colm's face seemed to soften and he said, "Tell me, Shay. Everything you told McCreevy."

So Shay told him and then blurted out, "I can get more information on this, Col — sir." Griffith was "Colm" to Shay in social situations, but he would always be "sir" on the job. "I can talk to people that . . . people who might not talk to the other guards."

"Because of your background, you mean."

"That's right. Rosie was a friend. She was always good to us, you know, the fellas in the flats. I just want to do right by her."

Griffith stood there, silent for a long couple of minutes. Shay's nerves were jangling. What was the detective sergeant going to say, and what would all this mean for Shay's new career? The confrontation laid bare for Shay just how important — how essential — it was to him to be Garda Seamus Rynne. The thought of losing this new identity, his future as a guard . . . Then Griffith said, "Here's what you're going to do, Shay. You will go and talk to people you think might have information. You'll do it alone, discreetly, and you'll report to me. Whatever you learn, you bring it to me."

"Yes, of course I will. Sir."

"You never mention it to McCreevy again. Or to anybody else."

"Right."

"And depending on what you learn, if anything, I'll decide where we go from there." With that, Griffith turned and walked out of the room.

We, he'd said. They were in this together now. Shay had Detective Sergeant Griffith's blessing to look into the case. Everyone had heard the rumour that Store Street's only detective inspector was on the road to promotion. And Griffith and McCreevy were among the most senior detective sergeants. Would one of them move up to inspector rank? Why would Griffith not entertain an ambition like that? Well, if Shay could help Rosie's family and help Colm Griffith at the same time, all the better.

☙

Shay and his family would always be grateful to Colm, especially for the way Colm had helped Shay's father over the years. But Colm wasn't the only member of the Gardaí familiar with Talkie's history. The other guards all knew that Shay's oul fella was Talkie Rynne, who had form for several offences, and Shay suspected that many of them were asking themselves: is Garda Rynne made of the same tatty cloth? And what is Garda Rynne going to do the next time his da has to be arrested and thrown in the nick? Is Shay going to spring him from his cell, get up in court, and say, "There is no evidence against this good man, Your Lordship?"

And he *was* a good man, was Talkie. A drinker, no question. He was more than that; he was an alco. But he was never nasty with it, unlike the fathers of some of the other lads Shay knew. Talkie was more likely to, well, do a lot of talking. And when he had loads of drink on him, he'd get sad. What would be a better word to describe how he'd be? Sentimental? Melancholy, that was it. Shay thought back to one time in particular. His mam was singing to the kids when it was time for the little ones to go to sleep. Deirdre Rynne's favourite song for them was called the "Cape Breton Lullaby." She had heard it on the wireless a few times and tried to remember the words. She remembered some and then made up some of her own. Part of it was in Scottish Gaelic, and Mam told them the song was from Scotland, and they would all get on a ship some day and go there. Shay learned later that Cape Breton is a part of Canada where they have the Gaelic. Anyway, Mam had on her big, pink, fuzzy housecoat that smelled like baby powder, and the kids were snuggled all around her in their pyjamas except for Shay, because he was older, nine or ten, and it wasn't his bedtime. The Gaelic lines sounded just like Irish and it was the mam telling her little son to "Sleep until day." And there were lambs in the song, and the da was out at sea working, but he would keep the teapot boiling or something like that. His wage packet would keep them from being hungry. And Shay asked his mother, "Is Da out on the sea, Mammy? Is he sailing on a ship? Can I go with him?"

"Eh, well, he's not really out on the sea. He comes home to us every night. But you know he works on the docks sometimes, unloading things the ships bring in."

"What does he do with the things he takes off the ships?" Was Shay a budding peeler even then?

"He loads them onto the lorries, of course, and they go to the men who ordered them in."

Not all the items got to the men who'd ordered them in, Shay would learn later in life. Talkie had occasionally come home with little treats or treasures that his mother knew then — and Shay knew now — had not been bought and paid for. Once it was bars of chocolate with writing on them in a language Shay didn't recognize, and a picture of a mountain covered in snow. Another time it was a little toy windmill. Sometimes it was bigger, more valuable items.

His father had walked in the door then, and Mam said, "Look at the cut of you! Why did you not put on the trousers and jumper I mended for you?" Shay looked and saw that his father's old blue jumper was frayed along the hem, and his trousers were too long in the legs and hanging down on his shoes.

"Ah," his father said, "it's no matter."

Shay said then, "What kinds of things d'yeh take off the boats, Da?"

And Talkie, who had drink on him, looked at Shay and then at Mam as if she'd said a bad word or taken the Lord's name in vain.

"Unloads the ships, love. I said he unloads the ships so we can buy the things here in Dublin."

"Take me there and show me, Da! Let's go there now."

"Ah, now, it's going to be dark soon." Shay later found out that Talkie had lost his job on the docks for failing to show up on time for work. "But let's the two of us go out. Not to the docks, but we'll go to the canal. Would you like that?"

"Yeah! Let's go."

It was a mild evening, the sun about to go down, and Talkie asked about Shay's classes at school and the football Shay enjoyed with his pals. They came to a tiny shop with crumbling bricks and metal bars on the windows, and Talkie said, "You stand out here for a minute and wait for me."

"What's in there, Da?"

"Just a little . . ." He left the sentence unfinished, went in the narrow door of the shop, and came out a minute later with a can sticking out each of the front pockets of his trousers. They arrived at the canal, and the water was high. Shay liked it that way: it reflected the lights of the streets and brick houses that lined the canal. They walked for a few minutes and then his father pointed to a bench and they sat down. Talkie took out one of the cans, popped it open, and took a long swallow. "Ahhh!"

"Is that beer, Da?"

"Sure, there's no harm in a little can of beer once in a while."

There were two cans, and it wasn't only "once in a while," but Shay didn't say it. Talkie was in good humour until he saw an Irish Army vehicle crossing the canal at the nearby bridge. "Fuckers," he muttered.

"Are they soldiers, Da?"

"Soldiers!" his father grumbled, and Shay could hear how the drink made him slur his words. "Soldiers are supposed to go to war and fight the enemy, not take a whip to their own people!"

"They don't do that! They fight for our country!" Shay replied, having no way of knowing one way or the other what soldiers did in real life, as opposed to in the stories, where they were heroes who had no fear of danger.

"*I* was a soldier, Shay. *I* was fighting for my country. Fighting to get the Brits off our island, after them occupying parts of it for nearly eight hundred years. And what did I get for that? Me and the other patriots that fought for our freedom? We got locked up in the Curragh, locked up in a prison camp!"

Shay stared at his father, who drained the first can of beer and cracked open the second. "Why did they lock you up, Da, if you were one of the soldiers yourself?"

"The Irish Army, and the men in power here, government men, they wanted to keep us down! And how do you take a man down and make sure he stays down? You lock him away in a prison, you humiliate him, make him feel like a criminal!"

"But you're not a criminal! So why did they —"

"Humiliate him, take away his dignity, and just for good measure, you go at him with a whip and tear shreds off his skin!"

His father's voice had a crying sound then, and Shay saw tears in his eyes. Talkie reached up with the hand holding the can and tried to wipe the tears away. But the can went flying and his father said, "Fuck!" as if something terrible had happened instead of just a can falling. And he made a dive to retrieve the can and then, "I'm sorry, Shay. You're my first son, and a father loves his son." That was a man's way of saying what your mam would say, *I love you*.

"And," Talkie went on, "I shouldn't be telling you about these terrible things. May you never, ever be hurt the way I was hurt." Talkie put his arm around Shay and pulled him close. "If anyone ever, *ever*, raises a hand to you, hits you, hurts you in any way, you come to me and tell me about the fucker. And I swear to you on all I hold sacred, I'll make sure he never gets near you again! Ah," he said then, "I shouldn't be talking. I had a few jars down the pub, and now . . ." He squeezed Shay tighter against him. "Forgive me, son. Forgive me, Seamus. I'm not . . . Let's get up for a walk again."

Shay had heard from some of his pals about the fathers getting langered, coming home and shouting, and some fathers thumping their kids and some even hitting the mothers. Shay promised himself and God that at Mass the next Sunday, he would send up a prayer to God and His blessed mother and thank them for making Talkie Rynne not ferocious and making him a good father in spite of the beer and the whiskey. And he would also pray that the men who hit his da with whips in that camp would get thrown down to hell. At that moment, standing by the Grand Canal, he wanted to throw his arms around his father and tell him he . . . tell him what? That he didn't care about the drink? That he loved his da anyway? He didn't know what a son should do, so he just smiled up at Talkie and said, "Yeah, let's walk."

Now, as a grown man, Shay could look at Talkie Rynne and honestly say to himself that he'd always been a good father. Talkie loved his children and his wife, and they had never doubted it. And during the good times, he'd have them roaring with laughter with his stories, some of them true and some of them, Shay knew, that just came out of his head at the time of telling. And since there was no way on earth to get Talkie off the drink, and since Shay enjoyed a glass or two himself, he and his father often headed off to the pub together and met up with Talkie's pals or Shay's and made a night of it. There were good times to be had with Talkie Rynne. Shay hoped and prayed that he would never have to deal with his father as a guard, rather than as a son.

CHAPTER III

S hay felt the need of a drink after the meetings with McCreevy and Griffith, and he didn't want to go to Reade's, where so many of the guards gathered to drink and tell their war stories. He had the next two days off work, so there would be no harm in enjoying a few pints. Now, it's a fine thing to have a godfather who's a member of the Garda Síochána, no question, but it's a fine thing as well to have a godfather who has his own pub. Well, it wasn't actually Finn Burke's pub; it was his da Christy's place. But Finn was often behind the bar at Christy Burke's, pouring pints, and so he was when Shay made one of his frequent visits to the much-loved drinking hole. It was at the corner of Mountjoy Street and St. Mary's Place, a cream-coloured building with a horizontal band of black above the door and windows. Inscribed within the band was the name Christy Burke.

Like many a Dublin pub, Christy's had a dark-wood interior, a long bar with pumps, and glistening bottles of spirits. You could sit on a stool up at the bar or at one of the tables along the wall, some of which were separated by wooden partitions. The 1916 Proclamation of the Irish Republic had pride of place on the wall behind the bar, and there were black-and-white photographs around the room as well. One of them was the famous picture of IRA gunmen patrolling Grafton Street in 1922, dressed in trench coats or jackets and ties, fedoras or peaked caps on their heads, rifles in their hands. The rumour was that Christy himself was one of the men in the photo, but when anybody asked, all they got from the old man was an enigmatic little smile. Finn was a younger version of Christy, with thick greying hair and grey-blue eyes that were often obscured behind a pair of dark glasses. Shay liked seeing Finn there, but he also liked the fact that it was on the north side, so he could enjoy a glass or two away from his old neighbourhood, and neighbours, on the south side of the Liffey. You might say it was his local away from home, if that made any sense.

And there was another pal of his in place that day, too, he saw. Finn's nephew Brennan Burke looked as comfortable in Christy's as if he was in the place every day of his life. In fact, though, Brennan and his family had emigrated from Ireland years ago for reasons that had never been made public. Whatever it was, Brennan's father Declan — Finn's brother — had packed up and bundled his family onto a ship bound for New York City. Brennan was just a young boy at the time, but he never lost his connection with Ireland and, as soon as he was old enough, started making the trip back home whenever he could. Short visits they usually were, but Brennan made the best of them, visiting his old friends and enjoying the craic at Christy's.

Shay had made his acquaintance a couple of years before. Brennan was a few years older than Shay, and he was an ordained priest by the time Shay met him, but he wasn't too holy to enjoy a night out with the lads. He and Shay had quickly become friends. Now here he was at a table near the back of the pub. Brennan had his back to him but Shay would have known him anywhere. Tall and black-haired, he was dressed in civilian clothes: a dark blue jumper with a lighter blue shirt collar under it. He had another man with him, a blondy fella around Brennan's own age. Shay approached their table and was about to greet them when two girls, young women in their twenties, came in the door and looked around for a seat. A rare sight, to see girls come into a pub without their men. Brennan and his tablemate looked up, saw them, and gestured to them to join the table. The girls introduced themselves as Clodagh and Louise; they said they had come to the bar to meet their uncle. He'd be along any minute. Clodagh laughed and said the two of them had decided to be bold and come into the place without the uncle at their side.

Shay watched as Brennan ground out a cigarette in the ashtray and got up to order drinks, but the other man took on that role himself. The girls were smiling with delight at Brennan Burke. It wasn't hard to see what women would see in him; he was a handsome-looking divil, no two ways about it. Shay was wondering whether, in that gathering, Brennan Burke was just Brennan, not Father. Maybe enjoying the attention without putting a damper on things by announcing his celibate priestly state. But no, what Shay heard was "I'm Father Burke. Brennan Burke."

Well! He wasn't hiding behind the absence of a Roman collar after all. Shay had misjudged him, and he'd have to do a better job of reading people if he was going to succeed as a guard.

Finn appeared behind the bar then and greeted Shay, who ordered a pint of Guinness. When it had settled, Shay took a few sips and then saw an older man come into the pub and wave to the girls at Brennan's table. They got up, said a few parting words to Brennan and his friend, and went off with the uncle. So Shay headed over to see his pal. They said their hellos and how've-yeh-beens.

"Shay Rynne, this is Paddy Healey."

Paddy and Shay shook hands and said hello. They made small talk for a few minutes and then Shay heard, "Hi yeh, Choc! Van! How are yis?"

Paddy greeted the new fella, and Brennan said, "I'm flyin', Colly, and yerself?"

"I've a thirst on me, to be sure."

"You're in the right place."

So another mate of Brennan's joined the table: Collins "Colly" O'Grady. Shay asked about the Choc and Van salutation and was told that the three had played Gaelic football together in school before

Brennan's family emigrated. Brennan had black hair and black eyes, and Paddy Healey was fair-haired with blue eyes, so they had been nicknamed Chocolate and Vanilla.

Colly said, "You could think of me as Butterscotch, I suppose." He had hair of a light brown colour and eyes only a bit darker than that.

"Sure, where were you," said Paddy, "when we were kicking a ball around behind the church in Rathmines? Too busy playing rugby, were you?"

"Ah, now, I came back to the oul Gaelic games at an early age."

"You did, sure, Butterscotch. But unless you want your nickname shortened like ours — which might necessitate you being called Butt from now on — I'd say stick with Colly."

"I will."

"Good decision, Colly!" Paddy agreed. "You'd not want the wife introducing you as 'my darling Butt.'"

"That decides the matter," Colly agreed.

Brennan said he tried to get together with these two friends whenever he came home to Dublin.

"These two hooligans were forever getting me in the soup during our school days, Shay," Colly said.

"Oh?" Shay asked. "Are these the sort of people I want to know?"

"Maybe not, if you're a priest of God like this fella."

"No, no, I'm nothing as strict and formidable as that. But I may be looking for your confession someday. I've joined the Garda."

"You haven't!" said Brennan.

"I have."

"Congratulations, Shay!" Brennan and the other two raised their glasses to the newly minted peeler. So the announcement didn't sour the mood at all.

When there was a quiet spell at the bar, Finn came over to the table and said, "The oul fella's on the warpath today, Brennan." Christy, he must have meant.

"Has he not been on the warpath his entire life, Finn?"

"He has. But he's wound up now about the refugees. He went up to Gormanston a couple of times last year, and he's talking about heading up there again."

Shay felt a pang of shame hearing that. Why had he not yet gone up there himself to offer assistance?

"Him going up there has me concerned," Finn said. "Christy has become a little less discreet in his old age, and I'm asking myself what he might blurt out in the presence of the soldiers there." The Irish Army men running the camp.

Brennan said, "You'd like me to accompany him, Finn. Keep an eye on him."

"I would."

"Well, I'd be serving my calling better by offering comfort to the refugees than by idling here in the family bar. Not to take anything away from the family business, now, Finn."

"Go early in the day tomorrow and you won't have to miss your shift in here. Before you can get Christy on the road to Gormanston, you'll have to break him out of the cell where they're holding him."

"Holding him!" Shay exclaimed at that. "What did he get nicked for? I never heard a word about it."

Brennan laughed and said, "No, he's in the Mater."

"Ah." The Mater Misericordiae hospital.

"That's what accounts for my presence in Dublin now. I'd been planning to come early next year, but I got a phone call from one of my great-aunts here, Cliona, the one I stay with when I visit. She told me Christy's in bad shape. He's in the hospital, and the family is concerned that he might never walk out on his own two feet. Or, as it was put to me, 'You never know when you tie your boots on in the morning who's going to be taking them off you.'"

"True enough."

"The oul fella had a stroke, but he insists there's nothing wrong with him, and he's being 'interned' for no good reason. Christy's a tough old skin but, after all, he's over seventy-five years old, so . . . Anyway, here I am. And it falls to me to spring him from captivity. Have you any time tomorrow, Shay? Care to go for a spin? I've a car on loan from the company." Burke Transport, the family's other business.

"Sure."

"Where will I find you tomorrow?"

"I'll meet you here."

"Half ten?"

"Good plan."

℘

Brennan was back in Christy's the next morning, nursing a pint while waiting for Shay Rynne. When Shay arrived, Finn asked him, "One before you go?" But Shay shook his head no. "We're going to transport a man across the county line, Finn. We'd best get on with it."

"Right," Brennan agreed. "We're off."

Finn said, "I don't see a Roman collar on you today, Father."

"Just as well, Finn. I don't want to go into the hospital looking like a bad omen. *Jaysus, Mary, and Joseph, who's the sagart here for?*"

Finn laughed. "You're probably right. They see a young sagart coming into the hospital, and they figure their nearest and dearest is about to depart this life."

So Shay and Brennan left the pub. A cold October rain was pelting down on them and they ducked their heads as they did a fast walk to the car, a red four-door Austin Morris Brennan had parked in a laneway. "Not a priestly colour for a car, I know," Brennan joked. "I may be mistaken for a cardinal, going about in red."

"Only fitting, Your Eminence."

"A fella could get used to that!"

They got into the car for the short drive to Eccles Street, and parked up. They entered the hospital, and Brennan led the way to his grandfather's ward. Brennan was not a man for hospitals, and it was clear from the face on Shay that he felt the same way. Brennan did his best to ignore the tubes and the charts, the monitors and other equipment ranged round the place, and focused on the fierce old man lying there, fuming. Christy had white hair that was only beginning to thin out.

Brennan had often been told that he had his grandda's hawk-like nose. But the old fella's eyes were not black but a cold-looking shade of blue.

"Ah, Brennan," he said. "Good to see you, my lad. And you, Seamus Rynne. But not like this. Get me the fuck out of here, so I can get behind my bar and stand on the two feet God gave me, and pour out for you the golden nectar God gave us, and you coming all the way over from America. I shouldn't be lying here taking a bed from some oul soul who's in need of it. Help me up here, lads."

It was soon clear to Brennan that "up" didn't mean a sitting position in the bed; it meant up, dressed, and out of there. In short order, Christy had discharged himself from the hospital's care, against the advice of the medical staff, scribbled something on a form, and left with Shay and Brennan. When they were out on the street, he said, "You know where I want to go."

"I do. Shay's coming with us."

"Is maith sin." That's good. "Gormanston today, and I'll be behind my bar pulling pints tonight, as I should be."

They made a quick stop for a few bags of food, loaded them into the car, and set their course for County Meath to the north of Dublin with Brennan at the wheel. Christy was his front passenger, Shay in the back. As they left the brick and concrete of the city for the green of farmers' fields, the rain let up, the clouds parted, and the sun came blazing through the rear windscreen of the car. It was a rare sight for Brennan, the countryside with its flocks of sheep, the cattle, horses, and ponies. It did him good to be reminded that there was more to the world than the great architecture of the cities.

He had the radio on, and there was a tenor singing "E lucevan le stelle" from *Tosca*. He sang along with it. He usually considered himself a baritone, but he had the range of a tenor as well. Lost in the music, he forgot for a minute that he had company in the car. "Sorry, lads, I tend to get carried away when I hear great music."

"You're a grand singer there, Brennan," Shay said. "You'd be as good on the stage as I'm sure you are on the altar."

"He's brilliant," said Christy. "The voice coming out of him would be enough to make a believer of you."

"Well, Grandda, to quote Beethoven, 'Music is the mediator between the spiritual and the sensual life.'"

"I'm somewhere in between there myself," Christy joked. "Just don't like to think which end I'm closer to."

Brennan glanced over and was struck by how frail his grandfather looked. But he was not about to mention it.

"Ah, here we are."

The Irish Army's camp at Gormanston had recently been modified to serve as a refugee camp for people who'd been made homeless by the attacks north of the border. Brennan and his companions arrived to see long wooden huts, each with a row of windows along the side, a door in the gable end, and a number over the door. They were greeted by a soldier, and there were a few formalities, then they handed over their groceries and began meeting the refugees. These were refugees within their own country, in Brennan's view and in the view of the entire Burke family; Irish republicans regarded the partition between North and South as illegitimate.

The three of them visited several of the huts and heard horrifying tales of what the people had endured the summer before. One woman, a Mrs. McCann, described what she had seen in her Belfast neighbourhood. "They set fire to our house, burned us out! Everything we'd saved for, destroyed. My mother's furniture that she left us when she died. Our beds and blankets. Our books and the children's toys. Everything we had. Lost. And the other houses around us, the windows smashed, and petrol bombs thrown in. We found out later that there were hundreds of Catholic families burnt out. Those hateful old bigots think they have the right to force us out of our own country. And not only that: they were shooting at us! I felt a bullet go whizzing by my head; I thought I was going to die of terror, right there on the spot. And there was a wee boy shot to death! And he wasn't the only one. Another young lad was shot, and some men killed as well."

A man joined in. His name was Donal. "And what do you think happened when we rang the peelers to put a stop to it? Nothing. We phoned in to the police. Did they come to save our houses?

Our people? We never saw a one of them. One of our priests went to the police barracks, him and another of the men. D'you know what the peelers said to them? Said they had orders to stay in the barracks! What's the use of them? Why have police at all, if they're going to stay sitting on their arses and let people be attacked and houses burnt?!"

This was painful for anyone to hear, but Brennan could imagine how painful it was for Shay Rynne, and him a peeler. Brennan was glad Shay wasn't in uniform. But then again, it was the Royal Ulster Constabulary in the North who had let the people down, not the Garda Síochána in the South.

"So then what happened?" Donal said. "The priest rang the headquarters of the British Army. Sure, the soldiers came out, but they went to the wrong place! When they finally found us and ordered the mob to stop, the mob ignored them, kept on calling us Fenian bastards and kept shooting and setting more fires. Lobbed petrol bombs at our places. What did the brave boys in uniform do? They fucked off. When they worked up the courage to come back again, they were ignored again. The mobs kept at it. And that's what we fled from; that's why we are refugees in the middle of our own island!"

Brennan looked over at his grandfather and saw the cold fury in the old rebel's face. He understood and shared the old man's anger. But Christy had just suffered a stroke; would these encounters put him in danger of another one?

ᏅᎣ

Brennan was happy to see Shay Rynne again, and he appreciated his company on the trip to Gormanston. It was plain that he was deeply affected by what he saw and heard there. That would stand him in good stead as a copper: he would have sympathy for people who had been visited with immeasurable suffering, and he would have a deeper understanding than many people in the South of what was happening in the North. Brennan was surprised — pleasantly so — at Finn's reaction to a young friend joining the Garda. Finn and his republican comrades did not always welcome the attentions of the police. Brennan knew, however, that the IRA had a policy of not targeting the southern state's police force. He knew as well that many in the Garda Síochána were sympathetic to the republican cause.

CHAPTER IV

Shay had been in Goss's Hotel before, not long after he heard of Rosie McGinn's death, and now here he was again. It was a four-storey brick building with rectangular windows. He went inside and nodded at the young receptionist; she was busy checking in a group of guests, so he had a look around. The lobby had sofas and armchairs in muted browns and blues, which matched the mosaic tiles on the floor. The bar was to the right as you stood facing the reception desk. The elevator was to the left, and the front staircase to the left of that. He headed up the front stairs, which were inlaid with the same little square tiles as the lobby floor. When he reached the first level, he walked along the carpeted hallway. The carpet looked new, and he remembered that the floor had been bare wood when he had last seen it. He started down the back steps and then stopped. Looking down, it was almost as if he could hear the clatter and thumping of Rosie as she plummeted down these stairs, terrified and in pain. Or was she in no pain by then? What about those marks on her neck? Was she still alive by this time or not?

He took a deep breath and told himself to get on with it. He began his slow descent. The steps here were made of iron, and they changed direction halfway down between the floors. Shay had the impression that if you stumbled and fell, you would not fall all the way down; your momentum would be halted at the wall as the staircase changed direction. But Rosie had been found at the bottom, so she had not merely slid down. She had either tripped and gone flying down, or she'd been thrown. On each side, where the iron staircase was embedded in the concrete floor, the concrete was raised a few inches in the shape of a square. Shay bent down and ran his fingers along one of the squares, feeling the concrete, the sharp corner, picturing someone's head — Rosie's head — being dashed against it. He drew his hand back. It was on one of these corners that she had fractured her skull.

〜

After viewing the scene of the crime, which he considered it to be, it was time to speak to somebody who had been there that night. The first witness he intended to question was the now-famous Mackey Walsh. Shay had played football against Walsh during their teen years, the boys from the neighbourhood round Fenian Street against the boys from the Liberties. And they'd had a nodding acquaintance after that, seeing each other in various bars and sports fields around the city. Shay had gone to hear Liberties Taken a couple of times as well. He liked their music and he was happy that they were starting to get the acclaim they deserved. The members of Liberties Taken spent most of their time across the sea in England, but they made the occasional appearance back home in Dublin. They'd had a Merseybeat sound in their earlier years, but more recently had turned to harder rock. Most of their "gigs," as they called their sessions, were done as fill-ins during showband concerts. Must have been a bit jarring for the audiences, long-haired rockers on stage right after the showband musicians in their suits and ties. Now they had a gig coming up at the

TV Club in Harcourt Street, and Shay wanted to catch Walsh before the show.

It was a warm evening for late October, so Shay was dressed in a lightweight jumper and blue jeans when he entered the building. He talked his way into the dance hall where the band was setting up. When he caught a glimpse of Walsh's shaggy dark hair, he raised a hand and walked over to him. Walsh recognized him and said, "How're yeh keepin', Shay?"

"I'm spot on, thank you, Mackey."

"Still playing football?"

"Once in a while when my mates get a match going. I'm wondering if I could have a word with you. Won't hold you up for long."

"Ah, I don't know now. I heard you're after joining the guards. Amn't I right?"

This brought on an ominous drum beat by Alex the drummer. Everybody laughed, Shay included.

"I swear he's not in any trouble, lads. And neither are the rest of yis." He fervently hoped that was true. "Just something I'd like to ask about."

Walsh gave a shrug, followed by a comical pat-down of all his pockets. Making sure there was nothing incriminating on him before he went off to the back of the room to talk to the peeler.

Mackey Walsh was tall and slim, and Shay could see why he was a favourite with the young girls. And not just the young. He had a fine-looking face on him, with bright green eyes that had the look of humour in them.

"First of all," Shay said, "and I know you've heard this countless times before, but your music is brilliant. Deadly. I've been listening for years, and loving it."

"Thank you, Shay. Sergeant. I appreciate the compliment."

"No sergeant's stripes on me yet, and somehow I suspect there won't be if I solve this case. Might piss off the powers above me."

"Oh, yeah? What case is that?"

"The death of Rosie McGinn."

"Ah, that was a terrible thing. A fine girl, a lovely girl." He peered at Shay. "Maybe I should be concerned here, a peeler taking me aside for questioning."

"No need for concern, Mackey, unless . . . unless you did something to be concerned about."

"Absolutely not. I knew her. I used to see her from time to time when we were playing or drinking at the hotel. I never . . . I never tried it on with her, that night or any other night. So, what brings you here to me?"

"I grew up with Rosie. She had a few years on me, but I knew her all my life. I'm hell-bent on finding out what happened."

"Good man. But I'm not sure if I can help you. They ruled it an accident, so."

"They did. But I don't believe it."

"So you think somebody did this to her?"

"What's being said" — by Shay's fellow guards — "is that she was off her head on drugs or booze and toppled down the stairs."

"When I saw her, she didn't seem drunk at all. And stoned? Not fucking likely. She was working, of course, for most of the evening, serving drinks and some snacks. And then later, well, she joined in the party. But nothing . . ." He shook his head.

"The party was in one of the rooms on the first floor, as I understand it."

"Two rooms, it was. Big ones, suites, right beside each other."

"And the registered guests were two county councillors from here in the city, I understand, playing host to councillors and TDs from out of town. I've heard that they gather from time to time, talk about their counties, their problems, gripes, all that."

"Yeah. Yer man was up there with them, Risteard Dermody." He was a Dublin County councillor. "Not sure if he spent the night there, but he was flying, I can tell you that. All of them were langered."

"Were any of them giving attention to Rosie?"

Walsh looked surprised, then said, "Not that I saw. But people were going back and forth between the rooms. You're not thinking one of them . . ."

56

"Not thinking anything yet, except that Rosaleen McGinn would not have got herself into a state where she'd go tumbling down the back staircase of her hotel."

"Right enough."

One of the band members came over then, with a harmonica in one hand, a cigarette in the other, and said to Mackey, "We're about to do a sound check . . ." He raised his eyebrows at Mackey.

"I'll be with yis in a jiffy, Johnno."

"Grand, so." And he returned to the front of the room.

"Who else was there? Besides the politicians?"

"Well, me and the other lads. Members of the band. Couple of business types from here in the city. Couple of fellas who work in the hotel bar. And, uh . . ."

"And?"

"Some young ones who, em, liked our music."

"Your music, was it? Anything else they fancied about you lot?"

"I suppose it wouldn't be stretching things to say they enjoyed our company."

"And you enjoyed theirs."

"We're single men. No wives or childer yet."

"None that you've acknowledged on paper."

"But I can assure you of this, guard: nobody in our circle did any harm to Rosie." He gave a little laugh, and then looked embarrassed. "Sorry. I was going to say, 'If you're here about a theft, I might be able to help you.' But I shouldn't bring up something so minor when you're here about a —"

"What was it you were going to say?"

"Just that, well, there's a girl who's been making me mental, for the last two years or more."

"Oh?"

"She's one of them that follow the band around, whenever we're here in Dublin. And she's got it fixed in her head that — Christ, how foolish to be talking about this with you now — she's got it in her head that me and her are star-crossed lovers! She always snags a front seat whenever we're performing; she follows me around after the show, writes me letters. Gets a puss on her whenever she sees me talking to another girl at a show."

"Were you talking with Rosie that night?"

"Sure. I talked to just about everybody there." He looked confused. "Where was I going with this?"

"You said something about a theft."

"Yeah, right. It was late. We'd been singing up in the hotel room. Then I went down to our van. The band's auto. To get away from this girl Merrilee. Then, don't I see her coming out the back door of the hotel and looking all around. She was standing under the light there at the back of the building, but my van was in the dark, so I could see her but she couldn't see me. I was having a smoke, but I crushed it out in the ashtray so she wouldn't see it glowing. She had something in her hand; looked like a couple of silver coins and she was looking at them. Then I heard a siren, and her head jerked up and she flung the coins away onto the ground. And she started to walk away, then stopped. She looked all around her and then snatched up the coins again, dropped them into her handbag, and took off at a run. I remember thinking that if the peelers came by, I'd inform on her, maybe get her nicked and out of circulation for a couple of months. But not really. I'm only joking you. Sorry, Shay, this isn't what you're here for."

"When you heard the sirens, was this the guards coming? Coming to the hotel after Rosie was found on the stairs?"

"No, no. This was before they were called in about that. We were finished and gone before the guards were called for . . . for Rosie. The sirens were for something else. I don't know what.

"When me and the lads piled into the van after our gig, they were slagging me about Merrilee. I'd left the room and she had, too, so I had to put up with that. I asked them if they'd lost any silver, and they went on: one of them had lost a watch, another a ring, another a silver flask. They were only coddin' me. We didn't know about Rosie dying when we were carrying on, you have to understand that. If it had happened by then, we didn't know."

"I do understand, Mackey. So. Anybody else there that night?"

Walsh looked him in the eye. "Couple of girls from down the canal."

"Ah. Who was enjoying *their* company?"

"Not any of us. Not the band."

"So that means —"

Walsh lifted his hand in a *don't ask* gesture.

"Do you know the names of the girls from the canal?"

"I don't."

"Recognize their faces?"

"I know I've seen them, down by the Pepper Pot church. Now, Officer, I hope I've been a good citizen, assisting you in your inquiries, but I have a guitar that needs tuning. Will you be staying to hear us?"

"I certainly would under other circumstances, and I will again. But tonight I have duties to perform."

"Good luck to you then. I hope you find out what happened. And I suppose I'm hoping you're wrong, and that it was just an accident. As bad as that would be, the alternatives are worse."

"True enough. Thank you, Mackey."

Shay let the band leader get back to work, while he, Garda Rynne, knew that the next phase of his investigation would bring him to the Grand Canal on Dublin's south side.

⁊

There were two cars idling beside the canal, one of them with a girl leaning in through the driver's window. Shay knew what she'd be saying: *Are you looking for business, luv?* Shay kept driving and parked up a few blocks away from his destination. He got out of his car and took a leisurely walk along Baggot Street to Fitzwilliam and then to Mount Street Upper, which brought him to the Pepper Pot church. Its real name was Saint Stephen's, but its cupola had the appearance of a pepper canister. And the saints who worked this part of the city were more Mary Magdalene than Mary the Blessed Virgin. Shay knew several of the girls, had grown up with a few of them. He spotted one of them now, Cora. Given that he was going to question her about a criminal matter, he didn't want anyone seeing them together. If she was going to be a source of information, he was going to protect her and keep their meeting confidential. So he sauntered around the streets again until he saw that Cora was in the clear. There was a brisk wind blowing, with occasional showers of rain, and he wondered how the girls could stand it, in skin-baring clothes when the weather called for an anorak. He walked towards her and she hailed him.

"Shay! Have you come to your senses at last? Going to walk me up to the altar in there and make me your wife?"

"Only if you agree to forsake all others, Cora."

"That means you won't be putting me out to work then, Shay." She came closer. "You won't be setting yourself up as my . . ." She glanced around to make sure they were alone, and whispered, "my *pimp*."

"I'd like to take a few of those pimps out of circulation," he said.

"Good luck with that! So what's it going to be? Marriage? Or twenty quid for my company in your car? Wherever you've hidden it."

"Ah now, Cora, you know me. I'm a sensitive soul and I only want to *talk*."

"Yeah, I've heard that one before."

"Could be worse."

"You're telling me? We get the fellas who want us to kiss them. I draw the line there. Shagging them is one thing, but something as personal as a kiss? Not on yer life! But that's enough of the shop talk. So?"

"How about I pay for your time and take you for a whiskey or a glass of wine?"

"Now, you mean?"

"Yeah."

"All right, so. No need to pay for my time. Just pay for my drinks, and I'll be happy."

He decided not to take her to Christy Burke's. This interview had to be done in private. "We'll go to my car and drive over to Conway's. Parnell Street."

"Sure."

They got into the car and, before Cora closed her door, she gripped the inside handle and pulled.

"You've not changed your mind so soon."

She shook her head. "Sorry. It's habit. Before we close the door, we always make sure it can be opened from the inside. If not, I bolt."

Shay pictured a girl in a car and the door locked against her; the image made him shudder. He looked across at her. "You're taking an awful risk, doing what you do, Cora."

"And that's how I minimize one of the risks!"

Cora was in her late twenties, but her face had already taken on a lined, hard-lived appearance. Her hair was a bottle blond with black roots showing. She was shivering in her short, silky black dress.

"You're in need of a nice woolly jumper there, Cora. Keep you from feeling the cold."

"And keep me from earning the few quid I make in the run of a night, me in a big, bulky gansey from the Aran Islands."

They arrived at the grand old pub, first opened in 1745, and he directed her to a table in the back. "What can I get for you?"

"Vodka and orange?"

"Coming up." He went to the bar, greeted the barman, and got a vodka for her and a pint of stout for himself.

When he was seated again, he said, "I'm here about Rosie McGinn."

"Rosie!"

"Yeah. I'm not satisfied that the Garda Síochána was up to the job before I joined. So I'm taking over the investigation."

"Are yeh jokin' me?"

"Well, yeah. But I'm looking into what happened. We could say I'm supplementing the investigation. Her death was put down as accidental, that she was legless with drink, and maybe drugs, and fell down the stairs."

"And you don't think that's what happened."

"Do you?"

"Well, I didn't know Rosie as well as you and your sisters and them knew her. But from anything I've ever heard, she wouldn't be acting the hippie and taking drugs."

"The party in the hotel that night . . ."

"Yeah?"

"Do you know any of the people who went to it?"

Her answer was "D'yeh have any fags on yeh?"

He opened his pack and they each took one. He lit hers and his own, and said, "So? Anybody you know at that hooley?"

"What do the Garda records say?"

"I haven't seen them. I'm asking you."

"You must have heard that a couple of the girls were there."

He nodded his head. "I heard. But I don't have any names."

"They'll skin me if I tell."

"They'll never know you told. I'll keep your name out of it."

"Well, I wasn't there myself, I can tell you that."

"But?"

She looked around her, as if the wrong person might be listening, even here in Conway's. Satisfied, she said, "Deena and Vivienne. And I'll bet they didn't give the peelers so much as their own names."

"You're probably right. I know the guards didn't get any information at all out of the girls, whoever they were."

"And you're hoping to do better yourself."

"I am."

"Just remember. You didn't hear it from me."

He tried to imitate the voice of an American mob guy out of the films. "This convahsation nevah happened, sweethaht."

⁊

Another conversation was never gonna happen whenever he could spot Deena Breathnach on the canal. Of the two working girls named by Cora, Vivienne was an unknown quantity. Deena, he knew. So he would be looking for her. But he would have to wait a night or two, because he had promised his oul fella he'd take him out for a jar. And it was never only the one, especially on a Saturday night. He collected Talkie at the old homestead on Fenian Street, and they made their way to Poolbeg Street, where they met Shay's best mate, Desmond Creaghan, in Mulligan's pub. Des was a big man with wavy blondish hair pushed back from his forehead; he wore glasses with heavy black frames. He and Shay had gone to school together and had been pals ever since. Now in Mulligan's, Des pushed a newspaper across the table to Shay and Talkie. And it wasn't long before they were nearly spewing the Guinness out of their mouths with the laughter, because Dessie had handed them a copy of the *Dublin Daily Knows*, and Shay was reading aloud from the front page of that all-too-popular tabloid.

GRANNY GULPS GEWGAWS IN GHASTLY GALA GAFFE
BY MICKEY JOE PAT MULLOOLY

Guests looked on aghast at this season's must-be-seen-at gala, as hostess-on-the-rise Pamela Pilkington-Poots suffered an oh-so-embarrassing moment. (Readers from the Corpo houses in Ballyfermot may have known PPP in her former life as plain oul Brenda Boyle, whose family moved out from the tenements to "Bally Far Out" so long ago that even Brenda herself has lost all memory of it.)

Anyway, the gaffe at Brenda-Pamela's new gaff in Ballsbridge: it happened at the hooley she put on at great expense for the Abbey Theatre. Pammy's table was alight with bone china (whose bones? The *Dublin Daily Knows* isn't squeamish; go ahead and tell us, so we'll know where *all* the skeletons are buried). And Waterford crystal — some say the crystal was *rented* for the occasion. To impress the quality, like. And quiche and a cheese log, along with multiple bottles of wine that had been aged in the hulls of ships coming all the way over from California.

At that very table stood Pamela PP's oul gran, Biddy Boyle, her eighty-year-old face bravely powdered and rouged, her watery blue eyes infested by two great black centipedes that fashionable folk assure us are nothing more hazardous than faux eyelashes. It was *so* sporting of PPP to invite the oul wan, what? And so sporting of

Biddy to put herself in the hands of PPP's makeup and wardrobe dominatrix.

And what could be more sporting for a poor old lady to cast her hungry eyes on the array of this year's must-have food on the table and ask herself about each morsel, "Wha' the eff is tha'?" Well, it's clear with unhappy hindsight that she didn't know wha' the eff those shining little snowball yokes were, but they looked like candied sugar or what's that fancy stuff they have over there, you know, over there in Europe? Marzipan, is tha' it? So she popped two of the yokes into her gob, much to the giggling amusement of the toffs in attendance.

But stop the lights! 'Twasn't candy at all, at all. Those two inviting, glistening little globs of glucose were in fact little figurines made of glass. So now what the quality are looking at, with their eyes out on sticks, is an oul wan bent over and choking her guts up, an ambulance screaming across the manicured lawn, and a formerly haughty hostess with her head nearly done in by the everlasting shame of it all. What would they be saying about Pamela Pilkington-Poots when her name came up in some of the better embassies in Ballsbridge? What would they be saying about her back in the old neighbourhood in Ballyer? Oul begrudgers, the lot of them! And what about oul Gran? No worries, gentle reader; she survived without any ill effects. But, more to the point, they bundled her out of the house before she could cause any more of a scene.

"Dessie, for fuck sake!" Mickey Joe Pat Mullooly was the pen name of the very man sitting across from Shay in Mulligan's. "James Joyce used to drink right over there." Shay pointed to the spot where the great man used to drink. "He did some of his writing in here. Let's hope his ghost doesn't swoop down and belt you in the head. How can you stand this shite?"

"Ah now, it's great craic," Talkie Rynne declared.

But Des did not stand by his body of work. "I can't. I can't fucking stand it, Shay. That's why I slag these people off whenever the occasion pops up. Though I have to tell you, it's great gas making up the headlines."

"I'm sure."

Shay then had an unexpected reaction to the foolish piece Des had written; he felt a pang of loneliness. How could something like Granny and the gewgaws produce a deep feeling in anyone? But what came to Shay's mind was the laughs he and his old love Allie had shared over the love comics she had found somewhere. They were comic books from America, called *Young Romance*, and they pictured girls and fellas in dramatic poses as they lived through the agony of young love. In one, he recalled, the male hero had a big square jaw on him, and a rake of glaring white teeth. His brown hair was swept back, with hair oil, no doubt. Allie had scribbled black curls over the hair and recoloured the blond locks of the heroine to ginger like her own. And she replaced the words in the conversation bubbles with a line like, "I don't care if you come from the Corpo flats and yer da is in the nick for stealing the Lord Mayor's motor car and the pig's head from the butcher's shop. I love you with a *passion that will never die*!!!" And the fella replies, "You and yer family and their grand notions and their *four-room* flat! They'll never accept the likes of me. Don't yeh see? It can never be! It's over between us. It's OVER!!" And the girl throws her arm over her eyes and cries out, "I'll never love another! I'm going to shut myself away in the convent!" And he walks away, turns, and says, "Yeah, I knew it. Knew yeh'd go for the place with the most rooms in it." Shite like that, and he and Allie would be in bits laughing over it. He still had one of the comic books. And he missed her as much at this moment in the pub as he had on the day she dumped him.

"But, come here to me," Des was saying, and Shay wrenched his thoughts back to the present time. "You'll never guess where I had an interview! An employment interview, I mean."

"With some even muckier, muck-raking, arse-wiping tabloid. In London maybe."

"Not at all. I had an interview end of last week with RTÉ!" Ireland's public broadcaster.

"You're havin' me on."

"I'm not."

"Good on you, Dessie! Best of luck with it."

He raised his glass and said, "I've no need of the luck; I have the job."

"What? That's brilliant, Des! So what got you the job? You brought to them copies of all those timeless classics you prepared for the *Dublin Daily Knows*?"

"Nah, they said that wouldn't be necessary."

"So how did they . . . what . . ."

"How did Raidió Teilifís Éireann come to invite the likes of me to an interview?"

Shay laughed. "Well, yeah. I mean I know you're a fine fella with words, and you know what's going on and that." Des had done three years at University College Dublin. Some combination of literature and politics. "But, Des . . ."

"They liked a couple of stories I did on crime, under my own name. And I came up with some suggestions for documentaries, you know, stories about real events, real situations, that yer everyday RTÉ listener doesn't get to hear. The dark side of Dublin sort of thing."

"Tales from the Corpo flats, kind of place me and you grew up in."

"Like that, yeah."

Talkie polished off his pint and made to get up for the next round, but Desmond said, "Lads, this round is on me. I'm the lord of the manor here tonight." And he went to the bar and got refills for all of them, even though Talkie was the only one who had drained his to the bottom.

"Thank you, Des," Talkie said, after taking a long, satisfying sip. "But what are we going to do without your brilliant reporting in the *Daily Knows*? How are we the citizens going to know what Biddy and Pamela and all that lot are after doing, if you aren't there to bring us the news?"

"Ah, well, my shoes are hard to fill, I have to admit."

"And I'm just the man to fill them!"

"Are you now, Talkie?"

"I am. Give me a minute here." He took a leisurely sip of his pint, looked around the room, then said his piece. "Dazzling Dessie Creaghan deserts his *Daily* post and leaves Dublin in the dark. The divil only knows what divilment the dockers and dowagers of Dublin are doing from day to day, and what dark and dastardly deeds they might dare to do, without Dessie to dish the dirt to da dirty and decadent denizens of Dublin city."

"Well done, Talkie, nobody will even notice I've gone when you slip in and take over for me!"

"I'll be happy to fill the gap, when I've a bit of spare time between my shifts at Jem O'Daly's new place."

"Right. You're working for him now. I should be cultivating you as an *inside source*!"

"Oh, don't expect me to dish out any dirt on yer man. It's oul Jemser that signs my paycheque."

"Yours and a lot of others as well. He's been working his tail off with the new company since he came back from New York. I wish I'd been writing for a tabloid in the Big Apple during his time there. If he's a big noise over here, I expect he was a big noise over there, or tried to be. Imagine the tales to be told about that!"

"Or not to be told," said Shay.

Jem O'Daly was one of the larger-than-life characters in Dublin. Known to one and all as a criminal, a gangster, a charmer. And now, it was said, a legitimate businessman. He had returned to the city a few months ago after spending a year and a half in New York City, doing God only knows what over there. And he had already bought out a big building contractor and was expanding the business and doing a good bit of hiring in the process. Talkie Rynne, who had known O'Daly since childhood, was now one of his (legitimate) employees, doing general labour and driving the vehicles belonging to O'Daly's outfit, which he had named Quo Day Building Contractors.

"Me here drinking with you," Talkie said, "and you writing about Jemser? He'd sack me from my job and bury me so deep they wouldn't find me till after the next ice age."

"Fair enough, Talkie. I promise never to quote you on the radio. But the *Daily Knows* would fold for good, go bankrupt, if it couldn't write about the recently returned Jem O'Daly and the recently sacked Charlie Haughey and all the other scoundrels who keep the yellow press in business."

Charlie had been the minister for justice years ago and more recently minister for finance, before being sacked in May for his alleged role in the Arms Crisis. He was charged, along with several others, with conspiracy to illegally import guns into the country. The arms — including machine guns, rifles, grenades, and ammunition — were meant to be used to defend the people in the North. Charlie and the others were sent to trial. Now, the trial was over; the jury had acquitted them. Everyone believed that the government had been well aware of the plan despite all the denials.

Desmond said, "I wish I'd been on assignment at the Four Courts yesterday when the crowd erupted with joy at the verdict." The scene was unforgettable. One of the defendants and some supporting political men were carried out of the court on the shoulders of court spectators. And the crowd chanted, "We want Charlie!"

"Ah, there will be other big stories for you, Des. We're never at a loss for newsworthy events in this country."

"True enough. But listen to this. The bosses at RTÉ more than hinted that my *accent* would have to be modified."

"What accent? You've no accent at all," Talkie said. "What were they on about?"

Then came a line of posh-sounding speech out of Desmond's mouth. "'Our listeners, well, they listen from all parts of this country, don't they? So we try to be as clear in our pronunciation as we can so that, you know, we can be understood all round the place.' I felt like saying to them, 'Good luck being understood in County Sligo sounding like that.' But, of course, I didn't. I just went along with the idea of listening to some of the presenters they suggested, so's I'd get the idea.'"

"I can't wait to hear you on the wireless sounding like that, Dessie!"

"You'll be hearing me. And don't worry: you'll know it's your old mate Des, with the posh new voice, because I'll be signing off 'Desmond Creaghan, RTÉ News, Dublin.' He paused to take a sip from his glass and light up a smoke. "You'll laugh, Shay, but for all the codding I do, all the rubbish I wrote up for that rag, I want to do serious reporting. *Journalism.* It's important that people know what's going on. And there's a hell of a lot going on right here on this island, and the truth shouldn't be shrouded in lies, or coated in sugar."

Shay didn't laugh. Any more than Desmond had laughed at him when he signed up with the Garda. They both wanted the same thing in their own different ways: they both wanted to do good.

ɛɔ

Desmond had to leave, but Talkie was not ready to call it a night. Not ready to put down a final glass and go home to the missus nearly as sober as when he'd left the flat. So Shay decided to take him to Christy Burke's.

Talkie had been to Christy's the odd time, but he tended to stick to the bars closer to home. So this was a bit of an outing for him. The place was fairly crowded when they walked in, but there were still a few tables unoccupied. Finn called out a welcome from behind the taps and asked what father and son would like to drink tonight. Shay ordered pints of Guinness for the two of them, plus a shot of Powers whiskey for Talkie. Shay spotted Brennan Burke on a stool down at the end of the bar. He greeted him and started to introduce his da, but it turned out that Talkie had met Brennan a couple of times over the years. They decided to take a table, and the three of them sat down. Talkie asked how things were going for Father Burke in New York, and Brennan told a couple of stories about life in the big city. Talkie had some amusing tales about priests he had known growing up, some of whom had given him a glimpse of a punishing hell, others who had given him a glimpse of the love of a merciful Christ.

The door to the pub opened, and Talkie looked over. "Sure, isn't it Christy himself!"

The publican was greeted by everyone in the place, and he nodded his head in acknowledgement. Brennan stood and beckoned his grandda over to the table, and everyone was happy to see him.

"You're looking well, Christy," said Talkie.

But he wasn't, not really. He was walking slowly and he grasped the back of Brennan's chair. Finn came over and said, "Are yeh all right, Da? Not dizzy, are yeh?"

"Don't be an oul woman, Finn. Go off and pour me a pint." Finn locked eyes with Brennan but said no more and went off for his father's pint.

Talkie said, "We were on the verge of prayer here, Christy, with a priest at the table."

"I would expect no less. The lads are on a break, are they?" he asked, gesturing to two tables where several musicians were sitting and sipping their drinks. Their instruments had a table of their own: a guitar, fiddle, bodhran, and a couple of tin whistles.

"They are," said Brennan, "but we'll be hearing from them again soon, I'm sure."

"You should give us a song yourself, Brennan," Shay suggested. "How about 'Ave Maria'? Or, since you'll be leaving Dublin again soon, how about 'The Parting Glass'?"

"I've a better idea. Let's hear from Christy."

"Ah, now . . ."

"Ah, now, nothin'. Get up there and give us a song or a recital."

"Would you consent to hearing the piece you once said 'isn't Yeats'?"

"I believe I said, 'It isn't Yeats, but I like it,' Grandda. And I do like it. Give us 'Tunnel o' Tans,' would yeh?" Brennan turned to Shay. "You know there's a tunnel underneath us here."

"Oh yes, I know that."

Christy was well over seventy-five years of age and on this occasion he looked every year of it, but he was up for a bit of entertainment. And Shay knew his history. Christy had fought in the Rising of 1916 and been imprisoned in Wales as a result. The prison camp over there was nothing if not a school for rebellion, and the men who came out of it soon took the next vital step in the effort to get the Brits out of Ireland. Christy opened his pub and fitted it with a tunnel where his fellow patriots — members of the Old IRA during the Troubles — could hide from the British forces who were determined to hunt them down. That was during the War of Independence, fought between 1919 and 1921. Some called it the Tan War, and that was because of the thugs the Brits sent over to supplement the Royal Irish Constabulary, who weren't able to handle the rebel threat on their own. The Tans were riff-raff; they got their nickname from their uniform, which was patched together with bits and bobs from the police and the army. They were famed for their brutality and hated in Ireland to this day.

And Christy had something to say about them. Finn brought him his pint. He took a mouthful, then walked over to the group of musicians, told them what he was going to do, and they cheered him on. He stood up straight, glass in hand, and launched into his recital.

> Come all ye Dublin men and women, and listen while
>   I tell
> Of a motley crew of misfits who were lifted out of hell,
> Dragged from hell and kitted out in rags of black and
>   tan,
> And sent to sort the Paddies out, child and woman and
>   man.
>
> They were hardly the cream of the English crop, what-
>   ever that might be,
> But a raggle-taggle band of thugs who fought us with
>   great glee.
> They burned our great Cork city, then so proud of this
>   were they
> That they pinned burnt corks upon their caps, and
>   shouted, "Hip hurray!"

They burned and sacked Balbriggan, as through the
    town they tore
Till it looked like a town in Belgium that was ravaged
    in the war.
And it's not just me who says so, but Asquith, a man so
    grand
That once he ruled the Sasanachs in their own princely
    land.

Christy interrupted himself to say, "The place was in cinders! You could see the smoke for miles around!"

But one dark night did they come my way, chased by
    our fearless boys
And into the pub they clambered and clomped, making
    a fearful noise.
They met no friendly faces here; we knew what the Tans
    were about,
So they ran round the place in a terrible state till at last
    they found their way out.

Into the tunnel they scurried like rats, Tan upon Tan
    upon Tan.
It left me to wonder about my own self, Who was I as
    a man?
Republican, sure, but publican, too, with an eye to shil-
    ling and pound
So what could I do but pour them a pint, round after
    round after round.

My cash box did ring as they gulped down the drink,
    but soon they were crying for home.
"Oh, Winnie," they shouted, "why did you forsake us,
    why leave us to cry and to moan?"

But Churchill was fine with the stories he heard, what
    the Tans did to woman and man.
So as far as I know, if you go down the tunnel, you may
    see the bones of a Tan!

All the punters in the pub roared their approval, as did Brennan
and the Rynnes, father and son, before Shay and Talkie said their
goodbyes and called it a night.

෴

Two nights later, Shay found himself once again loitering near the
Grand Canal. Until Deena Breathnach made her regular appearance.
Her dark brown hair was swept up in front and hung down in curls
beside her face. She had black lines painted around her eyes, and her
lips were a bright red, a stark contrast with her ivory skin. The temperature had plunged since yesterday, and she was wearing a white
furry jacket over her short black skirt.

Shay looked around and made sure there was nobody watching,
then he started walking towards her. His left foot slipped on the
slick carpet of fallen yellow leaves, but he managed to steady himself
without falling on his arse. He reached Deena and persuaded her to
join him in raising a glass. He headed to Parnell Street, thinking of
Conway's again, but when they arrived, Deena said, "How about the
Parnell Mooney? I like it there." So he parked the car, and they walked
over to the pub. Deena had grown up in a flat near his, and knew him
and his family. They spent a few minutes chatting over their drinks,
catching up on who was married to whom, how many kids they had,
and whether they'd stayed in the old neighbourhood or moved out
and up. Shay remembered his sisters describing Deena as a good student who did well in composition and music. How she'd wound up
spending her nights with the kerb crawlers who visited the canal Shay
had never understood. And any time he saw her, he knew better than
to ask. But he did ask about the fresh bruising around her left eye.

"Who did that to you?"

She gave him a look that said, *Do you think I'm daft enough to tell you that, and you a guard?*

"Let me know, and I'll give the same to him some night. I'll arrange it so he *looks at me the wrong way* and I'll give him a thumping."

"I can deal with him, if I ever see his sorry arse again. But it's not likely. The sleekit wee git is from ite of tine." Out of town. Shay laughed at her attempt at the Belfast accent.

Then it was time to get down to business. "Deena, I want to ask you about the party at Goss's Hotel the night Rosie McGinn died."

"What? Who says I was anywhere near the place?"

"You were there."

"Who told you that?"

"It's in the file," he lied. "You were there, and you're not in any trouble. I just want to know what happened to Rosie, and I don't believe it was an accident."

Deena looked around her, took in every face in the Parnell Mooney, and then said, "Is my name going to go in the files again now, because of this conversation?"

He wanted to assure her that it would not, but there were no guarantees if indeed she had information about the events that night. "I can't promise you won't be mentioned in the files, but you won't be the target of any aggravation."

She sighed, and then began to talk. "We heard something that we weren't supposed to hear." Shay started to interrupt, then thought better of it, and gestured for her to continue. "We know that that arse Dermody, the county councillor, rang up somebody and told him to go down the canal and get a couple of the girls. Bring them up to the hotel. It was me and another one, and we were promised good money to be with two culchie councillors that were in the city on business. Party with them first, have a few glasses, a few laughs, and then earn our money with them at the end of the night."

"Right."

She went on to tell him about Mackey Walsh and the band, the young women who were with them, the politicians, and the drinks supplied by the hotel. By Rosie. Deena said not a word about any drugs. Fair play to her, she didn't want to get anybody into trouble for that. And Shay wasn't interested anyway. This was a murder inquiry, even if it was his own; it was not a drug investigation.

Deena said, "We all heard there were marks on Rosie's neck. But we also heard she died from hitting her head, you know, from falling."

"Yeah, the state pathologist's report — I didn't see the report myself, but I know it said she died from head injuries. So those would be the same whether somebody pushed her down, or she tripped and fell. Nobody saw a man pushing or throwing her down the stairs, so that's what we were left with. Accidental death."

"Except — what did the report say about the marks?"

He thought back to what DS McCreevy had told him. "There were marks that appeared to be fingermarks on her neck, but she didn't die from strangulation. So our investigators seem to have written that off. Maybe some punter had his hands around her throat at some time, but that's not what killed her."

Deena leaned in closer. "Get the report. Or talk to the pathologist and ask him this: How many fingermarks showed up on Rosie's throat? How many fingers?"

"What?"

She smiled. "I'm talking about Risteard Dermody."

"Jaysus! What is it you're saying?"

"The fucker wanted my services at that party. Everybody else was in the other room right then, and he started fumbling with my clothes. And he doesn't have the use of the pointer finger or the middle finger on his left hand. I don't know why. But I remembered hearing that from one of the girls who used to work round Fitzwilliam Square."

Shay stared at her.

"So he was at me and trying to get my dress off, but I put the run to him. I didn't like him. If I was going to earn my invitation to the party, it wasn't going to be with him! He got in a huff and stormed out and returned to the other suite where everybody else was. I stayed behind because there were bottles of whiskey and wine, and I helped myself to a glass of wine. Then Rosie came in."

"Oh!"

"Yeah, and we knew each other from way back, you know, so she had a drink of wine, too, and we were having some laughs. I was telling her about Dermody and him being all over me. And she rolled her eyes up, as if she was saying, *What would you expect of him?* And I said to her, 'I'm not interested in him, or his money.' But I allowed as how he wasn't the worst of them, and I said, 'If you could have seen the oul corpse who kept at me for nearly two hours last night! It's almost enough to drive me away from the canal and into the parochial house as oul Father Kelly's housekeeper. My gran tried to get that job for me when I finished school. D'yeh think that line of work would suit me, Rosie?'

"'Sure,' she answered me, 'you'd be grand making the oul sagart's tea and his porridge, and washing his socks. And he's too old and feeble to be dropping the hand on yeh.'

"'Yeah, maybe that'll be my new life. Or, wait, I've a better idea. I'm thinking the solution is for me to be with Mackey Walsh tonight. Or if I can't get him, I'll take the bass player. Either one of them would give me a taste for the good life, something better than standing in the lashing rain on the canal and ending up with the likes of that old skeleton.' The conversation was something like that.

"'Good on yeh,' Rosie said to me then, 'good career planning for you, Deena. If I never see you again over by the Pepper Pot church, I'll know you're on the road with the lads of Liberties Taken. Or with oul Father Kelly.'

"So yeah, we were having a bit of craic like that. And then I heard somebody coming towards the room. And I heard Dermody's voice, him and another fella. And I didn't want any grief from Dermody again, and I whispered to Rosie that she might be saddled with him because he was drunk and he was eager to be ridin' one of us before the night was over. So I signalled to her to hide under the bed! And we got the giggles but we dived under one of the beds, where we were going to wait till those two amadáns left."

"First I heard of any of this!"

"Well, it wouldn't be in the Garda files, would it? I never told a soul until now. I was scared. I didn't want any attention from the guards. And I sure as hell didn't want Dermody coming after me. But now that it's you, Shay. And Rosie . . ." Deena's voice faltered then, and Shay saw tears forming in her eyes. "It was me he was after."

"Wanted you for a rub of the relic."

"No, I mean later. Me and Rosie were under the bed, right? So Risteard Dermody and the other fella were there — it was Ardan McClinchey — and they were into the drink and they started talking. Something about 'my plan,' that from McClinchey and 'you know it will benefit everyone.' And I couldn't make out whatever was said next, but I heard a rustle of papers and then McClinchey joked, 'It's all there, Risteard.' And then there was something about 'out the Ballyfermot Road' and the size of this or that, the dimensions. I couldn't make it all out. It sounded dull to me. Business talk. Then I heard one of them put a glass down on the desk. And McClinchey said, 'So I'll have it?' And Dermody said that after the next something or other, 'I'll move heaven and earth.' And McClinchey said, 'Well, earth anyway. I can send in the backhoe to help you there,' and they both laughed like a couple of hyenas. Then it was 'Right, so' from Dermody, and they made for the door."

"Holy Christ, Deena! By the sound of things, Ardan McClinchey just handed Dermody a fucking bribe to get permission for something. Well, he's got all those apartment towers in the suburbs and that new industrial estate on the Naas Road. Is that the kind of thing you were hearing that night?"

"Must have been, and that's why he wanted me dead. Dermody."

"Stop the lights! Back up a little here. What do you mean?"

"Just when they were leaving, I shifted myself under the bed and made a noise. Not very loud; my foot hit the bed frame. Something like that. And I heard their footsteps come to a halt. Dermody whispered, 'What was that?' And they were still, and didn't speak. One of them started to move back into the room, and me and Rosie grabbed one another. I looked into her eyes, and she was as scared as I was. We'd heard something we weren't supposed to hear, and they were on to us. But McClinchey just said, 'Come on the fuck out of here.' And they left."

Deena looked down at her empty glass and then at Shay's pocket where he kept his cigarettes. He stood up and went over to the bar, got refills, and then lit up their smokes. She took a long drag of hers and then a drink. He didn't rush her.

Finally, she said, "We eased ourselves out from under the bed, and Rosie said she wanted to be going off home. She walked over to the window and looked out and said, 'Shite! It's snowing out. That wasn't in the forecast!'

"And I said, 'It never is.'

"'I'm going to be walking home in that. I'll feckin' freeze before I get there.'

"I myself was going to stick around for a while. I was hoping the lads were going to maybe sing a few tunes for us before the party broke up. Mackey Walsh and them. And I wanted a bit more of that Italian wine. So I said to Rosie, 'Here, you take my jacket.' I had this gold-and-red jacket on, shiny gold threads on it. I thought it was quite flashy! I had a black dress on under it. I told Rosie to take the jacket for warmth, and I'd collect it from her sometime. 'It doesn't exactly go with your dress, but . . .' Her dress was a dark green. And she was laughing and saying here it was nearly Patrick's Day, and she looked like a feckin' Christmas tree.

"But, anyway, she left the suite with the jacket on, and I heard her heels clacking down the hallway. And I heard other footsteps, too, but God forgive me, I didn't think anything of it. Somebody walking along the hotel corridor. I just sat back on one of the beds, enjoyed my glass of wine, and then after that I went to the other suite where everybody was. Except Dermody and McClinchey. They'd left, but I didn't know when. Just figured they were off to do more drinking together or scheming. I never even thought . . ." The tears were flowing freely now.

"Deena, you couldn't have known what was going to happen."

"Or had already happened. Nobody would have been using those back stairs to leave the party. They'd use the elevator or the front stairs. The way I see it is that Dermody saw Rosie going by the door of the party suite, but what he saw was my bright red-and-gold jacket and the hair of a similar colour to mine. Hers was darker, coal black, but still . . . Our dresses were different colours but both dark. And he thought it was me. He knew I'd been in the other room, when he made his move on me, and that I hadn't been back to the party. He and McClinchey thought they heard something. He put two and two together and came up with the wrong answer. He knew I would have overheard that private conversation, and he went after me because of it. Except it was Rosie. But it didn't matter at that point; he was going to put the fear of God in — or was going to kill — whoever had been hiding in that room."

As terrible as it was, it made sense in a way that even Deena didn't realize: the marks on Rosie's neck and throat had been made by someone behind her. He must have tried to strangle her from behind. Or maybe it was more likely that he tried to hold her there and scare her. Who knew? But then when that failed, or when she struggled or tried to fight him, he pushed her down the stairs. *Threw* her down, it seemed, from the force with which she landed headfirst on the corner of the staircase at the very bottom. Alternatively, the man threw her down and followed her and tried to strangle her then. The head injury was to the front, so he may still have been behind her.

"Once you come out with this, Shay, that murdering bastard will be coming for me."

"If those missing fingers show up — *don't* show up, I mean — in the pathologist's report, that will be independent evidence, and it will obviously match up with Dermody as the killer, and the prosecutor might not need you at all."

"Might not. Half my life, Shay, has been made up of things that might not happen, but did."

CHAPTER V

DS Griffith shook Shay's hand and commended him on a job well done, when Shay reported to him on the Rosie McGinn case. "That was brilliant work you did, Shay."

"Thank you, sir." Shay managed to keep his dignity in the face of Griffith's praise, when his natural instinct was to jump with joy and call out to the other guards, *Did yis hear that, the lot of yis?*

"All it took was a bit of time chatting up a couple of the local brassers," Shay said then, "and the case was solved."

"But that's not the way we're going to present our report on the case, is it?"

"Of course not, sir, even though . . ." Even though, in Shay's opinion, it would serve them bloody right to hear the news that way. They didn't do their jobs.

"We're not going to rub anybody's nose in this, Shay. The girls refused to talk to McCreevy. Wouldn't even admit they were at the hotel. So I'll handle McCreevy. You will get the credit you deserve, and at the same time we are going to spare the feelings and reputation of the other men here."

"How about this, sir, as the way to present it? 'Sure, it takes a lad from the Corpo flats to get information from the girls from the Corpo flats, girls now working on the canal. Garda Rynne has many contacts in that segment of Dublin society, which should provide us with useful sources in the future.'"

Had to give Colm credit, he smiled at that. But then he said again, "I'll handle McCreevy."

⁊

Shay had no idea how Colm handled McCreevy, no idea how he reported the case to the other detectives. But a few of the detectives and the uniformed guards came up to Shay and offered their congratulations. DS Lar McCreevy, however, did not seem all that pleased to have a killer identified and, with any luck, taken off the streets and locked up. No, the identification of Risteard Dermody as the chief suspect didn't bring a smile to McCreevy's face at all. A red flush, more like, when Shay caught sight of him. But Shay was so chuffed with his accomplishment that when McCreevy beckoned him into the room where the uniformed guards awaited their assignments, Shay was ready and willing to do whatever shite little task was assigned to him. He would show McCreevy that he, Seamus Rynne, was not about to go into a corner and sulk over the way he was treated. He was better than that.

And the first task McCreevy handed him was far, far from the glamour of a murder inquiry. Shay was on the two to ten p.m. shift. And a man had rung the station to report seeing a couple of people, on more than one occasion, tapping the phone in a phone box in Marlborough Street. The informant could not offer a description of the miscreants, except to say that they were two girls, university students, perhaps. Phone tapping. Shay knew the trick. He used to do it himself with the other lads. You'd go to a phone box and you wouldn't put a coin in. Instead, you'd lift the receiver off the cradle and tap out the numbers on the cradle. Five taps for the number five, and on like that. You had to pause for a few seconds between numbers. And your call went through at no cost at all.

Gardas Rynne and Foley were sent out in the afternoon to find more concrete evidence that would lead to the arrest of whoever had robbed the telephone company of a couple of coins. Shay winked at Vince as they headed off to work, knowing this horrendous crime would likely never be solved. They knocked on a few doors and spoke to people in the street. There were no witnesses to the incident, and they stopped in at a café for coffee and a pastry, then returned to Store Street and reported to McCreevy. He gave them a blank look, as if he had forgotten all about it. But then he seemed to shake himself, and he said, "Man said it happened at night, too."

So out they went again in the evening to see, presumably, whether some of the same people who were out the night before were out again and had seen what happened. They dutifully went through the routine again. No luck.

But then, as they started back towards Store Street, they were stopped in their tracks by a shrill "Guard! Guard!" Shay turned and saw two middle-aged ladies bustling towards them, and a young man in a soiled grey track suit running away, tripping and falling to the pavement. Vince said to Shay, "I'll go after him; you see to . . ." He didn't finish but took off at a run. What he meant was that Shay would hear what the women had to say. Both women had their hair in tight curls, grey on one of them, brown on the other. They were dressed in wool coats and were clutching their handbags with vise-like grips.

"Everything I've heard about this city is true!" the grey-haired one said. She was barely able to get the words out, she was so short of breath.

"Are you all right, Majella?" the younger one asked.

Majella didn't answer the question but got on with her report. "That boy is on *drugs*!" She pointed to the young fella sitting on the pavement, with Vincent standing over him.

"Now, ma'am," Shay said, "just take your time and tell me what's wrong."

"I was confused, mixed up," said Majella. "We came in on the bus from Portrane. We're going to see a play. It's on at the Gaiety Theatre."

"No, the Gate," her companion said.

"Yes, the Gate. That's what I got confused about. The two theatres with such similar names. I've been to the Gaiety, but not the other one. We got lost trying to find it."

The Gaiety was over by Stephen's Green, on the south side. The Gate was here on the north side at the top of O'Connell Street. The women then talked about getting lost, walking along the unfamiliar streets, seeing scary, dodgy characters everywhere they looked.

"So, the young fella there," Shay began, pointing to him. "What happened with him?"

"It was terrible!" Majella exclaimed. "I was fishing about in my handbag, trying to find the newspaper clipping about the play, and my purse, my coin purse, fell out onto the pavement, and before I could even bend down to pick it up — I've got the arthritis, you see — *he* appeared out of nowhere! No arthritis on him! And he snatched my coin purse and started to run off with it. But he was tripping all over himself, and got up and tripped again. He's on drugs, I tell you. This city! It's a wonder anyone comes here at all!"

"Would you ladies wait here for a minute? I'll go and see to him." And Shay walked over to where Vincent was questioning the young suspect. The dingy tracksuit was old and stained. The boy had followed fashion and grown his hair long, but because it was blond and curly, it stuck out like wedges of cheese on either side of his head.

"I've got his name, his address. Donnacha Traynor. Donnie. Lives in Sean MacDermott Street. Saint Mary's Mansions."

Mansions, Shay said to himself. Overcrowded tenements, where families were crammed in together, several children in each bed. No privacy at all. Calling these places "mansions" was like calling a rat a stallion.

"He's on something," Vince told Shay, "but there's nothing on him." No drugs in his pockets, he meant. So, no charge of possession.

"And you were stealing a lady's coin purse," Shay said.

"She dropped it."

"Yeah, she dropped it. And?" Shay asked him.

"I only . . . I was off my head, with drink and . . . I'm off my head, not thinking right!" The poor lad looked ready to cry. "I never did nothing like that. Not before. Stealing from an old lady. Or from anyone! I just . . ."

Shay could tell from the cut of him, the defeated look in his eyes, the scrawny body in the too-large tracksuit, that his life was a rough one. If you shaved away the scruff from his face, the side whiskers, he'd have a baby-faced look about him. "How old are you?"

"Fifteen."

"Says he doesn't have form," said Vincent.

"I don't!"

"How'd yeh like it," Shay asked him, "if some young scut stole your mam's dinner money? Eh, Donnie? Would you like that?"

Shay expected to be told to eff off after presenting that scenario, but the young fella said, "No! I'm sorry! I'll go and sleep it off and I won't do it again!"

They'd all say that, Shay knew, but there was something about Donnie — maybe it was the lack of defiance in him — that convinced Shay he was telling the truth, at least as he saw it at the moment. The boy did not see himself as a future thief of ladies' purses. That might change as his life went on its dreary course. And it would certainly change if he was sent to an institution for juveniles.

Before he realized what he was going to say, Shay said, "Come with us. Come have a word with those two ladies."

"Wha'?"

"Get up. We'll see if we can get this sorted." The boy was reluctant, but he pulled himself up, stood, and walked ahead of the two guards. The women reared back when they saw him coming. He put his hands up in a gesture meant to convey that he would do them no harm. And he blurted out an apology. "I'm sorry, I really am. I saw it lying there and I just . . . I don't know, lost my head. I won't hurt you and I won't do it again!"

"Hold on a second, Donnie," Shay said, and then drew the women away out of hearing range and spoke to them. "I see a lot in my work as a guard." He tried to sound like an old hand who'd been on the streets for decades. "And I think he is truly sorry. He's only fifteen and he had drink on him and, you're probably right, some other substance as well. My impression is that he's not a bad fella. But, and I've seen this, too, if we charge him and he gets sent to one of those institutions, he'll come under the influence of a much harder breed of lads. If he didn't go in a criminal, it's a criminal he'll be when he comes out."

It took some persuading, and another apology from Donnie, but Shay was able to bring the incident to a conclusion then and there. He and Vince let Donnie off with a stern warning, and then they escorted the two women to the Gate Theatre. They were dismayed that they'd missed the first half of the play, arriving at the interval. But their evening was bound to be better than Donnie's.

This night's episode didn't have the glamour of a murder inquiry, but if Shay could give a break to a young fella who'd been raised with all the disadvantages Shay himself had endured, that was just as good a reason to get up in the morning and put on the uniform of the Garda Síochána.

ↄ৲

When he got home that night, the first thing he did was pour himself a glass of whiskey. The second thing he did was sit down with a pen and paper and write to Allie Cotter in Norway. "Dear Allie. There is no easy way to say this, so here it is: Rosie was murdered. Or it could come down as manslaughter. I know that you knew she did not get langered and fall down the stairs. No. Here's what I've learned so far. I think you'll remember Deena Breathnach?" And he set out the facts he had uncovered. Then it was time for a bit of boasting, but he tried to be subtle. It was Rosie who was important here, not Garda Rynne. But, still . . . "The detective sergeant who handled the inquiry missed important evidence, and wrote it off as an accidental death. I'm like you; I never believed that. So I conducted a murder inquiry of my own. I got the evidence from Deena and presented it to my superior officers. You know Colm Griffith? He was . . ." Shay wrote "delighted" and then crossed it out. There was no room for delight in a letter about Rosie's death. He considered "impressed" but that was a bit too boastful. In the end, he told her that Griffith was pleased, and the DS who'd fucked up the first inquiry was furious about being shown up. He signed it and put it in an envelope for tomorrow's post. He knew he'd be counting the days for a response.

෯

The following morning, the state pathologist's report in the McGinn case was exhumed and read again. Rosie died of a fractured skull. Her head had hit the raised concrete base at the side of the staircase. And sure enough, the marks on her neck, although faint, seemed to show four fingers and the thumb of someone's right hand, and two fingers and the thumb of the left hand. It didn't take long to confirm that Risteard Dermody's hand motions were those of a man who had at some point lost the use of the other two fingers. But when the information was presented to the state solicitor, the lawyer said that would not be enough to win a conviction at trial. The fingermarks may not have been made at or near the time of death. What was needed was a witness, or witnesses, who could testify about any contact Risteard Dermody had with Rosie McGinn at the party and his presence with her by the back staircase of Goss's Hotel.

What Shay had hoped to avoid could not be avoided: he needed the evidence of his friend Deena Breathnach. The lawyers needed to hear all about Councillor Dermody coming on to Deena, Deena and Rosie hiding under the bed, and the overheard conversation between the county councillor and the businessman, which appeared to involve an exchange of money for favours. Deena would have to testify about the councillor seeming to have heard a noise from under the bed and expressing his concern. She would recount how she had lent her brightly coloured jacket to Rosie for the walk home in the cold, and how she had heard Rosie's heels clacking down the corridor, and heard another set of footsteps in the corridor as well. Of course, the notion that Dermody had intended to frighten or kill Deena as a result of the overheard conversation and that he had mistaken Rosie for Deena, all of that was only speculation. But, even so, the case would be much weaker without Deena's evidence — her evidence of what she had actually seen and heard that night in the hotel.

There was no getting away from it: he would have to talk to Deena again. He had a quick word with DS Griffith, told him what he had in mind. Griffith gave him the nod and warned him again to be discreet. And so down he went again to the Grand Canal near the Pepper Pot church, and he strolled up and down the streets until he spotted her, looking fresh and nicely dressed for her night's work with a load of fellas she called "jockeys" who didn't deserve so much as a glance from a girl like Deena, or at least the girl Deena could be if she could give up her dangerous nightly occupation. But that wasn't for him to say. He walked up to her and asked her to come with him over to the north side for a drink.

"I'm only starting work, Shay. What would the boss say if I mitched off from the office at this time of night?"

Shay would like to get her boss alone some night in a secluded spot and put the frighteners on him. Or, better still, baton him into submission. But that wasn't his assignment tonight.

"I'm going to pay for your time tonight, Deena, no two ways about it."

"Wha'? Things are looking up. I'll not have to be buying my clothes from shoplifters anymore."

"Em, I'm not sure if I'll be able to cover that sort of expense. But I'll pay for your hours, and I really do need to talk to you."

"It must be serious. It's about Rosie, I'm thinking."

"It is."

It took some persuasion, but they were finally in his car and on their way through the south side of the city to the river. When they crossed over on O'Connell Bridge, Deena asked, "Where are we off to, Shay?"

"Christy Burke's."

"Oh yeah? I haven't been there in ages. My brother took me in there a couple of times before he fecked off to Liverpool and never came back. Fierce oul fella running the place."

"That would be Christy. Well, his son is Finn, and Finn was a friend of my father. Helped us out when Da was, you know, when he had his troubles years ago."

"Right, yeah." She turned to him. "If *you* go there, does that mean there's a rake of other guards that enjoy the place, too?"

He laughed. "Not much chance of that. The Burke family, let's just say, have not enjoyed a close relationship with the forces of law and order. Strong republican family, if you know what I mean."

"Oh, I see."

The place was jammed, the barstools all taken, and Shay wondered if there was any chance at all of a quiet table where he could have a talk with his witness. It was Finn, not Christy, on duty behind the bar, and Shay greeted him and introduced him to Deena. He ordered a Guinness for himself and a glass of red wine for his companion. Deena gave him a look when Finn turned to get the bottle of wine, and Shay whispered a reassurance that Finn was not a talker.

"Any chance of a seat in here, Finn? Popular spot tonight, so it is."

"There should be one in the back, Shay. Brennan's at a table back there. He had a couple of his mates with him, but they left a short while ago."

"Thank you, Finn."

They walked to the table and Shay raised his hand to Brennan in greeting. Brennan in turn hoisted his glass to the newcomers. Out of the side of her mouth, Deena said, "Sure, don't I wish there were some like *him* coming to mate with me down the canal!"

Brennan stood to greet them, and Shay made the introductions. "Deena, meet another member of the Christy Burke pub-owning clan."

"Howiyeh, Deena? Shay? I'm Father Burke. Christy's grandson."

Deena stared at him, then muttered to Shay, "Father? There's hope for me yet. Maybe I *will* see him on the canal someday. Wouldn't be the first."

"Ah, now," Shay said, laughing. So it was Shay, Father Burke, and Deena Breathnach at the table. A peeler, a priest, and a prostitute; it sounded like the beginning of a *walked into a bar* joke.

"I'm in need of another," Brennan said, raising his empty glass. "Anything for you?"

"Thanks, no," Shay said. "We've got our fill here."

What do I do now? Shay wondered. He had to speak to Deena, had to persuade her to give her name to the Gardaí and start the whole frightening process of going public as a witness against a very public man. So he took the coward's way out and delayed the inevitable with a line of chatter about the pub, the tunnel underneath it, and Christy's "Tunnel o' Tans" recital.

Deena was keen to hear about it, and said she'd love to hear the old fella do his party piece, but when the conversation foundered, she asked, "What is it you wanted to talk about, Shay?"

"Em, we'll wait a bit."

"That bad, is it?"

Father Burke returned to the table with a pint and a small one, that being a glass of whiskey. He took note of the serious looks on the faces and said, "Are you talking Garda business?" And to Deena, his tone light. "A banner, are you?" A ban garda, he meant, a woman police officer.

She looked straight at the priest and said, "No, not at all, Father. I work at a church."

"Ah, which one?"

"The Pepper Pot. I work along the canal there."

Brennan took the meaning and merely nodded in acknowledgement as if she'd said she worked cleaning the altar cloths and polishing the candlesticks.

Shay was surprised to hear her say, "Shay wants me to testify in court."

"Testify?" Brennan peered at her. There was still some discolouration around her eye, from the bruising she had taken. "Testify against whoever did that to you?"

Her hand flew up to the eye. "No, no, not about me. Something worse, so . . ." She caught herself then. Didn't want to reveal what she knew or who she knew it about, even to this obviously sympathetic listener.

"You two have things to talk about," said Brennan, "so I'll take myself off to the bar. There's a place empty now. And let you talk."

"No, you don't have to do that," Shay protested. "You were here first after all."

"That's right," Deena echoed.

"No worries," said Brennan. "And here's what we'll do. We'll move these chairs over to that table, so you can keep this table to yourselves." And he hefted two empty chairs from their table to the next, saying to the punters there, "More furniture for yis here, in case you decide to have a party." Brennan picked up his drinks, nodded at Shay and Deena, and went off to sit at the bar.

Now it was time for the talk. He outlined the situation for Deena. And she outlined the situation for him. "He'll fucking come after me, he will. Yis will find my body in the canal, and there will be no evidence against him. And it'll be written off as just another death of a brasser."

"No, it wouldn't be, Deena. I'd see to that. Am I not seeing to the death of Rosie, and her written off as a young one with too much drink on her? But Dermody won't get near you. We'll have him in the nick, and if all goes the way it should, he'll be sent away for life."

"If all goes well, right. If anybody believes my story about me and Rosie under the bed, recognizing Dermody's and McClinchey's voices, and then me knowing it was Dermody clomping down the corridor on his way to strangle Rosie and throw her down the stairs. What could go right with all that, wha'?"

Shay hated to admit it to himself, but he could imagine all too well how defence counsel would attack that story in court.

"I want to go now, Shay." She stood and swallowed the rest of her wine.

"Don't leave, Deena. You can help put that louser away. You don't want Rosie's death written off as if she was just —"

"You're making me feel even guiltier than I feel already. You know fucking well they won't believe me."

"They will."

"I'm leaving now."

"I'll give you a spin home."

"No, it's all right, Shay. Finish up there. I've a mate lives not far from here. I want to walk over and see her."

So off she went. Shay saw Brennan Burke give her a farewell wave. Shay finished his pint a couple of minutes later and got up to leave. He stopped by the bar where Brennan was enjoying a smoke and a whiskey. He said to Shay, "Are you going to charge whoever that low-life was who hurt her?"

Shay merely shook his head.

"Those girls," Brennan began. Ah, here it comes now, Shay said to himself, what my friend the priest really thinks of *those girls*. "The girls," Brennan said, "should form a trades union, protect themselves against those shitheads who mistreat them." Shay sent up a mea culpa. Once again, he had judged the man wrongly. He should have known better, knowing Brennan as he did now. "Couple more of these," the priest said, indicating his whiskey, "and you and I will go and hunt him down, teach him a lesson. I guess that's not the sort of thing to say to a guard."

"I suppose not, but I feel the same way about it, Father."

"Mind how you go, Shay. I'm heading back to New York two days from now, so if I don't see you, I will on the next visit."

"Right, so. Good to see you, Brennan. Till next time."

☙

But Brennan did not go back to New York as planned. His grandda took a turn for the worse, another stroke, and didn't recover. Christy Burke died on November 2, 1970, and his funeral was held three days later. Christy had surprised everyone by dying, as they say, "peacefully at home," not the sort of death that might have been expected, given the man's exploits over the last decades of Irish history. In addition to being a well-known publican and a member of the Old IRA, Brennan knew full well that he was a Provo — a member of the new Provisional IRA. When the violence had been unleashed in Belfast, the IRA had been woefully underprepared to defend their communities. Christy and his fellow Provisionals were determined to remedy that failing.

Brennan noticed Shay Rynne and his parents among the more than two thousand mourners, and they were fortunate to have arrived early enough to get a seat in the church. Many others had to stand outside under the grey and threatening November skies. Shay wasn't there in his role as a guard, though a large contingent from the Garda Síochána were on duty for the funeral and burial.

Christy Burke's history accounted for the presence of an IRA honour guard at the graveside, men and some women as well, dressed in tunics, berets, and dark glasses. A few had balaclavas over their faces; a few others had scarves. As Father Sean Murphy said the final prayer, and the coffin was lowered into the ground, a group of six men emerged from a white van. They were dressed like the members of the honour guard, and each had a rifle down by his side. They walked to the grave, raised their rifles, and fired a volley of shots in the air over the remains of Christy Burke. They quickly returned to their van and drove off. Brennan remembered a line from the great Irish patriot Michael Collins, who said that a volley of gunfire "is the only speech which it is proper to make above the grave of a dead Fenian."

Mourners crowded into Christy Burke's pub after that, Finn working the bar and Brennan assisting him, and everyone raising their glasses to the man who had been such a force in this part of the city. Brennan's good friends Paddy Healey and Colly O'Grady were there, and Colly said, "With so many of the Gardaí on duty at the funeral, it would have been a good time to hit a bank or two."

"Ah now," Brennan replied, "I was tempted, but I had my duties up on the altar."

"A missed chance it was. Well, there will be other chances."

"But did you see the peelers at the graveyard?" Finn groused to Brennan. "I'm sure they've enough photos of our lads to fill an album."

"I'm sure you're right, Finn. Good thing our lads and lasses are such an impressive-looking lot. Well, those who showed their faces. A lovely display it will make."

Shay Rynne appeared after a bit and came over to the Burkes to offer his sympathies. He squeezed in at the bar beside Colly and Paddy. As whiskey and porter were consumed over the course of the evening, people's memories were jarred — the pun was inevitable — and family and friends began telling stories about Christy and his daring exploits, and his repertoire of songs and recitals. Somebody promised to have a plaque inscribed with the words to "Tunnel o' Tans" and have it mounted on the wall. Musicians were among the gathering and they brought out their instruments and played rebel songs and laments. It was Brennan who closed the proceedings at the end of the night when he rose, glass in hand, and sang "The Parting Glass."

> Of all the comrades that e'er I had
> They're sorry for my going away
> And all the sweethearts that e'er I had
> They'd wish me one more day to stay.
>
> But since it falls unto my lot
> That I should rise and you should not,
> I'll gently rise and softly call
> Good night and joy be to you all.
>
> So fill to me the parting glass
> And drink a health whate'er befall,
> And gently rise and softly call
> Good night and joy be to you all.

CHAPTER VI

Shay had been warned by Detective Sergeant Griffith that crime was on the rise in Dublin, and the guards in Store Street Station were kept on the hop. But Garda Rynne was up to the challenge. He had been assured of Colm Griffith's faith in him. And Allie Cotter's as well. He liked to take out and reread the letter she had sent to him just before Christmas. Along with her Christmas greetings, she had praised him as Dublin's Sherlock Holmes. Or, as she put it, "Sure Lock'im up." But she went on to thank him for avenging Rosie and her family. And she wrote, "Sure, you're only brilliant, Shay. You're what all the guards should be." Ah, how he treasured that.

❧

In the middle of April 1971, there was a raid on a bank in Dorset Street. Two armed men in balaclavas entered the bank and herded all the customers over to one side of the room. Only one of the robbers had spoken, and he sounded young. Sounded like Dublin. He was short and thin. The other man was of medium height and athletic-looking.

He stood back and moved his gun from side to side, stopping to point it at each person in turn, while the younger fella demanded the cash from the tellers. The only useful description of the weapon came from a customer; he said the gun was a pistol with a "skinny barrel." It looked like a Luger he had seen in a film about World War Two. The pair of raiders got away with just under eight thousand Irish pounds, and made off in a dark-coloured Ford Cortina, no doubt stolen and soon to be abandoned.

Detective Sergeant McCreevy was in charge of the investigation. It took a couple of days, but McCreevy came up with a likely suspect, Duff Kenny, based on similarities between this incident and a previous raid by Kenny: the gun with the thin barrel, the way the gun was pointed at one person after another. Kenny had been in court on the earlier charge, but his lawyers had done some slick work on his behalf and got him acquitted. McCreevy swore he'd nail Kenny this time around, and he obtained a search warrant for his flat. The guard McCreevy had chosen for the job of searching the flat had taken ill, so Shay was the last-minute substitute. Kenny's place was not far from the flat where Shay himself had been reared. "Don't be stopping to gab with the neighbours there, Rynne," McCreevy simply had to say. "Take Hannaway with you."

McCreevy and some of the other guards were aware that Shay knew Duff Kenny, but they didn't know how well. Kenny was older than Shay, mid-forties, but he knew Shay and he knew Talkie. And there had been the odd night in the local shebeens, and whispered conversations about the situation in the North and what could be done about it. Well, Shay was not about to confess to a more than passing acquaintance with Kenny. Nor was he about to confess what he intended to do, apart from: "We're on our way."

Duff Kenny had two places he called home. The one out in Clontarf, which he'd bought with money he acquired in his "business dealings." Not money from the bank raids; he'd not dared skim anything off those, considering whose hands that money was destined for. Patriots' hands, as Kenny would see it. McCreevy and another guard would head out to Clontarf. Kenny's other home was his flat here in the city. Duff had put the flat in his sister's name but she was rarely in it; she was shacked up with a not-so-upstanding citizen across on the north side in Killarney Street. Duff still used the old place from time to time.

So Garda Bobby Hannaway got behind the wheel of the patrol car, and they headed over the bridge to the south bank of the river. The waters of the Liffey shimmered in the sunshine, and people were out walking, enjoying the bright spring day. Bobby was new to the Gardaí; with his round face and ready smile, he looked like a little boy with his first puppy. Shay assumed he had not yet been exposed to the darker side of crime and policing. Now, he was rabbiting on about the boldness of the daytime bank raid, and how did they think they'd get away with it. They'd got away with it before, and could well do so again, but Shay tuned him out. He had some thinking to do. He had to suss out what to do with Hannaway while he, Shay, went to work in Kenny's flat.

Shay might never have come up with his plan if not for the Arms Crisis the year before, when the two cabinet ministers were sacked for trying to procure weapons to defend the people who were being attacked in the North. The Arms Crisis began when the government here in the South appointed a subcommittee to coordinate intelligence and develop a policy for the North, and Charlie Haughey and another cabinet minister were put in charge. Haughey was also given control over a one-hundred-thousand-pound fund to provide aid to the victims of the violence in the North. What the men did was attempt to bring in a load of guns and ammunition. But instead of guns, what Haughey and four others got were criminal charges. Shay was far from alone in refusing to believe the government's claim that it knew nothing about the plot. In the end, the charges were dropped against one of the men, and the others were acquitted. In Shay's opinion, they should have been given medals. As far as Shay knew, Duff Kenny was trying to do what Haughey and company had tried to do last year, with Kenny's own little cache of weapons and the money from the bank raids.

Shay and Hannaway turned onto Sandwith Street Lower and drove past blocks of red brick buildings, some in good nick, others crumbling and in need of repair. Before they reached their destination, Shay told Hannaway to pull over. "It'll do us no good to have every resident of the Pearse House flats goggling at us from their windows. If we walk in, we might not attract as much attention as we would cruising in on wheels." So Hannaway parked up, and they took off on foot.

Pearse House was an enormous complex of four-storey apartment buildings surrounding a courtyard. The buildings were red brick on the lower parts, and beige cement, or some similar smooth finish, on the upper levels. They had rounded corners. Shay knew that Kenny's flat was on the second floor of the building fronting on Sandwith Street. He and Hannaway went into the building, and Shay knocked on Kenny's door. No answer. Knocked again, louder. Only one thing to do.

Something Shay always carried on his belt was a little leather pouch containing a set of picks to open locks, the kind Allie had shown him when they were young. The search warrant gave him the authority to break in. He took a quick look round, saw no nosy parkers in the corridor — contradictory impulses warred with one another in the souls of residents of flats like this, one impulse to be nosy, the other to avoid being called as a witness: *Sure, I didn't see a thing*. So Shay got to work on Kenny's lock, as Hannaway watched in fascination.

"I've never done that!"

"Your day will come. Now, watch a master at work."

It didn't take long, and in they went. The place was a kip. Looked as if all the junk Kenny didn't want littering up the fine house in Clontarf was stuffed in here. Clothes, boots, beer cans, cooking pots, a couple of old chairs with bockety legs. It was safe to say the sister hadn't been in residence for a while.

So, no member of the Kenny clan. Now to see the back of Bobby Hannaway. It was storytime for young Hannaway. "Bobby, I know this street. And I know the likely way Kenny will creep back here if he's thick enough to show up at his own place after committing a bold criminal act in the city centre. If he's of a mind to return here, it's likely he'll come along the quays. You'd best take the car to the quays and be on the lookout. You may be the first to spot him and even . . . and even what, Bobby?"

Hannaway gave Shay a little salute. "Get the arrest! Or a piece of it, anyway. What about yourself, though?"

"I'll follow orders and secure the flat. If McCreevy stops in here and I'm not on the job, he'll have me bollocks. So off with you now."

Bobby fairly skipped away, visions of glory and promotion filling his little ginger head. Shay had other matters to attend to.

He knew what was almost certainly hidden in Duff Kenny's flat, and he didn't want his fellow guards getting their hands on it. Did this make Shay a corrupt copper? He pushed the thought away and proceeded with his search of the premises. He made quick work of the obvious places where no man with any sense would hide any-thing, and then he got down to business on the floor. Specifically, the floorboards. Another item he carried in his day-to-day work was a pair of rubber gloves, so he pulled those on before feeling his way along looking for loose boards. And there they were.

Under the boards were three Colt 1911 pistols, one Browning Hi-Power, and an old Webley revolver. No sign of anything looking like a Luger, which had been used in the bank on Dorset Street. If the (other) guards found these guns, they would not link Kenny directly to the bank heist. Other offences, yes. But Shay consoled himself with the knowledge that nothing here under the boards could be considered evidence in the case of the Dorset Street raid. And if this cache were picked up by the (other) guards, it would be the Northern republicans' loss. Shay was fairly confident that his fellow gardaí would find other evidence to make the case against Kenny for the robbery. They had all the details of the previous, similar bank raid and Shay imagined that the state would lean a bit harder on the evidence this time in order to get a conviction.

So Shay had the guns. He lifted them out of the hole and put them on the floor. He grabbed a sour-smelling towel and tried to wipe away anything on the subfloor that might have carried a trace of them. Now, how to get them the fuck out of here? He heard voices outside. Footsteps. Coming his way? He didn't dare look out the window. He might be seen, and he didn't have the time. He opened the press and poked about; he was in desperate need of a container, so he'd not be walking out of Duff's building with five handguns dangling from his fingers. Now he heard a car driving slowly along the street. McCreevy? He hoped to God it wasn't him on the scene yet. Where could Shay find a container? There on the floor beside the refrigerator, a cardboard box with some tinned beans and corn and soups in it. He dumped them out and put the guns in the box.

Then he decided to engage in a little work of mercy, extend a little charity to the community. There were a couple of big paper sacks on the floor, so he chose the least torn and tattered and loaded the tinned foods into it. He spotted a large bag of crisps and added that to the grocery order. He carried the sack on top of the gun box and the manky towel, and left the flat. Made a point of not looking to the left or right; he walked out like any man setting out to do good works. No Garda cars in sight. Old Mary Riordan was a friend of the Rynne family, and she would be the recipient of Shay's kindness today. He prayed that Garda Hannaway was still keeping watch out there near City Quay, so he wouldn't catch sight of Garda Rynne hoofing it through the streets with a load of stolen food and guns. Mary lived in a tiny house on Erne Terrace Front, one of a row of little attached houses, some painted in bright colours, others in pastels. Mary's was a pale yellow with bright-blue trim.

He rapped on Mary's door and, thanks be to God, it didn't take her more than a few seconds to shuffle to the door. She'd be eighty if a day, and her white hair was done up in tight curls. She had on a blue-and-white flowery dress with a white apron over top of it. Behind her on the mantelpiece Shay could see a red-shaded lamp flickering in front of a picture of the Sacred Heart. His mam had one, too; everybody's mother did. Mary's eyes lit up at the sight of him. "Musha, is it yourself, Shay? Come in, come in. Garda Seamus Rynne back to see me, and him as handsome as a lord. Aren't you a dote in that fine-looking uniform? What's that you have there now?"

"I wish I had time to stop with you for a while, Mary, but I have to be off. Would you have a place where I can stuff this and I'll return for it later? And when I do, anything you want by way of food is yours to keep. Throw this old towel in with your wash, and keep it as well. And I'll be back for the other articles."

"Ah now, aren't you the angel coming to me like this?"

"But until then, Mary, don't let anyone see it. Don't tell a living soul I brought this here. That includes anyone on the street here, and includes the guards themselves."

"And you being one of them, sure you'd know what's best. I'll not be saying a word."

"And you didn't see me here today."

"I did not."

"I'll call in to you again soon, Mary. God be good to you."

"God bless. Mind yourself now, Shay."

Shay knew that if there was one person who could keep the secrets of her friends and neighbours, it was Mary Riordan. It was only after he got back inside Duff Kenny's flat that he noticed he was sweating into that fine-looking uniform.

☙

Three weeks passed and nobody had sniffed out the trail from Sandwith Street to Erne Terrace, and in fact Duff Kenny was charged with the robbery, after DS McCreevy received a tip-off and found the Luger out in Clontarf. So Shay made his next move. He emptied out a sports bag he had been using for football gear, and made an evening call on Mary. He arrived like a gentleman caller with a box of Butlers chocolates and a bottle of Jameson whiskey, and had a short visit with her. Shay then relieved her of the stash of weapons and stepped out into the street. He peered about him and saw nobody who looked overly interested in his activities, so he carried the Colts, the Browning, and the Webley in the sports bag to his Mini Cooper and opened the boot. He had a cardboard box all ready, a box marked Fegan's Frames & Photos. He dumped the guns into the box, closed it, and got into the car. He then headed to the river and crossed over to the north side.

He parked the car a few blocks from his destination, got out, and took a gander around him. Nobody out but young lads with some drink taken, and a young couple who had eyes only for each other's eyes. He opened the boot and took out his stash. He walked along Mountjoy Street and turned the corner to Christy Burke's. Finn was presiding at the taps. Shay held up the box and said, "Found some picture frames for you, Finn." Finn Burke merely nodded. Didn't ask what accounted for a load of picture frames arriving on the premises, just said, "Thanks, Shay. Put them in the back." And that was that.

⁂

Or so Shay believed. Until Detective Sergeant Griffith appeared before him, jerked his head towards one of the interview rooms, and stalked away with Shay in his wake. Griffith slammed the door and turned to Shay. "Did you log everything you found in Duff Kenny's flat, Garda Rynne?"

Garda Rynne, not Shay. Colm wouldn't have asked the question if he didn't already know the answer. If it was anybody else questioning him, Shay would have lied. He wouldn't see any alternative. But this was Colm Griffith; he could not lie to Colm. So he stood there, silent.

"Seamus, I *know* that Kenny had several pistols and a revolver stashed in his flat, guns that were not entered into the record of what you found. They were not there when our men went in after you and conducted a search of the place prior to laying charges against Kenny. What do you have to say for yourself?"

Shay racked his brain for something to say. Finally, all he could come up with was "If it was known here about guns, sir, somebody else knew about them, so . . ."

"You know I could have you sacked for this, Seamus."

"Sir, I —"

"I could have you sacked. But I won't. And I hope to God it never comes to that. I am the only one who knows about this. So far. Never mind how I know. And it seems you were able to gain entry to the flat without having to break the door down."

Oh Christ, the lock picks.

"But that's the least of it. Seamus, whatever your politics are, I don't care, but you do not interfere with evidence in a Garda investigation. Ever. Do you understand me?"

"I understand, sir."

"I'm giving you another chance here, Shay. Don't make me regret it."

"I won't, sir. I promise you!"

Colm Griffith left the room, and Shay stood there cursing his fate, his stupidity. He had taken the guns for the defence of the people in the North, and his troubles were negligible compared to theirs. But he had come within a hair's breadth of ending his career as a guard. And it struck him once again just how much it meant to him to be Garda Rynne, to be a policeman, a Guardian of the Peace, to do the right thing on the streets of his city. And he knew what his fate would be if it had been anyone but Colm who discovered what he had done. That was the worst of it: he had let Colm down, Colm who had done so much for Shay and his family. He felt sick to his stomach; he *was* sick. It was all he could do to maintain a walking pace as he headed to the jacks. When he got there, he spewed the contents of his stomach into the toilet. He hid in the stall for several long minutes before he felt able to emerge, wash himself, and return to work.

એ૦

And as if the gun fiasco wasn't enough, he was still a focus of DS McCreevy's resentment over being shown up in the Goss's Hotel case. Shite assignments, one after the other. Minor infractions that should just be ignored, not assigned to young guards out of favour with

Larceny McCreevy. Shite assignments? Literally, in one case. Dog shite, to be precise.

"Rynne!"

"Sir?"

"We've a complaint from a family in Mountjoy Square. New neighbour has a dog that keeps doing its business just outside their front door."

This was so low on the list of assignments a peeler could get that Shay suspected McCreevy of making it up, maybe even dropping his trousers and shitting outside the front door himself.

"Should we be mounting an armed response, sir?"

"Get the fuck over there now." He gave Shay the address and returned to, presumably, even more serious crimes to be solved.

Shay headed out, steaming. So to speak. He walked to the brick Georgian terrace, found the complainant's house, spoke with the old fella who came to the door. The man described the problem in detail and said, "Didn't I step in it myself the other day?"

"I'll go over and have a word with your new neighbour, sir."

So he did. The neighbour, a man in middle age, invited him inside. "My grandchildren," he said, pointing to the two little girls who were running about, squealing and chasing a little Scottish terrier. Shay repeated the complaint, and the man allowed as how he was aware of it. "Tell you what," he said. "D'yeh know what they used to do back in the day? The ancient laws?"

"The Brehon laws?" Those were the laws that were in force in Ireland for centuries, before being replaced by the legal system of the English overlords.

"That's right. When a dog fouled a neighbour's property, the owner of the dog was required to compensate the neighbour by removing the shite. Which I have done. And then by giving the offended neighbour a supply of butter, curds, and dough equal in weight to the pile of dog shite. Could I avoid a long prison sentence if I did that, d'yeh think?"

Shay laughed. "Couldn't hurt." And that's what the man did. Went to a grocer's shop, accompanied by Garda Rynne, and bought a quantity of butter, dough, and cheese curds — well in excess of the weight of the dog's doings — and took them across to the complainant with an apology. The man received the offering in good grace and began to laugh in spite of himself. And the dog owner said, "Buy you a pint? You, too, guard?" And they all went off to the nearest pub and had a pint and lots of laughs.

Shay enjoyed the story so much he rang Des Creaghan when he got home, and the tale ended up as a light little item on the RTÉ News. "Ireland's ancient laws recently solved a blistering row between two neighbours. A carrier bag filled with butter, dough, and cheese curd more than equal in weight to the droppings of a little Scotty dog was all it took to head off a legal dispute that might have escalated . . ."

It was McCreevy's turn to be steaming the next day. He looked as if his head was going to blow up.

✷

But the oul begrudger could not deny Shay's good work on some other cases over the next couple of months, including the attempted murder of a shopkeeper. Shay and Vince Foley questioned a number of witnesses and were able, as a result, to identify the culprit. The state solicitor put the case down for trial, and Shay would be giving evidence when the trial got underway. Another success arose out of his investigation of a series of burglaries; his work culminated in guilty pleas by the two men who had committed the offences. So, Shay the corner boy was exceeding expectations.

CHAPTER VII

S pring became summer, and rays of sunlight alternated with sudden showers of rain as was usual in Dublin. The parks and gardens grew lush with leaves and blossoms. But late in July, Shay's attention was directed to a less scenic part of town. Things had taken a turn he could never have expected. An enormous tract of land was bought on the Ballyfermot Road, in the western part of the city south of the Liffey, and remained just that: a tract of land with nothing on it. The news came out that one Ardan McClinchey had had a plan to develop the property into an industrial estate with sheet metal manufacturing, roofing, flooring, and other building materials, automotive supplies, and a slew of other businesses. But now he had no such plan. Apparently, he had been denied permission to develop the site.

Three weeks after hearing that news, Shay received a phone call at home from Deena Breathnach. She had something to tell him, and could they meet somewhere that night? "How about Christy's?" Shay suggested. It was the first place that came to mind, not surprising since he had become more and more of a regular there over the past couple of years. And had recently gone on the batter a few times with

Brennan's friends, Paddy Healey and Colly O'Grady. They had regaled him with stories about their young years with Brennan on and off the football pitch. On this night, Shay offered to collect Deena in his car, but she had a date she didn't want to miss — whether a work date or a personal date, she didn't specify — so she said she'd see him at the pub after that. He knew that Brennan was expected soon for his yearly visit, so they might be seeing him as well. When Shay arrived, Finn told him that Brennan had flown in two days before and had gone to the refugee camp at Gormanston, where he intended to volunteer several days a week while in Ireland.

Deena came in about an hour after Shay arrived, and they took their drinks to a table near the door. The fiddles and tin whistle started up, so they sat side by side in order to talk and be heard, and not interrupt the musicians. Deena wasted no time getting to the point.

"I think somebody's after me."

"What do you mean, Deena?"

"I was working last night. A man came along in his car. I'd never seen him before, or I don't think I'd seen him. He had a hat pulled down low over his face. He signalled to me, and I got into the car. He turned his head away from me then, looking out his side of the car. I did what I always do, what all us girls do, checked to make sure the door handle could be opened from the inside. And that checked out all right. But he didn't say a word to me. I tried to chat him up, get him to speak to me. But not a word out of him. Girls like me who do our kind of work, we know that the scariest clients are the men who stay silent, won't talk to us. We have to get the man talking, hear the tone of his voice, try and suss out what we're dealing with. This was a cold bastard. Still not a word out of him. I wrenched open the door and nearly tripped over myself getting out of the car while it was moving."

"What kind of a car was it?"

"A Renault. Green. Anyway, he drove away and I had a date with another fella, and then got cleaned up and went out again. And the Renault came by. I started walking away, and he crept along behind me. A true kerb crawler! Then he stopped the car and reached over to the passenger side and picked up a newspaper, and he flapped it open and sat there with it in his hands, as if he was reading it. I saw what it was, and that's what he meant for me to see. It was the front-page story, something about Risteard Dermody. Somehow, he knew I was a witness who might be giving evidence. Then, in case I didn't get the message, he put down the paper and drew his hand across his mouth, like zipping his mouth shut. My mouth!"

"And you don't know who he is. He wants you to keep your mouth shut about —"

"I've decided to testify. About Rosie's death."

"Oh!" Shay warned himself not to roar for joy; he was getting his witness. But she was being frightened. "What made you decide . . ."

"I'll do it if I'm not going to be the only one."

"So who else would . . . Who else would have evidence to give?"

She leaned in towards him. "Come here to me, Shay. I told you about that businessman who I thought handed over a pile of banknotes to the council fella."

"Right. Ardan McClinchey."

"Yeah, well, I heard through somebody — somebody I've worked with — that McClinchey is going to be charged with something about corruption, and he's going to plead guilty and get a deal for a light sentence." She sat back, took a sip of her wine, and smiled. "Guess why he's going to do the deal."

"You're havin' me on!" You didn't have to be a guard or a solicitor, or even a watcher of cop films at the cinema, to know that deals were frequently offered in return for evidence against another party to a crime. "He's going to turn on Risteard Dermody!"

"That's the story I heard." She took in Shay's reaction. "It's only yesterday I heard it, Shay."

In other words, if Garda Rynne was out of the loop, it might be because this was a brand-new development in the case. Or, he thought, it might be because the original investigator, DS McCreevy, couldn't bring himself to spread the good news around as far as Shay.

"But if some hard man is staking me out, Shay, I don't know if I can do it."

"Maybe we could increase the patrols —"

"More bother from the vice squad? Bad for business, Shay. The other girls won't be happy. That's not on."

"No, I guess not."

"I could move into a flat with some other girls, but if I can't tell them why, they'll have no reason to keep quiet about me living with them. And if I do tell them —"

"There's no guarantee that a big story like this won't get out."

When they had left the bar and Shay had stopped in front of Deena's flat, she told him she had arranged to take the bus out to stay with a cousin in County Wicklow the following night. "My cousin's married to a fella who works in the mines in Avoca there. They've two little girls. But there's a sofa in the sitting room, and they'll make room for me." She wouldn't, however, be able to stay off work for any length of time, so Shay had to figure out a way to keep his witness from harm. And having a Garda keep watch over her on the canal was not an option. When they were leaving Christy's, Finn had urged Shay to come back the next day, as Brennan and his mates were planning to get together there early in the afternoon. Shay had a couple of free days coming to him, because he had worked some overtime shifts. He would take one of those days tomorrow and spend a good part of it in his favourite drinking hole.

⁂

Brennan Burke had come back to Dublin in August 1971, staying as usual with his great-aunt Cliona at her place in Brunswick Street. She had two bedrooms and enjoyed company, so it worked well for both of them. So here he was on Saturday the twenty-first of the month, in place at Christy Burke's — it would always be Christy's, Brennan knew — with his pals Colly and Paddy on either side of him up at the bar. Shay Rynne walked in, and glasses were lifted to him in greeting.

"Barkeep, a pint of plain for yer man here," said Brennan.

"Barkeep, is it?" said Finn. "We'll see how bold you'll be, young Brennan, with your throat parched and your tongue hanging out and not a drop coming your way."

"Mea culpa, my good man."

"That's more like it."

But Finn had taken it all in good humour and poured a Guinness for Shay.

"You're off to Gormanston again, Brennan," said Colly.

"I am. They're in desperate need of assistance there. Assistance and comfort."

"I'm sure they are. We'll have to go up some time with you, Brennan. Eh, Paddy?"

"We will," Paddy agreed. "Help out if we can. Some —" He put his glass down and called over to Finn. "Can I use your telephone there, Finn?"

"Help yourself, Paddy."

"Excuse me, lads," he said and got up. He walked over to the phone and made his call, then returned to the bar. "Just rang home to clear it with the missus. I'm coming with yeh. You, Col?"

"Ah, I can't today, Paddy, but another time for definite."

Shay made up his mind in an instant. "Count me in."

So once again Brennan was at the wheel and on the way to County Meath, this time with Shay Rynne and Paddy Healey as passengers. And again he enjoyed the country scenes as they drove along: the green fields, the white stone walls, the cattle, and flocks of sheep.

"I can't stop thinking about what it must be like," said Paddy, "for all those families terrorized and disrupted. And them having to take refuge here in the South. Even a couple of children killed. If they were coming after any of my three, I tell you I'd be ready to launch a rocket at those murderous bigots."

"If Christy had been armed that day he came with me, I think he'd have tried to commandeer an army tank, drive it across the border, and launch his own invasion."

"The invasion Jack Lynch didn't launch," Paddy remarked. The Taoiseach had made a speech in the summer of 1969, making it clear that the current situation was the "inevitable outcome of the policies pursued for decades" by the government in place in the North of Ireland. Then came the words that made everyone in the country sit up and take notice: "the Irish government can no longer stand by and see innocent people injured and perhaps worse."

Brennan said, "Christy was still stewing about Lynch till the day he died. 'Jack's a lovely man, and was a great man on the hurling and the football pitch, but the government *did* stand by. Jack didn't have the bottle to go into the North!' I don't know how many times I heard him say that. But, Jesus, Mary, and Joseph, Ireland simply does not have enough men or equipment to take on the British Army. It doesn't bear thinking about." The state had established field hospitals along the border, but there was no invasion by the Irish Army into the North.

When they arrived at Gormanston and got admitted to the camp, they noticed a crowd around one of the huts, and were ushered inside. They saw that it was a special day for the refugees. Somebody had arrived with much more than goodwill to offer the refugees: tables were set up outside, and there were boxes of chocolates and toffee, oranges and grapes, packs of meat and bunches of vegetables. Another box was filled with children's clothing. And there were two new-looking bicycles. The man bearing gifts was Jem O'Daly, Dublin's most famous gangster turned respectable businessman. Talkie Rynne's employer. O'Daly was there with his wife and a couple of men in work clothes. Shay gave him a little wave and O'Daly waved back. Then one of the volunteers spoke up to say thanks.

O'Daly responded with a little speech, saying that the people living in the camp had fled crimes against humanity. "I know something about crime myself," he said, pausing a bit for the expected laughter. The people from the North might not get the reference, but the locals did and they smiled and laughed a bit. "But I never did anything like that, I assure you! Never burned people out of their homes because of which foot they kick with. And even the shenanigans I did get up to" — Brennan knew that "shenanigans" was putting quite a mild cast on O'Daly's criminal history — "the things I used to do, I'm not doing anymore. I've put all that behind me and I'm resolved to lead a good life, be a good husband and father. Amn't I right, Etty, my love?"

His wife gave a little jolt as if she hadn't been paying attention, and then she smiled. It looked a little forced, Brennan thought, but someone who'd been married to the likes of Jemser O'Daly for a couple of decades had no doubt gone through many periods of adjustment.

"And," O'Daly continued, "I am going to work very hard at being a good citizen, a productive businessman, and a generous employer." This time he looked at his two workmen, who both grinned back at him. "And, who knows, there may be even bigger things in store for oul Jem one of these days!"

Shay leaned towards Brennan and whispered, "There's talk of him going into politics, running for a seat in the Dáil in the next election."

Brennan nodded. "This does have the look of a campaign event."

"Yeah. Would you look at the jewels on yer one?"

Mrs. O'Daly had on a chunky gold necklace with bright red stones in it, and big, dangling earrings to match. Brennan noticed that a couple of times she batted the earrings back as if they were getting on her nerves. Not used to such baubles? Campaign decorations, perhaps. "But," he said, "how many of these refugees will resettle here and get onto the voting rolls?"

Shay shrugged. "This may make the news, and he'll be looking good."

O'Daly said his goodbyes then and promised a return visit. He took hold of his wife's elbow, and she backed away a bit. She said, "I think I'm going to stay."

He took her arm again and said, "Ah, now . . ."

"No, really, Jem. I'd like to stay and help out for a day or two. I know there are a couple of spaces that are vacant right now."

The chief volunteer spoke up then and said, "We'd love to have you, Mrs. O'Daly. We have room for you and we've no shortage of good things to feed you!" She pointed around to the newly arrived treats. "You won't mind if we keep her for a while, Mr. O'Daly?"

Shay whispered again, "Looks as if he does mind. Maybe he has a political announcement to make, and he wants the wife at his side!"

But the would-be politician's smile was back. "Of course not! She'll be a great help to you, so she will. And I'll just have to learn how to turn on the cooker at home. It's high time I learned!"

So he and his two workmen got into their van and waved goodbye, and Etty O'Daly walked off with the volunteer, saying, "All right, then. Tell me what you'd like me to do, and I'll do it."

Brennan and his companions turned their attention to the refugees and, once again, people had dreadful stories to tell, of terror and death and loss. They spoke to a young boy of fifteen, Peter, who was trembling with anger. His father was one of the victims of the Brits' new policy of internment without trial. The British Army had started raiding people's houses, breaking down doors, dragging men out of their beds, and throwing them in prison. Peter told them how his father was beaten and kicked repeatedly by the soldiers, while Peter, his mother, and young brothers and sisters looked on, screaming in terror.

Then it was a woman named Noelene McGlone. "My son is dead!"

Brennan put his hand on her shoulder and said, "I'm so sorry. Was he . . . How did he die?"

And she told him a heartbreaking story of her son Lanny and his bride-to-be, Trish, and the extra work the son had put in at the petrol station in order to buy them a house and fix it up for their future together. "Ach, it was a lovely house the way he had it done." She looked in Brennan's eyes. "It was in Bombay Street."

"And the mobs burned it down."

"Aye. And Lanny couldn't take it. Couldn't bear it. They lost the house and had to start all over. Trish was devastated, wanted to leave on the next boat out, go to Scotland. Lanny told her he wanted to join up with the IRA and fight back against the men who did this to us. But Trish said no, she was leaving. And she did. And Lanny couldn't get over it all. So just last week" — the grief in her face was nearly unbearable to see — "he took his own life."

Brennan reached over and put his arms around her. "I am so sorry, Noelene."

She clung to him as if she would never let go. Then she said, "They're holding off on doing anything until I can get there, but . . . but they're refusing him a Christian burial. They won't bury him in consecrated ground!"

"Noelene, I should have introduced myself more properly." He wasn't in his clerical clothing. "I am a priest, Father Burke."

She drew away from him as if he was a burning coal. "No!"

"Noelene, do you know what I think, as a priest?"

She looked at him in dread.

"I think that if there is anyone, anywhere, who will be received into the arms of God with love and mercy, it is those who were in so much pain that they could not go on living. I know what the Catechism says, but I have a greater faith in God than that. Our Lord is a God of mercy."

"Do you think so, Father?" She looked as if she was afraid to believe it.

"Yes. And Noelene, I promise you this. I'll see to it that, one way or another, your boy will have his funeral and will be buried in a Catholic cemetery." If Brennan couldn't find a sympathetic priest in Belfast, he would go up there and do it himself.

"Oh my God, can you really . . . but if the Church says . . ."

He leaned towards her and smiled and took her hand. "If I'm a renegade priest, will the sacrament 'not take'? I've heard some talk that the Church is going to change this, to take account of the person's psychological or emotional state when he made the decision to end things. Diminished responsibility, that class of a thing. The Church is nearly two thousand years old, and it moves slowly as we know all too well. But you may be sure of this: when Lanny has a Catholic funeral and is buried in consecrated ground, that ground under and over him will stay consecrated! Now I'm going to go and make a couple of phone calls."

And he went to the phone and rang Finn. He explained the situation. He knew Finn had connections in Belfast; surely, some of them would know a priest or two. Finn said he would make a few calls and ring Brennan back at Gormanston. It took a couple of hours, which Brennan and his companions spent commiserating with the refugees, but Finn came through with a contact for Mrs. McGlone. A Belfast priest she could rely on to do the right thing by her son and the bereaved family.

Mrs. McGlone expressed her gratitude over and over as Brennan, Shay, and Paddy prepared to leave. When they were heading for the door, Brennan heard her talking to one of the volunteers, asking how she would get to Belfast whenever the funeral was scheduled. Paddy turned around and said, "Mrs. McGlone, I'll give you a lift to Belfast and back. Just ring me whenever your plan is made." And he went over and gave the volunteer his telephone number in Dublin. And then they were off.

Back in Dublin, they drove to Rathmines and dropped off Paddy at home. Shay and Brennan decided to go for a bite to eat, and after that a pint at Martin B's, that being Martin B. Slattery's. When they were seated in the pub and had their first sips, Shay told Brennan that Deena Breathnach was now willing to testify in the Rosie McGinn murder case, but she was frightened. She was being watched and intimidated.

"We need her evidence to convict the man who killed Rosie. But Deena is in fear of her life."

"She's in need of a place to hide until that gouger is banged up in prison."

"If he does get banged up in prison. But as for the here and now, I have to think of a way to keep her safe until the trial. The post-trial situation, whatever it might be, we'll deal with that when the time comes."

"Can she talk Belfast? Maybe we know a place where she can hade ite for nye."

Shay started to ask something, then he caught on. "Gormanston, you mean."

"She's a refugee in a sense, is she not?"

"I suppose she is."

"But you wouldn't have to pass her off as a refugee from the North; she could go up there and help out as a volunteer. She'd have a place to stay, three meals a day."

"That's an idea. I'll see what she has to say."

⳹

Brennan was tied up with priestly duties on Sunday, so it was noon-time Monday when Shay collected Deena at her flat in Ringsend. He was dismayed to hear that she had not stayed with the cousin in Wicklow Saturday night; she told him she'd be in trouble of another sort if she didn't turn up for work beside the canal. The pimp again, Shay knew.

Shay had been in touch with Brennan, and they'd decided to go out for lunch. They choose the elegant Wynn's Hotel in Abbey Street. Deena was quiet in the car, which was no surprise. Shay decided to put off asking about the car-creeping man for now. He turned on the radio, and before long, he heard a familiar voice on RTÉ: Des Creaghan talking about the Garda Síochána. They had missed the first part of the story, but Des was now onto the subject of the state's women police officers:

> And, of course, anyone with eyes can see we've come a long way since women were first recruited into the ranks of the Gardaí. Back in 1958 when discussing the innovation of having woman police officers, Independent TD Frank Sherwin got up in the Dáil and said this about female recruits: "while recruits should not be actually horse-faced, they should not be too good-looking, they should be just plain women and not targets for marriage."

Shay looked over at Deena and they both burst out laughing. Des went on:

> Well, anyone with eyes to see has noticed that our ban gardaí are far from horse-faced. But, all that aside, the addition of women has been another positive change in our police force. And it looks as if we're going to need that police force more and more as time goes on.

Shay and Deena exchanged a couple of stories about Des, since they had both known him growing up, and then they arrived at

Wynn's. Brennan was seated in the warm, wood-panelled lounge with a glass of wine in his hand. He greeted the new arrivals.

"You look right at home here, Brennan," Shay said.

"And why would I not? This place was long a favourite with the Catholic clergy. Well, them and some of our rebels, and Yeats, and, well, I am humbled to be in such august company."

"Eh, you don't do humble all that convincingly, Brennan."

Brennan laughed. "Yeah, so I've been told. Now, what will you have?"

They looked over the menu and put in their orders for food and drink. Then, when they had their plates and glasses in front of them, it was time to get to the point.

Shay asked, "Have you seen anyone following you again, Deena?"

"I have. Same car as before, creeping by on the streets beside the canal."

"Well, Brennan here has an idea for you."

"Oh, yeah?"

"Yeah," Brennan said, "a place you can hide out before the trial."

"And after the trial, if it doesn't go well for me!"

"Sure. Now, if you're interested, I'll have to make the arrangements before I fly back to New York."

"New York City!"

"Right."

"Would I go at first as a tourist, like? And then fill out the papers or whatever I'd need to stay longer?"

"Tourist?" Brennan laughed. "In County Meath?"

"County Meath? Why would I be going there? Would I be able to find a job, maybe, in one of the fancy shops? What's the big street there, Fifth Avenue, is it?"

Shay and Brennan were both laughing then, as they caught on to her misunderstanding. But the hurt look on Deena's face brought the laughter to an end.

"What?" she said. "You think I'm not good enough to work in a shop in New York, me a little hoor from the canal in Dublin?"

"No, no!" Brennan assured her. He reached over and covered her hand with his. "I'd been thinking that you could go up to the refugee camp in Gormanston. Help out there and have a place to stay, meals, and all that, until the trial."

"Oh!"

"But, of course, I threw you off track when I mentioned New York. That's what got us laughing, the way I caused the misunderstanding. I meant the camp in County Meath. Anyway, I have to go back there, to New York I mean, wrap up my annual Dublin visit."

Deena was crestfallen. Not for long, though.

"But why not New York, Deena?" Brennan said. And her face brightened like the sun bursting out from the clouded Dublin sky.

Brennan spoke his thoughts aloud. "You'd come over as a tourist, yes, and I know people there who could find you a place to stay. And they'd allow you a bit of time before they'd come after you for the rent! And then, well, my father knows people who can help with the formalities, the papers you'll need for a longer stay, for working over there. He has assisted many an Irish émigré."

"I could start all over, leave behind my shite life here in Dublin."

"You could."

"And," said Shay, "fly back to Dublin for the trial, whenever that might be."

"And go back to New York again after. That creeper would not go all the way to America to hunt me down. But flights to America, they must be dear."

"They can be," Brennan allowed.

"How do yeh pay for your travel here, Brennan?" Deena asked. "The land of opportunity, they say. Maybe priests in America get a great wodge of banknotes in their pay packets?"

"Not at all." Shay knew from past conversations that the priest took on extra work in his New York parish in order to fund his visits to the old country. "I take on some extra teaching duties to supplement my earnings. I'd be happy to have you in one of my music classes when you get there, Deena!"

"D'yeh teach rock music?"

"How about Judas Priest?" Shay asked. "Black Sabbath?"

"We cover those in my night classes, but don't be telling the bishop," Brennan replied, laughing, and then turned to the cost of travel. He reeled off some possibilities for less expensive flights from continental Europe, if she took a ferry to the U.K. She said she had some things she could sell to raise the price of a flight from Ireland. Shay wondered what kind of things she had, and where she had obtained them, but he refrained from asking.

Anyway, in the end, it was arranged that Brennan would help her relocate, not to the next county over but to New York City. Whether for a short while, or forever, remained to be seen. This plan would keep her safe from threats over her testimony and, Shay hoped, would give her the opportunity to take up a new and safer way to earn her living. In Ireland in the meantime, she would be flitting between her own place and those of her friends, without staying long enough in any one place to have to explain why she was hiding.

CHAPTER VIII

S hay wasn't on the morning shift for Tuesday, August 31, 1971, but then he was. The phone jolted him awake at half eight in the morning. It was Colm Griffith, and he told Shay to get up, get dressed, and get to Darragh McLogan's house on Amiens Street. McLogan was a local politician; now he was lying dead behind his house. He had hosted a party there the night before.

McLogan? Couldn't be. He was a member of the Irish parliament, the Dáil. Shay had a lot of respect for Darragh McLogan, even if he was a politician. His background — his early life, anyway — was something like Shay's own. McLogan was a northsider while Shay was a southsider, but McLogan came from a poor family of six kids, and it was a struggle for his father to keep them all in shoes. The family, along with their old gran, had been crammed into a crumbling Georgian house on Amiens Street. McLogan was able to rise above the poverty, after working hard at school and taking any little jobs he could get. He helped support his family but he also got himself trained as an accountant. Eventually, he was able to start his own successful business, and he kept several people gainfully employed.

But unlike so many of those who rise up out of poverty, he never forgot where he came from. Never pretended to be from somewhere else. Didn't even move out of the old neighbourhood. He bought out his brother and sisters, and fixed up the old family home. He moved the kitchen up from the basement to the ground floor to give it more light, added a bathroom, things like that. When the adjoining house became available, he bought that one, too, and combined them.

And McLogan didn't start talking like a West Brit when he got elected to Leinster House, that being the home of the Dáil. He ran in the July 1969 election and secured one of the Dublin Central seats, on the city's north side. A man nobody would want to lose to a premature death. This couldn't be right; it sounded like a tale you'd hear in a public house after too much drink had been taken. Murder was a rare event in this country. Just over a dozen in the Republic the year before, three in Dublin itself. Plus a handful of manslaughter cases throughout the country. This wasn't the North; Dublin wasn't Belfast or Derry. And a member of the Dáil?

But Shay had the word from Griffith that he was dead. And Colm had said to Shay, "You've been doing good work, lad, and I want you working with me on this."

"Thank you, sir!" Surely this meant that Shay had been released from purgatory for the sin of taking the guns.

"I'll have more to say to you later. But for now, meet me at McLogan's place."

It would not have taken Shay long to walk from his place in Emmet Street, but he took his car to get there faster. When he pulled up at the house on Amiens Street, he saw Garda cars and an ambulance. Colm Griffith was there, and Shay greeted him and the other guards as he walked towards them. He kept walking with Colm through the house and out the back door, and there was Darragh McLogan, lying on his back. Shay recoiled at the sight, couldn't stop himself from gasping. He had never seen a dead body outside the safe confines of a wake or funeral. McLogan's face was swollen and cut, and there was blood on the ground by his head. Looked as if he had been beaten or kicked to death. His eyes were open, as if staring. What was the last thing the poor man had seen? Shay wondered. Whose was the last *face* he had seen?

Shay looked around and saw McLogan's wife, Muriel, standing with two other women trying to comfort her. It was plain that she was beyond comfort; her eyes were red from weeping, and they had a look of horror, of disbelief. The McLogans had four children, Shay knew, and he was now told that none of them had been here for the party. The oldest daughter was married and living in Cavan, the first son married here in Dublin, the second son at university in Galway, and the youngest daughter living in a flat near University College Dublin with two of her friends.

Griffith pointed to a young girl standing off to the side. "The young one over there, Stacy Magee, it was her found him this morning. She does cleaning for the family, and they had her in to serve the food at the party. She came back early this morning. Said she was doing the washing-up in the kitchen and looked out the window, saw a pair of shoes on the ground here in the back garden, and came out to see. Told me she nearly tripped over him lying there. She's too shaky right now to give any kind of coherent statement; I told her we'd come round to her house and speak with her. Now, it's time to talk to Mrs. McLogan, get the names of everyone who was here."

No copper likes talking to a widow or family member who has just lost someone they love.

"Mrs. McLogan," Griffith said, "I am very sorry for your loss. And I'm sorry that we have to talk to you at such a time."

Her voice catching, she said, "I know. I understand. But can we . . ." She looked to her house, and Griffith said, "Yes, let's go inside."

There were a few stains on the carpet and on some light-coloured upholstery, but otherwise there was little sign of an hours-long hooley. Stacy had done her job well, cleaning the place in the late hours. The living room had green-painted walls and dark-wood trim, and the trim around the front window looked newly touched up. There were embers in the fireplace, and fresh logs stacked up beside it. Family photographs were spread out on the mantel.

"I can wet the tea," Muriel McLogan said.

Shay wasn't sure whether they should trouble her, or whether this might be a comforting ritual for her. The latter seemed to be the case after Griffith thanked her and said a cup of tea would be grand. They waited until they were seated with their teacups before the questioning began.

"Now, Mrs. McLogan," Griffith said, "the first question that must be asked is this: do you yourself have any idea who would have done this?"

She began to weep again, and then said, "No, no, of course not. I can't imagine. It's not as if Darragh was, you know, involved with . . . troublemakers or the . . . you know, the groups. The factions."

"No, I understand."

"And . . . how it was done! How brutal!" She collapsed into sobs and said, "Oh, what am I saying? I don't know what I'm talking about. Sure, I'm not in my right mind. As if some other way, a bullet in his head . . . as if that would be . . ."

"No, we understand what you mean. Now, can you tell us if there was anything like a row between Mr. McLogan and anyone else last night? Or any kind of trouble recently that he mentioned? Did he seem troubled?"

"He never said anything. And there was nothing last night. Everyone was enjoying the party. Now it was a political gathering, so you'd see people huddled in corners talking with one another. You'd hear the occasional voice being raised, but that was entirely normal with the country in the state it's in now. What to do about the North, and all that. But as for Darragh, he just seemed his old self."

"All right now. Can you list off for us everyone who was here?" Griffith gave Shay the eye, and he took out his pen and notebook.

"I'll try my best. I may not be able to remember everyone. Well, I can start with family. Darragh's brother Cathal and his wife. Darragh's sister Etty and, of course, her husband is Jem O'Daly, and he was here. Life of the party as he always is!"

"Right," said Griffith, nodding his head.

"He's changed altogether now. We all know about his . . . his past. But he's a different man now, is Jemser. A great supporter of the party, a wonderful father to his and Etty's children. It's three they have. There was also a man who works for him, curly-headed fella." She looked at Shay as if trying to bring something to mind. "They were calling him by a funny name, but I can't remember it now."

Curly-headed man who works for O'Daly, and Mrs. McLogan looking at Shay. "Was the man's name Talkie, by any chance, Mrs. McLogan?" Shay asked.

"Yes, yes, Talkie. That was it."

"That's my —" Griffith caught Shay's eye, and gave him a quick shake of the head.

Griffith said, "He works for one of Mr. O'Daly's companies, Quo Day Building Contractors. Drives the vehicles, does some labouring work, that sort of thing."

"Right, that's what he said. He wasn't here very long. Left while the party was still going on."

That wasn't like Talkie, Shay thought, but kept it to himself.

"There were a few people I didn't know. No, only a couple, I suppose. Otherwise, it was just members of the party. I counted forty-two people, but I may have missed some. Of course, we had some of the Dublin TDs and their wives. They were still talking about the Ard Fheis back in February." The Ard Fheis was the Fianna Fáil party's annual convention. "Loads of drama there! The conflict between the Taoiseach and some of those other fellas. Feelings are still raw after the, you know, the Arms Crisis. But still, it meant so much to Darragh —" Her voice broke, and Shay and Griffith stayed silent. She resumed after a bit. "Darragh was such a strong supporter of the party. Fianna Fáil, you know, proud that it was de Valera's party, that Darragh and the others were keeping the flame burning, keeping the tradition and the principles . . ." After another little break, she recited a number of familiar names. "Even Charlie Haughey was here!"

"Ah," said Griffith. "Is that so?"

Charlie Haughey was the stuff of legend. He was the man who'd been minister for finance, who had been sacked from Jack Lynch's cabinet, charged with importing arms, and then cleared of the charges. Charlie's ambitions to rise once again in the party were known to one and all.

"So you knew everybody who was here, except a couple of the guests?"

"It was only a couple of fellas that I didn't know, but everybody else, yes."

"Were they party men, could you tell?"

"I'm not sure. I didn't recognize them but I don't know everybody, especially younger members or supporters."

Shay and Griffith once more expressed their sympathy to Mrs. McLogan and said they might have to speak with her again. The body would be removed once Forensics and the state pathologist had completed their investigations.

As soon as they were clear of the house, Griffith said, "So your father was there. Did you know that?"

"I only heard about the party and the death this morning, sir. Haven't been talking to Da for a few days now."

"We'll have to question him. I will, I mean. So, don't speak to him before I do."

"No, of course not, sir."

Shay could imagine his da's reaction when Detective Sergeant Griffith showed up at the door, not to pay a friendly visit but to question him in a murder inquiry. But Mrs. McLogan said he had left before the party was over. Before Darragh McLogan was killed.

"You'll be interested to hear this, Shay," Griffith said. "Jem O'Daly and his wife, Etty, stayed the night at McLogan's."

"Oh, they did?"

"They did. Etty was so distraught — her brother lying dead out there in the garden — that I let Jem take her home. Jem said he knew nothing about the killing until Muriel came flying into their room with the news. But you may be sure I had a good look at Jemser before letting them go!"

So that was their next destination, the home of Jem O'Daly. Everybody knew O'Daly, or pretended to. He was yet another of the legendary characters of Dublin, the hero or the villain of barstool reminiscences all over the city. He had started out in a Corpo flat like Shay's, his being in Boyne Street, not far from the Rynne family's place. He was the son of a boozing, sporadically employed father and a mother who wore herself out raising Jem and his seven brothers and sisters on the few bob that came in from Old Man O'Daly's occasional stints in the workforce.

Well, that life was not good enough for young Jemser; he was a lad with ambitions. He started his career robbing corner stores for cigarettes and small change, and supplemented his income by picking the pockets of the quality as they strolled along O'Connell or Grafton Street. And he became something of an employer of young workers, hiring little gurriers to steal for him and split the take. He never got fussed if he suspected the young fellas were holding back some coins from the business; he had bigger things in mind. So, when drugs began coming into Dublin in the mid to late 1960s, it was like manna from heaven for Jem. That's not to say Jem O'Daly was a drug dealer. He seemed to have the foresight that others lacked at the time.

When the coolest of the young set in Dublin considered these to be harmless substances that only enhanced the good times, Jem was far-sighted enough to see that no good would come of them, that people would suffer addiction and poverty if they got hooked on the stuff. So he didn't deal drugs, and he despised those who did. But still, there was a profit to be earned on the backs of those who did push the drugs. He made a point of robbing the dealers of their earnings, and he wasn't above using physical violence in the process. This became a risk for the dealers and should have been a deterrent. But, as soon became clear, the amounts of money to be made by young lads who had no other prospects and couldn't even have looked forward to owning a car, the enormous wads of money to be made ensured that the drug trade would never go away.

The other thing about Jem O'Daly was that he redistributed the wealth. Handed little old ladies a few quid for their shopping. Dropped off schoolbags and pens and notebooks and footballs at the doors of the poorer schools, for children whose parents couldn't hope to provide the things they needed. And he did this anonymously, though everybody knew it was him. He was also something of an enforcer; if anybody robbed or hurt a person Jem considered deserving of protection, he meted out punishment. He was feared and respected.

And he'd always been a lad people noticed. He was almost baby-faced, tall and fair-haired, and he had all the girls mad for him. The bride he chose was none other than Darragh McLogan's sister, Henrietta, better known as Etty. They'd been married for something like twenty-five years now and had three children. If Jem played away once in a while with Dublin lassies, it didn't seem to have affected his marriage. Etty must have known; everybody did. But the bond was strong between the two of them, as far as Shay had ever heard. After all, the thinking went, she knew exactly what she was getting when she said "I do" to Jemser O'Daly.

But the word was that O'Daly was telling the truth when he said he was going legit. He had many years of experience in the building trades, everything from carpentry to electrical work. And he had a head for business, for profit, as everybody knew. A year or so earlier, he had bought one of the building companies that had employed him. Paid cash for it. And then he set out to acquire some housing estates and office buildings. As a businessman, he came into close contact with the men who make the rules, the lawmakers, and it wasn't a great leap to think about entering politics himself. The rumour was that he would contest a seat in the next election. His party was Fianna Fáil, the party of that great and long-surviving patriot of independence, Eamon de Valera. The party was founded forty-five years ago and had held power in Ireland for more than thirty of those years.

Shay and Griffith drove out to O'Daly's house. He had long abandoned the inner city of Dublin. Griffith said with a laugh, "Isn't he grand now, yer man, living in Edwardian splendour. It's far from Edwardian splendour *he* was reared." Sandymount was one of the posh suburbs on the city's south side, on Dublin Bay. It was far from Sandymount Shay himself had been reared, but there was no need to remind Griffith of that. O'Daly's place was a semi-detached red-brick house with a front-facing gable and a rounded archway leading to the door.

There was no sign of any of Jem's fleet of pricey cars. He must have had one of them out himself, and the others would be at the site of

Quo Day Building Contractors. But Shay and Griffith went up to the door, and it was opened by Jem's wife, Etty. She was a tall woman, a little on the heavy side. Her face was pale, and she looked as if she'd had not a minute of sleep since her brother died. She was mentioned from time to time in the news, but this was the first time Shay had seen her in person since the brief sighting at the refugee camp. She was a pretty woman in a quiet way, with big grey eyes and straight light-brown hair that fell just above her shoulders. Her understated appearance never seemed to match the blazing gold jewellery she occasionally wore in public, the emblems of the wife of a man with money. Now she greeted the two peelers and invited them in.

She tried for a smile and said, "Sit yourselves down while I boil the kettle."

The sitting room, like Etty's occasional displays of jewellery, glittered with shiny objects. The arms and legs of a set of chairs were painted in gold; either they were antiques or were meant to look it. There were mirrors on all four walls, and these, too, were framed in metal painted gold. Griffith looked around at it all and gave Shay a wink. Shay started to imagine what Des Creaghan would write about the place if he'd still been working for the *Dublin Daily Knows*.

Mrs. O'Daly came back and served the tea in flowery china cups, which Shay couldn't quite picture in the big, powerful paws of her husband, Jem.

Griffith started things off with condolences. "We are very sorry about your brother, Mrs. O'Daly."

She nodded and said a weak "Thank you."

"And I am sorry we have to be here asking questions."

"No, no, I understand. I wish there was something I could tell you, but as I said to you earlier . . ." Her voice wound down and she stared at her teacup.

Griffith tried to put her at ease. "Your children?" He pointed to a brass-framed photo.

"Yes, that's our oldest, Niamh. She's married and living in County Carlow. She has a little girl. Our second daughter, Eimear, is away studying in France. Speaks French, loves it there. And our boy, Rian.

We'll just say he's out enjoying life! Lives in a little place in Glasnevin that Jem bought for him. Him and a crowd of other lads. We had our children when we were very young. I miss them when time goes by and I haven't seen them."

"I'm sure you do, Mrs. O'Daly. Now, first of all, is there anyone you can think of who would have had a reason — a reason in the man's own mind, I mean — to harm Mr. McLogan?"

"I can't imagine anyone wanting to do this. I don't know of anyone who wished him harm."

"You and your brother were close? A close family?"

Shay knew they were a close-knit family, from everything he'd heard about them.

"Yes, we were," she said. "There were six of us. Our big brother, Darragh; little brother, Cathal; and the four girls in the middle. Darragh being the oldest, he took care of us girls and Cathal. He protected us if ever any of the — well, as you know, there are some rough characters where we grew up — Darragh would calm things down, keep us safe as best he could."

"Yes, I'm sure he would," said Griffith. "And he was very well liked as a politician. Politics can be a tough game."

"It can."

"Did anything happen at the party? Did you see anyone being, em, hostile towards him? Arguing with him, that sort of thing?"

"Nothing out of the ordinary for a crowd of politicians. You'd see them having intense conversations, groups of them or a couple of them in little confabs together. They've so much on their minds now, it's no wonder that feelings run high. What do we do about the North? The terrible things that have happened to people up there!"

Shay got into the conversation then. "I saw you at the camp at Gormanston, you and your husband. And I think you stayed on to join the other volunteers, help out a bit."

"You were there?" she asked.

"I was." Shay figured that letting her talk about something of interest to her would relax her, make her perhaps more likely to open up. He looked over at Griffith, hoping he hadn't stepped out of line by questioning the witness. There was no look of disapproval, so he continued. "I went there with a priest friend of mine, Father Burke. A Dublin priest, transplanted to New York. He volunteers some of his time there when he comes home to visit. Brings them groceries, attends to their, em, their spiritual needs, that sort of thing."

"That's good. Good of him. I've been there a few times now, and there's a program run by a couple of the churches here in the city. They serve meals to the poor a few nights a week, and they use the big school over in Fairview. Saint Joseph's. There are some refugees who attend the suppers. So I go and help out. Oh, listen to me, rabbiting on about myself! It's taking me awhile to become accustomed to my new role in life — politician's wife! Or wife of a man who *hopes* to run for office. I'm not one for, well, appearing in public and all that. Getting myself all dressed up and posing for the cameras! But if I can be useful there in the camp, helping the refugees, I'll be doing something good for people, as my husband is trying to do." She shook her head then and said, "Ah, I'm sorry. My mind goes off on its own sometimes. What was I saying?"

"You mentioned some intense conversations at the McLogans' party," Griffith said.

"Right, right. But there was no shouting, and nobody storming off, you know."

"Was Darragh involved in any of those conversations? Or could you hear whether the talk was about him?"

"Well, there was one argument of some kind and Darragh was in it. But it was the other man who was . . . who seemed intent on having a row. I heard the man say something about the Ard Fheis in February. You know, they were all at the Ard Fheis in Ballsbridge."

"They were, yes."

"And that was still on their minds, and it seems the debates spilled over into the evening at Darragh's."

"Who was it, Mrs. O'Daly, the man you heard arguing with Darragh?"

Etty looked a bit shamefaced then. "I don't want to . . ." She didn't want to be telling tales about the man, informing on him.

"You can tell us, Mrs. O'Daly. After all" — Griffith smiled at her while saying it — "you are helping the police with their inquiries."

The woman tried to smile back. "Ah, I know. It was Jolly Roger Conaty." Conaty, Shay knew, was a TD from one of the northern suburbs. "He was having a go at Darragh, maybe about something that happened at the Ard Fheis. But Darragh wasn't in a wax about it; he was calm and reasonable, as he always is." She choked up a bit then. "Was! And it was my Jemser who was in between him and Conaty, trying to settle things down. Except when he called him a Blueshirt!"

"Who called who a Blueshirt?"

"Conaty said it to Darragh."

That was a name that still stuck to Fine Gael, the opposition party in the Dáil, because for a very brief time in the early 1930s, an earlier version of the party had flirted with what looked a lot like fascism. It was a law and order crowd, started up by a former Garda commissioner, and they wore blue shirts. It only lasted a couple of years, and that history was long behind the party. Some people, though, still used the word "Blueshirt" to slag off the members of Fine Gael. So for a member of Fianna Fáil to call someone a Blueshirt, it meant he considered that man a sympathizer for the opposition party.

"Jem tried to get them to back off each other, cool things down."

"Oh, is that right?"

"Everybody knows Jem's history. Of course they do. But what they might not know is that Jem can be very diplomatic, can calm people down."

"How about something in the past?" Griffith asked. "Anything that might have come back, got somebody fired up? After all, the way he was killed —"

She flinched at that, and Griffith apologized. "Again, I'm sorry, Mrs. O'Daly. It's just that the way he died has the look of a sudden passion, sudden anger. Not a premeditated killing, but that doesn't mean it might not have arisen from something in the past. Something that came up again, and set somebody off in a fit of temper."

The victim's sister was in tears by this time, as well she might be. But the questions had to be asked.

"I honestly can't think of anything. But I'm not thinking clearly now, anyway. If I think of anything —"

The door opened then and in walked Jem O'Daly. Etty looked over at him, and something flashed in her eyes. Shay read it as fear. But it was gone in an instant, so Shay may have been reading into it something that wasn't there.

"Jem!" she said. "Detective Griffith is here to, well . . ."

"Hello again, Colm." And then to Shay, "And I know Garda Rynne. I remember him from the days when him and the other little hellraisers used to jump into the canal and splash water on the decent folk walking by!"

Shay had a fleeting memory of himself and Des Creaghan doing exactly that.

"Guilty," he pleaded.

O'Daly had put on some weight over the years; he was heavy-set but not fat. His full head of fair hair was going a bit grey. There were a couple of faded scars on his face. He had on a pricey-looking blazer, a beige colour, and it looked like linen. Was that a silk shirt under it? Shay didn't know.

"Are yis getting anywhere with it? Any closer to finding the scut who did this?"

"We're gathering loads of information, Jem," Griffith said. "We'll have him. Don't be in any doubt about that."

"I'm just in to pick up some papers for a meeting over at my office, but I can come in to Store Street if you think I can help with anything."

"Thank you, Jem. A couple of quick questions now while we have you here?"

"Ask away."

"Well, the big question. Is there anything you can think of that explains this? Anyone who had it in for Darragh, or anyone who got himself into a fit of temper at the party?"

"Apart from the fact that political men always have people angry or dissatisfied with them, I truly cannot think of anybody who'd have done that to Darragh. Somebody did, but I sure as hell didn't see it coming. I have no fucking idea who did this."

"How about any arguments at the party, or at political gatherings recently?"

"Just the usual. Fellas jockeying for position, trying to get support ready in case of an election. Or" — he looked intently at Griffith — "a heave against Lynch."

There had been a rift in the party ever since the Arms Crisis, and there were some who would dearly love to oust the leader, Jack Lynch, and replace him with somebody more to their liking. Who? Charlie Haughey?

"And did any of that spill over on Darragh McLogan?"

"I can tell you, and you may have heard of it already, that Jolly Roger Conaty and Darragh had a bit of a dispute at the party. Words only, you can be sure. I can't imagine Conaty getting ferocious with Darragh. And anyway, I think I succeeded in pouring oil on the waters there."

"Good on you. What was it about, that little row?"

"Ah, something that had started way back at the RDS." The RDS was the Royal Dublin Society, the complex in Ballsbridge where Fianna Fáil had held the annual conference. "I'm not sure what led into it, but Charlie Haughey's name came up, and Conaty said something like, 'And you kissing up to Charlie as if you were a butler for the republican wing of our party, when really you have the heart and mind of a fuckin' Blueshirt!'"

"Painful for poor Darragh to hear that."

"To hear it on his last night amongst us. Look, officers, I have to go. But if I think of anything, I'll be in to see you, you may be sure."

He started from the room but then turned and said to Shay, "I had yer oul fella with me at the hooley, but don't be concerned. He was gone long before Darragh was . . . long before it happened." O'Daly left the room then, clomped up the stairs, and was back a few seconds later with a black leather carrying case. "All right. Goodbye for now. Etty, love, I won't be late."

Calming words but his eyes rested on his wife, and the look seemed to Shay to be one of warning. But, again, that may just have been the copper in him looking for suspicious behaviour in the wake of the murder.

CHAPTER IX

After their interview with Jem and Etty O'Daly, DS Griffith and Shay returned to Amiens Street and made the rounds, questioning the McLogans' neighbours, none of whom had heard anything useful. All they'd heard were the sounds of music coming from the McLogan house, and voices loud with drink. DS Griffith tapped two other guards to assist, and assigned them half the guests who had been enjoying the McLogans' hospitality the night before. Griffith and Shay set out to question the people on their list. Everyone offered bland assurances that they had not seen or heard anything that could account for the killing of McLogan. Griffith asked about the "Blueshirt" slagging, and a couple of people had heard it but didn't think anything of it. Just the kind of thing someone might say in a moment of exasperation, or as a comment on someone's politics. Nobody saw any punches thrown.

"Now, is it time to up our game a bit?" Shay asked when they had finished that round of questioning and were back at Store Street. "Are we going to talk to Haughey?"

"We certainly are." Griffith looked at his watch. "He should still be in his office."

"Could we wait awhile?"

"Wait?"

"Ever been to Abbeville?"

Griffith had to laugh. "Em, no."

"Now's our chance."

"Speaking of upping our game, Shay, I was quite impressed with your work on the Goss's Hotel case. Even though you started it off your own bat without permission! You'll not be doing that again."

Shay gave him a wary nod. "I won't, sir."

"And I've been impressed with other work you've done as well. I'm thinking of the guilty pleas for those burglaries and the charges laid in that attempted murder inquiry. I'm proud of you, lad."

The words glowed in Shay's mind.

"Here's what I have in mind. We put you in plain clothes and have you involved in more inquiries like this one. Crime is going up, not down, and there will be more bodies lying on the ground with their souls departed. Unfortunately. So, we'll have you working on more cases like this one. How does that sound to you?"

Shay stood there, gobsmacked. It was not a promotion to another rank, but it was a move upwards, no question. To be working serious cases, in plain clothes. And, though Griffith hadn't mentioned it, Shay would now be entitled to carry a gun.

"I'm a detective, young Shay. And I detect from the expression on your face that this idea is not unwelcome to you."

"Unwelcome, no, sir. Not at all. I'm honoured . . . delighted!" He felt himself blushing.

"Grand. We'll get that arranged."

"Thank you, sir!"

"Now, despite your new status, I'll be taking another of the guards with me to question another witness. Where would Mr. Rynne senior be at this time of the day?"

"He'd likely be out at Quo Day's headquarters, sir. Then home after that."

Shay's mind veered from joy over his new status in the Garda to concern over his father being questioned. But he had no choice except to wait and see what that questioning would reveal. He went into the room where his fellow guards were seated at desks doing their paperwork, and he sat and started on his own. He did his best to concentrate on the interviews they had done and record them accurately in his notes.

Late in the afternoon, Colm Griffith returned to Store Street and immediately put Shay's mind to rest. "Your father's account of himself fits with what we heard from O'Daly and Mrs. McLogan. He was at the party for a while, enjoyed a bit of the food and drink, chatted with people he knew, and left while everyone was still standing, including Darragh McLogan." Shay tried not to look as relieved as he felt. He avoided the eyes of the other guards who, he knew, had heard what Griffith said.

And then, that evening, it was time for a visit to Abbeville, time to see for themselves how far Charlie Haughey had risen from his humble beginnings. Charlie was one of seven children; his father had been disabled, and his mother had to raise her girls and boys on a small amount of pension income. But look at Charlie now. His imposing Georgian mansion was in Kinsealy, a few miles north of the city. The gods must have been smiling on the two guards because as they drove towards the massive house with its two-hundred-plus acres of land, there was Haughey himself, looking lordly, dressed in a tweed riding jacket, sitting astride a sleek brown horse with a black mane and tail. Posed against the light grey walls of his manor, it was as if he'd been expecting, not Rynne and Griffith, surely, but perhaps a crew from the telly come to film his aristocratic pretensions.

Or maybe the peelers after all. Griffith had left word at Store Street that he and Shay would be going out to Kinsealy; if ever there was someone who had fingers in every pie and maybe ears in every official office, it might be the former cabinet minister and man in the mohair suit, Charlie Haughey. But he pretended to be surprised at their arrival, got down off his (high) horse, walked it to a man standing some distance away on the property, and invited Shay and Griffith into the house.

Haughey was not a tall man, five and a half feet in height, and it was well known that he was self-conscious about it. Didn't like to be seen looking up at his opponents. It was also well known that he made up for it in other ways. What was the word? Compensated? Shay looked at the familiar face of the politician. Former politician. Haughey's hair was slicked back from a receding hairline, leaving a vee of brown hair on his forehead. He had a prominent, straight nose and hooded eyes. Still in his riding jacket, he brought his visitors into the sitting room. He knew Griffith, who introduced Shay. The place was as grand inside as out, with its high ceilings, mouldings, and elaborate furniture. Haughey didn't offer them tea. Shay didn't see anyone else in the house who might have made it. No sign of his wife, Maureen, daughter of the former Taoiseach Sean Lemass. Haughey said, "You're here about Darragh."

"We are," said Griffith.

"I can tell you I have no idea who did this, or who would have wanted him dead. He was well liked."

"True, but somebody didn't like him, and we have to question everybody who was there. What time did you arrive at the party, Mr. Haughey?"

"I'd say it was around half ten. And I wasn't there for long. Made the rounds and spoke to Darragh and Muriel, and most everyone else there, and then I left. Maybe forty, forty-five minutes later."

"Where did you go after?"

Haughey laughed. "Numerous people at Duffy's in Malahide can testify that I was there. You know Duffy's, used to be Hogan's."

"Are you aware of any arguments, any resentments, disagreements at the party or perhaps at the Ard Fheis back in February?"

He gave them a look as if to say *What would you expect?* "There was loads of that at the Ard Fheis, as you are no doubt aware. But this looks more personal than political."

"It does have that look about it, but it did happen at a gathering of the party faithful."

"I can't think of anything about our politics that could possibly explain a crime of such brutality." It seemed he had heard how McLogan died. Haughey leaned forward with a little smile. "After all, I was minister for justice. I wouldn't just let it go!"

Shay reflected as they said their thanks and goodbyes that he couldn't think of anything about their politics that could explain how a man on even a cabinet minister's pay, which he had been earning before he was sacked from cabinet, could afford to buy a palatial pile like this.

⅋

There was a bit of embarrassment for Shay the next morning when he arrived at Store Street. DS Griffith took a look at him and said, "Still in uniform, Garda Rynne?" Shay was thankful that nobody was within hearing distance because the reason he wasn't in plain clothes was that the only plain clothes he had of a workday type were second-hand, frayed, and worn. He was determined not to bring shame on himself in front of the other guards by appearing as a poor Dublin lad in worn-out clothes. He had not yet had the time to go to the shops. But Griffith was able to read his embarrassment and said no more about it, except to suggest that he work an afternoon and evening shift the next day.

The other Garda team reported that the politicians and wives they interviewed had nothing helpful to offer; they had not seen anything of a suspicious nature at McLogan's party. But Shay and Griffith did have a bit of luck with one of the Fianna Fáil TDs, Art Crilly. He jokingly said he fancied himself a bit of an artist with a camera, and he had taken a number of unposed pictures over the course of the evening. He offered to take the film in right away to have it developed. Griffith said, "If you don't mind, sir, we could take the camera and have the film done today." Crilly had no objection to that, and retrieved it from his desk and handed it over.

By mid-afternoon they had a packet of photos to examine. Shay and Griffith spread them out on a table and looked them over. Mostly, it was one politician chatting up another, or groups of them together. Shay noticed one shot of a man, taken from behind. The head of dark curls, the slope of the shoulders — it was Talkie Rynne in conversation with another of the guests.

As much as they hated to distress the widow again, they needed to have her identify the people Shay and Griffith didn't recognize. So once again they were at the house on Amiens Street. They told Mrs. McLogan about the photos and asked her to have a look. Her oldest daughter, Amy, was in the room with her, sitting on a sofa with her head in her hands. She looked up, opened her mouth as if to speak, but nothing came out. Not surprisingly, the pictures set off a wave of emotion again in the widow. Darragh was featured in several of the pictures.

It took a moment but Muriel cleared her throat and said, "Will you look at the pair of them!" She was pointing to a shot of Darragh with his brother-in-law, Jem O'Daly. O'Daly had his arm around Darragh's shoulder, and they grinned as they held up their glasses of whiskey for their colleague with the camera. "I know you, being the Gardaí, must look at Jem and think, well . . ."

"No," Griffith said, "we know he says he's changed his ways. He hasn't been in our sights lately at all."

O'Daly had a slew of ways that needed changing, but it was common knowledge that he had set his sights on a political career. His wife's brother, Darragh McLogan, had been one of his most loyal supporters, even though McLogan was a law-and-order type of politician. O'Daly was known to be sympathetic to the "subversives," the Irish republicans. O'Daly would not be in favour, for instance, of cracking down on the IRA. So, ideological differences between the two men. But family is family.

Other photos showed the wives of the politicians all dressed up for the occasion, and Muriel McLogan identified them one by one. Shay remembered that there had been a couple of people she didn't know, and she noticed one of them in the photographs. He was a short, stocky man shown from behind. She didn't know his name but said he had been friendly in conversations with the political people who were there. Shay and Griffith thanked Amy and Mrs. McLogan, and left the house, none the wiser for their photographic display.

"We're to see the girl who did the cleanup," Shay reminded the DS.

"Ah, you're right. We'll see her first thing tomorrow morning, em, afternoon. You took down her address?"

"I did. She lives with her parents in Liberty House."

☙

The death of Darragh McLogan was a tragedy, no two ways about it. But Shay could not help feeling pleased with himself; DS Griffith had selected him to work on a murder inquiry involving a well-known Dublin politician. A big case, and Shay was working it. Some of the young guards made comments like, "Good on you, Shay!" This gave him the feeling he'd always wanted, a feeling of being accepted in the Store Street Garda Station, a certainty that he was among friends. For the most part. Oh, there were a few, as always, who made cracks like, "Hope somebody checks the silver over there at the McLogans' place; make sure nothing goes missing." Shay did his best to ignore all that.

But someone he couldn't ignore was Detective Sergeant McCreevy. Shay was standing outside what he called the workroom, and there was a small group of guards around Colm Griffith, likely asking him about the McLogan inquiry. And here came McCreevy. He walked over to Shay and whispered, "Good man, is DS Griffith, taking on young guards and giving a boost to their careers. Only hope it doesn't damage his own career. Hate to see a good man shot down on his way up the ladder." And he walked away.

Shay felt as if his knees were going to buckle. He turned and walked into the room and sat at the first desk he saw. *Shot* down? Damage his career? Had McCreevy found out about the guns? How? An informer? Didn't matter how. The point was he'd found out. He must have. And he wanted Shay to know it. Shay was trembling. That hateful fucker could put an end to Shay's career. But even worse was the hint that McCreevy could damage the career of a rival, Colm Griffith, his chance for promotion. And all because Colm had given Shay a pass after discovering that Shay had taken Duff Kenny's guns. After all Colm had done for him, Shay felt like the worst kind of ingrate.

Shay had arranged to meet Des Creaghan and his wife, Fiona, after work, at Doheny and Nesbitt's pub in Baggot Street. Shay tried to put the gun debacle out of his mind. What would McCreevy gain by revealing it to anyone else? He'd have the satisfaction of seeing Garda Rynne sacked, Garda Rynne who had shown him up over the Goss's Hotel killing and had moved up to plain clothes and major cases. But then what? He would use the information against Colm Griffith in the competition to replace Detective Inspector Hennessy when Hennessy moved up. But according to the talk at Store Street, that wasn't going to happen any time soon. So, Shay told himself, McCreevy would wait. Bide his time. And what else could Shay do until then, but work as hard as he could on the cases assigned to him, especially the McLogan murder inquiry. He told himself to concentrate on the present. And the evening ahead.

Doheny and Nesbitt's was a drinking spot beloved of politicians and news reporters; the grand old Victorian pub was a well-known Dublin landmark. Des had taken to drinking there after he was hired by RTÉ; the very people with the most news value were to be seen here in D&N. Des was well on, by the look and sound of him when Shay arrived, so he might not be at his news-gathering best. But Fiona was, as always, sober and sensible. Shay sat down and took a swallow of the warm pint Des had waiting for him. God knows, he needed it. He looked forward to lifting a few more jars with his friends over the course of the evening. Fiona was a schoolteacher, and Shay had always enjoyed the amusing tales she would tell about the little mischief-makers in her class. She and Des had been waiting for little mischief-makers of their own, but no joy yet.

But the main topic of conversation was, of course, the murder of Darragh McLogan. Des was mad keen to hear all the details from Garda Shay Rynne. But Garda Rynne was still smarting from the balls-up with the guns; he was not going to bring more trouble down on his head by gabbing to a news reporter about the murder inquiry. All he said to Des was "They'll have me bollocks if I tell you anything."

Des understood, and he had other sources in the Garda Síochána who would not be shy about telling what they knew. But Shay did disclose the fact that his own father had been there; Des would find out sooner or later.

"Talkie there on the big night? He'll be my unnamed source!"

"Don't excite yourself now, Desmond. He was only there for a short time and left when everyone was still standing. And my fellow peelers know it." Shay managed a laugh and added, "But I may meet you on a dark street corner some night to tip you the wink if we pick Charlie Haughey as our suspect."

"Wouldn't that be brilliant? As soon as you give me the word, I'll start ringing publishing houses to bid for the book I'll be writing about your role in taking down Charlie Haughey."

"Ah, now, it's already been done. Jack Lynch took him down over the gun fiasco." Charlie's gun fiasco, not to be confused with Shay Rynne's little fuck-up.

"Charlie will rise again. I told you about him at the Ard Fheis."

Des had come away from the political convention in February with all kinds of tales about the Fianna Fáil party members, but Shay had forgotten all but a few snippets. "Tell me again."

"I will," he said, pausing to light a cigarette, "because I am not under the constraints which hobble you as a guard from blabbing to me. As long as you can convince me that you won't go running to my competitors in the news business, and reveal my insights to those less worthy hacks."

"We've already established that I'll not be talking to any newshounds, Creaghan, so get on with it."

"You should have seen it, Shay! Of course, the party's been split down the middle ever since the Arms Crisis. You heard about the crowd of them trying to shout down Jack Lynch. Him being the Taoiseach didn't win him any respect from the fellas who supported giving guns to the North. And then there was Charlie Haughey."

"There's always Charlie!" said Fiona.

"What a scene it was when he got up onto the stage with Lynch and them. And there were loud cheers for Charlie. And Lynch, what could he do with Charlie up there but shake his hand? Shake the hand of the man he'd sacked from the cabinet."

"Wish I'd been there to see that."

"I was there myself and I was only wishing I could multiply myself into a dozen Des Creaghans and sidle up next to all the secrets being whispered, the plots being hatched, the heaves being planned."

"Any murders being planned that you know of?"

"It's a wonder there was no blood spilt! But, no, if a man was beaten or kicked to death six months later, that doesn't suggest a meticulously planned assassination. Sounds more like instant rage."

"It does. But given that it was a gathering of politicians who had attended the Ard Fheis with all its fireworks, it may have been the end result of rage that had its source in earlier dealings."

"Very likely."

"So what *did* you manage to hear, or hear of, at the party conference?"

"All kinds of shite and blather, but what you'd be most interested in was the scene in which Darragh McLogan played a part."

"Tell me."

"Well, it was Charlie I was most interested in," said Des. "No surprise there. I was keeping an eye on Charlie, but he'd gone off alone, to the jacks maybe, and I wasn't about to follow him in there. But he had signalled to one of the other fellas as if to say, *I'll be joining you in a minute.* And it seemed that the fella he'd signalled was Jolly Roger Conaty. Conaty was with yer man McLogan in deep conversation, just inside the doorway to one of the rooms. So I lit up a smoke and positioned myself, oh so casually, outside the door where I could hear them gabbing.

"And it was Charlie they were talking about. Now they were both members of the Dáil, of course, in Jack Lynch's government. But the talk was, and this was nothing new, that Charlie wants to replace Lynch as Taoiseach. Taoiseach Charlie Haughey. Well, stranger things have happened. And Charlie, think what you will of him, has a charismatic air about him, and when he was in the cabinet, he brought in some policies that have made him popular with the people. So, as a politician looking ahead to the next election, you'd want to be associated with that.

"And, of course," Des continued, partly shuttering his eyes in an uncanny imitation of the hooded eyes of Charlie Haughey, "you'd not want to find yourself on the wrong side of him.

"So there was McLogan and Jolly Roger Conaty debating between themselves what to say about Haughey, what approach to take, whenever an election was called and they were out campaigning to hold onto their seats in the Dáil. Conaty said, 'Well, we'd emphasize the fact that Charlie is one of the people. Reared in poverty, but got his education, qualified in law and accountancy. Went into accounting . . .'

"And McLogan laughed at that point and said something about creative accounting. 'I'm an accountant myself and I'm not creative enough to see how Charlie acquired a grand estate like Abbeville!'"

Shay did not let on that he and DS Griffith had gone out there to question Haughey.

Fiona said, "Abbeville, right. If being a politician pays well enough to buy a palace like that, Desmond, I say you bid goodbye to RTÉ and put yourself forward as a candidate in the next election."

"Anything for you, love."

"Should I start looking for wallpaper? And buying you Charvet shirts from France?"

"I'd hold off on all that, Fiona. A politician's pay would be fine for the likes of us, but it couldn't begin to cover the kind of lavish life that Charlie enjoys. Anyway, Roger Conaty was saying something along the lines of 'Like everybody else in this country, I've been wondering about his financial dealings over the years.'

"And McLogan answered him, 'We're all asking ourselves the same thing: his lifestyle, Charlie's. How in the hell —?'"

Desmond leaned over and ground out his cigarette in the ashtray. "And then, Shay, who appears around the corner as if he'd just materialized in a cloud of smoke? Not there one minute, right there the next. Charlie. Looking at them with those eyes. I'd have been spooked, I'm telling you."

"Wouldn't we all?" asked Fiona.

"And then I had to ease myself away from there without being noticed. So I missed whatever else was said. But I saw the three of them not long afterwards, and it was Charlie smiling benevolently on Darragh McLogan, but giving the evil eye to Conaty, so perhaps we can conclude that McLogan apologized or sucked up to Charlie, and put the blame on Conaty for driving the conversation in the direction of slanderous remarks. But I just don't know."

Desmond lifted his glass and drained it, then lit up another smoke. He said, "Everybody knows that Charlie put in an appearance at McLogan's house."

"Yeah, apparently he made a grand entrance, but just went round the room shaking hands and who knows what? Promising favours? And disfavours to anyone who might turn against him? He was gone less than an hour after he arrived." Shay got up and ordered another round of drinks and returned to the table. "So that conversation you overheard at the Ard Fheis was one of many conversations you eavesdropped on, I imagine?"

"One of many indeed. But it was the only one that was in any way tetchy, with McLogan as part of it. Sure, I saw him chatting with all kinds of people but didn't hear anything controversial."

"How about Jemser? How was O'Daly received by the old party faithful?"

"I had the impression that some of them were leery. Others seemed to enjoy the reflected notoriety. To some of these public men, any publicity is good publicity. You'd have laughed if you'd seen this, Shay. Well, I shouldn't say 'laughed,' given what happened to Darragh McLogan. But later that day, there was McLogan at the edge of a crowd that had gathered around Jemser. Jem was regaling them with a tale about himself doing good works in his old neighbourhood.

"Remember that big storm we had last November, bucketing rain and the strong winds? And everywhere you'd look around the city, you'd see umbrellas that people had ditched because they'd been blown inside out by the wind. So Jemser wanted to help his old neighbours and he bought up a big supply of umbrellas. And for some reason he decided to make his deliveries on a bicycle. He had a cart attached to the bike and it was filled with umbrellas and he was riding it along the streets and stopping at the buildings. He'd go up and knock on the doors or call up to the people on the upper balconies to come down and get one.

"And as he said himself, 'Sure, wasn't I chuffed with myself, one of the three kings bringing gifts?' But then oul Mrs. O'Sullivan came out her front door, and started giving out to me. "James O'Daly, you ruffian! I knew it was you stole my Hugh's bike! You give that back or I'll have the guards on you!"' Jem said that everybody in the estate there knew old Hugh O'Sullivan had been in his grave for donkey's years, and his oul wan was away with the fairies. 'Gone senile, the poor soul,' says Jem. 'And then she started in on the umbrellas, said I must have nicked them from the Vincent de Paul!' It was something along those lines that Jem said and he put his hands up in the pose of a man who would never, ever steal from Saint Vincent's Society, and the people around us at the Ard Fheis were enjoying the performance."

"I can just see him getting them all laughing," Shay said.

"Right, and then who walks by but Jack Lynch? He was with a man I didn't recognize, deep in conversation. And what does Darragh McLogan do? He reaches out and snaffles onto Lynch's arm! The look on Lynch's face at being grabbed like that and him the Taoiseach. But he quickly covered it with an attempt at a smile. And he says to McLogan, 'Ah, you're entertaining the troops there, are you, Darragh?'

"And Darragh says, 'No, Taoiseach, that honour belongs to Jem entirely.' And he repeats the tale to Lynch, and then he starts in on some other gathering where Jem had been the main attraction, and the hundreds of people there, and all the support he has, one of the most popular men in all of Dublin. The simpering smile on the face of McLogan. Jack Lynch was clearly embarrassed. Even Jem O'Daly looked embarrassed, and that's something you don't see every day!"

"Sad in a way, isn't it?" Fiona said. "Darragh sucking up to O'Daly like that."

"He must have thought he couldn't advance his career on his own. Too much the quiet type, unprepossessing, I guess we'd say. But if O'Daly ever gets elected, McLogan may have thought he'd be sailing in O'Daly's winds. And O'Daly would be grateful, and throw something McLogan's way."

"And McLogan would have to be on the good side of the Taoiseach, whoever that might be following the next election," Shay said. "So one minute, you saw McLogan toadying up to Charlie Haughey, and the next minute he was trying to get Jack Lynch onside with O'Daly. Putting a bet on both horses there, so he could trot after the winner into the Dáil for a second term." Shay lifted his pint and finished it off, then said, "I wonder what Roger Conaty would have to say if asked about the earlier chat you mentioned, Conaty and Darragh. And the fallout when Charlie materialized in front of them."

Des merely shrugged. But Shay remembered that one of the other guards had questioned Conaty and had, unfortunately, come away with nothing.

"Oh, bloody hell."

Shay turned to see who had spoken. It was a girl in her mid-twenties, like him. Tall and slim with long, straight blond hair and light-blue eyes. A classic beauty.

Fiona whispered, "Amazing, isn't it, how they can sound posh even when they're effing and blinding!"

There was no need to ask who "they" were. The girl was as British as the crown jewels, and she had a look about her that said maybe her family had a box of jewels stuffed away up in a tower along with an old queen or two. What's this now? She was headed to their table.

"Excuse me," she said in a hushed voice. "Would it be all right if I sat here for a moment? I'm hoping to . . ." Her eyes slid over to the other side of the room.

Shay didn't wait for the explanation. "Sure, have a seat, won't you?" He stood and pulled out a chair for her, and she settled herself on it.

"Thank you ever so much. I'm trying to avoid someone. Which explains why I've come running into a public house all by myself." It was not a common sight, a young woman in a pub and no man with her.

Shay wanted to offer reassurance. "Sure, you're grand. We've loads of people avoiding *us*, so you've come to the right place. I'm Seamus, known as Shay, and this is Fiona and Desmond."

"Oh, hello. I'm Jane. Jane Blytheford." She began waving her hands around. "It's like a black cloud of death in here."

The smoke, she meant. Everyone in the place was smoking and, yes, there was a sooty cloud about the place. But you hardly ever noticed it; it was always like that.

"What would you like to drink, Jane?"

"Oh. Well, I . . ." She looked over to the bar.

"They have everything," Shay said. "A gin and tonic, maybe?" He had taken a guess based on oft-accurate national stereotypes and got it in one.

She knew it, too, but decided to play against type. "Normally, I would, but this time out I'll have, um, a pint of Guinness."

"Grand." He got up and went to the bar.

The three of them were having a friendly chat when he returned with the pint. When there was a break in the conversation, Jane asked Shay, "Are you from here in Dublin?"

"I am."

"Your accent is not as, well, as pronounced as some I've heard here. I can understand you!"

"He worked on it, so he could chat up posh birds," Desmond said in a voice so low that, thanks be to God, Jane didn't hear it over the noise in the pub. Nor would Jane be hearing that that was pretty well Shay's original motivation for taking up reading in such an intense way.

She asked them what kind of work they did, and Fiona said she was a teacher, her husband a news reporter. "Interesting! And you?" she said to Shay. "Do you and Desmond work together?"

Des replied to the question. "Ah, sometimes we work in tandem, sometimes we're at odds." She gave him a questioning look, and he said, "I'm with RTÉ and Shay here is a guard. A copper."

"Really!" said Jane, turning her attention back to Shay. "What sort of policing do you do?"

Des again gave the report. "He solves every kind of case you can imagine, from murders to dog shite offences."

Shay ignored him and asked, "How long have you been in Dublin?"

"Only a couple of weeks. I'm going to be a lecturer at Trinity."

"Oh! So, what will you be lecturing on? What is your subject?"

"The Victorian novel."

"Which one is that, so?"

She laughed. "No, I didn't mean a particular novel. I meant the novels of that period."

Shay felt like a right bollocks. He didn't let his eyes meet Desmond's.

"Hardy, the Brontë sisters, Dickens, of course. Oscar Wilde's *Picture of Dorian Gray*. All that lot, the usual sort of thing."

"So," asked Fiona, "who is it you're trying to avoid this evening?"

Jane flicked her hand as if to say it was of no importance. "Just a young man who, well, doesn't seem to realize I'm a Victorian!"

"Sure, we have trouble with that here," Des put in, "recognizing the Victorians."

"Fair enough. Perhaps I should post adverts about my lectures. Bring in people who would not normally make up my class list!"

Shay wondered whether he himself would make it on her class list, using the word "class" in its narrow and its wider sense.

As it turned out, she didn't find him all that objectionable. And didn't seem put off by the fact that he was a copper. The four of them had a lively conversation until Des and Fiona left the pub, and Jane stayed and started on another pint with Shay. He kept his own consumption down to a civilized level, put his work troubles out of his mind for the present, and managed to keep up his end of the conversation when it turned to literature. He made sure to stay with the familiar, the Irish writers whose books he had read. Jane had read some of the great novelists, poets, and playwrights but claimed to be deficient in O'Casey, O'Connor, and a few others.

"Did you know that several of our greatest writers lived only about two minutes from here?"

"I . . . no, I didn't. I haven't really got myself oriented in the city yet, but I'll want to see those places."

"Why wait? The sun won't be going down for a while yet. Let's go." The drinks had been paid for — her glass was still nearly full — and they left the glass and left the bar. "We'll head that way. It's only a couple of blocks from here."

It was a fine, clear evening, the sun low in the sky. Shay led the way to Merrion Square, with its magnificent Georgian houses surrounding a green park on three sides. The houses were of brick, and the colour was rich in the late-evening sunlight. The buildings were several storeys high, many with brightly coloured doors under fanlights. Shay knew where to look because one of his literature profs had taken the class on a walking tour.

"I suppose you live in a Georgian house yourself, do you? In England, I mean."

"No, no, we live in an old place. Nothing like these splendid buildings."

An old place, was it? Some of Dublin's Georgian places were built in the 1700s, others in the following century. Did Jane come from an "old family" in a house even more grand than these? Were the Georgians mere newcomers in comparison? He thought it best not to ask. As they walked along the south side of the square, he pointed to the houses where the illustrious Dublin men had lived. "AE lived there. George Russell, the poet. They say he was a bit of a mystical fella. I have to confess I've never read his stuff. Not yet, I mean. And Yeats lived right there."

"Yeats! I wish I'd brought my camera. I'll come back tomorrow."

And then, "Le Fanu. Even his name sounds like somebody who'd write about a vampire and ghosts, don't you think?" The name always made Shay think of fangs, but a more lit-class observation would be *He writes in the, em, the Gothic style.*

"I adore the Gothic," Jane said. "I shall hit the stacks at the library and get his works."

"And there's our Liberator. Daniel O'Connell."

"Ah, yes."

Did she know who O'Connell was? The man known as the Liberator because he was instrumental in bringing about Catholic Emancipation? The poor oul Catholic population of Ireland had been in great need of liberation after centuries of oppression and discriminatory laws passed by the Brits.

And speak of the divils, "There's your embassy." He pointed to number thirty-nine on the east side of the square, the British Embassy. "I can wait out here if you'd like to go in and say hello!"

"Oh, that won't be necessary. But if I get into any trouble, I'll know where to run."

"Sure, if you create so much trouble that you have me and a couple of other guards chasing you, this would be the place to take refuge."

She laughed. "Good to know."

"Now we'll go over there, Merrion Square North, to see the house where Oscar Wilde grew up."

They walked round the square to the corner house where the Wildes had moved the year after Oscar's birth, and where he'd lived until his twenties.

"Now, there was a fabled character," Jane said. "I've certainly read him. And Yeats, of course. Thank you, Shay. This has been a wonderful tour about. Have you any idea where James Joyce lived?"

"How much time have you got? Joyce lived all over the place!"

"Well, I suppose I . . . I'll look up the information and find my way to the Joycean places. I did have a bit of a walking tour of places associated with *Ulysses*. Fascinating, of course."

"Em, if you've got time some evening soon, I could take you round."

She smiled at him and said she would be delighted.

"He lived in many different places, so we might not get to see them all. At least, not on our first . . . Well, we'll see how it goes. Em, how will I contact you?"

She reached into her bag and drew out a scrap of paper, wrote down a number, and handed it over.

He'd have a lot of swotting to do before he'd be seeing her. He only knew a handful of places where the Joyce family had lived. He remembered hearing that there were something like twenty houses where the family had lived over time. Where were they all? He hit upon the idea of mitching off work one of these days for a half hour, and visiting one of the city's tourist bureaus. This was the sort of thing Des Creaghan would know, but Shay didn't want to set himself up to be slagged by Des about Jane and trying to impress her with his knowledge of the Joycean habitats. Knowledge Shay Rynne had never possessed.

But it wasn't the face of James Joyce that appeared before Shay's eyes in the dead of night. It was a face seen only in shadow, outside the window of a building where Shay knelt before a gaping hole in the floor. Some dark substance kept bubbling up and Shay kept trying to tamp it down, but it wouldn't stay buried. There was no more sleep for Shay that night. A line kept running through his head, something about sleep. Something he had read in school, or in his early bookworm days. Shakespeare? Yes, he had it: "Glamis hath murdered sleep."

He didn't remember who Glamis was, but if he was in Shakespeare, Shay knew he must have been a much grander figure than a resentful little bollix in a Dublin Garda station trying to take down a younger cop who once did the wrong thing for a right reason, and must never be allowed to forget it.

CHAPTER X

At ten o'clock that morning, Garda Rynne was making the rounds of the shops with a packet of pound notes withdrawn from the bank account he had opened when he began work at Store Street. He had pushed away the disturbing image that had murdered his sleep, and he looked forward to the task at hand. He had commandeered his sister Francie to assist in the unaccustomed activity of buying a suit, trousers and jackets, shirts and ties. It was painful, and some of his choices were quickly — and, no doubt, wisely — rejected by Francie. But by the time the Angelus bells rang at noon, Shay had what he needed. And he and his sister were still on friendly terms.

When Shay drove Francie back to the family home, she insisted that he come inside and show off his new wardrobe in front of their mam. "Go on in there and put the suit on!" Francie urged him. So he did. And Deirdre Rynne was thrilled at the new look of him, and he in turn was thrilled to have brought such a look of pleasure to his mother's face. His young nephew Kevin was home from school for his dinner. He didn't see what the fuss was about; where was Shay's uniform? But once it was explained to him, he got into the spirit of things. He declared that he wasn't going to waste any time reading school books. This from a boy just beginning his first term of his first year of school. Instead, he would be reading the newspaper stories about his Uncle Shay arresting the bad men and wrestling them to the ground. And Kevin knew what he wanted to do when he was finished with school. "I'm going to be a guard, too! I'll put handcuffs on the bad men and drag them into my patrol car and take them to jail and make them stay in there for twenty years." So Garda Rynne was as popular in Fenian Street — well, one small part of it — as he was in the Store Street Garda Station — with the exception of one small part of *it*. But he was feeling so delighted now, he would not give Lar McCreevy a minute's thought.

That afternoon, Shay in his new suit of clothes — grey suit, white shirt, and dark-blue tie — was on the job with Colm Griffith, who was kitted out in similar colours. They walked the short distance from Store Street to the Magee place in Railway Street. Liberty House was a housing complex with cement walls and red brick at the rounded corner of the building. The two guards walked up to the Magees' flat and knocked. A little boy answered the door, and his eyes nearly popped out when he saw them standing there, and they identified themselves. He hadn't yet learned not to trust a peeler, so he opened the door wide and let them in. They weren't that far from the McLogan place on Amiens Street, but they were worlds away from the comfort and elegance of that renovated Georgian house. Here, the mammy came out with a dishtowel in her hand; she looked as if she'd been working for twelve hours without a break, rather than just getting up to start her day. But she wasn't surprised to see the guards at the door; her daughter was a witness in a murder inquiry, after all.

"You'll be looking for Stacy. I'll get her out here for yis."

"Thank you, Mrs. Magee," Griffith said.

She went into one of the rooms, and Shay heard hushed conversation, then drawers opening and closing, and a few minutes later Stacy emerged, patting her long, dark hair into place and giving them a nervous smile.

"Hello again, Stacy," Shay said. "We've a few questions for you. It shouldn't take too long."

"Sure, all right. I'm . . . I'm sorry I had the janglers that first time when yis saw me there. I . . . I just . . ."

"We understand, Stacy. Who wouldn't be rattled?"

They soon had an audience, little faces with big eyes, looking in at them from the kitchen and the other bedroom. Mrs. Magee shooed them away, and Shay and Griffith sat down on a lumpy sofa while Stacy sat across from them on a bockety wooden chair.

"Now," said Griffith, "when we spoke earlier, you told us you'd been serving food at the party."

"I was. Usually I clean houses, and I clean for the McLogans. They asked me to come and serve the food to the guests. Hired me, I mean. So I was passing the plates of roast duck and French cheese around to all of them that were there. Fit for An Rí — it means fit for the king — that's the caterers, they provided the food. The McLogans knew the party would go on well past midnight, so they let me go home and asked me to come back in the early morning to clean up. And then I saw him. Well, yis saw him there yourselves."

"Had anything changed, with his body, I mean, between the time you first saw him and when the other guards arrived, and the emergency services?"

She shook her head. "Nobody went near him. He was only lying there and him with his shoes off and, well, you know how he looked, blood on his face . . . God help us!"

"Now, what can you tell us about the party?"

"It was all the politicians. The hooley went on and on. Seemed there'd be no end of it, and there was lashings of drink taken. But none of them were, you know, acting the maggot or anything. Just having laughs. A few whistles at me and at a couple of the young wives. And jokes and comical lines out of some of them. But lots of serious talk in corners, too. You'd think looking at them they were planning who'd be the next Taoiseach. If Lynch goes, that sort of thing."

"Did you see how Mr. McLogan was during the night? Happy or concerned, or anything you could see?"

A shake of the head again. "Just looked to me the way he always did, whenever I'd see him."

"Anybody arguing with him, or anything like that?"

"Not that I saw."

"Now, we have some pictures here, taken during the party."

"Right. One of the fellas had a camera."

"We'll set them out on the table there, if that's all right."

Stacy cleared some space on the kitchen table, and Shay spread the pictures out. Stacy bent over to look and rattled off the names of the well-known political figures and their wives, when she could put a name to them. She mentioned Charlie Haughey and the gangster-turned-good-citizen Jem O'Daly, and said those two attracted a lot of glances and whispered conversation over the course of the evening. "People were slagging Mr. O'Daly about a scarf he had round his neck. It was white and had a picture on it, a symbol or whatever you'd call it. It said 'New York Police Department.' And he said, 'Oh, didn't yis hear? They recruited me when I was over there last year.'

"And people made remarks about, you know, his reputation here in Dublin. Later on, he said I could wear it. I'd been in and out of the house. Some people were drinking out in the back garden and it was getting kind of cold out there. But I didn't want to take it from him, so then he put it on his wife, because she said she found it cold out there, too. And she laughed and said, 'Etty O'Daly, chief of police,' and everybody better behave themselves, jokin' around, like.

"Now, that fella," Stacy said, pointing to the stocky man Mrs. McLogan had not recognized. "I saw him talking to a few people, but I don't think they really knew him. He didn't look, em, he didn't look as if he belonged. His clothes were — not that I can shop in Brown Thomas or Switzers myself! — but his suit looked as if he'd bought it at a jumble sale."

Shay sent up a quick prayer of thanks that he wasn't there representing An Garda Síochána in a jumble-sale ensemble of his own.

"I had the impression he was a cadger. Got wind of the hooley going on at the McLogans' and invited himself in so he could pour the free drink down his throat and stuff his gob with all the fancy food. That's what it looked like to me." She laughed, and Griffith and Shay laughed along with her. But then, "I'm sorry! Here's me laughing, and Mr. McLogan getting attacked like that —" Stacy's voice failed her then.

Griffith waited for a moment before asking, "How long did he stay, do you know?"

She shook her head. "I left while the party was still going on."

"Is there anything else you can tell us?"

"I just don't know. I'm sorry."

"No, Stacy," Griffith told her, "you're grand. No need to apologize. It's terrible that you had to see that. If we think of anything else, we'll come by again."

"Sure, and if I think of anything, I'll ring you or stop by the station."

They thanked her and left, and were the objects of much attention from other residents of the tenements. The looks they got were not all that friendly.

℃℈

Shay and Griffith headed out to make the rounds of the McLogan party guests again, this time with the photographs in hand, but the pictures didn't spark any useful memories. Until they got to the home of Nell and Davis Fogarty. Davis was a TD for a constituency in the west of the city. He wasn't home, but his wife was. Shay had spoken to both of them on his first round of questioning, and neither of them had anything useful to offer. This time, on her own in the house, the wife did. She glanced at the photos and shook her head. But she had something else to say.

"I don't know if I should be telling you this, because it probably had nothing to do with it."

"Tell us anyway," said Griffith.

"I was . . ." She looked to the door in alarm, as a car stopped outside. But it started up again, and she appeared to relax. "I was upstairs in the house, McLogans', and I heard something. They were in the bedroom, and —"

"Who was it, in the bedroom?"

"Jem and Darragh."

"Just the two of them in there? O'Daly and McLogan?"

"Yes."

"What time was that, could you say?"

"It was only for a few minutes that I heard, half eleven or so. The party was still going on, with everyone there, everyone downstairs."

"And you were upstairs because . . . ?"

"I . . ." Nell sounded as if she was trying not to cry. "I was in the bedroom next to that one. I was just talking to somebody in there."

"Who were you talking to?"

The woman looked around as if someone might have come in and was listening, unseen, beyond the walls of the room. Then, "Rod McMullen. He works for Fianna Fáil, arranges events for them. He and I . . . not anymore, but we had a relationship. It was before I married Davis! But Rod, he never really accepted the breakup of the two of us, even though that happened five years ago. And while the party was going on, he was being . . . persistent in wanting to talk to me. I can't have anybody know I was in the bedroom with him! Even though we were just talking. My husband will think something was going on!"

"Let's not worry about that right now, Mrs. Fogarty. Tell us what happened in the next bedroom."

"I only started hearing them after Rod left the room, because when he was still with me, we were arguing. But when he went off, I stayed behind to . . . fix my face. I'd been crying, upset, you know. So I waited a bit, looked in the mirror, fixed my face and my hair. And that's when I heard what sounded like the end of a row between Darragh McLogan and Jem O'Daly."

"What did you hear?"

"O'Daly was giving out to McLogan, saying something like, 'We agreed on that. I had your word. Now what am I going to do?' Or, 'How do I go about trying to replace that?' I'm not sure. It was only a few seconds I heard, but at the end McLogan was sounding really apologetic. And then their wives came up the stairs, to collect them, I think, bring them back to the guests. And Muriel McLogan said,

'Come on, the pair of you. We've guests down there, remember?' Something like that. And then I heard Darragh saying, 'I'm sorry, Jemser. I'll make it right. I'm sorry.' He sounded really sorry, really upset. And the wives marched them downstairs!"

"This is very useful information, Mrs. Fogarty," Griffith told her.

"But I can't say I was in the bedroom there! Davis doesn't know I was in there with Rod. Just talking but —"

"Don't be worrying about that. We'll be careful with your information."

Shay and Griffith left after trying to reassure her. "Well, Shay, isn't that interesting? A row between McLogan and O'Daly at the party, after Jem and the two wives saying everything was coming up roses."

"Are we going to talk to O'Daly again?"

"We are, but not right away. And we'll ease into it by pretending we're there to ask him about something else. In the meantime, we go and have a word with Rod McMullen."

McMullen was of no use whatsoever. He denied being in the bedroom with Nell. Said he may have exchanged a couple of words with her somewhere that evening, but he'd had lashings of drink and couldn't remember where or what was said. He may have gone up to the jacks and seen Nell in the hallway and talked there, but sorry, he just could not remember.

"The jacks," Griffith said to Shay afterwards. Shay waited for more, but Griffith said nothing else on the subject.

"What about the jacks, sir?"

"She'd be more willing to talk, Nell would, if she was in the jacks on the other side of the bedroom where O'Daly and McLogan were. If she could say she was fixing her face in the mirror in the jacks rather than in the other bedroom."

If they could get her to alter her evidence, in other words. Shay hoped Griffith could not see the surprise in his face. Griffith was known to one and all as a straight-up, honest copper. But when Shay thought it over, this seemed a harmless enough alteration; nothing to do with the main point Nell Fogarty had addressed. If it meant that the witness would give evidence that would identify McLogan's killer, there was no harm done, not that Shay could see. Would there be another fear, though, that might take the place of her worry about her husband and the old boyfriend? Would she be willing to give evidence of a row between the murdered man and Jem O'Daly, evidence of some offence McLogan had caused O'Daly?

Next stop was O'Daly's office, the headquarters of Quo Day Building Contractors, located in an industrial estate northwest of the city centre. Shay rang to make sure he was there and struck a reassuring tone during the phone call. "We've some photographs taken the night of the party, Mr. O'Daly. We'd like to stop in and ask you to look them over, if you would."

"Sure, sure, I'll be here for a while yet."

O'Daly's building was new and sprawling; it was made of light-grey concrete and glass. The receptionist picked up her phone to tell O'Daly there were two guards there to see him. He came down in the elevator and brought them up to his office on the third — top — floor. The outer wall faced north and was all glass. Shay saw an airplane coming in for a landing at Dublin Airport. The tables in the office were piled with building plans and other papers. O'Daly sat down behind his desk, which was immaculate and well ordered, and he picked up a lit cigar from his ashtray. He put it in his mouth, took a long drag of it, and pointed to two chairs. "Have a seat there, fellas."

Shay took out the pack of photographs and spread them out on the desk. "Take your time and look them over. See if there's anyone there who . . . well, who maybe shouldn't be there."

O'Daly sifted through them and made some comical remarks about some of the politicians, what they were wearing, how much they had to drink. "Now there's a man never puts his hand in his pocket." Meaning he never pays for a round of drinks. "His name is Rooney. He's harmless enough; you just don't want him at the table with you down the pub. I didn't see him when he arrived. Or when he left, for that matter. But I didn't see him talking to Darragh at all. Probably avoiding him, since he was a gatecrasher in Darragh's home. Maybe he was there so he could brag of being in the company of the likes of myself and Charlie Haughey!"

Shay and Griffith laughed on cue, and Griffith said, "Thank you, Jem. We'll get everyone identified sooner or later. We won't keep you. But have you thought of anything since we spoke before, anything that might explain what happened?"

"You can be sure I've gone over everything in my mind, trying to bring back any little thing I might have noticed and then forgotten, anything that could explain how the fuck this could have happened. And I've not come up with anything at all."

"Politics can give rise to disputes, even among friends — strong opinions, strong feelings. Particularly with all the ructions going on in this country now."

"True enough."

"Any political rivalries or grudges you can think of that might have come down on the head of Darragh McLogan?"

"Nothing that would have led to this, nothing at all."

"But the killing certainly has a personal look to it, wouldn't you say? Maybe something closer to home rather than, say, an unparliamentary debate!"

"Unparliamentary, right!"

"So, anything personal you can think of? Family or friends not getting along?"

O'Daly shook his head no.

"How about the two of you? Political men and brothers-in-law. Any quarrel between the two of you that night?

"No."

"Or any time recently?"

"No quarrels, no fights, and I did not kill my brother-in-law."

"We have to ask these things, Jemser. You know that."

"I'm no stranger to being questioned by the guards. Yis know that, lads. And I hope your questioning gets results, and that you nail the scum that did this!"

They thanked him and said their goodbyes, and got back in their car.

"Well!" said Griffith. "Caught him in a lie. I believe that little woman who gave us her statement, Nell, a statement against her own interest. She doesn't want her husband finding out about her little tryst, or

160

'conversation,' in that bedroom that night. But she's a good citizen and told us about the row between O'Daly and McLogan. She is telling the truth. And O'Daly isn't. How's that for an example of *helping the police with their inquiries*, however unintentionally!"

☙

Once the state pathologist had completed his examination, McLogan's body was released and the funeral held on Friday in the Pro-Cathedral. Not surprisingly, there was a massive crowd, and Shay was one of several gardaí interspersed with the mourners. Darragh's widow, Muriel, sat with their children and the extended family in the first pews. The Taoiseach, Jack Lynch, was there, the members of his cabinet, former cabinet member Charlie Haughey, and politicians from all the parties. The Pro looked like the Greek temples you'd see in pictures, with the big pillars outside and the triangular roof at front. There were pillars inside, too, and it was all very elaborate. Lovely music as well.

Several people spoke about McLogan at the end of the ceremony. The politicians praised him for his quiet integrity and his ability to get along with people even with very different points of view. A peacemaker. And he never got too big for his old neighbourhood. Didn't flee to the suburbs for a big swanky house for himself and his clan. There were some glances exchanged around the church at this; many of the political men present had done exactly that. Nobody more blatantly than Charlie Haughey. Darragh's sister, Etty O'Daly, was one of the people who was scheduled to speak, but she was too upset. So her younger sister took her place and gave the congregation a loving portrait of the older brother everybody would want to have. He was the oldest in a family of six surviving children; one had died when just an infant.

"Darragh taught the other boys in the street to play football in the laneways, and kept them out of trouble when there might have been a temptation to rob a few pieces of candy from the shops. And he even made a dollhouse for me and Etty. He wasn't Joseph the carpenter" — she looked over at the archbishop in alarm when

161

she said that, and he smiled back at her — "but he did his best, did Darragh, with his hammer and nails. And me and the other girls painted it and found little toy tables and chairs to put in it. And most importantly, he always" — her voice broke but she carried on — "he protected us. We lived in a poor area, as everybody knows. When rough characters came round and threatened our boy cousins, or made dirty remarks to us girls, he called in his own friends and stood up for us and made the bad fellas go away. We always felt safe when Darragh was around."

Late summer light shone down on Darragh's sister through the high windows of the cathedral. Seeing her, hearing her speak of the family's love for their brother, Shay promised himself he'd do his very best to track down whoever had taken the life of this family's protector.

⁂

Shay had some time after the funeral to pursue his Joycean researches, so he headed over to a travel agent's shop in O'Connell Street. He wished he'd brought an anorak because, as it so often did, the weather changed from sunny to showers in the short time it took to walk to O'Connell. He shook the drops off himself as he approached a middle-aged woman in the place and told her he had family visiting, and they were keen on everything about James Joyce. The woman was friendly and helpful, and Shay came away with a couple of brochures and a map. He stood on the pavement and studied the locations before folding them and stuffing them in his pocket, then returned to Store Street. He decided that the evening's event would be a motor tour, to Rathmines and Rathgar, to Bray and Blackrock, the posher places where the Joyces lived when old John Stanislaus Joyce was still in the money. He'd leave the more humble abodes to another time. If there was another time.

He put in the rest of the afternoon going over witness statements in the McLogan case. Just before he left, the state pathologist's report was delivered to the station. Not surprisingly, it showed that Darragh McLogan had suffered injuries from blows to his body and head, apparently caused by a blunt object such as a boot or a shoe. McLogan had been rendered unconscious and died from a traumatic head injury.

❧

Shay rang Jane Blytheford, and they agreed to meet that evening at Trinity College. He drove across the river and parked up. Then sprinted into the quadrangle, where she was waiting, and they headed out together. The gods were kind; it was cloudy but there wasn't any rain. When they got to the car, though, he wanted to kick himself for not cleaning it out before going to get her. It smelled of stale cigarette smoke even to him, so how overpowering would it be to a non-smoker? And there was a wrapper from a not-so-recent order of fish and chips and a couple of empty beer cans. Not the most appropriate evidence to be found in the car, even the personal car, of a member of the national police force. He said, "Sorry," and leaned in and scooped up the items in his arms. He didn't see a bin anywhere, so he put the offending articles in the boot of the car.

What was it that had him concerned here, a car that wouldn't meet the standards of An Garda Síochána? Or the standards of Jane Blytheford? Did he still feel he hadn't been good enough for Allie Cotter, and now not good enough for Jane? He pushed the thoughts of Allie from his mind; the wound was still too raw.

As for the car, if Jane was bothered by the mess, she didn't let on. Shay only hoped her khaki-coloured trousers and light-blue jumper wouldn't get soiled from something mouldering in the seat.

He drove to Brighton Square in Rathgar as if he drove there every day, and they saw the fine brick terrace house where James Joyce was born in 1882. Then they looked at the lovely house on Castlewood Avenue in Rathmines, where the family had moved a short time later. The sea was flat and shining when they got to Bray and saw the Joyce house there. On the way back into the city Shay pointed out the Martello Tower, where the opening scene of *Ulysses* was set.

"They turned it into a museum a few years back."

"I'll be sure to come and see it."

Shay felt he was running out of conversation as they got nearer to the city centre. He remembered he'd told Brennan he'd meet him at Christy's. Brennan would be leaving for New York soon, so Shay didn't want to miss out on sinking a few pints with him. But he didn't want to miss out on more time with Jane, either. Bring her to Christy Burke's? He would have to think about it.

"Thank you so much, Shay, for our little motoring holiday," she said as they got close to Trinity College. "I shall take in the Martello Tower one of these days soon."

Take it in without Shay, by the sound of it. And then he was out of time to think things over. If he didn't speak up, she'd be gone. "Would you like to stop in at a pub for a drink?"

She seemed to think about it for a couple of seconds, then said, "Certainly. Why not?"

So he drove them over to Christy's. Shay opened the door for Jane, and she walked in. She looked round the place, and Shay saw her peering at the Proclamation of the Irish Republic, emblem of the 1916 Rising against British rule, and the photo on the wall, showing the trench-coated IRA men walking along Grafton Street with their rifles. Yes, dear lady, you have just entered a republican bar.

She turned to look at him but made no comment on their surroundings, so he decided to offer no comment of his own. "What will you have, Jane? Guinness?"

"Oh, I found the Guinness rather heavy. Too rich, I suppose. So I'll revert to type and have a gin and tonic, if I may."

"You may." If Finn has any gin. Yes, Shay looked up at the array of bottles and saw gin up there with the whiskeys and the other spirits. Finn came out of the back room and greeted Shay.

"Jane, this is Finn Burke. Finn, this is Jane Blytheford."

"How do you do, Mr. Burke?"

"Welcome to you, Jane. What can I get for you?"

"I'll have a gin and tonic."

"And the usual for me, Finn."

Finn nodded and proceeded to pour the drinks. "Brennan's over there with O'Grady."

"Ah, good."

When they had their glasses, they walked over to the table where Brennan was seated with Colly O'Grady. Brennan was all got up in grey trousers and a white shirt; a navy-blue jacket hung on the back of his chair.

"Where's the bride, Brennan?"

"Eh?"

Shay gestured to the clothes. "Just got married, did yeh?"

"Ah, right. No, I've been to the opera."

"Of course. I missed the opera myself today," Shay said, "but I'm there most days."

"The opera, in the afternoon?" Jane asked, saying "afternoon" as if she was saying *in the gutter*.

"I know, I know, but it was a preview, and you could buy a ticket. It opens tomorrow night, but that's sold out."

"Which opera was it?"

Shay interrupted at that point to make the introductions. "Jane Blytheford, meet Brennan Burke and Colly O'Grady." The two gentlemen stood to greet her, then invited the two of them to have a seat.

"The opera?" Jane asked again.

"*Don Giovanni.*"

"No! And I missed it. I've only been in the city a couple of weeks and I haven't kept up with the theatre listings, the concerts and all that. How was it?"

"It was brilliant. It's a company from Italy. I'd never seen them before. The voices were wonderful. And the tenor who sang 'Il Mio Tesoro' was excellent, though I couldn't help comparing his version with John McCormack's."

"Well, no, that comparison could hardly be avoided," Jane said. "So, Brennan, was it more seria than buffa or the other way round?"

"Well, that's the question that's trailed after this opera ever since it was composed, isn't it? But Mozart's music rises above all that, or flows beneath it like a dark river at times. That D-minor music! It leaves me at a loss for words."

"Where were you when all this was going on, Shay?" Colly whispered, but it was loud enough to be heard by the others. "At the track? The betting shop?"

"I'm avoiding the track these days, Col. Didn't do too well last time out. My horse took a fright and died just before the clubhouse turn, and I lost the house, the wife, the kids."

"Ah, yeh poor man. Drink up; you'll be feeling better in no time at all."

"I will. And I've a hooley coming up."

Shay knew that Brennan would be leaving Dublin early Monday morning. So what better way to send him off than to invite him to a party on Saturday night? The Rynne family were planning a surprise for his father, for Talkie's fiftieth birthday on September the fourth. Shay had already invited Finn along with Colm Griffith. Griffith couldn't come because his daughter was being married in County Clare that weekend. Finn was going to miss it, too, but he had a donation ready to go: a box filled with cans of beer and a couple of bottles of whiskey. Shay would be holding those back until the moment the party got underway, because the biggest challenge would be keeping Talkie off the drink before the guests arrived. It was going to be a surprise.

Now, with Brennan and Colly at the table, he would extend the invitation to them. And then there was Jane. He could hardly exclude her, but . . . Not that he didn't want to see Jane, and spend more time in her company, but, well, the opera, the "old house" in England — how would Jane Blytheford react to a night at the Corpo flats in Fenian Street? But it had to be done. "Yis are all invited to my family's place tomorrow night. Celebrating my oul fella's fiftieth birthday. Who'd have thought he'd ever make it this far?"

"Why, Shay?" Jane asked. "Has he been ill?"

"No. He's, em, he has lived life to the fullest, let us say."

"Well, thank you, I'd be delighted to attend."

Brennan said he'd be more than happy to come along. Colly said he'd love to, but he'd promised the wife they would spend the evening with her family. Des and Fiona were unavailable, too. Aside from Vincent Foley and another guard, Con Maloney, Brennan and now Jane, the party would be a gathering of family and neighbours.

A group of musicians began to gather at their usual spot in the corner. "Oh, good!" said Jane. "We're going to have music."

Shay glanced over at Brennan, who returned the look. Chances were that the music would have a republican air about it. Rebel songs were the usual fare at Christy's. But on this night, the session began with a couple of ballads, and Shay saw that the singer had Jane's full attention. This was followed by some rousing tunes on the fiddle and whistle, and she tapped her feet along with everybody else. Then one of the players said, "And now we'll be doing a piece yis all know, by Father O'Neill."

Father Burke and Shay exchanged a glance again. Father Charles O'Neill had written the song "Foggy Dew" after the Easter Rising of 1916, and the musicians took it up with great enthusiasm in Christy's pub. Shay noticed that Jane's smile faltered a bit when she heard the line "Britannia's Huns with their long-range guns sailed in through the foggy dew." That image had always sent shivers down Shay's spine — the massive ship with its guns materializing out of the fog — but he imagined that Jane's reaction came from a different source.

Shay was about to get up to order another round when he saw Deena Breathnach rushing to the table. She wasn't in her work clothes, Shay noticed, but had on a pair of tan trousers and a cream-coloured gansey that may have come from the Aran Islands. Her eyes were wide and she was nearly out of breath. "Shay. Good. I thought I might find you here."

"Deena, what is it?"

"He found me at Carrie's place. My friend Carrie. It's him again. Sitting in his car outside Carrie's flat." The man who had been following her, intimidating her. "I managed to shake him off as I ran through the streets to get here, but . . ."

Brennan stood up. "Deena, I'll take you somewhere safe."

Shay put his hand up. "No, Brennan. You stay here. I'll take Deena." He'd only had two pints, and a few sips of the third, so he was well able for the driving.

Jane looked from Brennan to Deena and then to Shay. "Are you leaving? I think I'd like to go home now."

"Ah, I'll just be gone for . . ." But he didn't know how long he'd be gone. He said, "Come on, Jane. I'll take you home. Deena, we'll find a place for you."

In Shay's opinion, the best place for Deena would be someplace out of town, like her cousin's house in County Wicklow, but whatever the case, he had to get her to safety. And it would do no harm to get Jane out of Christy's before the band struck up "Rifles of the IRA" amid cries of "Up the 'RA!" and raised fists among the punters in the room.

Before she left, Deena put her hand on Brennan's shoulder and said, "We'll be in New York soon. I have to keep the picture of the New York skyline in my mind. That will keep me going."

He covered her hand with his. "It won't be long, Deena."

Shay led the two women to his car, and they all got in. Shay saw Jane hesitate, but Deena immediately took the back seat, so Jane took the front. Before he started the engine, he said, "You know you're better off in Wicklow till you leave for the States. As long as you stay in the city, and keep returning to work, that man can find you. You know that."

"I know. And I do have a few pounds saved, to get me to New York. I could use more, but —"

"But it's not safe for you here."

"Yeah. Can you take me to my flat then, Shay, and I'll pack my things, and tomorrow I'll get the bus to Wicklow."

"I'll take you to your flat. You pack your bag. I'll take Jane home to her place and then come back for you. And I'll drive you to Wicklow tonight."

"Ah, Shay, I couldn't —"

"My word is law, young lady. Have you forgotten that?"

Deena turned her attention to Jane then. "I'm sorry, I'm wrapped up in my own troubles. I'm sorry about banjaxing your evening."

"Don't give it another thought, Deena. It sounds as if you're in a bit of a pickle, and you're better off away from here."

They arrived at Deena's place in Ringsend, and Shay assured her he would give her some time and then return to take her to her cousin's. She got out of the car, and Shay pulled away.

"Good Lord, Shay. That poor woman. What's going on? I take it she and Brennan Burke are embarking on a new life together in New York City, and the other bloke doesn't want to let her go. Some men just can't take no for an answer, and they can't comprehend the words 'It's over, old chap. Now, run along.'"

"No, no, that's not it." He started to laugh.

"Why are you laughing?"

"It's not funny, I know, but Deena and Brennan are not running away together. At least not in the sense you mean. They aren't a couple. Brennan is a priest, and Deena is, well . . ."

"The chap I met tonight in that bar is a priest?"

"He is, yes."

"I certainly wouldn't have guessed that."

"Most people wouldn't!"

"So, who is Deena, and why are they going away together?"

"Deena is a . . . She's going to be a witness in a criminal trial."

"Really!" Jane turned in her seat to look at him. "What kind of case is it? Political, subversives, that sort of thing?"

"No, no, nothing like that at all. It's a murder case." He turned to her in an effort to make light of it. "You'll be reading all about it in the papers, so you will. And my name will be mentioned. Stay tuned."

"I shall indeed. But what's the story? What sort of sordid occurrence did she witness? Do tell!"

Should he tell her or not? He was a peeler, and this was a police matter, so he should not be broadcasting it far and wide. But it wasn't as if Jane would be marching through the halls of Trinity College shouting about the case to all the professors and students and cleaning staff. But he couldn't stop himself from issuing a caution before he opened up. "You know this is, well, confidential, so . . ." Smooth, Rynne, smooth.

Jane was laughing at him, but her hand on his arm softened it a bit. "Shay, do I strike you as someone who blurts out everything she hears to the first pair of ears? I won't tell anyone."

"I know, I'm sorry." He gave her a pared-down version of the Goss's Hotel story without any names, though he could not resist highlighting his own successful efforts to have the case reopened.

"And Deena is one of your witnesses."

"She is. But a man has been tailing her, making gestures with a clear message: keep your mouth shut. In other words, don't testify. He has her petrified. And Deena doesn't scare easily. Well, she wouldn't, in her —"

"In her what?"

"Em, in her life. Anyway, that's why I'm taking her to her cousin in Avoca, to stay until Brennan can get her to New York. She'll come back to give her evidence."

"How far is Avoca?"

"Not very far. Next county over. To the south of us."

"Could I come along? Would that be all right? I'd love to see a bit of the country, even if it's dark."

Shay didn't think it would matter to Deena one way or the other. She had more on her mind than how many people were in the car taking her to safety. So he turned the car around and headed back to Ringsend. He parked outside her building and waited. It wasn't long before Deena came down with two cases filled with her belongings. Shay got out to help her lift the bags into the boot. "Would it be all right with you if Jane comes along for the trip? I don't think she's been outside of Dublin. You wouldn't mind?"

"No, you're grand. But it's a long way to Avoca, long way for you to be driving me, and it being the middle of the night! I should wait and get the bus tomorrow, Shay."

"No, you shouldn't. Settle yourself in the car, and off we go. I don't mind a little motoring holiday tonight. And this won't seem like a long journey once you've been in America for a while. The distances over there, hard for us to imagine!"

They covered the distance between Dublin and Avoca in just over an hour. Deena talked about the man who had been following her. "How much time has he been out there looking for me? He found me at Carrie's. He knows where I work on the canal. He was creeping along behind me there. Who's paying him? Risteard himself?"

"Have you had a better look at him now, Deena?"

"He's got thin brown and grey strands of hair. But when he parks up, he always has his cap pulled down so I can't make out much of him, except for the pointy chin on him with stubble on it."

"And he drives a green Renault."

"Right. I never got the tag number. I wasn't about to say to him, 'Excuse me, sir, could you stop for a bit, so I can memorize your number?'"

"No, I can see why that wouldn't have worked."

The conversation turned to other matters. Deena was interested to hear that Jane lived just outside London. Had she ever seen the Beatles before they broke up? She had. The Stones? She had. But, she said, she was more a fan of the London Philharmonic Orchestra than of the rock or pop bands, "so I'm a bit out of things!" She commented on the beauty of the countryside, what she could see of it in the dark, and said she'd make a point of seeing County Wicklow in the day-time. Deena replied that she herself had better appreciate it while she was here because she didn't expect to see many green fields in New York City. And so the time passed. Deena told Shay how grateful she was for his help, and he thanked her for offering to testify in the trial, and they all said their goodbyes.

Then, on the way back to Dublin, Jane gave voice to her plan. "You want to find this bloke, obviously, the man in the car. And charge him with attempting to intimidate a witness, or whatever the legal term would be."

"Ideally, yes, I would."

"Well, that's where I come in."

He shot a quick glance her way. "What do you mean?"

"I gather from what Deena said about working on the canal, that she is, well, a streetwalker. Canal walker, so to speak."

"Mmm."

"I shall take her place."

"You *what?*" It came out as a squawk.

Jane burst out laughing. "No, Seamus, I shall not be turning any tricks, if that is the phrase. I shall walk along the canal in Deena's place, in the hopes of attracting the attentions of the man you seek."

"Are yeh cracked? I can't believe I'm hearing this! The man is dangerous, Jane. Did you not cop on to that? It's not as if you're trained as an undercover agent!"

She laughed and then said, "You are going to be nearby, if you so choose." He started to protest, but she talked over him. "All I have to do is see this person, and note the details of his car. The plate number if possible. Then I walk off stage, never to be seen on the canal again."

"And if he attacks you?"

"He never attacked Deena, did he? No doubt afraid to be the next fellow to face criminal charges. He wants to frighten her. So I step into her shoes. Or shoes with a lower heel, since I'm a couple of inches taller than Deena."

"You don't look anything like her. Your hair is blond; hers is dark."

"We have the same build. Hair colour can easily be modified or covered by a hat. What would a woman do if she were afraid but also needed to keep working to support herself? She would try to disguise herself. She might take to wearing a hat, tucking her hair up inside it."

It was ridiculous. It was dangerous. "No, Jane. Thank you for offering to help the police with their inquiries. But, no." Finally, he was able to change the topic of conversation and he dropped Jane off at her place, telling her he would see her at his father's birthday party tomorrow night.

There was something to her idea, though, he had to admit. Not with Jane Blytheford playing the part, but with someone with long experience on the Grand Canal.

CHAPTER XI

Brennan had agreed to say the early evening Mass for a priest he'd come to know at, well, at Christy Burke's pub. Father Sloan wanted to visit a dying relative in County Kildare. By the time the Mass was over, Brennan thought he might miss the *Surprise!* moment for Talkie Rynne. But then again, most of the people Brennan knew here in the old country could never be described as neurotically fixated on punctuality. In any event, he decided not to bother going back to the Brunswick Street flat to change out of his clerical clothing. If the partygoers thought the presence of a priest would inhibit them, he'd soon put their minds to rest.

The block of flats in Fenian Street was typical of the Corporation housing in Dublin, brown brick with white trim, balconies running the length of the building, with dividers between them. The setting sun cast shadows over some of the buildings, and a warm glow on the red brick of others. He noted that the place did not bear a grandiose name like one of the other public housing blocks he had seen, that being the Fatima Mansions! He was about to enter the building when he caught sight of Jane, the English woman Shay had been squiring around. She was standing across the street, dressed in a pair of beige linen trousers with a long blue blouse over them. The blouse looked like silk. Her hair was swept up in an elegant knot. The expression on her face was perhaps to be expected in one who had arrived at the Corporation flats dressed in clothing of linen and silk. She was gazing about her at some of the dishevelled characters who stood outside, effing and blinding, smoking and drinking straight from the bottle. Then she looked up at the balconies where items of laundered clothing were hanging out and flapping in the breeze. Staring down at her were a few fellas who, like their counterparts on the ground, were enjoying a smoke and a drink, and eyeing Jane and making remarks that, mercifully, were inaudible below.

Brennan walked over to her. "Are you lost, young lady?"

She gave a start and then said, "Oh! Brennan! I, uh, just arrived and, well . . ."

"I imagine Shay had to get here ahead of time, get things going."

"Yes, yes, he did. I said I'd meet him here. I suppose I should go in."

He laughed. "Yes, I suppose you should. Shall we?" He extended his elbow for her to take, and she laughed along, and they entered the building.

Brennan had not, in fact, missed the surprise. Everyone was crowded into the little sitting room. The furniture was battered, the gold-and-green upholstery and the curtains patched. The family didn't have much, but great care had been taken with what they did have. The mantelpiece held a few family pictures in plastic frames, and there were a couple of fine-looking silver goblets on display. All the guests had drinks in their hands, none in silver goblets, so Brennan assumed they were for decoration, little touches of elegance in the humble room. He heard words of praise being heaped upon his uncle Finn, who was not present, and he remembered that Finn had supplied the liquid refreshments for the evening. There was a flowery patterned plate of shortbreads and two bowls of crisps on a table near the window.

Shay saw Jane and came over. She had a bright smile on her face and gave him a cheery greeting. Brennan moved away as they held a whispered conversation. Then Shay went to the drinks table and poured her a glass of white wine. Brennan heard her say, "Go on, Shay, attend to your guests." And she edged herself into a corner and took a sip of her wine.

Brennan saw one fella sidle up to Shay and say in a stage whisper, "Slummin', is she? Toyin' with a lad from the flats? Bet it's a new experience for her, righ'? Little Irish leprechaun for her to write home about!"

If Brennan heard the remark, had Jane heard it, too? From the mortified look on her face, yes, she had. Brennan moved in beside her and raised an eyebrow, awaiting a comment.

"Really, Brennan, I hope Shay's friends don't all think like that, the way that person put it. That I'm toying with Shay. I like Shay. It's no more complicated than that."

Brennan glanced over at Shay then, and heard what may have been the tag end of his reply to the lad who had made the remarks. And he was surprisingly good-natured about it. "She seems to be enjoying the experience. When she gets tired of it, I'm sure she'll let me know. And she'll be polite about it, unlike you, yeh tosser."

Shay caught Brennan's eye then and announced to the group, "This is Father Burke. But don't be getting nervous now. It only takes one or two jars or cans, and then he's just my pal Brennan Burke."

Everyone laughed, and a young woman who looked like a twin to Shay came over and introduced herself as Shay's sister Francie. She went to the makeshift bar and asked what he'd be drinking. Brennan saw a bottle of Jameson whiskey and said he'd be pleased to have a taste of that. People were telling stories about Talkie Rynne, and it was clear that he had been quite the rogue when he was young. "Get him to tell about the Monto!" someone called out. "Yis have to hear that one." It was agreed that the one about the Monto would be on the agenda.

It couldn't have been two minutes later when the door opened, and a woman came in, Shay's mother Deirdre, followed by Talkie. The crowd burst into a chorus of "Surprise!" and "Happy birthday!" and a few jibes about Talkie Rynne's great age. The man leapt back, looking almost frightened. Startled by the raucous welcome. Then he stood for a long moment, gobsmacked. Brennan once again noted the resemblance between father and son; Talkie had Shay's curly black hair, though now getting a bit thin and grey. He was shorter than the son and more wiry, and his face was lined. He looked older than his fifty years. Brennan knew from his own conversations with Finn that Talkie had not had an easy life. He'd been brutalized in the Curragh camp, had taken a long time to adjust after that. Spotty employment history, family to support, trouble with the drink and with the law.

But Talkie quickly got into the spirit of things, went about the room greeting the people he knew. When he came to Brennan, Shay walked over to them and said, "Be nice to the sagart now, Da. He rushed through his evening Mass just to get here in time."

"Ah, a short quick Mass, was it?" Talkie said. "I thought I knew you as one of the Burkes. But, no, you must be Father Flash Kavanagh, come back to us here."

"Flash Kavanagh?"

"Oh, he was a priest used to say his Mass at ten in the morning. That suited him perfectly, because the pubs opened at half ten. Sure, he'd have that Mass said and done by opening time, and he'd be at the pub in a flash. Day after day, he'd be in there. Father Flash Kavanagh! Welcome to you, Flash!"

Brennan greatly enjoyed the comical side to Talkie's personality. "I'll be more than happy to adopt that nickname as my own, Talkie. As long as you don't get me confused with another Father Cavanagh."

"Oh? Who would that be now?"

"He was the parish priest at Knock, at the time of the apparitions. Somebody came flying in to tell him what people were seeing out there, the images of Mary and Joseph, Saint John the Evangelist, and the lamb, but Cavanagh didn't bother his arse to get up and have a look for himself. Have himself inscribed in the history books. Missed the whole thing!"

"The oul liúdramán!" Lazy man. "I'm sure you're not one for missing things yourself, Father. Now, I see food and drink being put out for us, so help yourself. I'd best see to some of my other guests here."

"You go right ahead."

Brennan watched as he circulated among the crowd, with a line of chat for everyone in the room. He was in fine form, delighted that so many had come to celebrate his birthday.

Children ran about and played; everyone else sat on chairs or on the floor. Shay read out a greeting card sent by Detective Sergeant Colm Griffith, who wrote that he would be taking Talkie and Deirdre out for a restaurant supper when he returned to Dublin, to make up for his absence tonight.

The storytelling started up again as people enjoyed their drinks. And a call went out for the story about the Monto, Dublin's legendary red-light district of days gone by.

Talkie took a moment to light up a smoke, then smiled and said, "Ah, my uncle Conor used to tell me about the girls he'd see around there in the Monto. Beautiful girls, they were, and the madams would have them all dressed up and sparkling clean. And, you know, everybody appreciated them, even those who . . . well, the other people in the tenements, even the women, all had a friendly hello for the girls and the madams. They called them the 'unfortunate girls' but that was because they felt sorry for them. But they liked them. And little wonder about it, because the madams and their girls would give you anything. They'd give you food if you needed it, shoes for a barefoot child. And they did a great business, with sailors off the ships from all over the world. And some who — I'll not be naming names — would've been called *gentlemen* from right here in Dublin city."

He looked at Shay. "And there was more than one member of the Garda Síochána — from Store Street — who were legendary for their nights in the kips, enjoying the drink and the girls, and sometimes brawling in the streets!"

This brought whoops of appreciation and calls for names to be named, but Talkie was the soul of discretion. He was the gentleman now. He had a tale of his own, though. "I went up there myself when I was a little lad. Me and my brother Peadar. He's forever telling me the story, over and over. 'Mind yeh the time?' Our uncle Jeremiah was in for a visit. He had his tea and then said he had to go out to the shops for some messages. 'And I'll be going over to Pudding Street,' he said. Some of the family lived over there. And us kids, we liked the sound of that. Peadar asked him, 'Can we come with yeh?' But he told us no, not today. Some other day. After he'd left, Peadar signalled over to me. 'C'mon. Pudding Street! We'll follow behind him.'

"And so we did. We trailed after him along the streets and across the bridge, and then into the streets over there. Corporation Street, Railway Street. And Peadar says, 'I know these streets. Up here is the Monto!' And 'What's that?' says I, and he tells me, 'Never mind it. You're too little to know. But maybe we can get us a shilling or two.' And he told me what he'd heard, that the girls — whoever these girls were, he didn't say — way back they used to call them 'brass nails.' Maybe that's where the name 'brassers' came from. I've no idea. Anyway, the girls would be in need of a cigarette or matches or a bottle, and they'd lower a can down on a string from the window to the street. And young fellas like my brother would go and get whatever it was the girl wanted and bring it back and put it in the can, and she'd raise it up to her window and then send the can down again with a shilling or shillings. And you'd have the money to go into a shop and buy something good for yourself. So that's what we set out to do. We lurked in the shadow of a building, waiting for cans to come out of the windows. Only, an astounding sight greeted us instead. From one of the doors, out came a man carrying his clothes in a bundle, and him in his bare pelt!"

Talkie's listeners were spellbound, none more so than Jane; she looked plainly gobsmacked.

"And after him, out came Uncle Jeremiah, him with no shirt on and no shoes, and fumbling with his trousers and looking as if his wife or the Garda Síochána were after him. I couldn't believe my eyes, seeing it! My uncle like that! I don't know to this day if it was the guards that raided the place, or what."

"Or the Legion of Mary," Brennan interjected.

"Right enough. This was near the end of the glory days of the Monto. The Legion of Mary and the new Free State, they cracked down on the good times in the mid-1920s. But, anyway, there was me and Peadar, and he said to me, 'Come the divil away from here or he'll murder us!' Jeremiah, he meant. And Peadar grabbed me by the hand, and we ran away from there and me tripping and skinning my knee, but we kept on the run, all the way back across the bridge and home. And our mam asked us where had we been, and I said we'd been looking at the fellas with their bare arses sticking out in the Monto, and she cracked me across the arse for the filthy talk!"

The story was accorded a great reception amongst the guests, and there were other tales told, and it was a grand evening entirely. Then Talkie announced that it was time for some music. He left the room and came back with a concertina. Somebody else produced a tin whistle, and a neighbour left and returned with a fiddle. And the session began out on the balcony. There were songs and recitals, and music played with skill, and it turned into a fine old céilí. Brennan could hear people outside in the street, and he looked out the window to see them looking up. And so the céilí began to spill out into the street.

As he was about to step out onto the balcony to enjoy the ceol agus craic — the music and fun — he saw Deirdre Rynne standing at the entrance to the kitchen, so he walked over and introduced himself. She invited him to have a seat, and she asked him about his background, his family in Dublin, his work as a priest, and he chatted with her about all that.

After a few minutes, Brennan heard a telephone ring in the sitting room. He looked out and saw Talkie put down his concertina and answer the phone. "Who? Oh, right, yeah. Yeah, thank you. Sure, we'll see you in a minute." He put down the receiver, and then Brennan could hear the sound of a drawer opening and closing, and glasses rattling. It must have been the cabinet where the bottles were. Then he came into the kitchen with a worried look on his face.

"Who just rang, Talkie?" Deirdre asked.

"Fella by the name of Vincent. Says he's a guard, and him and another guard are on the way over here."

"The guards coming here?"

"No, not like that. Pals of Shay. They work with him at Store Street, coming as guests, that's all. And the fella made his apologies for coming late."

"That's nice, Shay's friends coming. What's troubling you, Thomas?"

Thomas now, was it? Thomas looked his wife in the eye and then looked down. She moved her left hand off the table. Then she said, "Never mind that." She returned her attention to Brennan.

"Can yis not hear the music?" Francie had come into the kitchen. "Don't be annoying Father Burke in the midst of the hooley, now, Ma. Come out and give us a tune on the concertina, Da."

"I will. Francie, there are two guards on their way over."

"Janey Mack!" She raised her hands and held them out as if to ward off terror. "Whatever will we do?"

"They're pals of Shay. Vincent somebody and another fella."

Francie laughed and said, "Don't be worrying yourself over it, Da. We all know you were at the McLogan party but you left early, so no suspicion is falling upon you."

Talkie was at McLogan's? Was the family concerned about . . . ?

"Oh, the guards know that. They came and asked me about it, and other people must have confirmed it for them, because they left five minutes after arriving."

Francie looked as if something had just occurred to her. "But Shay's Garda mates coming . . . is that why the silver's gone off the mantelpiece?"

Talkie's face darkened, but Francie just laughed. She looked at her mother, reached over and picked up her mother's hand. "And this?" Francie said. Brennan noticed then that a ring on Deirdre's fourth finger was now just a gold band; earlier he had seen a large sparkling stone in it. She had twisted the stone out of sight.

"Don't be concerned, Ma. Those young peelers are not going to recognize a few items that fell off a lorry . . . how many years ago? What anniversary was it?" She looked again at her mother's ring. Then looked at her father. "Get that concertina, Da, and join in with the session."

Talkie darted a worried look at his wife and daughter, but left to rejoin the party.

Deirdre Rynne looked mortified. "I . . . I never really believed he'd saved money to buy these things. I knew that they, well, as you said,

Francie, fell off a lorry. So I shouldn't have accepted them, but . . ." She gestured with her hands to indicate the cramped Corporation flat, the shabby furniture. Who could have blamed her for wanting a few touches of elegance?

Francie said, "Come on, yis, time to rejoin the festivities."

Brennan and Deirdre got up from the table and went out onto the balcony. There was somebody playing a fiddle in the street below, and somebody else playing a bodhran. A woman on the balcony joined in with her tin whistle. Beside her, Talkie added his concertina to the impromptu orchestra. A little boy came running out and grabbed the concertina and grinned back at Talkie. Brennan had heard him addressed as Kevin.

"I'm playing this now!" he announced, and a series of discordant squawks came out of the instrument. A few people laughed, and a bigger boy covered his ears and said, "You've killed it. You've fuckin' killed the thing!"

Kevin burst into tears then and thrust the concertina back at Talkie. The little fella started to run away, but Talkie grasped him by the arm. "Kevin, my lad. Stay here now."

"No, I can't play it! He said I killed it!"

Talkie put his arm around Kevin and said, "You didn't kill it at all. It's just that you're so strong. This is made for lighter fingers, not big, strong fingers like your own."

Kevin wiped the tears from his eyes and said, "Is that true, Grandda?"

"Of course it is, and you know what? I'm going to teach you every-thing I know about it. Private lessons, just you and me. Sound like a good plan?"

"Yeah!"

"You'll be brilliant, won't you, Kev?"

"Yeah!"

Talkie rubbed the little boy's curls and sent him off with visions of his future as a concertina player par excellence.

Brennan looked out over the gathering below, pleased with what he saw. Neighbours joined in the singing or stood by and tapped their toes. Two middle-aged couples did a step dance. Shay leaned over and greeted two men around his own age or a little older. You'd recognize them as guards anywhere, Brennan thought, though they were in civilian clothes. And they immediately joined in the singing and the dancing. Brennan thought Talkie had little to worry about with their arrival.

"Just like the rare old times," an ancient man said, and Brennan knew that back in the roughest days of Dublin's crowded tenements, with large families crammed into one room, this kind of event was frequent and brought much-needed joy to the poor people of Dublin. Even Jane looked as if she was enjoying herself, as Shay took her by the hands and got her up dancing.

Brennan was delighted to have this night to remember, this kitchen party in the street, before flying back to his new home in New York. Of course, the craic tonight made it even more painful to think of leaving Dublin on Monday morning.

CHAPTER XII

E arly on Monday afternoon, Shay was on the telephone listening to a long, moaning complaint from an old one who had her front window broken by "the sort of hooligans you see everywhere these days" and was demanding that the law be brought down on them in no uncertain terms. Vince Foley walked over and signalled to Shay that somebody wanted to see him. Shay finally got the window woman off the phone with promises that An Garda Síochána would pursue her complaint with the full rigour of the law. He scribbled a note to himself so he wouldn't forget about her thirty seconds after replacing the receiver. After all, he was working more serious cases now!

"Hi, Vince. What earth-shattering case is waiting for me today? A young couple sharing their love in the laneway behind Mrs. O'Finnicky's house? And her after watching them the whole time through her net curtains before ringing us? Or some lad who pushed a beer glass into the face of a louser who looked at him the wrong way?"

"None of the above, Shay. A young one here for you, or at least for the guard investigating the McLogan murder. She wouldn't tell me anything once she found out I'm 'not the man in charge'!"

"Good enough then. You run along and let 'the man in charge' handle this." The other man in charge had left the station a few minutes before.

Foley laughed and left him to it. Shay went out to the entrance, where he saw a girl in her late teen years, by the look of her, or maybe early twenties. She had long black hair framing a freckly face that looked as if it belonged on a ginger. And she had a nervous, flighty look about her.

"I'm Garda Rynne. What can I do for you today?"

"Em, do I have to give yeh my name?"

"Let's just hear what you have to say, and we'll see about names later."

"But . . ."

He was going to talk to her there in the station, but she had such a case of the janglers that he said, "Let's go outside and have a walk." She didn't want to be seen standing by the Garda station, so he led her down to the river and along the quay for a ways, then turned and asked, "Now, take your time, and tell me what's on your mind."

"It's a man I saw and him nearly knocking me down with his car."

Nearly. Shay could see promotion coming his way in the wake of this heinous offence. Detective Sergeant Seamus Rynne, Guardian of the Peace in the Republic of Ireland.

"Were you hit at all?"

"I wasn't, but I nearly was."

"And where did this happen?"

"On Amiens Street."

Shay smiled at her, in what he hoped was an encouraging way. "Whereabouts on Amiens Street? It's a long street, so."

"At the corner of Seville Place."

That wasn't far from Darragh McLogan's house. And she had asked for the man investigating the murder. This might be interesting after all, if . . . "When was this?"

"The night he was killed. The TD."

Now Shay was interested. "Ah. And what time would it have been?"

"It was late, morning really, it was. After the Dock Rocks Club closed. It closes at two o'clock."

"So you were out on the street at two o'clock." That was the wrong tone to take with her, as was clear when her face seemed to shut down on him. "I mean, I'm just trying to clarify, get the exact time. I know I've been out at that time of night, too!" He smiled at her again, as if they were both in on a mischievous little secret. He could see her relax a bit. "So this was late in the night or early morning. August thirtieth or thirty-first."

"It was."

"And you were —"

"Me and this fella. He moved into one of the flats near where I live with my ma. And I knew he goes to the club. And me and some of my pals were together that night, having a few laughs and some . . . We'd passed a couple of bottles around, me and the girls. But I wasn't gilled or anything. Just had a bit. But I decided I'd like to see if this lad would be coming out of the place after closing time." Her face was a painful red by this time.

"Sure, you liked this young fella and you were in the area anyway, so why not see if he'd be there. I know what you mean. So then what happened?"

"He wasn't there. I waited kind of outside and away from the Dock Rocks door where I could see. But no sign of him, so I started to walk home. And I was at the corner, and I started out across the street, and that's when this fancy silver car came roaring along and nearly put the heart crossways in me. And I jumped out of the way and I fell on me arse and I was effin' and blindin' about the man and his car."

"I'm sure we'd all do the same. So he was speeding, you'd say?"

"Going like the divil out of hell!"

"And then?"

"And then I'm down on the street, and I heave myself up and get back onto the pavement. And he pulls his car over, parks up, and comes back to me."

"Is that right?"

"And he's saying, 'Are yeh all right there?' And 'I'm sorry, I was driving too fast and wasn't paying attention. Are yeh hurt?' And I wanted to say I broke my leg, but there was nothing broken and I wasn't really hurt at all, just fierce annoyed at him. So I said, 'I'm the picture of health, but no thanks to you!' And he said again that he was sorry, and he went to the car. But then he came back to me with a whack of banknotes, and didn't he hand over fifty punts to me!"

"Well, you don't see that every day, do you?"

"And he says, 'Please don't say anything about this to anyone. It wouldn't do for me to be arrested for driving while under the influence!' But he was sort of smiling when he said it. Yet he looked as if the nerves were going on him. He was alarmed about the whole thing. And then it was 'The wife would have me bollocks,' and I couldn't help but laugh. And then he walked back to his car and drove off."

"And now you want him charged with careless driving, dangerous driving, something like that?"

"No, no, that's not it." She looked about her then, as if someone might overhear. "It's just that when I heard the next day about the TD being killed, Mr. McLogan, and this happening so late at night near his house, and this man — the man in the car — it being a rich man's class of a car . . . But the man, well, he didn't look or sound like a man who'd have a car like that. And this happening so close to Mr. McLogan's house. Oh, I don't know what I'm doing here. I'm probably making a big mistake."

"What did you mean, that he didn't seem like a man who'd have a car like that?"

"Well, he didn't sound posh or anything like that. Just sounded like any of us here. And he didn't look like a rich man. His suit, wherever he bought it, it wouldn't have been dear. More like from a bargain shop. And that mop of curls on his head. He may have been the man, the rich man's driver. You know, a fella who worked for him."

Shay was getting an uneasy feeling. He knew that Jem O'Daly occasionally bought new and pricey cars for his businesses, most recently an Aston Martin. And the image of a curly-haired man, a driver of O'Daly's cars and lorries, a *servant*, fit a man Shay knew only too well: his own father. Talkie had been at the McLogan party. That in itself was not a matter for concern; DS Griffith was satisfied with what Talkie had to say. And it was not all that strange for him to have been at McLogan's house that night. He worked for O'Daly, and O'Daly was angling for political advantage, no doubt wanting to look as if he was still a man of the people. Talkie Rynne was one of the people.

But a driving offence was a small matter compared to a murder, and McLogan was alive and well when Shay's father left the house. Shay returned his attention to the girl beside him.

"So here I am now," the young one said, "talking to the guards, informing on the man. And he gave me money. Do I have to give yis the money, give it back, like? 'Cause I don't have it anymore. I needed it for . . . necessaries."

"No, no, don't be concerning yourself with that. But I do need your name."

Her light-brown eyes were as wide and round as penny coins. "This will get me in the soup with whatever man was driving that swanky car. Telling tales about him, and all he did really was drive too fast. And he didn't leave the scene! He stopped and . . ."

And paid for her silence.

Shay finally got her name out of her, Mary O'Neill, and he assured her that they wouldn't be throwing her name around. She didn't look like a person who had been reassured, when she walked away from him down the quays, glancing around her to see if she was being watched.

Shay walked back to Store Street, reminding himself that, yes, a driving offence was a small matter compared to murder.

&

Shay wasn't in on the preparations, the flight reservations, the termination of the lease on Deena's flat, or any of the rest of it. Father Burke may have called on the Man Above for assistance but, however he did it, he got Deena Breathnach out of Dublin and to New York.

And Shay had taken Jane's script for the play on the canal and handed the role to another actor. He told himself he would inform DS Griffith about the plan after the fact. If it was productive. He had loitered near the canal until he spotted Cora, walked her to his car, and suggested the plan to her. He said nothing about the Dermody trial, just said a man in a green Renault had been following Deena and frightening her. As a result, Deena was going away for a while. Cora wasn't all that different from Deena in height and build, and she was familiar with Deena's clothing and mannerisms. She would be strolling the canal anyway, and she knew the dangers. She had long experience in taking care of herself. Not that there was any guarantee of safety in her line of work, but, as she said herself, this little pantomime would be no riskier than any of her other nights around the Pepper Pot church. He offered to be nearby for her during this assignment, but the look she gave him said, *This is my world; I can live in it.*

Shay told her not to turn down any dates while waiting for the Renault but, well, he'd leave it up to her to decide how to carry out her mission. He said he would pay for any lost time, and she accepted his offer. So he gave her his home phone number, thanked her profusely, and let her get back to work.

He heard nothing from Cora for the two nights after that, but the stunt paid off on night three. Cora rang him at home just after eleven. She told him she'd seen a green Renault approaching at low speed. She made a point of staring at it, and it stopped. She took note of the Dublin plate number, and then she turned and walked away. The car followed, and she peered in at the driver. Deena had said the man wore a cap pulled down over his forehead, but she had been able to see a pointy chin and straight thin brown hair with grey strands under the cap. Cora made the same observations. And then the man did a double take, obviously realizing that she was not Deena Breathnach. And he sped away. And that was that. Shay told her how grateful he was and that she could send him her account.

"Ah, go on out of that," she replied. "I'm just glad I could help Deena."

When Shay got to work in the morning, he went through the process of identifying the owner of the Renault. It was a man he'd never heard of, Ivor Gilday, but he made a note of the details in case they would be useful in the trial. Or in case he decided to charge the man with threatening or intimidating a witness. He would keep the information to himself for now.

Shay knew Jane would want to hear that her scheme was successful, even if the starring role went to someone else. So he got in touch with her and invited her out for supper. He walked to the city centre and they chose a place not far from Trinity College. As they ate and drank at the table, he thanked her and filled her in on Cora's canal walk, and the crucial information it produced.

Then they chatted about other things, their childhood days, and Shay was surprised to learn that Jane was a bit of a sportswoman. She used to coach young girls in hockey, hockey played on the field. And that led Shay to speak of his love of hurling. They ordered more wine, and Shay could see its effect on Jane. Her face became flushed, her eyes a bit bloodshot. She returned to the subject of Deena Breathnach. "How did you get to know Deena, or should I ask?"

Shay smiled at her. "No reason not to ask. I've always known her. She grew up near me. Another former resident of Fenian Street."

"*Fenian* Street." Jane laughed when she said it. "Named in honour of those blokes who carried out the dynamite attacks on London all those years ago?"

"Mmm."

"Strange that they've kept that name for the street, that they haven't changed it to something more, I don't know, neutral."

What? "Why should they?"

"Sorry, Shay, perhaps I've offended you. I don't mean to."

"I'm not offended."

"I get the impression that you're, well, sympathetic to all that. Republicans. The Irish Republican . . . that sort of thing."

That was the sort of thing you did not speak of in an Irish bar or restaurant. You did not say these things out loud. He put his right index finger over his lips and shook his head.

"Oh! Secret stuff, is it?"

"Jane, there are certain words, and certain initials, that you don't say aloud in a public place."

"I'm sorry. I'm a — What do you call it here, a blow-in? And I don't know the local customs. The local taboos."

"We should finish up and get on the road."

"Before I become too much of an embarrassment! Well, then, let us be off." And she lifted her glass and downed the rest of her wine. "Why not come over to my place? We can have another glass, and nobody will hear me if I say the wrong thing."

He was all for going to her flat, though not for more conversation about sensitive matters. "Sure, we'll have another at your place."

They got up to leave, and she was a little unsteady on her feet. Shay took her arm, and they walked to her flat. The place was small, but she had managed to fit in two large bookcases filled with books. She brought out a bottle of white wine and they started in on that, sitting side by side on a brown leather sofa.

Jane turned to him and said, "I'm sorry. I'm usually better behaved. And I usually stop at two glasses of wine."

"Not a bother, Jane, no need to apologize. I myself have been known to take more than two glasses!"

"So there are some things that are not to be spoken of where other ears might hear."

"That's right."

"But in a place like — What's the place we went to? Burke's?"

"Christy Burke's, you mean?"

"Yes. That's clearly a, well, a republican bar. The pictures on the walls, the songs they sing. Rebel songs, I guess you'd call them. Nobody's hiding their true colours in there."

"That's different."

"How so?"

"That's not naming names, or talking about somebody's history or who's been . . . active. It's just . . ." This was not a conversation he wanted to get into, not with someone he really didn't know all that well.

"I'm under the impression that you're a frequent visitor to that establishment. You like it there. So it's very sporting of you to be seen in public with an English girl!" He didn't know what to say to that, so he said nothing. "All right, Shay, darling, I get it. I'll shut up. Except, well, if you do support the Irish republican . . . point of view, that must put you at odds with your fellow coppers, I should think."

He could have said, *Not all of them.* But that was definitely something that should remain unsaid. He didn't want Jane Blytheford's colleagues at Trinity College, at their next wine and cheese social, hearing, *Oh, did you know there are IRA sympathizers in the Garda Síochána?*

Shay felt her hand on his arm. "I'm sorry, Shay. I shouldn't have said that. I apologize. If we are out together again, if I haven't put you off entirely, I promise to imbibe no more than two glasses of wine, and you won't have to fend off any more outré remarks or questions."

"Ah, I'll get over it."

They got on just fine after that, particularly after she said, "Well, Shay, you didn't permit me to play the part of a canal walker, but would you be interested in a more amateur production?" At first he didn't catch on. Then he did.

As he made his way back to the north side on foot, he tried to sort out his feelings for Jane. He liked her, no question. He enjoyed her humour, and he had sure as hell enjoyed her tonight when she abandoned that famed English reserve. But it wasn't really anything like love, was it? No, not yet. Love was what he'd had with Allie, and that feeling had never gone away. Ease off on the drink, Rynne, he scolded himself.

CHAPTER XIII

T he next development in the McLogan case was a report from
Forensics. The report showed that the wounds on McLogan's
face and body were a match for his own shoes. Someone had put on
McLogan's shoes to do the kicking. There were fingermarks on the
shoes, but the prints were so smudged that they would be of no use in
trying to match them to any one person. There were fibres and hairs
on the victim's clothing, but these could have come from the close
contact he had with many of the people who attended his party.

There was, however, one finding that stood out. McLogan's body
was found outdoors behind his back door, and the evidence at the
scene indicated with a high degree of certainty that he was killed
there. There was construction going on next door, and in the back
garden there were wood shavings, scraps of old paint, dust, and small
bits of mortar and brick. Traces of these materials had been found on
one sock that had been linked to one of the men at the party. And
that man was Jem O'Daly. Jem and Etty O'Daly, being related to the
McLogans, had been invited to stay over the night of the hooley. They
had packed one bag with their belongings and had it in the bedroom

they were using. As Colm Griffith said, "It's a good thing for us that Mr. and Mrs. O'Daly are good, clean people, and put on clean underwear and socks in the morning! We took the overnight bag from Jem as he was leaving the house. Told him, 'Nothing can leave the house yet, sir.' In case he might have been smuggling the murder weapon out in the bag!"

"How did he react to that?"

"Just shrugged and said, 'Sure.' If it bothered him, there was no sign of it."

In the course of their investigation the morning the body was found, Forensics had gone through all the rooms looking for evidence, and one of the things they searched was the O'Dalys' bag. They found the sock with the construction debris on it and took it in as evidence. Tests now showed that the debris matched what was in the back garden. This was no small thing, given that whoever had killed McLogan had put on McLogan's shoes to do the job. So the man had taken his own shoes off, and most likely had done this near where McLogan was lying.

It was time for another chat with O'Daly. Shay and Colm Griffith found him in his office on the top floor of Quo Day Building Contractors. O'Daly had a crowd of other fellas with him, all of them with cigars in their mouths, and they were enjoying a laugh about something. But when he saw the police at the door, he shooed the other men away and stood to greet the guards. If he was disturbed by their arrival at his office, he didn't show it.

"What can I do for the Gardaí today? Can I get yis something? Coffee, tea, or . . . ?" He gestured to a well-stocked bar at the side of the room.

"No. Nothing, thanks, Jem. We've a couple of questions for you."

"Sure, sure. Sit yourselves down." He sat at his desk, and Shay and Griffith sat facing him.

Griffith wasted no time. "Jem, what were you doing in your sock feet in McLogan's back garden the night of the party?"

"What was I doing . . . What is it you're asking me?!" He looked more amused than upset.

"The Forensics guys, as they always do in these cases, went through the house that morning and examined everything, and they found a pair of your socks in your travel bag. And the socks had material — scraps and rubble from the repair project next door — on the soles of them." It was only one of the socks, but that didn't matter right now.

O'Daly was shaking his head. "I've no idea what you're on about, Colm. I wasn't walking around the place, inside or out, with my shoes off. Next question, Officer."

"If you were out there for some innocent reason, you'd best tell us now."

"Everything I did that night was innocent, apart from having too much drink on me and telling a few jokes that might have sounded rude or scandalous to more sober ears."

Shay was expecting Griffith to ask again whether O'Daly had argued with McLogan that night, but quickly realized that it was wise not to repeat the question. They already had O'Daly's dishonest answer to that question from the previous interview. Better to let it stand as a lie than to have O'Daly come up with a less guilt-laden reply.

O'Daly leaned towards them. "I didn't kill my brother-in-law, lads. We're not that kind of family!" He laughed when he said it, knowing that Griffith and Shay and every other guard in the city knew what kind of a family O'Daly's was, until he had made his about-turn and decided to go legit. Nobody, however, had ever suggested that Darragh McLogan was in on any of O'Daly's schemes or offences.

O'Daly said goodbye as if they had just stopped in for a friendly gab. He looked, or managed to look, unconcerned. But could he really be that unconcerned about the fact that the evidence pointed to him having taken off his shoes outside McLogan's house where McLogan's body had been found?

When they were outside the building, Griffith said, "This evidence puts him squarely in the frame for this, Shay." O'Daly in the frame, not the man who'd been speeding away from McLogan's end of the street the night of the murder.

"What reason," Griffith continued, "could he possibly have for walking around out there with only the socks on his feet? You can bet there is some reason O'Daly wanted his brother-in-law out of the way. It may be something that just came up and set O'Daly off, or it may be something that had been simmering for a while, and O'Daly got himself worked up at the party, and him with the drink on him. There's a motive out there, and we're going to find it."

⁊

The second weekend in September was bright, warm, and sunny, and some of Shay's mates from the old neighbourhood got together for two afternoons of football. Followed, of course, by marathon sessions in a couple of the local pubs. Shay had rung Jane's number on the Friday but got no answer. Tried the next morning, no answer again. He concluded that she had gone away for the weekend. But his own weekend was loads of fun, so he didn't feel left out of things. As the workweek got underway, though, Shay was a worried man. A worried son.

On Tuesday evening, he sat brooding over his pint in Christy Burke's, brooding about the incident involving a man who had the characteristics of his own father, zooming around in a pricey car in the early hours of August the thirty-first. Yes, Jem O'Daly's sock had debris on it from the back garden, but you could be sure he would come up with an innocent — or innocent-sounding — explanation for that. Shay knew he couldn't put it off any longer. He had to get his father alone and ask him what happened the night of McLogan's party, McLogan's death. He didn't want anyone else around, so he left Christy's and called in at the flat on Fenian Street and invited Talkie out to wet his throat. Talkie would never say no to an invitation like that.

They got into Shay's car and headed over to the north side, but their destination was not Madigan's or Christy Burke's or Walsh's. Their destination was Emmet Street. Shay pulled up near his own house and reached behind him to the back seat. His father jerked away as if he was afraid of — what? Being hit? This still happened from time to time, Talkie being spooked by sudden movements or loud noises. The ordeal he'd suffered in the Curragh camp could still make him jumpy decades later. Shay told him he was reaching for

195

a bottle of whiskey he'd bought at the off-licence, and Talkie said, "Good man." They went into Shay's house, and Shay poured them each a generous helping, and handed Talkie his glass. He produced a pack of fags, and they both lit up. Shay told himself to stay calm, to lead into the subject without alarming his father or raising his hackles, to take it easy.

But despite his good intentions, the first words out of his mouth were "What the fuck were you doing, speeding along Amiens Street in Jemser O'Daly's car the night of the murder?"

His father looked as if he had taken a bolt to the heart. "What?"

"You heard me. Now you do the talking."

"I wasn't —"

"You were. You had one of O'Daly's cars."

His father's eyes shifted away. "Well, that was it, so. Jemser got the new Aston Martin — a beautiful machine, it is — and he gave me the car for the night, because he'd be stopping overnight with the missus at Darragh and Muriel's. He wasn't going to be driving it, and there were a couple of deliveries he wanted me to make. And I did those, then dropped in at the party, early on and only stayed for a short while, and then I . . ."

"How about McLogan?"

The shifty look again. "What do you mean?"

"Were you talking to him? How was he?"

"He was grand, so he was."

"But not for long. Somebody put the boots to him before the night was over and left him dead."

"Well, it sure as fuck wasn't me! I'm asking myself who I'm talking to here. Is it my son, or is it *Garda* Rynne?"

So there it was, his true attitude to Shay being a peeler. But no, what man wouldn't get his ire up being questioned in this way by his own son? But question him, he would.

"What happened, Da? You left the party early. Why'd you do that?"

"Because it was filled with a lot of fellas with a warm welcome for themselves, and I had the chance to be off by myself in an automobile fit for a king! I was of a mind to drive it around the city, stop to have a jar or two, and then take the car back out to the Quo Day office. And take one of the old bangers home to our place, the way I always do. So I went to an off-licence and got myself a bottle of Powers, and I drove round the city, enjoying the sights and enjoying a few sips from the bottle."

"But at something like two in the morning you were racing up Amiens Street and nearly ran over a young one standing there."

"Oh, that was an awful thing. I knew then I'd had too much drink on board, and I'd be in trouble."

"And that's why you paid her off."

"I didn't pay her off! You're making me sound like a . . . somebody in the Mafia! Or a —"

"Or a politician."

"Yeah, like one of those fellas. Shay, I didn't want to be reported for drink driving and nearly bringing harm or even death to the young one there. My mind was scrambled."

"Where did you get the fifty punts?"

"I had it with me."

"You were carrying fifty punts in cash with you."

"I got fifty for some work I did. Some of my work is paid in cash, Seamus."

If Talkie Rynne had fifty Irish pounds in his pocket at the end of the workday, there was no chance under heaven that he would still have fifty pounds on his person or in the glovebox of O'Daly's car several hours into the night. He'd have drunk some of it away, maybe put some on the horses; he would not still have it on hand to pay off a near victim of his reckless driving. So it wasn't his money.

This was all so foolish, so contrary to common sense, that it had a faint ring of truth about it. Leave it to Talkie to end up in a situation like this and then make an awful hames of it. Shay wasn't looking forward to the other guards hearing this tale from Garda Rynne's own father. He tried to salve his conscience as he told himself he would report the conversation to DS Griffith. Eventually. But he wanted to learn a lot more about what happened that night, and who had acted even more suspiciously than Talkie Rynne, before he came clean about the interview he had just conducted. He was determined to stay with the murder inquiry; he didn't want to be turfed off it, which would happen once the car story came out.

Before that happened, Shay wanted to be along for the questioning of witnesses, the discovery of evidence; he wanted to know right away when a suspect was identified. He did not want to be cast into the outer darkness, where he would have no idea what might be happening with the case and with his father. So he put on hold the plan to come clean with his superior officer.

⁊

The talk was all about Jem O'Daly next day at Store Street. Detective Sergeant Griffith had the reformed gangster at the top of his list. Shay, thinking ahead, could see the day when he himself would want O'Daly in the dock for this. But once the news about his own father's actions came to light, he wouldn't want it remembered that he'd been pushing for O'Daly to wear the prison shackles. So he would play down his interest in O'Daly. He said, "No doubt there's a list of things that O'Daly's a good suspect for. But this? Weren't the two of them working together? O'Daly gets the support of somebody respectable like McLogan, and McLogan gets more publicity by appearing with the notorious, promised-to-sin-no-more Jemser O'Daly."

"I don't have to remind you, Shay, how quickly even the best of relationships can go sour, how quickly tempers can erupt."

"There's truth in that, so. But wouldn't O'Daly have found a better way to knock somebody off than kicking a man to death? O'Daly probably has a closet full of guns from his former life."

"As I say, tempers can erupt in an instant."

CHAPTER XIV

S hay couldn't put it off forever. And he knew he'd be getting stick
for putting it off this long, for questioning his father about the
night of the murder, and then waiting nearly a week before reporting
the conversation to his superior officer. But now it was time. Shay had
Talkie in his car, and told him to sit tight while he went into Store
Street Station to break the news to DS Griffith. As if it wouldn't be
bad enough, Lar McCreevy was there with Griffith. Shay hemmed
and hawed and tried to think of a way to get Griffith alone. But
McCreevy was not for moving, and Shay didn't have the authority to
tell him to get lost. So Shay took a deep breath and made his confession. McCreevy's face was like the dense black clouds they must have
seen in biblical times just before the forty days and forty nights of
bucketing rain. Colm Griffith's face was impossible to read.

McCreevy spoke first. "So. Rynne. You took it upon yourself to
question your own father as a possible suspect in the murder inquiry."

"I questioned him about a reckless driving incident, which happened to —"

"Which happened to happen around the time, quite possibly, that the murder was committed. Then you waited as long as you could, hoping to have a rake of other suspects in play, before telling us about your father."

"He has a perfectly innocent — well, not innocent when it comes to the way he was driving — but otherwise innocent explanation. And I've brought him in to give you a statement."

"Isn't that decent of you, Rynne."

Griffith broke into the conversation then and said, "I'll handle this, Lar. I'll be in touch about the other matter when I have the information."

So, with that, McCreevy was dismissed and went off to wait for the other matter, whatever it was. Went off to wait. Or to gloat?

Griffith said to Shay, "You understand that you'll not be taking part in the interview with your father."

"Of course. I understand that, sir. I'll fetch him for you now."

So Shay delivered his father to his interrogators, Detective Sergeant Griffith and whoever else Griffith would be bringing into the interview room. And then Shay waited. And hoped and prayed that Colm Griffith's long-standing support of the Rynne family would make this ordeal a bit less harrowing for Talkie. But Griffith was first and foremost a detective, and he was questioning Talkie Rynne in connection with a murder. Shay was supposed to be filling in reports on a couple of incidents from the week before, but he wasn't able to concentrate. He was waiting to see what his father would look like when he emerged from his ordeal.

When that time came, when Talkie was released by his questioners and Shay was given the word to go and collect him, Talkie had the look of a man well pleased with himself. Once they were seated in the car for the short drive back to the family home, Talkie said, "I told them what happened. And, as you can see, I'm a free man!"

"You told them what you told me."

"Because that's what happened."

"Did anything else happen, besides what you told me?"

His father turned to look at him. "Like what?"

"I don't know, Da. I wasn't there."

"Don't be troubling yourself about it. I answered their questions and they let me go. So let that be the end of it."

℃

But that was not the end of it. The sky fell on Talkie Rynne two days later.

The day began like any other, with Shay and a new detective sergeant, Scully, questioning witnesses about a series of burglaries in one of the housing estates not far from the Garda station. When he returned to Store Street in the afternoon, he knew that something was off. People were avoiding his eye. And then Colm Griffith came to him with the news. "We've brought your father in again, Shay, this time as a suspect."

"What?!"

"You understand that your participation in the McLogan murder inquiry will be over now. But, as a courtesy, I'll let you have a look at what we found after we talked to him the first time." And he handed Shay a report. The look he gave Shay was not unsympathetic, but Shay knew his own participation in the case was indisputably over.

He took the papers to a desk and started to read. Tried to stop his hands from shaking. The first thing Griffith and his team had done was go out to the Quo Day headquarters in order to examine the Aston Martin. Jem O'Daly was away in Portlaoise for the day. Visiting an old pal in the prison? Shay wondered. But there was no reference to that, only the fact that he was out of town. One of his managers at the office handed over the key to the Aston Martin, so Forensics could see what evidence it might yield. And yield it did. Talkie's prints were on the door handle, the steering wheel, and the gear stick as expected, and also on the glovebox. Was that where the fifty pounds had come from, a stash of the readies kept by O'Daly and his men?

But what nearly made Shay stop breathing was the fibre evidence the Forensics guys had found in the car, around the driver's seat. Small fibres, not in great abundance, but they came from the tweed jacket Darragh McLogan was wearing the night of the party. Griffith and another guard had gone over to see Muriel McLogan and asked her, "Do you know if Darragh was ever in Mr. O'Daly's new Aston Martin?"

She shook her head. "I'd have heard about it. Darragh was a man who loved cars. If he'd been in a brand new car like that, he'd have been brimming over about it. So, no, he was never in an Aston Martin."

Then came the second interrogation of Talkie Rynne. A cautioned statement. Shay began reading the transcript. Griffith didn't begin with the car; he began with the party. Yes, Talkie had been there for a short while. He was long acquainted with Darragh's brother-in-law, Jem O'Daly, and he did various kinds of work for O'Daly's company.

"There were forty or so people there. Did you have a chance to speak with Mr. McLogan?"

"Ah, I'd only a quick conversation with him. 'How are yeh keepin', Darragh? Grand party,' that sort of a thing. I've a bit of a reputation, as you know yourself, Col — Detective. I'm known as a man would talk the hind legs off a donkey, so I wanted to be sure not to do that, and him with so many other guests to be greeting."

"And what time would this have been?"

"Half eleven, midnight maybe."

"Right. Happy to see him? Did you shake his hand, clap him on the back kind of thing?"

"No, no. No physical contact with him at all."

Shay nearly banged his head down on the desk at that. Who besides a peeler would use a phrase like "physical contact"? To Griffith, it would have had the sound, as it did to Shay, of a man anticipating an accusation or a troublesome fact and rushing to deny it. In language that would not come naturally to a man like Talkie. So instead of fibres being transferred from McLogan's jacket to Talkie because they were in close, friendly physical contact, even for a few seconds, the fibres were transferred by some kind of contact that Talkie said never happened. Check that box and move on.

Next it was the car. And Talkie gave them the same story he'd given them before, the story he'd given Shay. He was cock-a-hoop about having the Aston Martin for the night, so he stayed at the party for a short while, then went off in the car. Stopped for a bottle of whiskey, and drank from it while driving round the city. He was half-gilled and was driving too fast and nearly hit young Mary O'Neill. Worried about getting caught driving his boss's car while guzzling from a bottle of whiskey and endangering the life of a pedestrian, he apologized and gave her some money for her trouble.

"Mr. Rynne. We found something in the car." Shay could imagine his father tensing up at that. "As you may know, our Forensics unit can find things that we don't always notice, because the things are so small. Like fibres from someone's clothing. Mr. Rynne?"

"Yeah, yeah, sorry."

"We found fibres from Mr. McLogan's tweed jacket in the car. But Mr. McLogan was never in the car. You were in the car. Would you like a glass of water?"

"No, no, I'm grand."

"How do you explain the presence of those fibres around the driver's seat of the car?"

"Em, some other fella must have —"

"And that's not all."

Oh God, what else was there?

"We also found traces of dust from mortar and a tiny chip of paint on the floor of the car, on the clutch and the brake pedal."

Shay was torn between the urge to rush in, too late, and save his father, or strangle him with his own hands. He kept reading with a feeling of doom coming down on him.

"What kind of stuff are you talking about?" asked a desperate Talkie Rynne.

"Debris from the repair project next door to the McLogan house. Back of the house, where he was killed."

"I didn't kill him! Some other fella must have been there and then was in the car!"

"Nobody else who's been in the car since that night had contact with Mr. McLogan, or the place where he died. You can be sure we've checked into all that."

Had they? Or were they just telling him that to squeeze him into a corner? What about O'Daly himself? Wasn't it possible that he had been in close physical contact with his brother-in-law while he was wearing that tweed jacket? And that he'd been right there where McLogan was killed? There was the material found on O'Daly's sock. Shay would raise that possibility if it got to the point where . . . But no. Talkie reacted by doing what he always did: talked too much.

"This is what happened, and it was innocent altogether. The reason I didn't tell you . . . I knew it would look bad, even though —"

"Just tell us, Mr. Rynne."

"All right, so. I was at the hooley. A bit late, I was. I'd been out having a few jars. Got to McLogan's after eleven o'clock, I think it was. And I talked a bit to the other people there. I didn't see Darragh, so I looked around, then went downstairs to a little office he had. And wasn't he in there with a young fella? It was dark in that room. And there was a conversation going on, Darragh and this other fella. And I knew I'd seen that lad before, but I couldn't place him. Anyway, I'd missed the first part of whatever it was they were saying. All I heard was something like, 'After this, O'Daly won't be el presidente of Quo Day Building Contractors any longer.' And he handed an envelope to Darragh, and Darragh put it in one of the pockets of his jacket. And the young lad said, 'Think of it as a bloodless coup!' And Darragh smiled, and I thought it was a sly smile, like.

"And I had drink on me, as I told yis, and I thought, 'Some shower of shites are taking over Jemser's business! He's going to lose it, and I'll be out!' I lost the run of myself entirely. And so when the young fella walked out, I jumped at Darragh and I grabbed his jacket and tore the pocket, and I got hold of the envelope, and I fucked off with it. Ran out of the house, got into the Aston Martin, and roared away.

"And I took myself off to the docks, and I turned on the overhead light in the car and started reading the papers, and I realized what was going on. The papers were from Jem O'Daly's solicitor's office, copies of the real documents. And I remembered then where I'd seen that young fella. Lorcan somebody. He was from the solicitor's office, worked for the solicitor and sometimes came out to Quo Day to

204

drop things off or collect things from Jemser. And anyway, I read the stuff. And it turned out it wasn't a crowd of other fellas going to take the businesses away from Jemser at all. It wasn't a move against him. It was a legal scheme to put control of his companies under another company. A holding company or something, and it was meant to protect Jemser himself, and was supposed to protect the businesses, from claims or anything that might come up from Jemser's past. It was to shelter them all from harm. And I knew then that the smile on Darragh's face wasn't that he was going to benefit from the 'bloodless coup.' It wasn't that at all. Lorcan was just being comical using those words. It was all to help Jem and his companies, and Darragh was pleased about that."

"Yes?"

"So I went off in the car and had some more of the whiskey, and this kept going round and round in my mind, and I decided to go and give the papers back to Darragh. And tell him I was sorry, and patch things up with him. So I returned to his house and went in. I don't think the place is ever locked. But the party was long over. Nobody around. I was in the kitchen and I looked out the window, and thought I saw a pair of feet out there in the dark. That didn't make any sense, so I opened the back door and went out. And I saw him fucking lying there! And I was fucking petrified, and I got into the car and blasted off in it, and that's where the girl came into it. And I took the fifty punts from the glovebox where Jem kept some banknotes and papers for the car. I've a temper on me, and some-times I don't wait to get the whole story about something. And that accounts for the bollocks I made of things that night!"

"And where are those papers now?"

Here it was noted in the file that "Mr. Rynne said nothing for a count of ten."

Then, "Mr. Rynne? The papers."

"I . . . I put a match to them."

Talkie Rynne had just put a match to himself.

There were notes at the end of the report, showing that Lorcan at the solicitor's office denied giving any papers to Darragh McLogan.

And well he might deny it; it would cost him his job if he'd been handing over confidential documents, or copies of documents, about a client. Losing his job might be the least of it; nobody would want to be the man who crossed Jem O'Daly by revealing his confidential plans. And then it was O'Daly himself being questioned. And he denied that there was any change coming to the companies, and he had no idea what the guards were on about. Again he, too, likely had reason to deny any shakeup in his business empire. Any big move like that tended to benefit some and hurt others, maybe some of his managers and investors, and it wouldn't do to have it all leaked to the public, whatever it might have been. O'Daly might now be on the search for a new firm of solicitors.

Were all these denials genuine? Had Talkie made up yet another one of his stories to cover his own guilt? Shay had no idea how he was going to deal with these revelations. But he knew he didn't want to complicate things for himself or his father, didn't want to be accused of conniving with his father, or coaching him, if there were to be further interviews at Store Street, which there almost certainly would be. So he stayed clear of the family home that night.

ഇ

First thing next morning, DS McCreevy came up to Shay and said, "You may want to station yourself by the window there. Or you may not." And he walked away. What was it McCreevy wanted Shay to see? It wasn't long in coming. A Garda car pulled up outside. The guards opened the rear door of the car. One of them reached in, put one hand on a man's head, and with the other pulled him out. So Shay had the agonizing experience of seeing his father under arrest for the murder of Darragh McLogan. Talkie must have resisted, fought the arrest, because they had his hands cuffed behind his back. Even from here, Shay could see that his father's eyes were bloodshot. His hair was mussed and his shirt tail was half out of his trousers. He looked as if he'd spent the night on the batter and hadn't been to bed. The scene brought sidelong glances and nasty remarks Shay's way, of course. The general theme was "What would you expect coming from the slums of Dublin?" But others, his friends in the station, made a point of commiserating with him, and he was so grateful for this, he had to fight the onset of tears.

It didn't take long for the news to get around, and Finn Burke rang Shay at home and offered his unconditional support. "I've a brief who should do a better job than the fella your da used the last couple of times. And here's his phone number at home." This was a solicitor who was up to the standard required to beat a murder charge. Shay expressed his gratitude to Finn and rang the man immediately, apologizing for the phone call after work hours. Brian Kelly assured him that he was used to nighttime calls, and he would give Mr. Rynne all the assistance he could.

And indeed he did. Talkie was released the day after his arrest, on the grounds that there was not sufficient evidence to maintain a charge of murder. The guards had the fibres and traces of construction rubble, the crazy drive from McLogan's house, the lack of corroboration of Talkie's claim about the business papers. But there was nothing that connected Talkie to the attack on McLogan. Not enough to take it to court and win, was the feeling. But that didn't mean Talkie was innocent in the eyes of the Store Street Gardaí. It was made painfully clear to both father and son that the father was *the* suspect in the case.

After his shift was over, Shay headed across the river to the family's flat. Talkie was fluthered; he must have started drinking as soon as he was released. But who could blame him for that? And Garda custody wasn't the only thing he'd been released from.

"He fuckin' sacked me!" Jem O'Daly had sacked Talkie from his job at Quo Day.

"What?! Oh, Christ. Because he thinks you really did it? He's known you long enough to know you'd never have killed Darragh!"

Or had O'Daly known Talkie long enough to suspect he'd lost the rag for some reason and done exactly that?

"Because of the drink driving I did that night! And the money. The fifty punts." The money Talkie had claimed was his own. Well, Shay had never fallen for that chapter of the story.

Now Talkie gulped down another glass of whiskey, and kept saying over and over, "I didn't do it. I didn't kill him."

Francie was sitting with her arm around their mother, who was distraught. She must have taken Kevin over to one of the neighbours. Shay stayed with them for an hour or so, trying to reassure them. When he rose to leave, his father pleaded with him, "Find who did this, Shay. Find him and get me out of this fuckin' hell."

And then Shay was sitting with Des Creaghan in Delaney's bar in Smithfield. This was one of the times they tended to avoid Des's local, Doheny and Nesbitt; that's where Des usually wanted to go to rub shoulders with those in power and those writing about them. But when it was just Shay and Des talking out of school, and likely being indiscreet, it was better to go another pub. There was no shortage of places to go; Dublin had hundreds of drinking spots to choose from. And they both liked Delaney's.

"Christ, Shay, I can't believe they brought your oul fella in for this, and still have him as their suspect."

"Abair é!" Say it!

"You've a houseful of suspects for the killing of McLogan, forty-some Fianna Fáil politicians and hopefuls and family members at McLogan's house. How did they come up with Talkie as the man to cuff for it? You can be sure I won't broadcast anything you tell me here tonight."

So Shay gave him a short summary of the facts that had condemned his father. "The case may be put on the long finger for now, Des, but as soon as my fellow guards can find the evidence they need, they'll be coming for Talkie and will have him for the murder. And I'm off the case, so what can I do?"

Des leaned in close to him and said, "Stay on the case. Just don't let them know you're on it."

They didn't make a night of it at the pub. Des went home mid-evening, but Shay was restless and halfway to langered. He dreaded lying down and facing a sleepless night fretting about his father. He wanted company, female company. He thought of Allie Cotter. What would she say about the calamity Talkie had brought down upon himself? She'd always liked Talkie, Shay knew that, and Talkie had always enjoyed chatting with her. She was well able to hold up her end of the conversation, even with someone as voluble as Talkie Rynne. What on earth would she say now? Shay would never know.

He tried to put her out of mind, as he flagged down a cab and took it to Jane Blytheford's flat over by Trinity. She looked more amused than disturbed by him showing up at her door, unannounced, in the state he was in.

"Come in, come in. I really do think tea would be in order."

"Have yeh got an'thing else?"

"I have a nice bottle of Cab Sauv, if you'd care for a glass."

He had no idea what it was, but anything in a glass sounded good right now, so he said yes. He plunked himself down on her sofa, and soon she returned with two glasses. Ah, it was wine. Red. He lurched forward to seize it and only just missed spilling it.

"It's from Bordeaux," she said, as she seated herself at his side.

"I would expect nothing less," he replied, and she laughed.

"This is not your first glass tonight, I gather, though perhaps your first of Cabernet Sauvignon."

It was his first glass, ever, of Cab whatever-she-called-it. And oh, it was fine stuff, indeed. He had it down in two swallows, and she raised her eyebrows.

"Another? To sip on and savour?"

"Ah, yes, another would be grand." Sip and savour; take it slowly, in other words. He would.

She returned with the second glass, and he took it but didn't immediately bring it to his gob.

"You seem a bit rattled tonight, Shay."

"It's me oul fella," he burst out.

"Me oul fella?" she repeated, in a semblance of his own way of speaking. "What about him?"

"They nicked him for McLogan. Well, they've let him go. But he's still their suspect."

"What? Shay, slow down and tell me."

So he gave her a shortened version of the catastrophe that had befallen his da, and took a couple of sips of the wine. He cautioned himself not to pour it all down his throat at once. "Ah, this is lovely stuff, so it is."

She laughed again. "I'm chuffed to hear that you approve. So, getting back to your father, they think he did it because of that business with the papers, but they've had to release him because they don't have sufficient evidence."

"Right. They have it in for him, I know they do."

"Oh? Why is that? Has he been in trouble before?"

He took a long "sip" from his glass. "Ever since he was interned, he —" No, he told himself, don't get into all that sad history. The state Shay was in, he might end up in tears over it.

"Interned?" she asked. "When was this? Where was he interned?"

But he waved off her questions. And finished the last of his wine. She brought him another, and he drank deep once again.

"So your fellow police officers have it in for your father. It must be rough for you, working with them and knowing that."

"They've got it in for me, as well."

"What? Why is that?"

"Because I'm a Dub and because of me taking those . . . the situation in the North and me finding that cache of —" Shut your gob, Seamus! he scolded himself again.

"Cache of what?"

"Ach, I'm hammered, Jane. Can I just lie here for a bit? I'm legless here."

"You lie there till . . . till you feel better. I'll bring you a blanket." He watched as she left the room, and then his eyes were closing.

The sun was up when he came to consciousness again. He had a blanket on him, and a ferocious headache. Where was he? At Allie's place? Or was it only a dream? It was a dream, and a blissful one it was. If he fell back to sleep, could he bring it back? It was about him and Allie walking the strand at Bray, eating ice cream, and talking over each other, they had so much to say. When he woke up, he was seized with longing for her. And this was not the first time; he dreamed of her often. He raised his head and looked about him. What had he been drinking? How much did he have?

When he came to his senses, he realized he was in Jane's flat, and she had already left for work. It was painful but he got himself home, washed, and off to Store Street, where he spent a rocky, unproductive day, which seemed to last for a week. Every once in a while, he had a flash of memory, of guzzling red wine and talking about — what? His father? Himself? What had he been going on about? Had he been telling things he shouldn't have been telling? Had he blurted out his fear of McCreevy and the stranglehold he had on Shay? What did Miss Jane Blytheford think of her Dublin boyo now?

CHAPTER XV

At the end of September, there was a flicker of light in the darkness around Shay Rynne. Two flickers, actually. The first light moment came when Shay noticed DS McCreevy with a puss on him, and it wasn't Shay who had put him in foul humour this time. A couple of guards arrived at Store Street near the end of the day shift. They had come from Counties Longford and Leitrim, searching for a suspect in a series of car thefts in their part of the country. They introduced themselves to a few of the fellas in the station, and then the Longford man called out. "Larracy! How are you keeping?"

"Grand, Mulvey, grand," McCreevy replied, and he took a great interest in the papers he was holding. He gave a distracted wave and disappeared into one of the interview rooms. A man with important business, not to be interrupted.

The two visiting guards exchanged a glance, and the one from Longford rolled his eyes. Then he asked the others, "Where do you drink?"

"Reade's" came the answer. "See you there in half an hour or so?"

Shay joined the group heading over to the pub and was soon seated with a pint in his hand, listening to tales of what passed for crime in the counties of Leitrim and Longford. Not a patch on the crime the Dublin lads had to deal with, but he made the appropriate comments at the appropriate times. What he really wanted to hear was how the Longford man, Mulvey, knew DS McCreevy, and why McCreevy had turned away. When the others at the table were deep in conversation, Shay said to Mulvey, "I guess you know McCreevy, right? He didn't linger for a long chat, I noticed."

"I hardly know the man," Mulvey said. "I started at the station not long before he left."

"Left Longford, you mean? I didn't know he was a guard there before Dublin," Shay prodded.

"He was."

"So you didn't know him well. But you might have expected a warm welcome, if you both worked in the same station."

"Larracy McCreevy doesn't have the reputation of a man of warm welcomes!"

Shay pointed at Mulvey's glass. "Get you another?"

"I wouldn't turn it down."

So Shay got up and ordered them both another pint. When he returned to the table, he returned to the subject of the crabby detective sergeant. "I don't find him that warm a man, myself. I wonder why he's like that, do you know?"

Mulvey shrugged. "As I say, I didn't know him well. But Garda Glennon had a run-in with him. She's no fan, I can tell you."

"Glennon?"

"Nora Glennon. A ban garda in our station. She's on the car theft investigation, too, but she's not in Dublin today. Coming sometime in the next couple of weeks, as far as I know."

A run-in with McCreevy. What had he done? How could he meet Ban Garda Glennon? "Will she be coming to Store Street?"

"I think so. Our suspect had been sighted here in Dublin, on the docks."

It was time to turn to more pleasant topics, like crime. So Shay got himself into the general conversation, but his mind was on Ban Garda Nora Glennon, and how to make sure he met her when she came to Dublin. When he was back at Store Street, he put a word in the ears of Vince Foley and Bobby Hannaway that he would like to meet Nora Glennon whenever she turned up in Store Street. So, if they had a sighting, let Shay know.

ↄ৲

The second and much brighter light that shone for Shay was the news that Risteard Dermody would be going on trial for the murder of Rosie McGinn. The trial would begin in the Central Criminal Court on the twenty-fifth of October.

Deena Breathnach's information about Ardan McClinchey turned out to be correct; the property developer had agreed to plead guilty to charges relating to bribery and corruption. And in return for a lighter sentence, he turned on his co-conspirator Risteard Dermody. Dermody had not come through with the promised permission for McClinchey's planned industrial estate, and McClinchey found himself in dire financial straits as a result. Whether Dermody had turned his back on his pal after the money changed hands, or he tried and failed to secure the permit — whatever the case, McClinchey was now Dermody's worst nightmare.

Shay thought Jane might like to attend the trial or parts of it, given the fact that she had met Deena and had even wanted to impersonate her on the canal to find the man who had been trying to intimidate her. It took Shay by surprise that Jane showed little interest in attending. She said she had a lot of work to do, a couple of journal articles to write, so she wouldn't sit in. She wished him good luck with it, and they left it at that. But he couldn't help but wonder: Was it Deena's case Jane had lost interest in? Or was it the drunken bowsie who'd stumbled into her place barely able to talk sense to her?

Along with the other guards who had worked the case, Shay attended several meetings with the prosecution solicitor, Cormac O'Flaherty.

O'Flaherty was short and slight with a sharp-featured face and grey eyes that radiated a shrewd intelligence. He immediately inspired in Shay a feeling of confidence. He gave a summary of the evidence that would be presented at trial. McClinchey was going to testify about the party in the suites of Goss's Hotel, about his deal with Dermody and the cash he handed over in return for the promised favour. He was also going to tell the court about his and Dermody's anxiety when they suspected that Deena Breathnach had been hiding under a bed and had overheard the exchange. And the businessman was going to go further than that: he said he saw Dermody stalking down the corridor towards the back stairs and, a few minutes later, Dermody reappeared looking as if he'd come face to face with the devil, and said, "Don't you ever breathe a fucking word about our talk in there!" And then he bolted for the front stairs "as if the hounds of hell were after him." The solicitor asked McClinchey if he had seen Dermody attack Miss McGinn and he said no.

But there were the fingermarks on her neck, and there was Deena's evidence about Dermody's weak or injured fingers, which matched the pattern of the marks. And the state pathologist's report showed that the fracture of her skull was caused by her falling onto the sharp corner of the concrete base at the side of the staircase. She had fallen on it; she had not merely "slid" down. The momentum of her descent was such that she had practically "flown" down the stairs.

O'Flaherty said that all of this was good, though he was wishing for something more direct. He acknowledged, of course, that this was unlikely to surface: the killer would not have acted if there had been a witness standing by.

⁊

A few days later, Shay was writing up his notes about another case, not a murder but a purse-snatching outside the Connolly train station, when Garda Bobby Hannaway came in with another guard beside him. He introduced her to Shay as Ban Garda Nora Glennon from Longford, and Shay stood to greet her. She was a tall woman, taller than Shay, with blond hair pulled back from a wide, friendly face.

Now, how was he going to broach the subject of McCreevy? He settled for asking if he might have a word with her. She smiled at him, and he had the impression that she knew what he wanted to talk about. The other guards from Longford had likely tipped her off. They arranged to meet at four o'clock at the archway into Stephen's Green, the lovely park in Dublin's city centre.

Nora was under the arch when Shay arrived, and they decided to start off with coffee from Bewley's in Grafton Street. They ordered their coffee to go and talked about their work and their families as they walked back to the park. The flowers in the beds were still in bloom, and the leaves were beginning to turn to yellow. Before Shay could think of a way to bring it up, Nora turned to him and said, "I hear you work with Larracy McCreevy."

Shay laughed and said, "When I can't avoid it, yeah. You know him yourself, I understand."

"I do."

"Why is he such a pain in the arse?"

Nora looked around and said, "Let's have a seat on the bench over there, by the pond."

They sat down and watched as a family of ducks glided by on the water, and Shay said, "Do you know what happened here during the Rising of 1916? The rebels were entrenched here and the Brits were firing on them from outside. But there was a ceasefire when it came time for the park keeper to feed the ducks. The firing stopped so the birds could be fed."

She turned to him, wide-eyed. "You're having me on."

"I'm not. It really happened."

"Must be a lesson in there somewhere, but I don't think we've learned it. So. You were asking about McCreevy. I take it you've had some trouble with him."

"I have. And you as well?"

"Right."

"What happened to put you on the wrong side of him?"

"He thought I was out to get him."

Shay smiled at her. "And were you? Out to get him?"

"Not at all. I wouldn't bother me arse about the likes of him."

"Why did he —"

"I knew something about him that he didn't want revealed."

Ah, maybe there was something in this for Shay if, as he feared, McCreevy had somehow learned about the gun heist and was reserving that knowledge for use against Shay in the future. If McCreevy had done something wrong himself, and Shay could hint that he knew about it, they might arrive at a situation of . . . What did the Yanks call it? About the nuclear threat from both sides. Mutually assured destruction, that was it. He and McCreevy . . . He returned his attention to Nora Glennon.

"It was a case of theft from an accountancy office in Longford town, big whack of money stolen, and the thief set up a scene to make it look like a burglary. McCreevy was a newly minted detective, and he headed the inquiry. The man suspected of the theft was the son of a very prominent farmer and landowner, fella by the name of Keenan, a pal of McCreevy's father. Of course, nearly everyone in town claimed a close friendship with the local squire, Keenan. It looked as if Keenan the younger would be arrested any day. And then nothing happened; the suspicions seemed to go up in smoke." She moved her fingers to illustrate something vanishing into thin air.

Did McCreevy have something to do with the suspicions going away? Shay wondered. Was he offered an incentive by the big man in town? More, perhaps, than an incentive?

"Suspicion had been redirected to a fairly new employee of the firm, a blow-in from County Armagh."

"Why was this new fella suspected?" Shay asked.

"There was evidence against him. Something of his was found in the fake burglary scene, part of a shoeprint or something. I can't remember the details now."

Another suspect to take the focus off the rich farmer's son. Real evidence, or something planted, maybe? Shay scolded himself for getting ahead of things. All he said was, "That must have come as good news for McCreevy!"

Nora Glennon looked confused. "Good news for McCreevy? Why?"

Shay didn't know the story, so he just said, "Sorry, go on."

"McCreevy had missed it. He had tunnel vision, focused entirely on Keenan. He was so convinced of Keenan's guilt that he missed the importance of evidence pointing to the other suspect, the man who had really stolen the money."

McCreevy was going after the squire's son? The son of a friend of McCreevy's own father? This was not what Shay had expected to hear. "So," he said, "it was not a case of corruption?"

"Corruption? On the part of . . . ?"

"McCreevy."

"No! Incompetence, not corruption. And he was shunned for it in the Garda station, let me tell you. The other guards would pass him in the halls and give him a look of disgust. Or, maybe worse, mockery. Bullying from a couple of the other lads. He was never put in charge of a big case again."

Not what Shay had expected to hear, for sure. He thought back to what Nora had told him earlier. "You said you had trouble with him yourself."

"That was because of what I saw one night outside the station, soon after all this had happened. McCreevy was sitting in his car . . ."

"Yes?"

"He was crying. Slashing his hand across his eyes to wipe away the tears. And I was passing by and saw him. And he saw me. And the face on him! He looked as if I'd caught him robbing Father Murphy's collection plate!"

The last thing Shay had expected, or wanted, was to feel sympathy for Larracy McCreevy. He tried to push the feeling away, but it wouldn't go. Not entirely.

"I never told anyone until now, Shay. Never said a word. Why would I? But he obviously thought I had blabbed it around, that he'd been crying. As if I would have gossiped about something so personal. Or maybe he was just worried that I might. So, whenever he had the chance, he assigned me to cases that required me to work a different shift from him. And the few times I protested or questioned him about one of the cases — humble uniformed ban garda that I was and still am — he'd bluster at me and tell me to do what I was told. Not long after that, he got a transfer to Dublin. I think his da did some finagling; the father was friendly with the guards there and maybe here as well."

"Must have been rough on his oul fella, having to push for a transfer, and everybody knowing why. Having his son leave home."

"The father was ashamed of him, couldn't wait to see the back of him. At least, that's what I heard. Anyway, one day shortly after all this unfolded, McCreevy was gone. There was no farewell piss-up down the pub for him. He was just gone."

ᖱ

Shay drove out to meet Deena Breathnach at the airport when she flew home from New York City for the Dermody trial. He saw her in the midst of the other new arrivals, and she smiled and waved. She looked like a sophisticated traveller in her dark-grey suit and high-heeled shoes. Her hair was long and straight with a fringe down to her eyes. When she reached him, she gave him a hug, and he took her travelling case. He wondered how she'd been able to lift it. She had been in New York for over a month and a half, and she told him she was loving her time there. Loving it so much that she was making plans to stay. Brennan's father had connections who had helped with the formalities of living and working there; she didn't know the details but everything had gone smoothly so far. She was working in a coffee shop in Manhattan but was looking for a job in one of the big department stores. Saks Fifth Avenue, she said, or Macy's.

Deena was much more relaxed than she had been when she left Ireland; she had arranged to stay with a cousin in one of the Dublin suburbs, and did not seem all that concerned about whoever had been following her before she left Ireland. Shay asked to go over the evidence she would be giving about the night at Goss's Hotel, and she recounted it to him again in the car. It was all consistent with what she had told him first time around. But there was one thing she mentioned now that he didn't recall hearing before. Or had he heard it? There was a familiar ring to it.

"What was that you said about your jacket, lending it to Rosie?"

"She wanted to get away, after we'd been hiding under the bed and hearing that fella giving the bribe to the council man, but she looked out the window and it was snowing. It was going to be a cold walk home for her, so I took my jacket off and gave it to her. And we laughed because of her dress being dark green and the jacket being red with the shiny gold threads on it, and we said something about her looking like a Christmas tree. And Rosie put it on and said, 'Oh, does it clash frightfully? Should I have worn my best gold tonight?' It was her necklace she was pointing to. It was silver. Silver discs, like."

"Silver discs."

"Yeah, hanging from the chain."

What had Shay heard about silver? There was something. He turned to look at her.

"What's the matter, Shay?"

"Nothing, nothing, Deena. It's just that somebody —"

Then he had it. Mackey Walsh had told him about silver coins being thrown . . . right, the girl who was mad for him, always trying to seduce him. Walsh had gone out to his van to get away from her, and he saw her come out of the back door with silver coins in her hand. But could it have been a silver necklace?

He left Deena at her cousin's place and told her to ring him if she had any trouble. And then he set out to find the lead singer of Liberties Taken. He knew that the band had been playing at the TV Club again, so Mackey Walsh was in town. Shay knew some people in the Liberties — the Liberties neighbourhood — and did some asking around. Eventually, he located the singer in Jack Cusack's pub in the Coombe. He was sitting up at the bar with a couple of fellas Shay didn't know; they weren't members of the band.

He spotted Shay and broke out in song. "Woke up this mornin', and never knew this day would be my last." He hesitated for a minute, took a sip of his pint, and continued, "Till the sheriff came and took me in for something I thought buried in my past. How's that for an on-the-spot composition, lads?"

"Sure, you can do better than that, Mackey!" one of them said.

They laughed and so did Shay. "Wondered if I could ask you something, Mackey. Won't keep you long."

He turned to his companions. "Don't worry, boys, your secret's safe with me." Then, to Shay, "Is it about Rosie McGinn?" Shay nodded, and Mackey explained to the others, "I'll tell him anything I can, if it means nailing the fuckhead who killed that young lady."

The others seemed to understand and did not look as if they'd be walking out on Mackey for talking to a peeler.

He got up and followed Shay to a quiet corner of the room. "You remember telling me about that lassie who has a grá for yeh?" Love for him.

"Oh, yeah. She's still at it."

"What's her name? You may have told me."

"Merrilee Cranitch."

"You saw her come out the back of the hotel and she had something in her hand."

"Right. She had something and she stashed it in her handbag. What was it? I'm trying to remember."

"Coins, was it?"

"Yeah, that was it. Looked like a few silver coins, like maybe she'd robbed them off somebody. Otherwise, I remember thinking, Why did she throw them away? I'd seen her come outside and then look at what she had in her hand. Then she jumped as if she'd been jabbed with a cattle prod. That's when I heard the peelers, their siren wailing. She threw the coins down. But then she checked over her shoulder, looked all around her, and bent down, grabbed the coins, and dropped them into her bag. She took off at a good clip away from the hotel."

She had something that, on her first reaction, she thought she couldn't keep. Shay asked Mackey, "Could it have been a necklace with silver discs on it?"

"I suppose it could have. All I remember seeing was round things and they were silver."

"Thanks, Mackey."

"So what's the story, Shay? Why the interest in her? This necklace . . . Oh, fuck!"

"Yeah, it may have been Rosie's."

"And Merrilee took it off her? When would she have snatched it? You don't mean —"

"Don't repeat any of this, Mackey."

"I won't."

"Rosie still had the necklace on when she left the party to go home."

"So Merrilee robbed it off Rosie lying there dead!"

"Could be. Now, I have to track down this young admirer of yours. Where would I find her?"

"You won't have to think very hard about it, Shay. Me and the band are playing tonight at the TV Club."

"And she'll be there."

"As sure as night follows day, Merrilee follows Mackey."

"What does she look like?"

"She looks like a little brown-haired girl made up to look like a tart, and she'll have her attention one hundred percent focused on the band."

But trying to interview a witness in a murder inquiry in the midst of a show on Harcourt Street with a crowd of people around, and his witness focused one hundred percent on the band, would be far from ideal. "Would you happen to have her home address?" How likely was that?

"Oh, I have it."

"Really!"

"Don't be looking at me like that, Seamus. I've never been there, but that's not because I haven't been invited. She writes me love letters with her address and a drawing of the street prominently displayed. It's a ground-level flat in Dominick Street. The number escapes me right now, but you can ask someone when you get there. Don't tell her I sent you."

❧

What were the chances that Merrilee Cranitch still had the silver necklace she took off Rosie McGinn's body two and a half years ago? Would she wear it around the streets of Dublin? Or would she have sold it? Pawned it? And, for the purposes of convicting Risteard Dermody, would there be a fingerprint on it? Shay knew that prints on some surfaces could last for years. Depending on how the item had been handled, would he have a major piece of evidence that would leave Detective Sergeant Colm Griffith gobsmacked over Shay's brilliant work on the case? And leave DS McCreevy fuming with resentment once again, once the news got round?

What if McCreevy decided to act on his resentment, and go over Colm's head and tell Detective Inspector Hennessy about Shay taking the guns? Shay now knew something about McCreevy: that he had left the Longford Garda Station under a cloud, leaving behind a reputation for incompetence. How would he like that news to get out? But, Shay told himself, everybody makes mistakes, misses things. McCreevy had done it again with the Goss's Hotel case, only to be shown up by young Garda Rynne. McCreevy was a prick. But the image of him sitting in his car, weeping, gave rise to a feeling of pity in Shay. Was that scene something he could throw up in McCreevy's face to shame him, make him back off? Shay couldn't see himself doing that, even to McCreevy.

He crossed the river to the north side and parked the car at Store Street, went inside and — with a sense of optimism that might not be justified — picked up a couple of evidence bags for his visit with Merrilee Cranitch. Should he tell DS Griffith what he was doing? Probably. But what if nothing came of it? Better to find out whether the necklace still existed, and then whether it might constitute good evidence for the trial. He made his way on foot to the complex of boxy flats in Dominick Street Lower.

Since he was in his own clothes, he assured himself that he wouldn't stand out as a peeler in this rough and peeler-unfriendly street. Or did the new plain clothes send a message to others, as they still did to Shay when he looked in the mirror, *Newly promoted Garda*? But even without uniform or baton, he met with resistance when he made his first inquiries. If you don't know who lives where, what the fuck are you doing here; that seemed to be the feeling. Nothing new there; he was well used to it. But finally, an old dear pushing a grandchild in a rickety pram pointed to one of the buildings and said, "Yer one lives in there." She pointed to one of the ground-level flats. "But she's not home."

"Have you any idea when she might be back?"

She shook her head and kept walking. But Shay knew that Mackey Walsh and Liberties Taken would be playing at the club in Harcourt Street. Surely Merrilee, Mackey's most enthusiastic fan, would come home and get herself all dolled up for her evening out. He would wait a couple of hours and try again.

When he returned, sure enough there was a light on in the flat. He rapped gently on the window. Rapped again, and a pale young face peeked out from behind the curtain. He gave her what he hoped was a reassuring smile and pointed to the door. It took a few minutes, but she finally came to the door and let him into the building.

She was short and slight, with long brown hair and big brown eyes. The scent of shampoo came off her. She was wearing a pair of bell-bottom blue jeans and a frilly pink blouse. Getting ready for the night out. Now, how was he going to handle this? Accusing her of robbing the dead would get him nowhere. Would she respond to an appeal for help?

"Hello, Merrilee. I'm Garda Seamus Rynne." As you might expect, that brought on a look of fear as she stared up at him. "Don't worry now," he said and smiled at her. "I'm not here to arrest you for anything at all. But I'm thinking you might be able to help me with an inquiry."

"Ah, no, I couldn't."

"You'd be surprised, Merrilee, how the smallest bit of information can sometimes help. Can sometimes get a killer off the street."

"A killer? Round here?" He saw a mix of fear and something that might have been fascination.

"Could I come in for a few minutes? I won't take up much of your time. Are you heading out for the evening?"

"I'll be seeing Liberties Taken!"

"Oh, they're a great band. If I didn't have to work tonight, I'd be there to see them myself. You're the lucky one. Have you ever seen them before?" That got him an invitation to her flat.

She led him down the corridor and opened her door. She ushered him inside, saying, "I see them all the time! I'm a friend of Mackey Walsh!" She managed to caress his very name.

The furniture was drab, but the walls were a blaze of colour, with rock band posters and album covers, featuring the Beatles, the Rolling Stones, Bob Dylan, Donovan Leitch, Janis Joplin, and, of course, Liberties Taken.

"You're a big music fan, I see."

"I know all the new music. Look here, here's me and Mackey." She picked up a framed picture showing a beaming Merrilee and a glassy-eyed Mackey Walsh with his arm around her. You could see a crush of people around them in a smoky bar. Merrilee's hair was much shorter than it was now, and Mackey's was longer; the picture had been snapped some time ago.

Shay used Mackey as a lead-in to where he wanted to go. "He's a fine fella, Mackey, from everything I've heard. And I actually met him. I tell you I was excited about talking to him, even though it was about something terrible that happened."

"Oh, yeah? You talked to Mackey? He wouldn't do nothing bad!"

"No, of course not. It wasn't about him doing anything. It's about this crime I'm investigating. D'you mind if I sit down?"

"Have a seat, sure."

So they sat facing one another, and he got into the subject in a way he hoped would attract her interest and her sympathy. "Mackey is fierce upset about a man who committed a murder and who might get acquitted and be allowed to go on living in our midst." He was laying it on thick with her, but he thought a lack of subtlety wouldn't be fatal with this witness.

"Mackey hates injustice. Sure, doesn't he sing about it? D'yeh know his song 'Thomas Street Blues'? That's about the poor and the injustice that's against them."

"Right. Great song it is. Well, the case I'm working on is about the murder of a girl who grew up poor and, through hard work and determination, got herself a good job in one of the hotels here."

Recognition set in then, and she took on a wary look. She didn't say a word.

"I'm talking about Rosie McGinn, of course, and her death at the hands of a very rich and powerful man. There's injustice for you!" She nodded but remained silent. "I myself grew up in a Corpo flat, in a street something like Dominick Street here. And I know the people in the flats; well, nothing is ever given to them, you know? Sometimes you have to take what you can get, because nobody's going to do you any favours. I know I took some things when I was a kid, stole a few things. And, oh, a couple of times, the peelers caught me at it, but they didn't put me under arrest or anything. They knew what it was like for a lad growing up in the poor parts of this city."

Merrilee's eyes never left his face as he gave her the spiel. She knew, or at least suspected, what he was getting at.

"Anyway, Merrilee, I can tell you something in confidence here." The guards had never made public the fact that there were finger-marks on Rosie's neck; all they had put out to the news reporters was that she was found dead at the bottom of the back stairs of the hotel, and that they considered the death suspicious. And that they now had Risteard Dermody charged with murder. "This fact has never been made public, Merrilee." She now looked keen to hear the secret. "We think somebody — somebody important — tried to *strangle* her before he pushed her down the stairs."

Merrilee's eyes were wide and unblinking.

"Now I have to emphasize this, Merrilee: you are not going to be in any trouble. At all. You in fact could be one of the most important witnesses we have."

"Me? A witness?"

"In the trial. You could help make the difference between seeing this man get away with murder, and seeing him convicted and sent away to prison." Fear was giving way to fascination. So he fed into that. "I have to tell you, your name may well be in the papers. As someone who helped put this killer away!" Merrilee Cranitch, the toast of the town. "As I've said, Merrilee, you'll not be in any trouble yourself. We know about the silver necklace, and —"

Her hand flew up to cover her mouth. "Who seen —"

"And that could be one of the most valuable pieces of evidence in the trial." He was almost afraid to ask the next question; what were the chances? "Do you still have the necklace, Merrilee?"

He could almost see the debate she was waging within herself. And that suggested to him that she still had the thing. She gathered her thoughts, and then came out with it. "I didn't know she was dead! I thought she was only passed out from the drink. And" — here she gave him back what he had fed her — "like you said, us that are poor, we never get nothing. I knew she worked at Goss's and she'd have money and could just go out and buy it again. But I wouldna robbed it off her if I'd a known she was dead! And then I found out she was dead, and I knew I couldn't take it to the pawn shop because the peelers might . . . Somebody might recognize that it was hers. And then I thought . . . it's so awful being poor and living in a place like this!" Go ahead, Merrilee, milk it for all it's worth. "I never wore it. I hid it away. I thought maybe someday I'd sell it, when, you know, when people would have forgot that it might have belonged to the one that was killed."

Shay left Merrilee Cranitch with assurances that she would face no charges and that she would be supported in her appearance in court. Perhaps left her with a fantasy about fame as a courtroom heroine, someone Mackey Walsh would be reading about. And he walked away with a necklace of silver discs on a chain in an evidence bag. A necklace apparently untouched since the night of Rosie's death.

CHAPTER XVI

T he jury trial of Risteard Dermody for the murder of Rosaleen McGinn got underway in the Central Criminal Court on October 25, 1971. Shay and the other guards were called to testify about their investigation. When it was Shay's turn, defence counsel tried to make it sound as if Shay was personally involved in the case because of his friendship with Miss McGinn and therefore went into the investigation with blinders on, refusing to see her death as an unfortunate accident. The defence team took the position that there was no proven connection between the marks on Rosie's neck and her death on the staircase. She could have been in a confrontation with someone, or even a friendly game of sorts with a boyfriend. As for the state pathologist's report on the missing left-hand fingermarks, that proved nothing. Was the prosecution suggesting a standard that is always met in cases of strangulation?

That's when Shay thanked the Man Above that the forensic examination of the necklace had come up aces. There were fingerprints on the silver discs: those of Rosie herself, those of a third party who would be testifying before His Lordship, and two prints — partial but identifiable — belonging to Risteard Dermody. Witnesses from the night at Goss's Hotel gave evidence that they did not see anyone else put their hands anywhere near Rosie's neck that night, most importantly Dermody himself. Nobody had seen him touching her; the closest contact between them was when Rosie handed him a drink. If he touched her necklace, he did it out of sight of all the others at the party that night.

Deena came forward in her dark-grey suit with a white blouse, and her makeup was subdued. She looked like a woman solicitor entirely at home in a courtroom. Well, Shay reminded himself, much of her work life had required her to play a role. She got into the witness box and told the judge and jury about Dermody trying to touch her, fumbling at her clothing with his damaged fingers, and about him storming off.

Then she and Rosie were in that room, just the two of them, while everyone else was in the room next door. She and Rosie were enjoying a couple of drinks together and having some laughs until Deena heard Dermody's voice and that of McClinchey when the two men came towards the room. Laughing together, the two young women dived beneath one of the beds to hide from the men. That's when Deena heard the conversation between Dermody and McClinchey, and she recounted that conversation — the exchange of money for favours relating to something to be built in Ballyer (Ballyfermot). Then, she said, she banged into something under the bed, it made a noise, and she heard Dermody say in a very quiet voice, "What was that?" She and Rosie were frightened; they had heard something they were not supposed to hear, and one of the men knew they'd heard it. Shortly after that, Rosie decided to leave. It was cold and snowy, and Deena lent her the sparkly red-and-gold jacket she'd been wearing. Rosie and Deena were around the same size with similar colour hair. Wearing the jacket, Rosie could easily have been mistaken for Deena.

The cross-examination was a rough one. "What do you do for a living, Miss Breathnach?"

"I work in a coffee shop."

"Oh, is that right? Where is the coffee shop?"

"New York."

"I see. And before that job, what did you do?"

She glared at him.

"Well?"

"You know."

"Tell us."

"I worked along the canal there."

"You are a prostitute, is that right?"

"I was."

The barrister turned his wigged head to the jury and gave them a look. Shay was sure that everybody read the same thing he did in the lawyer's face: *How can we believe the likes of her?* But she stuck to her story, and when the prosecuting counsel conducted his redirect, Deena made the point that she was not in this courtroom to enjoy herself, that she had been afraid to get up and tell the truth, that somebody had been following and watching her, and that's what prompted her move to New York, where she had begun a new life. (She had told Shay she had no interest in seeing the intimidator charged in court, and her having to return to testify about that.)

Then it was Merrilee Cranitch in the witness box. She was dressed for the occasion in a dark-blue dress and matching jacket, her hair in a knot atop her head. Her demeanour alternated between nervousness and an almost manic excitement. She came off as properly remorseful about taking the necklace off Rosie's neck and repeated her assertion that she had had no idea Rosie was dead. She had thought Rosie was just passed out drunk. And she put on the poor mouth again, quite convincingly: "A girl from Dominick Street would never be able to get silver jewellery like that. But I should never a done it. I'm sorry."

But, yes, it had come directly from Rosie, lying at the bottom of the stairs at Goss's. So the court had evidence that the necklace had been on Rosie during the party, was still on her when she was lying on the back staircase, and it went directly into the possession of Merrilee Cranitch. It had not come into the possession of Risteard Dermody at any other time. So there was no innocent way to explain away his prints on it.

And, finally, the big moment came amid a rustle of excitement in the gallery: Ardan McClinchey got up and told the judge and jury about the bribe he had given Dermody in the hotel room, the assurance the politician had given him for his planned industrial estate, the panic when the two men realized there was somebody under the bed listening. And then, he testified, "Risteard saw the girl walking towards the back stairs, and he went after her. He thought it was the . . . Miss Breathnach. I went back to that room where nobody else was, and I threw a glass of whiskey down my throat. The nerves were going on me. And then Risteard came back, and he looked as if he'd seen the devil himself. He was shaking, and he said, 'We have to get out of here.' And I followed him to the front stairs and down and out of the hotel, and I said to him, 'What happened?' And all he said, and I beg the court's forgiveness, all he said was, 'Fuck!' and then 'Not a word about this night. Ever!' And he was gone."

The defence counsel, of course, brought up the lenient sentence McClinchey had been given for his role in the bribery. "You bought that sentence just as you tried to buy permission for your industrial estate, didn't you, Mr. McClinchey? You would have said anything to get a more lenient sentence, wouldn't you?"

McClinchey replied, "I was and am guilty of the corruption charge. I am embarrassed and ashamed of what I did, though I'm not by any means the first and won't be the last. Sometimes that's what you have to do in order to get business done with this . . . with the way things work in this country. And many other countries. Unfortunately. I told the truth to the court when my own crime was dealt with, and I am telling the truth here today. A young woman's life is of much greater importance than any business plan, and I would not have got up here and lied in front of Your Lordship, the jury, the people of this city, and, most especially, the family of Rosaleen McGinn."

Everyone was in suspense about whether Dermody would give evidence in his own defence. He did not. Must have been convinced that whatever he might be asked, and however he might respond, would cause him more harm than remaining silent and hoping the case could not be proved against him.

All that remained to be done on the morning of October twenty-eighth was for the judge to give his instructions to the jury. Once he finished and sent the jurors off to deliberate, Shay and DS McCreevy and the other guards met with O'Flaherty, the prosecution solicitor.

"Our witnesses did well," O'Flaherty said. "We've no eyewitness evidence, of course, of Dermody putting his hands around her throat or throwing her down the stairs. Nobody saw that. But then again, that's often the way. The most direct evidence we have is his finger-marks on her neck and his prints on the jewellery. As you heard the judge explain, in order to find him guilty of murder, the jury must be satisfied that Dermody committed the act that resulted in her death, and that he intended to cause her death or cause her serious injury. There is a presumption in law that the accused intended the conse-quences of his act. The accused may rebut that presumption, if he can convince the jury that he did not intend what happened — for example, that it was an accident. Dermody would have had to testify to that effect, and he did not. The jury will be wondering what he has to hide, which would account for him not getting up there and giving evidence to avoid a life sentence for murder. To at least get it down to manslaughter.

"I'm not sure how this would go if we had a judge alone, but I think all the circumstantial evidence in addition to the fingerprints may just do it for the jury. We'll have to wait and see."

Shay had never been good at "wait and see." He stepped out to a chipper and brought his lunch back to the station. And waited. He wrote up reports on other cases. And waited. Went out for coffee and came back. And waited. By mid-afternoon, he found himself pacing the floor like a father-to-be waiting for his wife to give birth.

Finally, the call came in to Store Street nearly five hours after the jury went out. The jurors had returned with their verdict. Not guilty of murder. But guilty of manslaughter. It was not what Shay and the other guards wanted, but it was the next best thing. It was a convic-tion, and Dermody would be going to prison.

There was plenty of glory to go around, and much of it glowed golden on the head of Garda Seamus Rynne for not letting his friend's death go unavenged, for digging up the evidence to put Risteard Dermody away. DS Griffith said, "You did brilliant work on your first murder inquiry, Seamus. You're a credit to Store Street, and I know this is only the beginning for you."

DS McCreevy put it this way: "Good on you, Rynne. Your contacts in the dark corners of Dublin society stood us in good stead, and will again in future." He smiled at Shay, but it wasn't the smile of a man congratulating another for a job well done; it was the smile of a man who knew that Garda Rynne's father had murdered a politician and would someday slip up, and provide the evidence needed to convict him. And what about those five handguns that had gone missing from the scene of a Garda investigation? Did McCreevy really know about that? Would he use it someday to destroy Shay's future as a guard?

In the midst of the celebration of Shay's success, he felt a spike of fear that those guns could be fired at him at any minute of any day. Would Shay have any warning if that was about to happen? Would he use what he knew about McCreevy to stop him in his tracks? Would it work if he tried? But never mind that now; this was Shay's time to savour his triumph over Risteard Dermody.

Sweeter for Shay was the rousing cheer that met him when he walked into the old Pearse Street bar, Moroney's, where his neighbourhood mates always gathered. The lads in the pub, those who had been slagging him without mercy since he joined the Garda, raised their glasses and belted out their Fenian Street theme song: "Glory o, glory o, to the bold Fenian men!" They wouldn't let him pay for a pint all through the night. It was one of their own who'd been killed, after all, and one of their own who had avenged her. The killer was in the nick and would be for years to come.

☙

If Shay was feeling more at home than ever in the Garda Síochána, he was soon reminded that home is not always a safe place to be. He was in Christy Burke's one night, as he so often was, and Finn had news

233

for him that was nothing short of stunning. Finn ushered him into the little room behind the bar, where they would not be overheard. And he said, "I've heard, Shay, and I think there's some truth in it, that the Brits have spies here. The Secret Intelligence Service."

"They have, sure. When have they not? We know MI6 have spies all over the world. We're a foreign country, so they have people here."

"Not just 'here,' Shay. If the rumour is true, they have somebody close to the Garda, maybe inside the Garda Síochána itself."

"*What?*" Shay nearly choked the word out. "How do you know that?"

Finn put his hands up as if to say, *Don't ask.*

Shay tried to digest what he had just heard. "We're obviously not talking about a fella sounding like Ringo Starr, or like a lord of the manor, in one of the Garda stations; wouldn't be hard to spot a bloke like that! So it's one of our own men passing secrets to . . ."

"One of your men, or someone close to your men, passing secrets to his British handler, or whatever they'd call him. And I don't imagine the traitor is driving out to Dún Laoghaire every day and putting a sack of secret Garda documents on the ferry to Holyhead. So the British handler is here amongst us, near at hand."

"Maybe they've got a tape recorder spinning in a dark corner of Reade's pub where the Store Street guards do their drinking!"

"Maybe so, Shay. Have a gander around next time you're in there. But anyway, we can assume that, yes, the Brit who's running him and collecting the information is here in Ireland."

"Christ!"

"From what I've heard, the Brits have information about certain things the guards here have been up to, and the people they've been investigating, which they wouldn't otherwise know."

"Fuck. I think we can assume it's not purse-snatchings or drink driving cases they're interested in."

"No, that wouldn't be it at all."

"So, who's their target, Finn? Republican subversives or us peelers ourselves? Is our police service not up to the task, as far as the Brits are concerned?"

"Both, maybe, republicans and the guards. Sure, the Saxons know we're all alike, sitting around all day telling stories and plotting and rebelling. That's what they used to say about us in their newspapers back in the day. And not just back in the day. It's no stretch of the imagination to think that Her Majesty's Government thinks *our* government is not tough enough on those dastardly plotters and rebels here in the South."

Finn himself was one of those plotters and rebels, as Shay well knew.

"Now, it's better the divil you know than the divil you don't, so my advice to you, Shay, is not to change your behaviour in any way. If there are sudden changes in procedure, people being careful, people hushing up, that, of course, tips off the spy. And then the fella or fellas running him will take a different tack, and then nobody will ever know what they're up to, or who they've recruited."

"But I have no idea who it is, Finn. So he's not the divil I know at all." He caught Finn's gaze. "Do you know who it is?"

Finn shook his head. "I don't know. I don't think anybody does. But the chances of uncovering this *secret agent* are greater if he continues on thinking he's safe. The longer the same man stays at it, following the same patterns of behaviour, the better the chances of his identity being discovered. If he gets spooked and gives up, and the Brits replace him with somebody else, they'll be even more clever and careful, and then we'll have no clue what's going on."

There was no need to ask who "we" were. Finn's comrades in arms must have had a source of their own. Where? In England? Belfast? This was way beyond Shay's capabilities as a humble guard.

"Now, go out there and enjoy the craic and don't be worrying yourself over what you've just heard."

"Ha! I'll forget I ever heard it. I wish!"

"But you didn't hear it, did you, Garda Rynne? And you sure as hell didn't hear it from me."

"I didn't hear a thing, Mr. Burke."

಄

As the year 1971 drew to a close, the McLogan murder inquiry was left in limbo. There was not enough evidence to charge anyone for the killing, "anyone" meaning Thomas "Talkie" Rynne. Not enough evidence *yet*. Shay saw Jane Blytheford once in a while, not very often — she had taken on a couple of time-consuming research projects — but when they were together, she always tried to bolster his spirits about his father. One good thing happened, thanks to Finn Burke, God bless him. When he heard about Talkie being sacked by O'Daly, Finn found a job for him at Burke Transport, maintaining and cleaning the cars, vans, and lorries, and delivering them from place to place. There was, of course, one condition, which was perfectly understandable: Talkie was never to get behind the wheel of a vehicle when he had drink taken. Talkie was so grateful, Shay hoped and prayed that he wouldn't scupper his opportunities there by bending the rules, or the elbow.

As for other possible suspects in the murder, the lead about Roger Conaty and his little spat with McLogan led nowhere in the end. McLogan was still on his feet when Conaty left the party. Conaty drove home and ended up drinking at a neighbour's house for several hours after that. There were three other men there, and all attested to Conaty's presence. As for Jem O'Daly, there was not enough evidence to bring him to court. This left Shay desperate to find some incriminating detail that would elevate O'Daly to the top of the list.

CHAPTER XVII

Nineteen seventy-two got off to a fine start for Deena Breathnach. Shay heard about it in the middle of January, when he got a long-distance telephone call from Brennan Burke in New York.

"It's near midnight where you are, Shay, sorry if I woke you. But I thought you'd like to hear that Deena is getting on just fine here."

"Sure, you're grand, Brennan. I wasn't asleep. What's the news?"

"She kept applying to work at Macy's department store and it's paid off for her. She's just been hired as a sales girl. She rang me to say thanks to you and to me for helping her settle here in New York."

"Good on her. That's brilliant."

"And she's made a new friend here. My sister Bridey. I'd been telling Bridey about a girl named Deena coming over from Dublin, wanting a new life in New York. I didn't get into the reason why, didn't spread any gossip about Deena's former occupation. It was a bit comical the day I introduced them. Bridey and I arranged to meet at Macy's, and I'd make the introductions. But my sister is not the most punctual person, so I was there by myself and decided to find Deena in the store. I was in my civilian clothes and I went into the department where they sell women's coats and jackets. There was a young one working there, and I asked for Deena.

"'She's not here anymore,' the one says to me.

"'What?'

"'She's not in this department. Try lingerie.'

"The last thing I wanted, Shay, was to try lingerie." Shay had a good laugh, picturing the scene. "But she pointed me in the right direction, and I went on my way. And wouldn't you know it, there were several women, young and old, examining the merchandise, holding lacy things up against themselves and looking in the mirrors. A mother was there with her young daughter. The mother caught sight of me and gave me a look that would curdle cream. Me, the only man in sight; I stuck out like a square pr—

"Then I heard, 'Brennan! May I help you? Is it something for yourself, or for that special someone?' Deena, laughing her face off. 'I'd never have taken you for the blushing type, Brennan.' Anyway, it was gas, the whole scene. And then Bridey found us, and I introduced them. And they've become good pals. I've gone out for supper and a few drinks with them, and my little sister didn't bat an eye when Deena started talking about her former life. Bridey's been taking her around the city, Times Square, a Broadway play, the bigger-than-life New York life. And Deena's loving it. She's wishing she was earning a better pay packet, so she could have an even bigger bite of the Big Apple, but it's all good."

‸

The new year did not dawn quite so brightly for Shay. There were parties and great sessions of beer over the holiday, and long nights in the pubs. He couldn't bring the details into focus, but he knew the craic had been mighty. Jane had gone to London to spend the holiday with her family, and she gave him her parents' phone number for a Christmas call. They got together when she was back in Dublin, and he was happy to see her again, though he still wasn't sure what their future held. If anything. And he was haunted by other news he had heard about the holidays. A friend told him that Allie Cotter had come home for Christmas and had gone off with her family to the grandparents' home in County Wexford. This brought on a pang of loneliness and loss that, try as he might, he couldn't shake. No other woman, at least not yet, had been able to fill the void that Allie had left.

And then there was the evening with Talkie. It started on a high note. Dublin had come almost to a standstill because of a heavy snowfall. Shay knew that countries accustomed to snow had snowplows and another type of big machine that ground up the snow off the streets and blew it into banks along the sides. People had special tires for their cars in the winter. Not so in Dublin. Equipment here was very limited. So Shay and the other guards had to deal with accidents where cars had slid off the roads, and there were a few ambulance calls for people who had slipped and fallen in the street. But the city had a magical look about it whenever the sun came out from behind the clouds and glistened on the white blankets of snow. And Shay's little nephew Kevin was spellbound by it all.

The day after the storm was a day off for Shay. His sister Francie had to work, so Shay drove over to Fenian Street in the morning — nearly becoming a casualty himself as his car swerved and almost completed a U-turn on his way across the city. When he entered the family home, Kevin came barrelling towards him. "Take me out in the snow, Uncle Shay! We'll go sliding! We'll go skiing!" Of course, there were no sleds or skis anywhere on the premises; Shay had never laid eyes on sleds or skis anywhere at all. But he scooped the little fella up in his arms and said, "Let's make you a sled. And if we don't have any dogs to pull it, I'll be the dog."

"Yeah, you be the dog!"

Talkie emerged from the kitchen then, a cup of tea in his hand. "What's the craic?"

"Grandda! You be a doggie, too!"

"Doggie?" Talkie looked down at his grandson, uncomprehending.

"We're going to make a sled for him, Da, and since we don't have dogs or a horse to pull it, me and you will do the honours. You up for it?"

"Ehhh, I . . ." He looked weary, as if he'd had a long night. But then he seemed to rally, smiled down at Kevin, and said, "Sure, we'll have a sled for you."

They looked around the flat, and the best they could do was take the old wooden crate Kevin played with, pretending it was a train, and rechristen it as a sled. Talkie opened a drawer in the kitchen and brought out a length of clothesline and got to work attaching the ends of it to the crate. Deirdre got Kevin dressed in his warmest clothes, and he was jumping up and down with excitement.

Minutes later, they were out on the snow-covered pavement, Kevin seated in the box, shouting with glee as he urged his husky dogs on through the snow. Shay's feet were freezing in his shoes, but he wasn't going to let that slow him down. What did slow him down was the makeshift sleigh. Its square corners kept getting stuck in the snow. He knew a real sled would have something underneath, smooth and curved up to make for swift passage. But he and Talkie did their best to drag it dashing through the snow, and Kevin was squealing with delight. Talkie's eyes sparkled and he had the look of a much younger man; he grinned and waved to the neighbours who came out to watch the show. Soon, other children came running from the flats, jumping onto the sled with Kevin or pulling other kids by their arms or legs.

At one point Talkie reached down and grabbed a handful of snow, patted it into the shape of a ball, and threw it at one of the boys. From then on, everyone was engaged in a snowball fight. Somebody labelled it the Snow Battle of Fenian Street. It was great fun seeing the kids laughing and taunting each other and pitching snow at one another. But even better, from Shay's perspective, was the sight of his father, his cares momentarily forgotten, laughing as he was pelted with snow. It brought back memories of the good times with his da, Talkie's playful side, when he'd take the kids for walks along the canal or for a day of sand and surf at Sandymount Strand.

That evening, after supper in the flat with his parents, sister Francie and a beaming little nephew, Shay and Talkie stood on the balcony, each with a can of beer in hand, looking out at the flakes of snow falling in the darkness. "I was a good father to you, wasn't I, Shay?"

Shay turned to him. "Of course you were, Da. You were and you are. Just as you're a good grandda to Kevin. Why would you even have to ask?"

Shay could hardly bear to see the pain in his father's face. Tears welled up in Talkie's eyes, and he turned his face away. "I didn't do it, Shay. It's destroying me. You know yourself I didn't do it."

"I know, Da." And he was ninety percent certain that his father had not committed the murder. What reason would Talkie Rynne have to kill Darragh McLogan? But reason may have played a very small part in the killing.

"I can't work on the case, you know that. Not openly. But you can be sure I'll be doing everything I can, from the sidelines, to find out who killed Darragh and left you in the frame for it." He reached over and put his hand on his father's shoulder.

Talkie looked at him and nodded. His eyes started to fill up again. This time he didn't look away. "I know you will, Shay. If only there were more guards like yourself."

And it struck Shay yet again just how important it was to him to be a guard, to try to do the right thing. For his father and for all the other boys and men who had grown up in overcrowded tenements with no guarantee they would ever escape their poverty. No guarantee they would ever be able to shake off the prejudice that met them every time they tried to make a better life for themselves and their families. As for his own father's trouble, would Shay be able to find anything in the McLogan case that would point to another man's guilt?

✍

But Garda Rynne's work left him little time to brood. He had an unexpected call to duty on Monday, January 31, 1972. Crowds were massing in Merrion Square, in front of the Georgian terraced building that was home to the British embassy. The people were there to express their outrage at the Brits for the massacre in Derry city the day before. On Sunday, January thirtieth, British Army soldiers had opened fire on unarmed civilians marching to protest the new policy of internment, the new policy of throwing people into prison without a trial. The soldiers shot and killed thirteen people; more than a dozen others were shot and wounded. When Shay arrived in the square, he joined the lines of gardaí standing along the railings and on the steps of the embassy, facing the protesters. A strange calm settled over the crowd as they began singing Ireland's national anthem, "A Nation Once Again." Shay, like the other guards, stood to attention as the people sang.

The siege continued and grew. Thousands upon thousands of protesters came, carrying placards: "British Troops Out," "British Pigs Out," and, referring back to that earlier shower of brutal British troops, "Black and Tans Out."

Shay, of course, wondered how Jane Blytheford was reacting to what was happening at her embassy. He hadn't seen much of her in the last couple of weeks; she was busy with her research and lectures. Or was she just too busy for the likes of him? Well, now was hardly the time to run off to a call box. And he could not imagine how he would handle such a conversation.

The standoff continued into the next day and the next, as the crowd grew larger. People brought coffins to represent the thirteen dead, and Shay and his fellow gardaí let them through to place three of them up against the embassy door. Shay heard the reports of hundreds of people offering support to the IRA and Sinn Féin, people queuing up to offer their assistance.

Over and over again, Shay heard a clattering sound and the tinkling of broken glass, as the crowd threw bricks and stones and bottles towards the building. Eventually, the guards could no longer hold the crowds back without using force, so there were times when they were given the order to use their batons on the protesters. The closest Shay came to that use of force was to lift his baton and hold it over a few heads, and shout at the people to back off for their own good. He could not bring himself to club a person for demonstrating against the killings by the Brits when he was in complete agreement with the protest.

It wasn't only bricks and bottles; there were dozens of petrol bombs hurled over the guards' heads at the building. Whenever a bomb found its mark, the crowd cheered as if they were cheering on the Dubs in a football match at Croke Park. Shay was looking up as a flaming bomb sailed overhead, and a drop of burning petrol hit the side of his neck. He let out a yelp and staggered sideways. The pain seared into his skin as if his nerves had become burning matches. He was only one of many guards and demonstrators who suffered facial and other injuries, and many of them were much more serious than his own little burn.

And then a man broke through the crowd and lobbed an incendiary bomb, which hit its target and blew the door off the embassy building. Everyone was rocked by the deafening blast of the explosion. It sounded to Shay as if the entire sky had erupted in an immense, thunderous crack.

Events in the square came to a climax when three men got onto the balconies of adjoining buildings and made their way along, till they reached the embassy. One of them managed to hoist the Irish tricolour to half-mast on the embassy flagpole. The other two used axes to hack away at the upper windows, opening them up to the petrol bombs. Soon enough there were flames licking through the windows on the top floor. The crowd blocked the fire engines from getting in and they disabled the hydrants, though they allowed the ambulances in to treat the injured civilians and guards. The flames burst through the embassy roof. Finally, the roof collapsed and the crowd was showered with sparks. In response, the people cheered and whistled their delight.

The embassy was burning. And the Garda Síochána made the decision to let it burn. The decision to stand back and let the embassy burn was supported by the ministers for justice and defence. They knew that to fire bullets into the crowd could have resulted in dozens of people being killed. Bloody Sunday all over again, this time with Irish citizens being killed by Ireland's own police and soldiers. The consequences were simply unthinkable.

༄

After a few days of calm, Shay rang Jane's place and was stunned to find that her number had been disconnected. He set out immediately for her flat and found not Jane, but cleaners preparing the place for new tenants. He managed to track down one of the literature professors at Trinity, and the man confirmed it: Miss Blytheford had packed her bags and moved back to England. Shay was thrown into turmoil by the news: he felt sympathy for her, anger at her for leaving without letting him know, confusion over whether he would miss her, or whether what they had together was not substantial enough to last anyway. But he certainly wanted to speak with her, so when he got home he rang her parents' number in London. Her mother, sounding to Shay's ears like a person not accustomed to taking phone calls or anything of that sort herself, asked for his name. When he gave it, she asked for it again, then said she would tell Jane he had rung.

He heard from her an hour or so later. "Hello, Shay."

"Jane! You've left for good? Your job at Trinity —"

"Of course I've left for good! Do you think any English person would feel safe in Dublin, anywhere in Ireland, after what happened?"

He should have replied, *Of course, they wouldn't feel safe. I understand that.* But what came out of his mouth instead was "D'yeh think the people of Derry feel safe after so many being killed or wounded by British soldiers? And where can they go?"

"Our soldiers were defending themselves."

"Against a bunch of unarmed demonstrators."

"That's not the way people see it here."

Shay couldn't stop himself. "Maybe they should open their eyes and look again."

"Do you think burning our embassy is the proper response to what happened in Londonderry?"

"The proper response to what happened in *Derry* would be the arrest and conviction of the soldiers who killed all those innocent civilians. But I don't imagine that's going to happen in our lifetime."

There was a long silence, and he was not sure whether she was still on the line. But then she said, in an obvious effort at lightening things up, "So, Shay, besides all that bother, what *else* is new?"

What else could there be? What else could you discuss with someone who had fled Ireland after the firebombing of her country's embassy?

The other things that occupied Shay's thoughts these days were not things he wanted to bring up to Jane. The fact that his father's drunken manoeuvres the night of the murder had kept him at the top of the list of suspects? He didn't want to get into that again. And rumours of British spies and spy handlers taking secrets from the Irish police? He could imagine her reaction to that. *Brits under every bed, eh what? Under there with the communists, I suppose. Or lurking in the shadows in the Dublin streets, eavesdropping on all your lads come spilling out of the pubs.* She'd have a good laugh at him.

Or what about the crackdown that was sure to follow in the wake of the embassy attack? Would the Irish Republic become as repressive as the North in trying to snuff out anything that looked like subversion?

All he could say in reply to her was a lame "No, nothing else to report here." The call ended with "Do keep in touch, Shay. I shall miss you and who knows? Maybe we'll meet up again someday in happier times."

Happier times, right. "Goodbye to you, Jane," and he hung up the phone.

છૈ

The days rolled by with enough work to keep Garda Rynne occupied, but there were no developments in the McLogan case. Shay felt the threat of it ever hovering, over his father and over Shay himself. The saying that "no news is good news" offered little comfort. Because you never knew when the newsboys would be out in the street, shouting, "Read all about it! Fenian Street man rearrested for politician's murder!"

245

PART TWO

CHAPTER XVIII

On Thursday, August 24, 1972, Shay was on his first airplane flight ever, and it was transatlantic. He was on his way to an adventure that he hadn't anticipated, but grabbed at when it came his way. He and Des Creaghan had met one evening at Bewley's for a coffee and cake, and Des told Shay he hoped to make a radio documentary about Dublin's infamous gangster-turned-politician, Jem O'Daly. It was an open secret that O'Daly was planning to run for a seat in the next election.

"Will this be part of a series on criminal politicians, or only the one who's been caught at it, penalized, and who's admitted it in public?"

"Ah now, Seamus, I'm only one man. And there are only twenty-four hours in a day, seven days in a week. I can't possibly cover them all. O'Daly will keep me busy for now, especially if he ends up with a murder charge levelled at him."

"So, are you hoping he'll be charged? Convicted? I mean, if you can't have Charlie! Will a murder charge make a better story for you?"

"That would be an interesting angle, no question. But just as interesting would be O'Daly suspected of murder, and then being in the rare position of an innocent man falsely accused."

"Which would you prefer?"

"I'm a journalist, Shay. Neutral and fair to a fault. I just report the facts, wherever they may lead. If I find myself engrossed in the subject, I may even write a book about him."

"Can't wait to read it, Des."

"Oh, you won't have to wait. You can take part in the research."

"How's that now?"

"I'll be tracing O'Daly's footsteps in . . . New York!"

"New York?! You're having me on!"

"I'm not. You have reason to be interested in Jem O'Daly's activities wherever they may have taken place. And you have holidays banked up, if I'm not mistaken." He smiled and raised his glass to Shay.

"You're thinking . . ."

"Last week of August."

"I'm in."

"Knew you would be. So I've brought something for you. Over the years, like any other journo in Dublin, even the tabloid muckrakers like me, I've written the occasional piece on O'Daly and his exploits. You know that stuff already, but you may have missed this one. O'Daly was in New York for over a year. Year and a half, it was. Early 1969 to mid-1970." He reached into his pocket and pulled out a folded piece of newsprint. It was one of his comic bits from the *Dublin Daily Knows*, dated July 30, 1969. "Have a read of this."

PRATIE-FREE MENU STUMPS PADDIES IN THE BIG APPLE

BY MICKEY JOE PAT MULLOOLY

It was exotic fare that was served in La Mia Suocera restaurant in Little Italy, exotic at least to the guests of one Dublin bowsie-made-good, now living the high life in New York City. Jemser O'Daly, who is no stranger to faithful readers of the *Dublin Daily Knows*, is now strutting the streets of New York in his camel-hair over-coats and mohair suits (sorry, Charlie, but you can't expect to lead in matters of fashion and not be followed), and broadening his circle of acquaintances beyond the Paddies and Mick-Yanks who inhabit the warm and cozy neighbourhood of Hell's Kitchen on Manhattan's West Side.

Our Jem, who has sampled everything from the delights served during afternoon tea at the Shelbourne Hotel (eyebrows were surely raised when the likes of him slipped into a seat there) to the prison fare on offer in the Joy (where nobody was surprised), is now a con-noisseur of fine Italian wines and food. But not so his guests, who might as well have been culchies in from Ballybejabbers in remotest rural Ireland, so gobsmacked and socially gauche were they when they plunked their arses down at La Mia Suocera with Jemser. Jemser and his recently acquired, heavily old-world accented Italian associates.

Visiting our Jem were Mary St. Gobnait O'Blarnaighey and her husband, Fuller, and Mary St. Midabaria O'Leprecha. Our Irish friends had a couple of days in the sun before the big dinner date, and one of the two ladies was showing the effects of the unaccustomed sunlight on her alabaster skin. The Italian men were quite taken with le sue lentiggini, her freckles, which had been brought to prominence by the blast of sun available to those who live at the 40th parallel.

The first faux pas, the first bit of embarrassed befud-dlement, came when it was time to order the wine. They were looking at a wine list as long as the odds against Ian Paisley sitting down for a pint with the Pope. What shall we have? A noble red Barolo? A Barbaresco? Or perhaps a white La Scolca? Flustered by the choices, our visitors deferred to their wine-familiar hosts, and the bottles began arriving. Our Irishmen and ladies, according to a reliable source, felt they were in the midst of a religious experience, a mystical taste of heaven, so brilliant was the taste and effect of the magnificent wines that filled their gobs and gullets.

But what about the food aspect of the meal? A look at the menu, filled with strange and impenetrable items, gave rise to distress amongst the insular guests at the table. Mary St. Gobnait was heard to say in a tremulous voice, "Where's the praties? Where's the boiled cabbage?"

This brought a sneer and a rolling of eyes on the part of their lordly waiter. But the superior attitude was short-lived, and the poor oul Oirish visitors had no more social shame to fear. Their hosts were described to this scribe as tall, dark, muscled, and dangerous-looking, with origins on an island off the toe of Italy. One of these powerfully built and connected men said to the waiter, "Either a bowl of mashed potatoes, or your brains, are gonna be on this table." And after forty minutes or so, the waiter banged the bowl of white mush down on the table, turned on his heel, and stalked away.

"That's great gas, Desmond. Who are these Italians you've got in here?"

"Have you seen the film *The Godfather*?"

"Not yet. I'd like to see it."

"One of the greatest films ever made. All about the Sicilian mob. The Mafia. It's based on a book by that name, *The Godfather*, by a man by the name of Mario Puzo. I'd read the book not long before I wrote this. Loved it. Wish I could write something like that."

"Maybe you will."

"Yeah, right. So anyway, that's where the references and, em, the tone and language come from."

"So you're saying O'Daly was in league with members of the Mafia?"

Des raised his shoulders in a big shrug and said, "Ay, it was just dinner, okay? I'm not sayin' nothin' more than that."

That must have been the way the characters talked. Shay would have to see that film or read the book. "And you are going to expand on the research you did for this insightful piece of literature?"

"I am. Now you wouldn't think, reading this piece of serious and arduously researched journalism, that there is anything more that could be said on the subject of Mr. O'Daly and his time in New York. But you'd be wrong. I intend to go above and beyond that preliminary effort, and see what else can be learned about the man and his time abroad."

"How are you going to get more information? How did you get this . . . this . . ."

"This drivel? I tarted it up, but it's based on fact, believe it or not. Names have been changed to protect the embarrassed. Mrs. O'Daly — Etty — and her travelling companions took advantage of the services of one Philip Durnahan, who's an old friend of mine. He grew up in Stoneybatter and went into the tourism business. He moved to New York some years ago. Lives in one of the suburbs there, and he conducts tours for Irish people going over to see the USA. New York and Boston, mainly. Arranges their flights, their hotels, buses to take them around to the sights, all that. I've been in touch with him, and I'll see him when I get there. He found me a cheapo hotel in Brooklyn. That's one of the five boroughs of New York. Two beds in the room. So there's one for yourself."

"Really, Des, are yeh coddin' me?"

"I'm not. Desmond and Seamus are going to New York."

"Brilliant, Des! I appreciate it, and I'm going to start making my plans."

"Good man."

Shay pointed to the news article. "You say there was another couple who went over on the tour with Mrs. O'Daly."

"Right."

"These foolish names are for O'Daly's wife and guests."

"They are."

"Why did you name O'Daly and not the rest of them?"

"Wanted to have some fun with their predicament but wanted to spare them the ridicule. His wife and two other people I respect."

"So who are they?"

He looked Shay in the eye and said, "Mrs. O'Daly's brother and the brother's wife."

"Darragh and Muriel McLogan!"

He nodded his head in reply. "They flew off for a New York holiday three weeks after the election in 1969. Must have been to celebrate McLogan's election as TD. So, another reason for your intrepid reporter, Des Creaghan, to go snooping about in New York."

∽

So there was Shay Rynne crossing the Atlantic Ocean on an Aer Lingus flight to New York City. He had arranged to take just over a week of holidays. He told his employers that, like everybody else, he'd always wanted to see New York, and he had a chance to go there with a mate of his. He had another motive, but he kept that to himself. Des was not the only one who'd be looking into Jemser O'Daly's life in the big city. It wasn't likely that Shay would find anything linking him to a murder in Dublin more than a year after he left New York, but he might learn more about his criminal career. At the very least, that could prove to be useful information for a peeler to have. On the off chance that he did uncover something connecting him to the murder of McLogan, it would eliminate Talkie Rynne as the prime suspect.

Finn Burke had been in touch with Brennan about meeting Shay at the airport. Des was in the city already. He had flown out the day before. Shay wasn't sure whether the nerves would go on him, flying over the ocean, and this his first time up in the air. But no, he was as excited as a little lad on his first trip to the playground. He loved it, kept gawping out the window even when all he could see was sea and sky. And then coming in over land, seeing scads of buildings and not knowing whether that was New York or not. What was that line he'd read in one of the books? Myles na gCopaleen, was it? No, it was Merriman. Like the man in the poem, Shay "goggled and gaped like one born mindless."

Brennan, dressed in civvies, was waiting for him when he landed at Kennedy airport late in the afternoon. "How's the form, Shay?"

"Grand altogether."

"Now, you'll not be needing that sports jacket. This is New York. It's August. The sun is splitting rocks out there. If I weren't trying to cut such a dignified, priestly figure myself, I'd be running the streets of the city in nothing but the skin God gave me."

When they left the airport and began walking to the parking lot, Shay understood what he meant. He had never been in such sizzling heat; good thing he'd brought along some short-sleeved shirts and lightweight trousers. Brennan led him to a modest-sized black car. Shay noted the modest size because the rest of the cars looked like enormous barges, so long and wide and flat they were, and in every colour imaginable.

"How d'yis have room on the roads for these big boats of cars?"

Brennan laughed. "Ay, whaddya tawkin' about? Yeah, our cahs are big. Ya wanna make somethin' of it?" Shay stood back a bit, and then he laughed. "Ya gotta get used to the way we tawk heh in N'Yawk."

"Ach, I've my work cut out for me here if I have to take language lessons."

Returning to his normal Dublin speech, Brennan said, "Everything is big over here. I wonder what Freud would say."

"Eh? Oh, right!"

Brennan took Shay's bag and placed it in the boot, and they got into the car. He put the key into the ignition and turned to his passenger. "Now I've a question for you," he said.

"Ask away."

"Are you a man to have his name immortalized in the papers at home in Dublin? 'Well-known Garda Seamus Rynne,' that class of a thing?"

Shay had to laugh at that. "I've no fame to my name. It's a rare old day indeed when my name gets into the papers."

"How about Desmond Creaghan's reports for RTÉ? Does he give you some free publicity once in a while?"

"Rare again."

"Maith go leor." Good enough. "While you're here, you are a news reporter. No, make that a researcher for the famous Desmond Creaghan of RTÉ, here to assist him with the story he's writing about Jemser O'Daly."

"Why is that?"

"Instructions from my oul fella. Declan can put the two of you in touch with people who might have some information about O'Daly's time here, but he can't be seen to be putting the police on them. They won't talk if they know you're a copper, and they won't cast too kind an eye on Declan for making such an arrangement. A nosy parker for a newspaper or the radio, that would be fine, as long as you don't go public with any of their names."

"Understood. I'm now undercover. Sometimes, I'd like to stay under. Em, Brennan, I don't know whether the news travelled over here about my . . ."

"Your father. Yes, we've heard about it. There's a news agent near the family's place in Sunnyside, and he brings in a couple of the Irish papers. A bit late, but nobody complains about that. Paper said Talkie was arrested but then released without charge, buíochas le Dia." Thank God.

"But they still think he did it, Brennan. He's their chief suspect. It's like waiting for the guillotine blade to fall."

"I'm so sorry to hear it, Shay. I like your oul fella, and I hope to Christ the suspicion goes away. Falls upon somebody else."

God bless Brennan, Shay thought. He didn't ask whether the oul fella had really done it. All Shay said was, "It won't come as a surprise to hear that I'm interested in Jemser O'Daly for the most obvious of reasons. I'm not just making it up out of whole cloth, either, Brennan. There was physical evidence on O'Daly's clothing that places him near the body just outside the house. Anyway, enough of that for now."

"Grand. Now where is your pal Desmond?"

"He's got us a room at some little hotel in Brooklyn."

"Are you sure? I could find a place for you at the parish house if you like. Saint Kieran's. Or, of course, my mam has offered space for the pair of you in the family home in Queens."

"Thank you, Brennan. I appreciate the offers, but I might as well stay on course with Dessie." And Shay had only stayed in hotels — rundown rooming houses, more like — a handful of times in his entire life. And this was New York.

"Right. I understand." And it seemed, from the look of amusement in those black eyes, that he did. Shay pulled out his notebook, consulted it, and rattled off the address of the hotel, and they headed out.

Brennan took a quick glance at the notebook and said, "Get a new one." He was right; this was obviously a policeman's notebook.

They drove through Queens and into Brooklyn, and the new boy gaped at the size and scope of the place. "Christ Almighty! And at home we think Dublin's the big city!"

"Nearly eight million people here."

"That sort of puts it in perspective. We have, what? About ten percent of that number in Dublin?"

"Sounds about right."

They pulled up at a dodgy-looking place in Brooklyn, at the address provided by Des, and Shay thought maybe he'd been too quick to reject the invitation to stay with Brennan and his fellow priests. But it wasn't all that bad when they parked and went inside. The desk clerk rang Des's room, and he was soon down to greet them. Shay introduced him to Father Burke. Des had heard of him, from Shay, but they had never met. The two shook hands.

"Come on up to the room, lads." So they followed him up the stairs to the third floor. The room was plain, but when had Shay ever known grander accommodation? It looked clean enough and had two beds, a wardrobe for their clothes, a sink, and a small table that Des had set up as a bar. The toilet and shower were down the hall. The room was hot, and a rickety fan wasn't doing much to cool it off.

"We'll all have a short one?" the host asked, and the two newcomers nodded yes to a glass of Jameson whiskey.

"So, what did you see last night, Dessie?" Shay asked. "First night in the Big Apple."

It was a rare occasion when you saw Des Creaghan looking embarrassed, but that's how he looked now. "Em, I was . . . you know, pretty well shattered after the long flight and —"

"Don't be telling us you stayed in this little barracks all night, and slept through your first night in New York!"

"No, no, not that. But there's a bar round the corner, and I stopped in, you know, and then I was going to get on the train or the bus into Manhattan, but I had a bit to drink and then Phil Durnahan came and joined me. And there was a crowd in the bar, and they were pestering me to tell them stories about the Troubles in our native land and, well, the time just flew past."

"And you never got off this block for the entire night."

"But we'll make up for that, now that you're here."

"We will." Shay turned to Brennan. "Would you like to join a couple of bogger tourists on their first day in Manhattan?"

"I would."

And so, after Shay deposited his things in the room and had a wash, the three of them headed out. When they got to Manhattan and Brennan found a parking spot, they left the car and began walking through the legendary city. It was early evening by this time, but still steaming hot, and people were out on the pavements. Shay thought he was going to snap his neck, goggling upwards at the towers of concrete and glass, and then returning his gaze to street level where the lovely women passed by in their fashionable summer dresses and sandals with high heels, and the tanned skin on them. He looked over at Des, who said to him, "You look every bit as gobsmacked as myself, Shay. Have you ever seen the like of the birds here in New York? You'll have to put a fucking gelly bomb under my arse to get me out of here!" He turned to Brennan then. "How do you do it, Brennan?"

"I don't," the priest replied and put his hands together as if in prayer.

Des laughed and said, "Sure you must be a saint, Father."

"Ah, now . . ."

But Shay had heard enough about Brennan and his history to know that he had been intimately familiar with what he was giving up when he gave it up.

He treated them to a little talk about a few of the places they were seeing. "You probably recognize that one." Shay did. The famously tall place with the spire was the Empire State Building. "It was the tallest building in the world until they started on the World Trade Center. Two very high slim towers being constructed in lower Manhattan. You'll get a fine view of them when you're down there, or if you happen to be sailing the Hudson River." He pointed out a few more buildings he liked, older ones, then said, "I won't go on about buildings anymore. I was all set to study architecture before God reached down and grabbed me for the priesthood."

"Is that right, Brennan?" Des asked.

"It is."

"Then you must thank the Man Above every night of your life for delivering you to this architectural heaven. Glad to be out of poor oul Dublin."

"No."

"No?"

"I love Dublin, including much of the architecture. If it had been up to me, we'd never have left."

"But it wasn't up to you. You were just a little boy at the time. So it was your father's decision to sail from the Old World to the new."

Brennan gave him a look Shay couldn't quite read. "Wasn't his decision, either."

"So, who —"

Brennan raised his hand to ward off the question. "He doesn't talk about it."

"Ah."

"Now, are we hungry, lads?"

They acknowledged that they were.

"What would yis like to eat?"

Shay didn't know what to say, not being accustomed to a lot of choice in the matter, but Des spoke up. "Are we far from Little Italy, by any chance, Brennan?"

"It's in Lower Manhattan, but it won't take us any time to get there. We'll take the car."

"Now that I'm on a roll," said Desmond, "would we be able to find . . . What's the name of the place? I have to think . . . Soosera?"

"Suocera?" Brennan said. It sounded like *swo*chaira.

"Yeah, that's it."

"La Mia Suocera. I know it. It means 'My mother-in-law.'"

"I hope they don't cook like my mother-in-law. But, one way or another, this meal and our libations are on me. My treat." He waved off their protests.

Brennan said, "Well, the food is brilliant. You won't be disappointed. Andiamo, ragazzi!"

"And that means?"

"Let's go, lads."

"You know Italian?"

"Only a little bit. I want to learn more. I love the language. I'm hoping to study in Rome, maybe as earlier as next year if the stars align in my favour."

When they arrived at the restaurant, Shay felt as if he was one of the non-sophisticates Des had had so much fun with in his *Daily Knows* article; there were so many choices on the menu, none of them familiar at all, that Shay had no idea where to begin. But finally he went for the richest-sounding combination of pasta and sauce and meat that he could find. And Brennan ordered the wine.

Des looked around the place and said, "Anybody get murdered here, Brennan?"

"Murdered?"

"There was a mob killing in one of the places here a few months ago."

"Ah. Umbertos Clam House. Not far from here."

"Right. Ever been there?"

"I have, as a matter of fact. With my sister and with . . ." He looked at Des and then at Shay and said, "Deena."

"Des knows the story," Shay said, in reply to Brennan's unspoken question. He had filled Des in on the circumstances surrounding Deena's testimony in the Dermody trial. "How's she doing?"

"Grand when I saw her last. Told me she's enjoying the work at Macy's."

"Good."

"But," said Des, "yis weren't in the Clam House when the man got killed, right?"

"No, we were there a couple of weeks before that."

"So, who got the chop? A mob fella, wasn't it? Joey somebody?"

"Joey Gallo, in April. Killed on his birthday. It was the third gangland murder in a twenty-four-hour period."

"Whoa! Tough town you're living in."

"Sure, there are some rough characters."

"Like the Mafia."

"But remember: for many, many years after our own people started arriving on these shores, we were despised. There were signs all over, for job opportunities, signs saying, 'Help Wanted: No Irish Need Apply.' And Italian people face the same prejudice, the great majority of good people being judged by the actions of a few."

"True enough."

"And don't forget: we've a powerful Irish mob in the city, too."

"And that's one of the aspects of New York life I'll be looking into, as I dig into the life of our man Jemser O'Daly."

They returned to their rigatoni and tortellini and gnocchi. The food was the richest, most delicious, best stuff Shay had ever tasted. And the red wine, the Barolo, was heavenly.

"Do the priests in New York get this for their Communion wine, Father?" Shay asked.

"We get plonk."

"Aren't you being a bit sacrilegious there, Father Burke?" Desmond laughed. "Dismissing the blood of Christ as plonk?"

"Oh, no, not at all. Once I consecrate it, it leaves even Barolo in the dust."

Now Shay wanted to know whether Desmond had learned anything more from his tourist guide pal about Jem O'Daly and his guests during the visit back in 1969. "So you saw Phil Durnahan last night."

"I did. And he said to ring him tonight, and he might be able to join us for a bit. Should I get him on the phone?"

"Sure," Shay replied. "Why not?"

So Des got up and asked if he could use the phone. He was back a couple of minutes later. "He can't make a night of it, but he's going to come over for half an hour or so."

"Grand."

"We'll order another bottle of this." Des held up his glass of wine. Shay and Brennan seconded the motion.

"So, Des, did Durnahan have anything to tell you about Jemser O'Daly's time over here? Aside from his family's tastes in food and wine, I mean."

"As a matter of fact, he did. He told me that O'Daly took to the high life here in the city."

Shay asked, "Anything about the visit of the wife and in-laws?"

"He left me with more questions than answers, I'm sorry to say. But we'll hear about it when he gets here."

The conversation then turned to Brennan's life in New York, his parents, sisters, and brothers, and his efforts to maintain a high standard of music in his parish church.

"Desmond!" Shay heard the voice behind him and turned to see a short, wiry-looking fellow with a head of light-brown curls and a bright, smiling face. He knew he'd seen him around Dublin. May have met him through Des sometime in the past.

"Phil, come and have a seat. Phil Durnahan, this is Shay Rynne and Father Brennan Burke."

The second bottle of wine had arrived by then, and everyone had a glass. Only a half glass for Brennan now, as he'd be driving. They asked Phil about his tour business and they talked about that for a few minutes. Then Des brought the conversation around to Jem

O'Daly and his visitors in the summer of 1969. Phil already knew about Desmond's journalistic interest in Dublin's renowned gangster; nothing was said about Shay's own interest.

"I don't know much, Des. All I overheard was a bit of a row between O'Daly and McLogan."

A row between the two of them. Shay certainly wanted to hear about that.

As if reading his mind, Des issued a note of caution. "It was a row that took place three years ago, two years before Darragh's death. And it's not as if they've been on the outs with each other ever since. But let's hear it, Phil."

"Well, the day before that happened, I gave them a bus tour round Manhattan, and we stopped in front of some of the famous shops here. Bergdorf Goodman, Saks Fifth Avenue, places like that. Following the bus tour, the group would have the afternoon to see the sights or to shop on their own. O'Daly and his wife were sitting across the aisle from McLogan and his wife in the third or fourth row in the tour bus, and I could see the women's eyes sparkling as they talked about which shops they'd be going to. Jem O'Daly had a big grin on his face, and he called across to the women, 'Yis will be kitted out like Jackie Kennedy, girls!' I saw Darragh McLogan eyeing O'Daly, and he wasn't smiling at all, and I was close enough to hear Darragh whisper to Jemser over the sound of the bus's motor. He said something like, 'Maybe you didn't hear me the first time, Jem. Where did the money come from?' Given the timing, I had the impression that McLogan was talking about the money for the women to go shopping in these pricey places."

"What did O'Daly say to that?"

"Some smart-arse answer like, 'Ask me no questions; I'll tell you no lies.' So we're no further ahead about that money, whatever was going on there. But then there was the row in the hotel corridor at half one in the morning."

"This, we have to hear."

"The two couples had rooms side by side. And I was staying on the same floor. Some nights I stay in hotels with the tour groups;

sometimes I go home. Anyway, on this occasion, I was in the hotel in a room across from the McLogans. The whole group had gone out to dinner somewhere, and then people split off to go about on their own. The McLogans went for a walk and then came in for an early night. Jemser and Etty O'Daly went somewhere else. I didn't know where, but I think somebody came by in a car and collected them. I knew that two or three of my pals were drinking in a bar nearby, so I went out to join them. I got back to my room around one o'clock or a little before, and it took me awhile to get to sleep. Drink puts some of us to sleep, but it's never had that effect on me.

"So I'm lying there in bed and I hear a door open and somebody shouting. I'm jolted upright in the bed, wondering if it's one of my crowd in trouble. But before I get myself dressed to go out into the hall, I listen for a bit. And I cop on that it's Darragh McLogan giving out to Jem O'Daly. Something like this, McLogan saying, 'What did you think you were doing, sending a woman back here in the middle of the night in a taxi? In a dangerous fucking city like this?' If yis knew McLogan, it was a rare thing to hear him effing and blinding, so you know he'd really lost the rag with O'Daly. And O'Daly replies that he knew she'd be fine, his friends knew the cab driver and he was reliable.

"But then O'Daly says, 'Did you see her face?' And Darragh says, 'No, I heard her at her door, and looked out. She had her back to me, and I asked her where you were, and how did she get back to the hotel, and she told me a taxi, and went into the room and shut the door. What did you mean about her face?' And O'Daly replies, 'You'll see a great red blotch on her cheek. Beginnings of a bruise.' And Darragh, of course, says, 'What in the hell are you talking about?' And O'Daly explains what happened. They'd gone to see some man. I didn't catch the name if he even said it. And then, 'He had a great bulldog of a man looking out for him.' Or an animal of some kind, and it was clear he meant a bodyguard.

"And O'Daly goes on to say they had come up on this fella and spooked him or got too close to the door or whatever it was, and this big gorilla — yeah, that's what he said, gorilla — lunged towards

O'Daly, and O'Daly, being quick on his feet from the experience of countless brawls, backed off. But he said the missus had stepped forward as if to give out to the man, her not knowing how dangerous some of these people are. And the punch landed on her. On Henrietta. Etty. And O'Daly shouted and shoved the guy to the floor. Then the man he was there to see came to the door, and there was a ruckus with the bodyguard. And the man told the gorilla to get the fuck out of there, and invited O'Daly in. Whatever their business was, it sounded as if O'Daly and this man, this gangster maybe, didn't want the little woman there for the meeting, so they sent her home in a cab."

"Jesus, Phil!" Shay exclaimed. "And this row between O'Daly and McLogan was being carried on in the hotel corridor?"

"Better than in one of the rooms with one of their wives."

"And did Mrs. O'Daly really have a bruise?"

"Yeah, something that would be turning black and blue. And so did Jem. Plain as day next morning. It's not every day one of my tourists has such a real New York moment!"

"Good thing, or you'd be out of business."

"I would. Or maybe I'd attract a very strange group of tourists, out for the thrills."

"So," said Desmond, "McLogan was standing in the corridor hearing this crazy tale about his sister!"

"Yeah. He wasn't best pleased. But O'Daly got him calmed down, assured him that he'd knocked the bodyguard out of contention, and protected his wife, McLogan's sister. And then he got a bit huffy, O'Daly did, and he was telling McLogan that no matter what he, O'Daly, had done in his life, he had always protected Etty and their children, left them out of things. Anyway, the man had assured O'Daly that his taxi driver was sound. The wife would be safe. I was standing by my door mesmerized by all this. I know I missed some of it, but you get the gist."

"We do."

"And then I heard McLogan questioning O'Daly about the company he'd been keeping till after one in the morning. I didn't hear a reply to that; maybe there was a *significant look*, or something, because McLogan got off the subject. And O'Daly said, 'And haven't I always been good to you yourself, Dar?' Or words to that effect, with a bit of a sting in them. I know we've all heard that some of McLogan's electoral support came in the form of money from O'Daly's pockets. Anyway, they managed to patch things up by the end of it, McLogan even sounded apologetic to O'Daly. 'I know you tried to protect her, Jem.' That sort of thing, and it was over.

"Now the next day, it was comical in spite of what had happened. Because O'Daly was telling everybody about his fearless wife, that she was a descendant of some kind of Irish warrior-goddess, that she'd stepped up to fight off the attacker and protect her husband, so nobody'd better mess with Etty. And she tried to take it in good humour, but she was still shaky. Who wouldn't be?"

Shay considered the scene that Phil Durnahan had witnessed, or at least overheard. It didn't sound like something that would have continued to smoulder two years after the fact. But he was certainly curious about whatever it was that Jemser O'Daly was doing in the middle of the night with people who employed jittery gorillas to guard their doors.

Phil had to leave, and they thanked him for giving them the story. After everyone had shoved every morsel and every drop into themselves, and Desmond had paid the tab, they walked to Brennan's car. There was a parking ticket stuck under the windscreen wiper. Brennan picked it up and shrugged, in the same way Shay had seen people shrug things off all over the city. They got in, and Brennan said, "Declan tells me he can meet up with you tomorrow. To, he says, 'give them whatever information I have.' I have to warn yis: my father never gives 'whatever information' he has, not to you or to me or anybody else. Keeps his cards close to his vest, does oul Dec, but he'll likely direct you to some people who may open up a bit more. So now . . . You've seen the brilliant, shining face of New York. But this city has a darker side, as you've no doubt heard."

"Dublin has a darker side these days, too," Shay said, which earned him a look from Brennan, the kind of look you'd get from the schoolmaster when you'd been particularly thick about the subject of the lesson. Brennan put on a New York accent again and said, "You don't know from dahk!" Then, "Would yis like to have a look?"

"We would," Des replied, his eyes fairly gleaming at the notion of it.

So they set out for a nighttime tour of Manhattan.

‿

Shay could hardly believe what his eyes were seeing. Gaudy neon signs and pictures of naked women advertising porno movies and porno shops and live sex shows. On some streets, girls and women in high heels and skimpy clothes leaned against the porno places or other buildings, sashayed along the street, or beckoned to men passing by on foot or in cars. Some of the girls stood with big, muscular men in brightly coloured, garish clothing and large-brimmed hats. There were people lying on the pavements — sidewalks, as they were called here — people seemingly unconscious, with rubbish strewn about them. Others sat up with begging cups in their hands.

Then Brennan drove past rich-looking terraces with brownstone buildings and apartment blocks with uniformed doormen outside. But not long after that, they crossed a river and saw block after block of burnt-out buildings. Windows were boarded up, or merely left open to the night. The place had the appearance of a war zone, with crumbled masonry and streets filled with rubbish. There were cars that had been stripped of their wheels, mirrors, and doors. Shay looked to his left and saw flames shooting from the roof of a building.

"Brennan, there's a building on fire!"

Brennan didn't even turn his head. "There's always a building on fire."

"What?"

"The Bronx is burning every night."

"That's where we are, the Bronx?"

"Yeah."

"What do you mean, it's burning every night?"

"Landlords torch their buildings. They can't afford to pay the taxes or the other expenses. The economy's in the shitter."

"So they set fire to their own properties!"

"Well, sometimes gangs burn the buildings."

"This must be what hell looks like," Des muttered. "Or the planet Earth after some apocalyptic war we've brought upon ourselves."

Again, Shay saw people lying on the sidewalks, and others stepping over them. When Brennan's car slowed down, men approached the windows, holding out bags of stuff — drugs, obviously. Sirens wailed all around and never seemed to stop. More than once, Shay saw police cars and ambulances screaming down side streets. Brennan came to a red light and honked his horn and sailed right through it.

The Garda in Shay protested out of habit. "Red light, Brennan!"

"Out of the question, to stop here."

Looking around him, Shay had to agree.

"What the fuck is going on here, Brennan?" Des asked. "This is America. This is the place people come *to* in order to get away from whatever shite they had to live with in their home countries. And *this* is what they come to?"

"Land of the free, Des," Brennan replied. "'Give me your tired, your poor, your huddled masses yearning to breathe free.' Well, I'm sure you're familiar with the inscription on the Statue of Liberty out there. You can come to the United States of America. Doesn't matter if the arse is out of your trousers and you don't have a cent to your name. Doesn't matter if your father was a lord or a peasant. You land on these shores, you have the same chance as anybody else. Secure for yourself the American dream. In theory. The flip side of that, *in theory*, is: if you don't make a success of your life, you've nobody to blame but yourself. It's your own fault. So those who have succeeded, who have raked in tons of cash for themselves, look down on those who haven't. And in any society, not everybody can make it. Some of the richest people in the world live on the Upper East Side of this city. In the same city as *this*." He pointed to the desolation around them.

"What kind of numbers are we talking about here, for crime, I mean?" Des asked.

"I don't know how many assaults, rapes, burglaries, or things like that we've had. Big numbers, you may be sure. I did hear that there were well over fourteen hundred murders in this city last year."

"Fourteen hundred in one year!" Des exclaimed. "How many murders did we have in Dublin, Garda Rynne? Do you know?"

"I've seen the Garda commissioner's reports, yeah. In the Republic of Ireland, in 1971, there were fourteen murders."

"Ha," said Brennan. "You're making that up because I said fourteen hundred, right? Well *over* fourteen hundred."

"It was fourteen murders. Plus a couple of infanticides and a handful of manslaughters. Five or six."

"And what's the population of our hard-won Republic, three million?" Des asked.

"Yeah."

"Well, here in New York it's eight million," Brennan said, "so New York should have had, what? How many murders? Not even forty. What about Dublin itself last year? With one tenth the population of New York."

"Three murders in Dublin. You can do the maths!"

So that was Shay's introduction to life on the streets of New York.

CHAPTER XIX

S hay and Desmond were to meet Declan Burke on Friday, so Brennan collected them in the late afternoon and drove them to Sunnyside in Queens. He asked them what they had done earlier in the day, and Des told him, "We got sunburns." Which was true. Another fiery hot day. They told Brennan about the bus tour they'd been on, around Manhattan and over to Staten Island on the boat, and Des imitated the New York voice of the tour guide to great effect. They pulled up in front of the Burke family home, which was half of a two-storey brick house with white trim, situated on a corner lot with a hedge around it and trees in the yard. A young girl came flying out of the house, caught sight of the visitors, and said, "I'm late!" Brennan introduced her as his sister Bridey. She had dark-red hair and hazel eyes, and she was a sweetheart. "Sorry, but Sharon and Janet are waiting for me!" And she took off on the run.

"She's always late." Brennan laughed.

Shay and Des followed Brennan into the house, and they were introduced to his mother. Teresa Burke was tall and slim, with dark eyes and black hair streaked with silver, pulled back in a kind of knot. A lovely-looking lady. "You'll have tea," she said, and they thanked her.

"Declan!" she called out. "Brennan's here with Mr. Creaghan and Mr. Rynne."

"Oh, call me Desmond. Or Des."

"And I'm Shay."

Mrs. Burke invited them to have a seat in the living room while she made the tea. The room was filled with fine-looking chairs, a sofa, and end tables made of dark, gleaming wood. There were photos of the family in silver frames on one of the tables. The sun streamed in through the window. Shay could hear a television in another room, a news report about the Vietnam war. Somebody snapped off the set and then the da came into the room. Shay and Des stood to greet him. Declan Burke was a man who gave the impression of being in command of any room he entered. A few inches shy of six feet, with a muscular build, he had thick white hair and cool-blue eyes that scanned the newcomers before he uttered his welcome. He shook their hands.

Teresa looked at her husband, and it was the look of a worried lady.

"It's going to wind down, Teresa," said Declan. "He'll not be in it."

Brennan explained. "My brother Terry has finished university and he's working out at JFK. The airport. What he wants to do is join the air force as a pilot. Says it's the best training for a career in civil aviation. But Ma wants him to wait until the shambles in Vietnam runs its course."

"He'll be sent over there."

"He won't be, Teresa," Declan said again. "The Yanks will have to pull out of it."

The Yanks, says a man who's been living in America for more than twenty years. Shay guessed that he hadn't quite taken on a new identity. As a Yank.

"They should have pulled out of it before they pulled in," Brennan remarked.

"Let's enjoy our tea," said Teresa.

Shay and Des got on to the purpose of their visit, and Shay let his pal do the talking. Des said, "As you may have heard, one of our TDs, Darragh McLogan, was murdered at a gathering of Fianna Fáil last summer. No charges have been laid but his brother-in-law, Jem O'Daly, is regarded as a possible suspect. I understand that the name is familiar to you."

"It is," Declan conceded.

"A well-known, some might say notorious, Dublin character. And he made something of a name for himself over here, I understand."

"He did."

"So I've been doing some research into his background, his history, for RTÉ. Of course, there's so much material on him in Dublin, and so many characters who are delighted to bend my ear about him, that the difficulty will be paring it down for broadcast. I have no idea how much I'll be able to learn about his time here in America, but I'll do my best. Shay here is in town on a fact-finding mission as well."

Brennan spoke up then. "Shay will be looking for anything that might have happened here that would account for him killing his brother-in-law."

"Sounds like a stretch to me," Declan said. Shay assumed that, like Brennan, Declan was in the know about the arrest and release of Talkie Rynne, but nobody mentioned it.

"It does, Da, I know. But the brother-in-law, McLogan, came over here for a short visit when O'Daly was living here. If anything happened during that trip that might have soured things between them, Shay will want to know about it. But he'll be undercover, as a researcher working with Desmond on his news story. Nobody will know he's a guard." Brennan looked over at Shay and said, "In fact, the Gardaí don't even know what he's here for."

"That's right. They think I'm spending a few days in New York with a pal. Nothing more than that."

"You'll be in the soup if they find out you lied to them," said Declan.

"I've been in the soup with them before." Declan merely raised an eyebrow, the way Shay had seen Brennan do, but he made no comment. Shay was not going to confess to the ill-fated gun snatch, or the delivery of the guns to Declan's brother Finn. "But if I do a good job on the McLogan murder inquiry, that may keep me out of the soup pot from now on." There was no need to add *And keep my oul man out of prison.*

Brennan said, "I'll take them to some of the bars frequented by the, em, the fellas from the West Side. Give them a bit of the atmosphere."

"Take him tomorrow," Declan said.

"Tomorrow?"

"Tomorrow night. Go to the Avenue. The White House Bar."

"A bar, is it? That's one way to get an Irishman into the White House again!" Des joked.

Declan made no comment on that but said, "There will be something going on there, and it may be of interest to a man looking into the history of our people here in New York."

Nobody asked for more information. Shay was content to go along and see whatever the Burkes thought would be of interest.

"We'll do that," Brennan said. "How about O'Malley's now, Da? That's our local," he explained.

"Sure, I'll join you for one. That is, I'll go with you as long as I can be assured that my name won't be used in any story on RTÉ!"

"Certainly, Mr. Burke. Declan."

"And nothing that could identify me, even without my name."

"You have my word."

"And mine," Shay added.

⁂

They said their goodbyes and thanks to Mrs. Burke, and started off on foot for the family's local pub on Queens Boulevard. There it was, O'Malley's. There were three men working the taps and pouring the shots, and Brennan asked what everyone would be having.

"It's on me, Brennan," Desmond said.

"Thanks, Des. The usual for you, Da?"

"The usual."

"A Guinness for Declan. Same for me, and add to that a double Jemmy." A double Jameson. Shay and Des decided on the same, and when they were poured, the group made for a table near the back of the pub.

"You fellas wouldn't feel out of place here, I'm thinking," said Brennan.

"Just like home," Shay agreed.

O'Malley's was typical of a smoke-filled Irish bar, long and narrow and done up in dark wood. On the walls were photos of boxers and other sportsmen, and there was a glass case filled with memorabilia at the end of the room. The punters were all men, each of them with a cigarette or a cigar, and a pint of plain or a glass of whiskey. A number of them greeted Brennan and Declan, and Brennan asked them how their families were and how they'd done with the horses. Betting appeared to be of great interest in O'Malley's.

"So, have you and your family always lived here in Queens?" Des asked the Burkes. Shay wondered whether Des really didn't know the history, or if this was the news reporter's way to get the information flowing.

Brennan took out a pack of cigarettes and offered them around. Everybody took one and lit up. "Our family left Ireland," Brennan said, "and washed up in Hell's Kitchen. You've likely heard of it, a tough Irish enclave on the city's West Side. Our fellas had to be tough, at least starting out. Our people were hated when they got off the famine ships in the 1800s. Last thing the WASPs wanted, last thing White Anglo-Saxon Protestant America wanted, was a horde of poor, starving, desperate Irish Catholics. As I mentioned before, 'Help Wanted: No Irish Need Apply.'"

"Nobody was going to give the Irish fuck-all," Declan added, "so they had to take it."

Brennan returned to his family's history. "We spent some months in a ratty tenement there before the gods smiled on us, and our father came up" — he gave his father a pointed look — "with the money for that fine brick house here in Sunnyside." Shay knew Des well enough to know he was dying to ask for the identity of those benevolent gods and why they took a sudden liking to the Burkes of New York, but Des managed to stay quiet. Brennan continued, "Hell's Kitchen is the area between Eighth Avenue to the east and the Hudson River to the west between Thirty-Fourth and Fifty-Ninth Streets. Times Square and the Theatre District are right there on its eastern flank; the waterfront is its western boundary, with all the rackets associated with organized labour, shipping, and cargo. You'll see the Kitchen for yourselves tomorrow night."

"Looking forward to it," said Des. "How did it get the name?"

Brennan shook his head. "There are many conflicting stories. One is that Davy Crockett — the American folk hero and politician — had this to say about the Irishmen he had met in another rough part of Manhattan: they were *savages* and were 'too mean to swab hell's kitchen.' Whether that slander migrated up as far as today's Hell's Kitchen I don't know. As I say, there are competing theories."

"And some of the fellas on that side of town may have known Jem O'Daly," Shay said.

"Apparently so."

Declan gave a quick nod of agreement, then asked, "How seriously is he suspected in the murder of his brother-in-law?"

Shay had no desire to keep the truth from Brennan's father. "You've probably heard this, Declan. My father is a suspect. He was on the drink and he did something foolish that night, at McLogan's. I don't for a minute think my da killed McLogan. As for O'Daly . . . Before my father came into their sights, my fellow guards were all but sure it was O'Daly who had done it. There was physical evidence connecting him to the scene of the killing, and he lied about a crucial element of the case. And there's something else that inspired them to want O'Daly put away. McLogan was one of the TDs for Dublin Central. He's a law-and-order type, so that sits well with some of the Gardaí. But his sister married Jem O'Daly, and O'Daly has helped him out on the campaign trail. Family ties and all that. O'Daly, of course, is anything but law and order. Until now, anyway. He is, as we all agree, a colourful character."

Desmond chimed in. "To say he's a colourful character is to paint him all too drably. As you may know, there are manoeuvres to get rid of Jack Lynch. So the politicians are all positioning themselves, in case there's a heave, to win favour with whoever replaces Jack as Taoiseach."

"You don't mean O'Daly!" Brennan exclaimed.

"No, that would be a long way off for O'Daly even if he got elected. But he has a high profile. If he can convince the voters that he really has given up his criminal ways, he'll be a force to be reckoned with in government. Now, looking back to the time before McLogan was killed, O'Daly sees his relationship with the well-respected Darragh McLogan as a clear advantage in getting where he wants to be. But it goes both ways. McLogan sees reflected glory for himself if Jem O'Daly gets in. O'Daly will almost certainly show his gratitude by angling for a bigger role for McLogan than he has — than he *had* — up to now."

"Now, you, Des," said Brennan. "Are you enjoying your work with RTÉ?"

"I am. I'm still amazed that they took me on!"

"Why's that?"

"My previous employment was with the *Dublin Daily Knows*. Are you familiar with that rag, Father Burke?"

"Are you having me on, Desmond?"

"I'm not. I wrote under the pen name Mickey Joe Pat Mullooly. So in those pages, a story about you would go like this, if you had the good fortune to be featured in the *Daily Knows*. 'The beauteous broads on Broadway were bug-eyed as black-haired, black-eyed Bible boyo, Brennan Burke, bulled his way to the betting shop where he bet the farm on Bright-Eyed Betty, only to lose big time. And then our Brennan had to answer to the bishop,' et cetera, et cetera. How would you like that kind of fame attached to yourself, Father?"

"The life of a celibate recluse in a small, humble, wooden chapel would be preferable to that, I'd have to say. Your work is a bit higher-toned these days."

"As am I, myself." Des laughed as he said it. "But there is also the fact that I have some insight into the working and not-working classes of Dublin, since I was reared amongst them."

"Good on you."

"Brennan on the moor!" The voice came from behind Shay, and he turned to see two men, one of them a big hefty fella with short curly ginger hair, the other smaller, slimmer with dark hair. Both of them greeted Declan. And it was clear from the hellos and raised glasses around the place that the two were regulars at O'Malley's. "Join you?"

"Sure," said Brennan, and they pulled two chairs and another table up next to theirs. Brennan introduced the new arrivals as members of New York's Finest, sergeants Bernie Silverberg and Michael Cadigan. It was clear that Shay was to maintain his cover even in this company, as he and Des were introduced as two reporters over from Dublin.

"Reporters, is that right?" Cadigan asked. "So, what are you reporting on over here?"

Des was quick with his reply. "We heard you've developed a bit of a crime problem here in New York, so we're here to see if there's any truth to that rumour."

"Crime?" said Silverberg. "I'll give you crime."

Cadigan asked, "How about this one for the folks back home in Ireland? The incident that was called in to us a few nights ago. You know the one I mean, Silver, guy from outta town. Only a tourist would call in something like this."

"Yeah. A schmuck from someplace nobody ever heard of."

"Silverberg, if it's two miles outside the five boroughs of New York, you never heard of it."

Silverberg turned to the rest of them. "No, really, where this guy was from, he said it's called Dogtown. I thought he was shittin' me."

"No. It's in Georgia or Alabama or someplace like that. Guy had this accent, like a hillbilly from down there."

"Okay," said Silverberg, "so we get this call and we go to see this hick at his hotel. I say to him, 'What the fuck were you doing walking around Hell's Kitchen by yourself at twelve thirty at night?' Guy's in town for a sales convention, and a bunch of them went out on the town, and this guy fucked up the address when he tried to get back to the hotel. Anyway, he says to me, 'What did you say's the name of that place?' I tell him, 'Hell's Kitchen.' He thinks I'm makin' it up. Him coming from *Dogtown*. Like I said, a tourist. So anyway, he comes across a robbery in progress on Fifty-First Street. He sees these two mutts go up to two guys who are coming out of Franny Mulvaney's. You know, the bar where they all —"

"Yeah, where all us Micks drink," Declan said. "We know it well."

"Right. The marks are a middle-aged gentleman and a taller younger guy." Silverberg shot a glance at Declan and Brennan. "Fucking perps, one of them's got a gun, points it at the two marks, and the other perp goes for the pockets of the younger of the two men. Our tourist sees this going on, and he's all agog at this bit of New York real life, but he's practically crapping in his jockeys. Doesn't know what to do. Wants to help but doesn't want to get his head blown off."

"Yeah," Cadigan agreed. "We've all been there."

"But," Silverberg said to Shay and Desmond, "don't worry too much about the two marks, the two victims here. Turns out they don't need no help. We'll call the younger guy Brennan. Brennan notices that both these shitbirds have their eyes on him. Thinking he is the one to watch, probably dismissing the older fella — we'll call him Declan — as less of a threat. Ha! Dec turns toward Brennan, and this must'a made the gunman relax a bit. Which he shouldn'a done, because Dec, quick as a flash, reaches over, grabs the gun, and twists it out of the perp's hand, then uses it to belt the guy across the head, and the guy goes down." Silverberg bowed his head to Declan and said, "Declan Burke, fearless exemplar of a fearless tribe. Then" — Silverberg turned to Brennan — "the other mutt throws a punch at Brennan, but Brennan dodges it. He replies with a couple of punches worthy of Rocky Marciano, and then wrestles him to the ground."

"So, what does he do, our boy from Dogtown?" Cadigan asked, playing along.

"Well, he's smart enough to know that the two mopes on the ground might just get up and rob *him*. But he thinks he should do the right thing, so he hightails it to a payphone."

Cadigan rolled his eyes. "Payphone. Hell's Kitchen. Twelve thirty in the a.m."

Silverberg laughed. "I know. Fuhgeddaboudit. But somehow this phone was in working order. There was nobody passed out in it in a pool of puke, and nobody came up and jumped into the booth and grabbed his wallet. So he called it in."

"Yeah, well, he'll get stars in his crown in heaven, but we don't have a vic. The two marks, our two friends here, were well able for these two mooks. Declan points the gun at the two of them, bends down to one of them, and whispers something into his face. Our good citizen described the perp now as 'honest-to-God scared to death!' And who wouldn't be, with one guy looking like the chief of staff of the IRA, and the other like a soldier in the Roman legion! Then our two would-be victims turn and walk away. Declan pockets the gun."

Silverberg took a good, long swallow of his beer and said, "I wonder where that gun is now. Do you have any idea, Sergeant Cadigan?"

"Not a clue, Sergeant Silverberg," Cadigan replied. "Could be on the other side of the Atlantic, far as I know." He reached over and clinked his glass against Declan Burke's.

"So there you have it, a report of yet another violent crime on the island of Manhattan." It was Silverberg's turn to look at Declan and Brennan. "And the two putzes who ended up on the ground, having the fear of God put into them? We'll not be hearing from them. No arrest, no charges. No crime worth reporting when you think about it."

Shay looked over at the two Burkes, and he could well imagine them putting the fear of God into any unlucky gobshites who thought they could intimidate and rob them. If only Shay could send them over to Dublin to scare the shite out of Lar McCreevy some dark night outside Store Street.

To underscore the point he had made, Sergeant Cadigan sang out, "Brennan on the moor, Brennan on the moor. Bold, brave undaunted was young Brennan on the moor." To Declan he said, "A few more fluid ounces of this and I'll come up with a song for you, too, you old Fenian."

There was a bit more discussion amongst the characters at the table, and their respective tribes, and then the talk turned to Darragh McLogan and Jemser O'Daly. Shay gave them a short history of the case, leaving Talkie Rynne out of it altogether and according a prominent role to O'Daly.

"Right," said Silverberg. "I get the idea. And the vic was O'Daly's brother-in-law."

"Who else are the cops over there looking at for this guy's murder?" Cadigan asked.

Shay didn't look at Creaghan or the Burkes. "They're looking at political rivals, people who wanted to take McLogan's place in the Dáil. And the hooley at McLogan's house that night was filled with ambitious men."

"But the way he was killed," Des said. "He was kicked to death. Not exactly a skilful execution."

"That's right," Shay agreed. "That's another reason the guards are looking at O'Daly. It has the appearance of something personal, and they are family. Brothers-in-law."

"And are you the only two, em, journalists," Brennan asked, "who are curious about O'Daly's time over here? Wondering if there might be a connection?"

Shay had already heard about one incident between the two of them here in New York, but they seemed to have patched things up that very night. Shay said, "There's been lots of talk about O'Daly's time here, no question. There may be things he doesn't want known back home. And McLogan, being O'Daly's wife's brother, may have had better access to stories about him than other people would have had. Did McLogan know something, and O'Daly wanted to shut him up?" Shay put his hands up, even though nobody had voiced an objection. "It's all speculation, I know."

"So," said Des, "O'Daly made a name for himself here in the big city. Made himself right at home with his fellow Irishmen, from what I hear."

Brennan answered, "His name was known in Hell's Kitchen."

"And you lived over there yourself."

"We did, for a short time, eh Declan?" he said to his father, then turned to Shay and Des. "That part of Manhattan has been home to Irish criminal gangs since before the century began. There were

Dutch and Germans in the neighbourhood, too, and from my reading of the history, they were frequently scandalized by the fighting and the carrying-on amongst some of us Oirish. But eventually, things got better organized. And more lucrative. The U.S. government's greatest gift to the criminal fraternity in the United States of America was Prohibition. I still can't believe it: the Puritans in charge of this country actually amended the *constitution* to outlaw liquor! The Eighteenth Amendment, it was."

"Sounds as if you're still feeling the pain of it, Brennan," said Des.

"I didn't take it personally. That amendment was repealed in 1933. Well before my time."

Des stood and called for a toast. "Here's to the repeal of the Eighteenth Amendment."

The others at the table responded, "Hear, hear."

"One thing about O'Daly," Cadigan said then. "He was squiring this broad around, I know that."

"Was he now?" Desmond asked.

"Yeah, well, from everything I heard, the women liked him. But this broad in particular, she was a showgirl. Chorus girl in one of the Broadway shows. Or Off-Broadway, whatever it was."

"Who was that?" Silverberg asked.

"Whatsa matter, Bernie? You got a stable of these fillies and you're scared one of them was stepping out on you?"

"My broads don't go for any of you Irishers with your bejabbers and your begorra and your uncircumcised shillelaghs. They got standards."

"Yeah, well, Jem O'Daly had standards, too. Tall, gorgeous blond came to New York for the high life. Came from somewhere in the Midwest."

"Where?" Silverberg asked. "Dogtown?"

Cadigan corrected him. "Dogtown's in the South, Bernie, and this girl was no dog, let me tell you. And a sharp dresser, too. Is that what you say about women? A fashion plate, I guess you'd call her. Word was she was engaged to be married to the producer of some of the shows on Broadway." He raised his hand to ward off an objection. "No, I don't think Myron Lastman flew over to Ireland, tracked down — not O'Daly, but his brother-in-law, and got into a fight to the death over O'Daly's fling with this dame."

"I'm sure you're right," Desmond said. "Considering what kinds of things O'Daly's wife had to close her eyes to over all the years she's been married to him — the crimes he committed, the years he was in prison, and who knows what else — something like this New York fling wouldn't lead to McLogan calling down death on himself for his sister's honour on August thirtieth or thirty-first of last year."

CHAPTER XX

Declan retired early but Shay, Des, and Brennan stayed on the batter till the wee hours and so it was painful waking up the next morning. It was a Saturday, but Shay knew that Brennan was going to be getting up to say Mass at Saint Kieran's. The Latin Mass, not the new one in English. Shay had told him he'd be there. As it turned out, Shay got to the church before Brennan did. He walked inside, trying to ignore his hangover. It was a beautiful old stone church with stained-glass windows in bright colours. Shay hadn't been to Mass in a while, but he didn't even have to think about the lifelong rituals: he dipped his hand in the holy water, blessed himself, walked to a seat halfway up, genuflected, slid into the pew, and then knelt down to say a prayer. It wasn't much of a prayer, but he said a few words on behalf of his family and then sat up again.

He could hear voices overhead in the choir loft. Sounded like young fellas, so he figured it was Brennan's choir. He heard the door open behind him, and then, from above, "Shhh! It's the assassin! My dad told me a coupla guys jumped him. In the middle of the street. Him and his old man."

"Your dad's a cop, right?" another boy asked.

"Yeah, and he told me about Burke gettin' mugged!"

"Here he comes now."

The assassin?

"And we don't even have our books out. Get them, Dickie!"

"Yeah, yeah. What are we doing today?"

"*Mass of the Angels*, dummy! Don't you remember? He's singing the *Sanctus* himself."

"Who's singing the *Sanctus*? Robbie?"

"No, the assassin himself. Shut up, here he —"

"There's not a mark on you!" The young boy's voice slid up the scale. "We heard you got mugged! Did you get hurt?"

"It was nothing." The voice was Brennan's, Father Burke's. "You should have seen the other guy. Needed a priest." They all laughed.

"So. Gentlemen. Music for today's Mass. First, the *Kyrie*. What is it we're praying for when we say 'Kyrie eleison'?"

"Lord have mercy," one of the boys piped up. "Even *I* know that much Latin."

"No, you don't," Brennan responded.

"What?"

"That part of the Mass, the *Kyrie*, is Greek. What school did you go to, Duffy? If it were Latin, it would be 'Domine, miserere.' Or, more likely, we'd say 'Miserere, Domine.' Right?"

"Uh, yeah."

"So. We're talking about the mercy of God."

"Bet you showed a lot of mercy to whoever tried to take you down!"

Laughter again.

Then, "Facts, Giuseppe: me oul man was with me. The individuals who jumped us are still alive. That was a lesson in mercy, whether our attackers realized it or not."

"Your old man? How old is he? Did you have to do the fighting for both of you?"

"You've never met my father, have you, Giuseppe?"

"Unh-unh."

"Well, let's just say those two gurriers are lucky they still have their kneecaps."

"Huh?"

That had gone right over the heads of the lads in the choir. But Shay got the joke.

"Now, I missed rehearsal this week, but surely you fellas remember the Mass parts from all the practising we did the week before."

"Yes, Father."

"All right, then. We'll just go over the *Salve Regina.*"

Jesus, Mary, and Patrick, what a beautiful sound from that choir of young boys! And then the brief rehearsal was over. People had been coming into the church, and it was now half full. Shay turned in his seat and saw the assassin, in his black soutane, gliding up the aisle on silent feet. Sure, Shay could see how he might have earned the nickname. He didn't exactly look the part of the kindly parish priest, with that haughty-looking face and those black eyes that could condemn you to the fires of eternal damnation. So he didn't look like a cherub. But from what Shay had heard of some of the new music in the church these days, if a hard man was needed to keep standards up, well, Burke was yer man.

He nodded hello to Shay and others in the church, then bowed before the altar and disappeared into the sacristy. Two minutes later he was at the back of the church in his vestments. He had on a long green cape with the design of a crucifix in gold down the back. Shay couldn't remember the name of it. Started with C but wasn't cape. And a biretta on his head, the black cap with the ridges on top. Father Burke processed up the aisle again, at the end of a line of altar boys in their black cassocks and white surplices. He sang the Mass parts, and the boy choir responded. The singing was brilliant. The sermon wasn't about hell and damnation, Shay was relieved to hear. It was about some of the stories in the Bible. The priest billed it as "What they wouldn't have made up if they were making it up" and there were giggles throughout the congregation.

"It's not surprising that some people claim that the stories in the Bible were inventions by the Christians of the time to convince people

285

to follow them. But we have an authority who had no love for Christians at all. Tacitus was a Roman who lived in the first and second centuries AD. He was a politician and historian, and in his *Annals of Imperial Rome*, he referred in an almost off-hand manner to the Crucifixion. He wrote that exquisite tortures were meted out to 'persons hated for their iniquities, whom the common people called Christians. The author of that name, Christus, had been put to death by Pontius Pilatus, during the reign of Tiberius.' So, no fan of Christians was Tacitus, and yet he documented the execution of Jesus Christ.

"Now, for the Christians themselves. One thing that strikes the reader of Scripture is that some of the disciples are portrayed as less than holy and heroic. Jesus was so exasperated with Peter at one point that he cried out, 'Get thee behind me, Satan!' Other disciples are depicted at times as dim or cowardly, a bunch of thicks, a bunch of schmoes. Is that how you'd create a legend?" The congregation laughed at the picture this presented. "Wouldn't you paint them as a much higher class of people, more admirable, if you were making it up to convince people to change their lives and follow you?

"And now, the Resurrection. In all four Gospels, who finds the empty tomb? Women. The Gospel accounts differ as to how many women were there early that Sunday morning, but they all agree on the presence of Mary Magdalene. And she was, let us say, a woman with a past. So: women! At that time and place in history, women were not accepted in law as witnesses. Now, in 1972, we still have a long, long way to go with respect to women's equality. No question. But back then, women being given the credit for witnessing the greatest event in world history? Fuhgeddaboudit!" The Irish voice had turned New York, and again the congregation enjoyed a laugh. "The men at that time would *never, ever* have made this up. Other accounts presented a more acceptable version. Saint Paul makes no mention of the women at all. The story would sell better that way! But the writers of the four Gospels all had the women on the scene. Because that's the way it happened. You wouldn't make it up!"

The priest made a seamless shift from the lighthearted tone of the sermon to the solemn dignity of the rest of the Mass. There was more great singing, especially when Brennan did the *Sanctus* by himself. One of the finest melodies Shay had ever heard in church, and he remembered it from his days as an altar boy. But he'd never heard it in a voice as good as this. Not an assassin now, but a man sounding like an angel of God. Hard for Shay to believe this was the same man who had flattened a couple of muggers on the West Side of New York.

∽

Brennan invited Shay to his parents' place for dinner — lunch, over here — but he was too tired and hungover to make polite conversation. What if he fell asleep in front of Brennan's ma at the table? Brennan was no stranger to hangovers himself, so he understood and drove Shay to his hotel. He'd have a bit of a sleep and then there was somebody else he wanted to see in New York.

"Have you seen much of Deena, Brennan?" Shay realized immediately how the question might sound to the man who had just said the Confiteor and had sung such a beautiful Mass. But Father Burke just laughed.

"I've seen her a couple of times. That evening with Bridey at Umbertos in the spring, and then a couple of months ago, again with Bridey. Haven't heard anything lately. Bridey is studying maths in college, and she was offered a summer job at a math and science camp for children. She's been busy with that. I imagine she'll link up with Deena again when she has more time."

"I'll go see her. Would she be working today, I wonder?"

"It was a Saturday that time I saw her in the shop, so she may well be."

"I'm going to have a little snooze and then I'll head over to Manhattan. Macy's. Everybody's heard of it, so it should be easy to find."

"It's in Herald Square. West Thirty-Fourth Street. Ask anybody around there, and they'll point the way."

He thanked Brennan, got out of the car, and went up to his room. Des was out, so he flopped down on the bed and slept for a good two hours. He awoke refreshed, got himself washed, and asked the man at the desk how best to get to Herald Square. The man told him where to get the subway, how to get the tickets, and all that, and once again, Shay was the gawping tourist. Another new experience, hurtling along under the earth in a subway train, which he found fascinating. Then he was above ground again in the blistering heat. He strolled around Herald Square for a few minutes, again marvelling at the buildings and the crowds, and then made his way to Macy's department store. It was massive, several storeys high, and seemed to take up an entire city block.

He went inside, relieved to get out of the heat, and was dazzled by all the goods on display. He was wishing his ma and sisters were with him to enjoy it all. Them and . . . no, he didn't want to think about Allie Cotter. He put off asking where the ladies' knickers department was, and took himself for a walk around. Rode up and down on the escalators, which were made of wood. Now, who should he ask about the knickers department, a man or a woman? Young or old? He decided on a young woman at one of the cosmetic display cases.

"Excuse me. Could you tell me where I can find the, em, ladieswear departments, you know, the nightgowns and all that? It's for . . ." He could feel the blush going up his face.

The young one laughed and said, "It's for your sister. She broke her leg and can't get out shopping, right?"

"No, no, I know a girl who works in it, but I've never been to Macy's before."

"Never been to New York before, by the sounds of it. That's okay." And she gave him the directions without any more slagging.

He thanked her and headed in the right direction. When he found the place, he felt like a man who'd spent his entire life in a monastery. Women were walking around wearing these things? He should try for a date with a New York girl before returning home to Ireland. Again, an image of Allie flashed through his mind, but again he banished the thought of her. He walked up to the girl working the counter, and said, "Excuse me. Is Deena in today?"

"Deena? Who's Deena?"

"Deena Breathnach."

"What? Brannock?"

"Em, she works here, in this department, and —"

"Yeah, sure she does. Do you know how many creeps come in here and say they're looking for Susie, and 'Oh, she's not here right now? That's okay, I'll just hang around and wait.' And look at all the stuff on our racks. There's no Deena here, so why don't you take yourself off to the men's department, or go buy yourself a dirty magazine to be your girlfriend tonight. Your *Deena*."

Oh, God, she thinks I'm a creep, a pervert, Shay said to himself. But what about Deena? "No," he said, "you've got it all wrong. Deena works here, I know that, and —"

"No, she doesn't."

"Can I ask you then: how long have you worked here yourself?"

"I've been here nearly two months, and I never saw or heard of anybody named Deena."

"Could you do me a favour?"

The look on her face said that if she did him any kind of a favour she'd come away from it crawling with bugs.

"I just mean, could you ring the manager, or somebody, and ask if Deena is working in another department?"

She obviously decided that was her best hope for getting rid of him, so she went to the phone, made a call, asked her question, and gave a *just as I thought* nod at the answer. She thanked the person on the phone and said, "She used to work here. Now she doesn't. She quit." The salesgirl turned from him then. "Oh, hello, ma'am. Do you need some help there?"

Shay the creep crept away.

CHAPTER XXI

B rennan was the wheelman Saturday night with his da, Shay, and Desmond as his passengers. They were headed for the West Side of Manhattan, where they planned to enjoy a drink at the White House Bar in Hell's Kitchen. Fortune smiled down in the form of a parking spot a couple of blocks from the bar, which was located on Forty-Fifth Street and the Avenue, that being Tenth Avenue. The bar was jammed, but the men behind the bar were able for it, and Brennan and his companions did not have long to wait for their pints and whiskey. They stood by the bar and looked around. There were as many women as men in the place, and most of them were dressed to the nines.

Shay said, "Good thing me and Desmond here put on collared shirts and jackets, well, like yourselves." He nodded towards Brennan and his father. "We wouldn't want to disgrace ourselves by looking as if we just came off trotting the bogs of Ireland."

"Sure, you're grand," Brennan assured him. Then, to Declan, "What's going on here tonight, Da?"

"Wait for it," Declan replied, and then began quizzing Des Creaghan about his family in Dublin and his work with RTÉ. Des was in the midst of one of his goofy alliterative news headlines when he interrupted himself to exclaim, "Jesus! Is that Elizabeth Taylor just walked in?!"

Brennan whipped around to see the stunning woman who had just appeared at the entrance and was being greeted by a throng of people around the door. She did indeed look like Elizabeth Taylor, and he could understand why Desmond and Shay were goggling at her. But Brennan knew who she was.

Declan explained. "That's Maureen Spillane, married to Michael. Their wedding anniversary is tomorrow, but that's Sunday so they're having the hooley tonight. And here comes himself."

The man at the door, who would stand out anywhere for his black Irish good looks and his pricey suit, was instantly recognizable as Mickey Spillane. The Gentleman Gangster. Brennan had met him on a couple of brief occasions, but knew him more from the newspapers. He was just under forty years old, Brennan knew. The couple looked like, and were treated like, royalty.

Des and Shay continued to gawp at them, and Declan laughed. "Haul your eyeballs back into your heads there, lads. If you behave yourselves, I'll introduce you. Mickey Spillane runs things over here." Declan didn't elaborate, but everybody in the room, including Garda Rynne and the man from RTÉ, knew that what Spillane "ran" were the rackets on New York's West Side. He was the head of the Hell's Kitchen Irish mob. What Brennan didn't know — had never known — was just how well his father knew Spillane and his associates.

"And," Declan continued, "his lovely wife is the former Maureen McManus. Her father is Eugene, one of the McMani, as they are known here. The McMani pretty well control the political fate of the people in this area through their leadership of the Midtown Democratic Club. Politics marries the street. Everyone seems to agree it's a fine match."

A few minutes later it was time for the introductions. Declan stood and motioned for Brennan and the two visitors to follow. Spillane turned from the group surrounding him and had a big smile on his face. "Declan! Good to see you. You've met my lovely bride. Maureen, you remember Declan Burke."

She turned her dazzling smile on him and said, "Of course I do. How are you, Declan?"

"Couldn't be better, Maureen. Congratulations, the two of you. You did well for yourself, Mickey."

Spillane laughed and said, "I sure did."

"I believe you've met my son, Brennan."

"How's it going, Brennan?"

"Fine altogether, Michael. Congratulations to you and Mrs. Spillane on your anniversary."

"Thank you, Brennan."

"And this is Desmond Creaghan," Declan said. "Des is a reporter with RTÉ back home. And Shay here works with him. Watch your words now, Mickey."

"Oh, we won't worry about that. No news to write about in this city. Nothing ever happens here!"

Declan made a bit of small talk with Spillane and the lovely Maureen, and then noticed all the other well-wishers queued up, so the Burkes and their guests said goodbye and returned to their table.

"I can tell you," said Declan, "that when Jem O'Daly was here on the West Side, he took to dressing like Mickey there. He had suits tailored to fit him perfectly, made of some sort of costly wool, and his shirts were a brilliant white. May have been silk, I don't know. And his hair was brushed over like Mickey's. Oh, yer man O'Daly cut quite a figure on the streets of New York."

"Must have been earning a good wage to afford all that clobber," Creaghan said.

"He was a good earner, from everything I heard," allowed Declan.

The word "wage" would not have been all that accurate to describe how O'Daly had been earning his living, Brennan reflected. It wasn't a clock he'd been punching during his time in Hell's Kitchen.

A few minutes later, Declan got up and went over to a hefty-looking, dark-haired man, sitting at the other side of the room.

Des said, "Well, that's star quality, what?" He was referring to Mickey, Maureen, and their attendants. "There's nothing surreptitious about yer man Spillane. He doesn't skulk around in the shadows."

"True," Brennan agreed. "Everything my oul fella told you tonight is common knowledge. Or he'd not have said a word about it. Not a man for loose talk is Declan Burke."

"I can well believe it," Shay said. "I know from long acquaintance with your uncle Finn that Declan's time in Dublin as an . . . well, all I'm saying is that Finn was never an open book about your da."

"As you say, I can well believe it."

Brennan was sure that his father's history as an IRA man in Dublin was a subject never broached in Christy Burke's bar, even though Christy's own exploits were still sung during music sessions in the pub. Brennan wondered what conclusions Shay Rynne and Des Creaghan had drawn from the fact that Declan Burke and Mickey Spillane were first-name pals. As far as Brennan knew — and with oul Dec you had to read between the lines in order to approach anything close to knowledge — any working relationship he and Spillane may have had was in the past. Declan was a legitimate businessman. But then there was Shay's father, back in Dublin, a first-name pal of Jemser O'Daly. And he was a suspect in the killing of O'Daly's brother-in-law. What was the real story there? Not for the first time, Brennan reflected on what we don't know about our fathers, who art in line for heaven. Or elsewhere.

Declan returned to the table with the man he'd gone over to see, a man Brennan had never met. Everyone was introduced to Davey — no surname offered — and Shay maintained his cover as an RTÉ researcher. Davey grabbed an empty chair from another table and pulled it over. Declan asked what he was drinking and got up to buy the round. When they all had fresh drinks in front of them, Davey inquired as to the kind of things Desmond and Shay reported on. Des did the talking and made himself into a wide-eyed, dazzled cub reporter who hoped to write about the colourful life of Jemser O'Daly in the Big Apple. And he hoped to get a glimpse of the New York that his readers and listeners could never hope to see for themselves!

Davey took on the role of man about town, a role he seemed to slip into without effort, and he talked about the different neighbourhoods in Manhattan, rich, famous, infamous, poor, dangerous. Then he lowered his voice and said, "Things are a little touchy here on the West Side these days. These years. The Spillane-Coonan war, you know. Now there's no doubt about my loyalty to Mickey, but for me to be seen gabbing away to strangers . . . No disrespect intended, Declan. Or to you guys, either." He looked from Shay to Creaghan. "But how about we move over to the Landmark? The centre of the action tonight is here in the White House. I'm not going to spill any secrets, 'cause I don't want somebody hearin' about it and spilling my guts out on the sidewalk! But, even so, I'd feel better talking to you away from everybody here."

"Sure," Declan said, "we can meet you there, Davey. Why don't we take our leave first? Say our goodbyes. And then you follow half an hour after us."

"Yeah, that sounds good."

So Declan walked over to the Spillane table, where congratulations were offered again, along with good wishes for the future. Brennan had to give Creaghan a little nudge to tear him away from the aura surrounding Maureen McManus Spillane. Well, what man wouldn't stand in awe?

⁕

The Landmark Tavern was a brilliant old Irish pub in Hell's Kitchen, Eleventh Avenue. Been there since the 1860s. It had a tin ceiling and a well-stocked, long mahogany bar. Brennan and the others made their selections from the glimmering bottles and taps, then found a table and sat down to enjoy their drinks. Declan warned them that they might see a ghost, that of a young girl from Ireland, who had come to New York during the Famine and then died up on the third floor, where her spirit remained to this day. She sometimes wandered along the halls. There were other ghosts, too, or that had always been the rumour.

Then the talk returned to earth. Des Creaghan said, "It sounds to me, Declan, as if Jem O'Daly kind of modelled himself after Mickey Spillane. Wanted to be seen as another Gentleman Gangster. I don't recall seeing O'Daly in his early career in Dublin swanning about in suits and shirts that would cost a few months' wages for the regular working man. Now, sure, he's Mr. High-Fashion Avenue, but not back then."

"I imagine that's what he did," Declan agreed. "He'd have taken a look at Spillane: he'd have seen heads turning whenever he walked by, and he'd have said, 'I want some of that.' And Spillane probably took his cue from one of our earlier characters who made a name for himself in New York. An Irish family who came here from Liverpool. You'll have heard of Owney Madden."

"Oh, yeah."

"He had a violent history, did Madden. Left a few skeletons behind him before he'd left his youth behind him. And he got in with a criminal gang here called the Gophers. They were battling it out with another crowd called the Hudson Dusters — cokeheads back in the early 1900s."

"Coke!"

"That's right. Cocaine even back then. Hence the name 'Dusters,' I suppose. But Owney really came into his own with Prohibition. He imported booze from Canada, from Cuba. Bootleg liquor, rum-running, speakeasies, and tributes from shopkeepers and businessmen who didn't want their shops burnt out, that's where Owney made buckets of money. And he was a fella with ambitions to move up in the world. In society. That's how it was that many of our people managed to succeed. They came in off the ships as dirt-poor immigrants with no prospects. The rackets, gangsterism, that was the way to make money and move up. And if anybody moved up, it was Owney 'The Killer' Madden. When he wasn't out there shooting a rival, he was seen in the speakeasies, the clubs, the dancehalls; he became known as the Duke of the West Side. You know the film star Mae West? Well, she was Owney's mot."

"No!" Des exclaimed.

"Yes. And all kinds of other stars came to his club. And in the early 1930s, he made an alliance of sorts with a fella by the name of Lucky Luciano, a Sicilian. This opened the way to cooperation between the Italian and the Irish . . ."

"Communities?" Brennan said.

"Smart arse," his father countered. "Owney was a sharp dresser. The rich-looking suits, the stylish overcoat, the fedora on his head. These fellas became glamorous figures, partying with celebrities. The ultimate city sophisticates. You've seen films with James Cagney? Well, Cagney modelled himself after Owney Madden."

Brennan enjoyed hearing his father expound on New York life. It was a rare occasion when Declan Burke was so talkative. But Brennan knew that every word of it was public knowledge; otherwise, the newcomers would not have been treated to a talkative Declan Burke.

"I'm going to need more than a radio broadcast for all this, Declan. I'm going to need my own show on the telly."

"Sure, you'll make your fame and fortune out of this little excursion." Declan turned to Shay then. "Not sure how much you'll get out of it, Seamus."

"Ah, we'll see. But it's been worth the trip already, even if I never hear another word!"

That's when Davey arrived over from the White House, got himself a drink, and sat down at the table. They chatted a bit about the Spillanes' anniversary party and the power of the McMani in the Democratic Party in New York. Then the conversation turned to Jem O'Daly.

"O'Daly, right. He sure enjoyed the advantages the mobs have to offer here in New York: booze, broads, and betting, as they say. He was friendly with Mickey Spillane and his boys. And he looked to Spillane for inspiration. I know O'Daly has been described in Dublin as a Robin Hood type. Well, here it was people coming to the White House bar, and telling Mickey Spillane their troubles. Like one of the old chieftains back in Ireland, head of the clan, dispensing favours and, well, maybe some disfavours, too. A son got mugged? A member of somebody's family had medical bills to cover? Mickey listened and helped if he could. And O'Daly tried to do the same, make a big name for himself, during his time here.

"Too bad he wouldn't haul his ass back over here and assist Spillane in his time of need. I mean the war that's going on between

Spillane and Jimmy Coonan's gang. If you saw Coonan, you'd not believe he's a vicious little fucker; he looks like an angel with his blondy hair and his baby face. But he's brutal and, bad luck to us all, he's the new breed that's coming up behind Spillane. So Mickey's gotta watch his back with Coonan's boys out there. And, of course, he's got that touchy relationship with the Italians. You know who I mean."

Everybody knew who Davey meant. There was the Hell's Kitchen Irish mob, and then there was *the Mob*.

Davey leaned over and said in a quiet voice, "I'm talkin' about the Five Families. But the West Side rackets have kind of, you know, been divided up between their mob, their various families, and our lot, Mickey's gang. And it works, as long as Mickey pays up where he has to. The Italians get their cut; the Italians don't fuck with Mickey."

"Sounds as if you'd have to be a diplomat as well as a hard man to survive in all this," Desmond said.

"Now, Mickey Spillane, he's no choirboy either; he's got a long sheet, long criminal record, God knows. But he doesn't deal in drugs, and he doesn't have that extreme violent streak you see in Coonan. Not that he's never raised a hand to anybody. And some of the other guys, well . . . You being Irishmen like myself, you'll enjoy this: the guys in *their* mob think *our* guys are fearless. The Italians think us Micks are crazy brave! There may be a touch of violence they see in some of our fellas. And that's not a bad thing to have them thinking." He lifted his glass to his fellow Micks and drained it. Des went to the bar and got him another.

"Thanks, Des. So anyway, Jem O'Daly made a splash during his time here. And then" — Davey snapped his fingers — "just like that, he was gone. And he didn't go around shaking hands and saying goodbyes, and having people waving at him as his plane took off from JFK. The fact that he didn't do that suggests that maybe, just maybe, somebody was on the lookout for him, and he couldn't take the chance even of being spotted at the airport."

"What do you mean?" asked Des.

"I don't think it was his decision to leave our city."

"Ah."

"One day O'Daly was here, in the neighbourhood here, and next day he had vanished. And then he popped up in Canada."

"Canada! First I've heard of this! What was he doing there?" Des asked. "What part of Canada?"

"Montreal. Somebody spirited him outta here. Got him across the border. For his own protection. I have a pal up there, and he called me on the phone one night and said, 'What the fuck's with this guy O'Daly? I've been asked to hide him up here till he can get a flight out.'"

Brennan saw Davey shoot a glance towards Declan, meeting nothing but a blank look in return. But Declan must have known about the Montreal connection, if he knew Davey was the man to ask about all this.

"What I heard, and I don't know if there's anything to it, was that his disappearance had something to do with the Italians!" Davey pitched his voice even lower. "One of the Families? I dunno. That's as much as I ever heard."

CHAPTER XXII

It was Sunday afternoon, and Shay looked on as Desmond engaged in a furious debate with himself. "O'Daly took a detour to Montreal. That means my story took a detour to Montreal. I'd like to go up there but, Christ, I've only a few days in New York. And then Phil Durnahan's taking a crowd up to Boston, so I want to do that as well."

"There's no guarantee you'd get anything useful if you fecked off to Montreal, Des."

"Yeah, I'm sure you're right. But you'll be going around with Brennan again, I imagine. And if you see Declan again, or Davey . . ."

"If I hear any more about it, you'll be the first to know."

"Good man. I'll stay here in the USA."

All the talk about Jem O'Daly's time in New York, the men he associated with, and now the mysterious detour to Montreal, this all gave rise to hope in Shay, hope that O'Daly was too immersed in his criminal ways to ever give them up. A man like that would be a much more likely suspect in a murder than a man with weaknesses, a man who'd been dealt a bad hand in life. A man like Talkie Rynne. How on earth was Talkie doing these days, with suspicion of murder

299

hanging over his head? Shay had a sudden urge to speak to him. It was evening in Dublin, and a Sunday. His father would almost certainly be home. It was time for a long-distance telephone call.

He rang the hotel's reception desk and told the man he was going to make a call to Ireland. The man told him to go ahead, and the long-distance charges would be added to the bill for the room. Shay's mother answered the phone. "Ah, Shay, what a delightful surprise, you ringing all the way from New York. Is it everything they say it is?"

"Everything and more, Ma! I can't wait to get home and tell you all about it." He gave her a few of the highlights of big city life and then asked her to put his father on the line. He hadn't told his family the real reason for his trip to New York, just told them he and Des were off on a spree.

"Shay!" Talkie said. "How many punts will they be taking off you for this call? Dollars, I should say."

"Nothing to worry about. I'm wondering how you're doing, Da." Shay could tell from his voice that he'd been drinking.

"Well, they haven't sent a posse after me yet. Isn't that what they do over in America?"

"Haven't been around to ask questions or anything?"

"They haven't."

Talkie chatted a bit about his work for Burke Transport; he was enjoying it and he liked the other lads who worked there. There was a bit more conversation and then Shay said, "Take care, Da. I'll be seeing you soon. Put Ma back on the line, will you?" Talkie said goodbye and told Deirdre to take the receiver again.

"How's he really doing, Ma?"

"Em, he's —"

"I'm on the pig's back, Seamus!" his father shouted into the phone. "Don't be concerning yourself."

But he was concerned. They ended the call, and Shay was left with the certain knowledge, just from his mother's tone of voice, that his oul fella was not doing well at all.

But Shay had somebody else to worry about here in New York. He turned his mind to finding Deena Breathnach. This was a city of eight million people, and he had no idea where to start. He didn't want Des in on this; it had the makings of a great story for the news, and Des might find it hard to resist. So Shay would speak to Brennan alone. Shay had the phone numbers for the Burkes' home and the parish house, so he announced that he was going out for a little walk, and walk he did, until he found a working phone box. Didn't attempt his old phone-tapping trick there. He reached Brennan at Saint Kieran's.

"Brennan, I'm sorry for bothering you again."

"It's not a bother, Shay. You think a few nights out on the town skulling pints and listening to stories is a spot of bother?"

Shay laughed and said, "When you put it that way, no, I guess not. It's been great craic seeing New York with you and your oul fella, not to mention the other characters you introduced me to. The cops and robbers, one might say."

"And there are some who are in both categories at the same time. What are you up to today?"

"Well, that's why I rang. Didn't want to mention this last night, but I went to Macy's earlier in the day."

"Yes?" The tone of his voice suggested that he knew what he was about to hear.

"No sign of Deena in the, em, department where she'd been working. I spoke to a young one who's been working there for almost two months, and persuaded her to ring somebody in management to see if Deena had switched jobs in the store. All I got back was 'She used to work here, but she quit.'"

"Fuck," said the priest.

"So I'm wondering how the hell I could go about finding her."

"I'm sure your thinking is the same as mine, Shay. She's returned to her former profession. The girls make a fortune here; of course, most of it is handed over to the pimps."

"Fucking leeches."

"Yeah. So you're wondering how we can find her."

Shay liked the sound of that "we." Brennan was going to help him yet again. "I wouldn't know where to start, Brennan. It's not like the Grand Canal in Dublin. Considering the size of New York City and the population, posing as a john wouldn't get me anywhere near her! So tell me what you think of this: I don't want to get her in the soup, don't want to get her arrested, but would it make any sense to ask somebody in the NYPD? Mike Cadigan maybe? Him being Irish and her —"

"Him being Irish hardly makes him unique in the New York Police Department! You can't swing a cat in this city without hitting an Irish cop. So no reason to think Cadigan would know a particular immigrant from Ireland. But Bernie Silverberg might have some ideas. I know from some of his tales in O'Malley's that he used to work vice. It was years ago, but couldn't hurt to ask him. He works here in Queens, and he works weekends. I'll ring you back if I have any luck tracking him down."

"Thanks again, Brennan. I owe you big time."

Brennan put on a rough New Yorker voice and said, "Ya betta be careful who ya owe favahs to. Somebody may try to collect on that debt someday."

"What's that now, Brennan? If it's still Brennan Burke who's speaking to me."

"Yeah, this is Faddah Boik tawkin'. Someday I may came after you with a collection plate, and you betta pay up."

"Ha! You can be sure I will."

"Sit tight now. I'll ring you when I've got hold of Bernie."

"Sure. Ring me at the hotel."

☙

A couple of hours after that, Shay and Brennan were sitting in an air-conditioned coffee shop waiting for Sergeant Bernie Silverberg. Shay said to Brennan, "If I'm going to be asking a favour of a police officer, I'm not going to feel right about lying to him. You know, keeping up this pretence that I'm a reporter, or a researcher for Des Creaghan. I'll want him to know I'm a guard."

"That won't pose a problem for you. Bernie will have done undercover work himself, no doubt. If not, he'll be well familiar with fellas who do. Won't be a problem."

So, when Silverberg arrived and they were all sitting with cups in front of them — coffee for Shay and Bernie, tea for Brennan — Shay apologized for his deception and explained why he had maintained the fiction during his visit. "It wasn't done to pull the wool over your eyes or those of Sergeant Cadigan; it was more for, well, other people we were going to meet. On the West Side of the city." He stopped well short of saying, *Some of Declan Burke's underworld acquaintances in Hell's Kitchen.*

Silverberg just shrugged with his shoulders and hands, then said, "Nu?"

Whatever that meant, he didn't seem in the least offended. So Shay decided to get on with his request. "What I'm trying to do, Bernie, is find a girl who came over here last autumn. Brennan may have explained all this. She's from Dublin, worked as a prostitute over there. She witnessed something, a crime being committed in Dublin, and was the target of some intimidation. Thanks to the efforts of Brennan here, she was able to get away, come to New York, start a new life. She was working at Macy's, but . . . now she isn't."

"You're afraid she's returned to the life she knows best. Except New York is a much bigger stage for a girl to play on. Much more dangerous. I'm not saying it wouldn't have been dangerous for a hooker in Dublin; it's like that for working girls wherever they are in the world. But, well, everything's bigger and badder here in New York."

"Right. I'd really like to find her."

"Think you can change her mind again?"

"Hoping."

Silverberg looked skeptical; what New York cop wouldn't? "Have you any idea how much some of those girls earn in a year? Sixty, seventy thou a year, some of them. Lot more than being a sales clerk in a department store."

"Christ, that's a whack of money! But the girls don't get to keep it all."

"That's for sure. They're making their pimps rich. If a girl tries to rip off her pimp, fuhgeddaboudit! He'll beat the shit out of her. Prostitution is big business in this country. Couple a hundred thousand hookers — there's several thousand of them here in New York — at least twenty bucks a transaction, five or six transactions a day, maybe more. And there's the guys who run the hotels; they get their take from renting out the rooms. And there's the massage parlours. And then there's the girls that are higher up the ladder. They look down on the ones on the lower rungs. Those girls up near the top, call girls and them, they make way more than your regular little ho. And above that you have the women who run the ritzy houses and charge big bucks for the services their girls provide. Add all that up? Comes to billions of dollars a year. In a country founded by a bunch of Puritans!" Silverberg turned to Brennan. "The ones who came over on the *Mayflower*. In the 1600s. Weren't they even purer than the regular Puritans?"

"A breakaway sect, that's right. Began calling themselves Pilgrims."

"Wonder if they had any prossies on the ship, eh, Brennan? Well, buying and selling sex is big business here, and has been for a long, long time. And those who make their living from it are in no hurry to give up the wads of cash they earn from it night after night."

"But even if I can't talk her out of leaving the street," Shay said, "I'd like to see her."

"I'll ask around, Shay. Give me all the details."

"I will, but I wouldn't like to see her get, em . . ."

"We have bigger fish to fry than some poor girl working her tail off. We get an average of three to four murders a day here. So don't worry about a girl out there doing the oldest tricks in the book."

"Thanks, Bernie." So Shay gave him her full name, age, physical description, anything he could come up with, and his phone number at the hotel, and Silverberg said he'd do his best.

❧

Shay and Desmond spent Monday touring around Brooklyn, and then Des, a lifelong sports fan, said he wanted to see the baseball stadium where the New York Yankees played. That meant another trip to the Bronx, but this time it would be daylight. They asked the man at their hotel's front desk which subway to take, and he looked at them as if they'd lost all sense. "You guys wanna go *where?* And you wanna go on the *subway?* Are you shittin' me?"

"Em, no, we're not," Shay answered.

"Do you value your life?"

"Are you suggesting that others might not value our lives?"

The man was shaking his head at the idiocy of these two tourists. "Listen, a pal of mine drives a cab. I'll call him for you. He'll take you there and bring you back here. You guys agree with him on a fare for the round trip. And don't get out of the cab in the Bronx, okay? Stay in the car with the doors locked. Got it?"

"Got it," Des replied.

The man made a call, and his pal the taxi driver arrived shortly afterwards. The hotel man gave the driver a look that could hardly be missed. It said, *Take these two lunatics to the Bronx, and bring them back alive.*

Well, it wasn't long before they saw his point. And the taxi driver drove the point home even more, by starting the tour on Park Avenue in Manhattan with its posh apartment buildings, glitzy shops and automobiles, and its richly groomed inhabitants. A very different story on the other side of the Harlem River, where they found themselves on Park Avenue in the Bronx. The picture was even more stark in the light of day than it had been after dark. Again, they saw an expanse of burnt-out or abandoned buildings, yards full of rubble, and people hanging around or lying in the debris, looking as if they'd never heard, and never would hear, of the American Dream. Des got his look at Yankee Stadium, but it was overshadowed by what he'd seen all about him in the Bronx. When he and Shay were back in their Brooklyn hotel with drinks in their hands, Des said he didn't know whether to write a story or incite a revolution.

"They already had one."

"Yeah, the American Revolution. I can't decide whether that's an historical fact or a contradiction in terms."

"Well, whatever you'd like to see happen here, Des, it will take more than a shocking exposé on Ireland's public broadcaster."

"You're right, of course. Maybe I could do more with it if I was back with the *Dublin Daily Knows*. 'Posh Park Avenue poseurs don't pay their portion of taxes to prop up the poor . . ." But his heart wasn't in it. He recognized a hopeless situation when he saw one.

He looked at his watch. "Half four. So, half nine at home. I told Fiona I'd ring her today." He picked up the phone and went through the rigmarole of making a long-distance call to Ireland. It took a few rings, but she answered. "Fiona, love, I'd have rung you earlier but we had a chance to see Yankee Stadium. Baseball, yeah. You did? Well, that's where we were, me and Shay. Oh?" Des turned to Shay and had a grin on his face. "That sounds interesting. He's right here. You can tell him yourself." And he handed Shay the receiver.

"Hi, Shay. I tried to ring you and Des earlier, but you were out. I'd better get to it, since you fellas are paying for long distance! Guess who's back in town?"

The first name that came to mind was Jane, but he was not about to say that. "Who, the Black and Tans?"

"Ah, no, they're in the North. No. It's Allie!"

"What?" *Allie!*

"Yes, Allie Cotter is home from Norway."

A quick intake of breath, and then Shay tried to sound casual. "Oh, is she?"

"She is. I saw her."

"Home for a little visit?"

"Home for good, sounds like."

"Ah."

"And yes, if you're wondering, she did mention your name."

"Was I wondering?"

"Well, I thought you might be. And it was funny, Shay. She asked about me and Des, and several of the people we grew up with. Then, oh so casually, as if it was an afterthought, 'Oh, how is Shay Rynne these days?'"

"An afterthought. I get it."

"You should get it, Garda Rynne. You've questioned suspects, have you not? And when they blather on about some things and then pretend to be offhand about something else, pretend it's no big thing at all? You suspect it's something important, amn't I right?"

"Mmm."

Fiona continued, "And she was just as offhand when she said, 'Married now, is he? Houseful of little Rynnes?' And I just as off-handedly said you were not. She is living with another girl. I didn't recognize the name, but they've a flat somewhere in Drumcondra. Which is convenient for the bus or a walk to work, because our Allie is working at the Gate Theatre. Box office and I think other jobs there as well."

"Brilliant!"

"Des and I saw *The Importance of Being Earnest* there last year, and there's another Wilde play coming up in the autumn some-time. Anyway, you'll know where to find her. And there you have it. Breaking news. Missus Desmond Creaghan, RTÉ News, Dublin."

"Thanks, Fiona! I'll give you back to Des."

Des spoke to her for a couple more minutes, told her he'd be seeing her soon and then ended the call.

Fuck! Now what? Shay had acted calm while talking to Fiona, but he wasn't calm at all. Allie was back in town, living with another girl, not with a princeling of the Norwegian royal family, and she had asked about Shay. What should he do when he got back to Dublin? Walk over to the Gate Theatre, and say, *Hello. A ticket for my usual seat. Wait a minute, don't I know you?* No, he'd have to resist the temptation. She was the one who'd left; let her be the one to come and see him. Hold on here, stop the lights! He had no reason to think she'd be coming to see him. She'd asked about him, sure, but it would have been a bit odd if she hadn't, after asking about the rest of the old gang.

And what would he do if she did show up at his door? It would no doubt be nothing more than an old friend coming to say hello. Just because he still had a grá for her after more than two years apart didn't mean she still felt anything for him. But pretend for a minute she did. What about the other girls he'd walked out with? What about Jane Blytheford? What had he felt for Jane? He'd enjoyed being with her, no question, enjoyed her company and their talk about books and all that. And he sure as hell liked her when they were alone together and she abandoned that cool, calm, British stiff-upper-lip demeanour. But what was really going on there? Shay had thought all along that Allie had left him for someone better, someone a few classes above him and herself. He thought she was determined to rise above him and their upbringing in the Corpo flats. She was out to find a man taller, fairer, better than Shay, and she'd found a Norseman who met that need.

But then the question arose, something that would be obvious to anyone reading his mind, to anyone who knew the two of them at all: Is that what he himself had been doing? Chasing after the Trinity girls, the educated class of girls, and then the English bird? Lecturer at Trinity College, no less. Were he and Allie trying to rise above each other? Above themselves? Above their station in life? The suspicion of it filled him with shame. But no, that couldn't be right. He did not think that way. Allie? He had no idea what she was thinking, now that she had returned home to Ireland.

As for Des, he would be flying home on Wednesday night, and he wanted to see Boston before he left the country. So he boarded Phil Durnahan's tour bus on Tuesday morning for the trip to Massachusetts. He would have one night in Boston, and Phil offered to take him directly to the airport the following night for his flight home to Dublin.

❧

The phone rang for Shay on Tuesday afternoon. Bernie Silverberg. The good news was that he'd found Deena; the bad news was that he'd found her working the streets of New York. "I think it's her, Shay. I asked around, and my sources tell me there's a girl calling herself Diana, but she's Irish and fits the description. She's working Eighth Avenue. If you cruise along there tonight, you may spot her. If not, wait around, 'cause she may be up in one of the rooms servicing a john. The hotel she uses is a dump called Bobbi-Sherleen's, on Eighth near the corner of Forty-Sixth Street."

"I really appreciate this, Bernie."

"No problem. Be careful out there. Where you got hookers, you got pimps, junkies, muggers. Guys'd stick a knife in ya for fifty cents or a pack of smokes. Whaddya expect?"

"Right. I'll keep an eye on things. Thanks, Bernie."

So that night, it was Garda Rynne and Father Burke out cruising for hookers. They drove to the West Side and then walked along Eighth Avenue. There was no shortage of working girls, and the other characters on the avenue were just the sorts described by Sergeant Silverberg, except for the respectable-looking couples making their nervous, edgy way to the restaurant or the theatre. And there was Bobbi-Sherleen's hotel. It wasn't the Waldorf; it wasn't the Shelbourne. Not that Shay had ever enjoyed the luxury of staying in, either. But he'd sleep rough on the street before he'd lay his head on a pillow in this place. He saw a couple of girls go in with men, but no sign of Deena.

Shay noticed Brennan eyeing a bar across the street from the kip. "A small one would go down nicely now," he said, "and we can keep our target in sight."

"Sure, might as well."

So they walked into the bar, which wasn't all that bad, got two glasses of whiskey, and sat down at a table with a view of the street. Shay was sure he wasn't the only one tempted to down the whiskey in a couple of swallows, but they nursed the drinks and kept watch.

Brennan said, "I hope to God we can find her and help her out. I don't mean save her from a *life of sin* or any of that roaring-from-the-pulpit sort of thing. I mean, save her life. It could well come to that here on these streets."

Shay's fingers tightened around his glass, and he looked out at the street. No sign of her.

They had just paid for and started in on their second glasses when a man came down the steps of the hotel. He was dressed in a light-weight summer suit and looked like a banker or an insurance man.

"A businessman from out of town who hasn't researched 'places to stay in New York,'" Brennan said, "or a client of the girls — there she is."

They bolted up from their seats. Shay put his unfinished whiskey on the table, Brennan finished his, and they rushed out of the place and across the street in a blare of car horns.

"Deena!" Shay called to her.

She turned and saw him. "Shay, for fuck's sake! What the fuck are you doing here?"

"You seem surprised, Deenie. A pleasant surprise, I hope!"

"A pleasant surprise, in yer hole! Oh! Father Burke!"

Deena was wearing a red miniskirt and a shirt in a black, white, and red pattern. The shirt had a high collar. Shay imagined a much skimpier top under the shirt. But he didn't dwell on it. Her clothing and her hair were clean; she didn't look much different from the other girls, the non-prostitutes, he had seen by the thousands on the streets of New York.

"What are yis doing here, or am I going to be sorry I asked?"

"I'm here researching recent Irish émigrés in the city, so what a happy coincidence —"

"Oh, yer bollocks, Shay. Howiyeh, Brennan?"

"Come with us for a bit, will you, Deena?"

"To Mass, Father?"

"Well, if you'd like. But I was thinking of a restaurant. We could all sit down for an evening meal."

"And a talk about my life on the streets of the big, bad city."

"No doubt it will come up in conversation."

"All right, all right. I'll follow yis. Where are we going?"

"I know of a good place a couple of blocks over."

She said no more as Shay fell in beside her, and they followed Brennan a couple of blocks west. He turned in at a nice-looking restaurant, and they all went inside. They focused on the menu and gave their orders for meat pie, fish and chips, lamb stew, and the beer and wine paired with them.

Then, "Fair play to yis. You caught me out."

"We weren't trying to catch you out, Deena," Shay said. "We're worried about you."

"Why don't you leave that to my mother?"

"I'm thinking the dangers you faced on the canal back home are multiplied many times here in New York. And your mother would have no idea."

"I'm a big girl, a grown-up. I can take care of myself."

His heart went out to her when she said it. Shay was a grown-up, and he'd never have fooled himself for a minute that he could take care of himself if he was outnumbered by a gang of thugs or out-weaponed by a gun-wielding psycho on these streets in the dark of night.

Then he noticed what she had done when she'd made her claim of invincibility. She had reached up and tugged the high collar of her shirt tighter around her neck. Maybe she hadn't even realized she was doing it. Shay glanced at Brennan. He had caught it, too.

"What happened, Deena?" Shay asked, nodding towards her collar. "You're with friends here."

He expected the usual defiance or a smart-arse remark, but no. She started shaking and said nothing for a moment, then, "If he finds out I've been talking to a cop, he'll kill me. That's something you just don't do; you *don't sign on your man.*"

Shay didn't bother to state the obvious: that he was a Dublin cop and had no jurisdiction here. He got to the point. "What did he do to you, Deena?"

"This is nothing compared to what's been done to some of the other girls."

"Show me."

It took her a few seconds to decide, then she peered about the room. Satisfied that nobody else was looking, she undid the top couple of buttons of her shirt and pulled it away from her back. Twisted around for them to see.

"Fucking hell!" Father Burke muttered in a low, deadly voice. "Who did that to you?"

Her upper back was covered with red welts. Shay had a vision of Burke doing a lot worse to whoever had hurt her like that. And Shay would have been right there with him.

"I can't tell you that," she whispered.

"What did the scumbag use on you?" Shay asked her.

"His belt." Tears started from her eyes, and she swiped at them with her wrist. "I'm telling you, other girls got it worse than this. One of them, this poor little one from a farm somewhere in the west of the country, her man burned her with a cigarette, all over her back! And d'yis know what she said to me about it?"

"I know what I hope she said."

"Yeah, right, Shay. You wish she described it in great detail at a court hearing for his sentencing. But no. She said, 'I deserved it. I stepped out of line.' I wanted to belt her myself!" Deena slapped her hand over her mouth and said, "No! I don't mean that. I didn't want to see her hurt at all. But how could she think she fucking deserved it? Then she went on about a girl needing a man to protect her, and she owed him for that, and she'd do whatever he told her to from then on. And that's what I'm expected to be! Grateful that my man is taking care of me! In return for the stash of banknotes I hand over to him at the end of every night."

Shay glanced over at Brennan, and those black eyes looked like burning coals. Shay was seeing Burke the assassin here, not Burke the kindly parish priest.

Deena spoke up again. "I'm not saying we weren't roughed up when we worked the canal back home. A pimp is a pimp, bad cess to them all. A lot of the girls were beaten there, too. But the scene is so much bigger here, so many people involved in it, and everybody seems so hyped up. I . . ."

"When did you get back into it?" Shay asked her. When, but he meant why.

She looked down at the table, avoiding his eyes.

"Deena?"

"I allowed myself to be *seduced*! That's how stupid I am. I fell for a clever line of flattery and promises." She lowered her voice and muttered, "Fucking eejit." Shay and Brennan stayed silent, waiting for more. "I met somebody at a bar not far from here. Got to talking about work, money, not enough of it, the great roaring times to be had in New York if only you could afford it. Went back to the bar, same crowd again. I mentioned a beautiful watch I'd seen in a shop window, with diamonds in it. Said I wished I could have one, but I was laughing when I said it. I could never afford something like that in a thousand years. And — it's a miracle — I could have it! And I did. Or one that looked quite like it. And I put it on and, ah, the luxury of it. And there was more where that came from. Tickets to Broadway shows, rock concerts. I could repay my kind benefactor later on, once I had the money for it. How could I make that much money? Easy."

She looked up at Shay and Brennan, and it was plain how wretched she felt. "Have yis ever met anybody as thick as that? As me? I'm so fucking stupid, I'm not good for anything but walking the street!"

Brennan spoke up then. "Deena, you're not stupid. And you are good enough for whatever you decide to do. We've all had the experience of falling for a clever line of gab."

"Who was it?" Shay demanded to know. "Who chatted you up, gave you the watch, promised you more? What's the man's name?"

There was a little burst of laughter from her then. "Man? D'yeh think I'm daft? It was a woman. You don't think I'd fall for any line a man would spin me, do yeh? Not at all. I can see right through a man."

"A woman!"

"Sure. She was brilliant. And there was me, thinking I'd met this wonderful new friend; we'd be mates. But of course she was working for a man, sent out to do some recruiting. And I'm such a . . . such a schmuck!"

"If we can come up with a plan to get you out of here," Brennan asked, "will you go along with it?"

She was weeping now and merely nodded her head. Shay noticed that people at nearby tables were sneaking glances at her. This wasn't Deena as Shay had known her. As a girl, and as a girl on the canal, she was never at a loss for words. Always had some defiance in her. Not now. Now she was broken.

"This is the big city, Deena," Brennan said. "There are people who live in one or the other of the boroughs who hardly ever go out of them. Fellas in Queens who rarely set a foot on the streets of Manhattan. It won't be hard to find you another place where you'll be safe."

"I don't think I could . . . I wouldn't really be away, though, would I? I'd hear the news, see the papers, I'd know what's happening on the streets. And in the shite hotels where all this goes on. And how could I resist coming into Manhattan, the shops, the theatres . . . I'd be afraid the temptation would never go away. But the price to be paid . . ."

"You'll find other work."

"I know, Brennan. And I really appreciate what you fellas are trying to do for me. But I just want to get away from here. If I go back home, though . . ."

Shay knew that her safety couldn't be guaranteed back home in Dublin. If it was a crony of Risteard Dermody who had tried to intimidate her out of testifying, would he go out and punish her, now that Dermody had been convicted? And even without that, it would be difficult for her to avoid returning to her well-worn path along the canal, once her old friends knew she was back in town.

Brennan said, "You may want to take some time to make a big decision like that. But you need a safe place to stay for now. My father knows a man who has rooms he rents out. Rents them to old folks, so it won't be exciting. But it'll be safe."

"I've had enough of exciting for a while!"

"I'll make the arrangements."

"Thanks, Father, for trying to save me from my sinful ways!" She was trying for a bit of her old bravado, but she couldn't quite pull it off.

Their meals arrived, and they concentrated on those. Brennan said there would be a place for her at the Burke family home in Queens until they could find an apartment for her. But she was having none of it. "I'll stay in my flat till I can find a place to rent."

"But won't that . . . Won't the man you're working for come looking for you if you don't turn up for work?"

"If he does, I'll give him a story he'll believe. Tell him I'll be out on the street again Wednesday night, and I'll make it up to him then. Remember: I'm good at play-acting. It's part of my job!"

"So it is," Brennan agreed, if reluctantly.

They exchanged telephone numbers and Brennan and Shay split the bill for the meal. Then they parted for the evening, Deena insisting that she would take a taxi home.

The following day, Brennan was sitting across from his father at the family's kitchen table, the two of them enjoying a smoke and a cup of tea. Brennan had just told Declan about Shay's interest in talking to Davey again, this time about Jem O'Daly's sudden urge to visit Montreal.

"Well, go ask him. Davey's not what you'd call elusive quarry, Brennan. You can find him any night of the week at the Landmark. He has his supper with the missus, then he heads out for the night."

"Grand. We'll see him there. Now, I've another question for you." And he filled his father in on Deena Breathnach and her urgent need for a new place to live.

"She has to be somewhere safe until she decides whether to stay or to leave New York. She doesn't want to leave. She's enthralled with the city, but she'll never feel secure as long as this man, this pimp, thinks he owns her. And she's certain he'll try to get her back. He's already . . . been violent with her. It's a matter of pride as much as money with these fuckers; doesn't look good in front of the other men in the trade if he can't keep his woman in line."

Declan Burke looked as if he'd like to get violent with the man who thought he owned Deena Breathnach. "Get me his name, and where to find him."

"Da! Surely, you're not thinking of confronting this man yourself. That would be —"

"Brennan. Just get me the name and where he can be found."

God help us, thought Brennan, surely his father wasn't of a mind to walk up to this dangerous individual and . . . and what? But Brennan would go along for now. "I'll get the information from her."

"Go maith." Good. "And, in the meantime, I'll have a word with my pal who has the places for rent, see if he has a place available for her."

෴

Davey, as predicted, was not in the least elusive. Just after eight o'clock that evening, Brennan collected Shay in Brooklyn and they drove to the West Side of Manhattan. They went into the Landmark Tavern, and there was Davey sitting at a table with two other men. He lifted his glass in greeting. They ordered their pints and found another table across the room. Brennan put his glass down, got up, and walked over to Davey. He nodded to the other men and said, "When you have a minute, Davey, could you stop by and answer a couple of questions for our tourist friend there?"

"Sure."

He joined them a few minutes later, and they exchanged a bit of small talk before Shay said, "You mentioned a pal of yours who'd seen O'Daly in Montreal?"

Davey looked around, then answered, "Yeah. Buckley Whelan. You might be able to talk to him. They call him the Boxcar. Don't know why. Montreal has its own West End gang, like here. Irishmen like us. They call Montreal the 'Bank Robbery Capital of North America.' In some years, they did more bank jobs than in the big cities here in the USA."

"I didn't know that!" said Shay.

"They're fucking good at it, and some of the jobs were done by the Irish gangsters." Davey was full of talk about the fellas in the Point Saint Somebody, Montreal's Irish mob, the schemes they'd carried out. They were very good at what they did; they timed things precisely, got in and got out. "A veteran of these bank robberies is this guy Whelan. He was one of the best. You could talk to him. Tell him your old man — Brennan's old man — is a friend of Nicky the Shirt. Don't know how he got the name, but anyway, him and Whelan were partners a few years back when some goods came into the Port of Montreal and then were transported down here."

"What kind of goods?" Brennan asked.

"Stuff that guys like you and me would never shoot into our veins."

Davey saw something in Brennan's expression, and said, "Don't worry, Brennan. You'd just say that about your father to ease your way in with Whelan. Declan Burke would no more approve of heroin than he would of handing the USA back to the English. You can be sure of that."

Brennan had never thought otherwise, but it was good to have it confirmed.

"And besides," Davey went on, "Mickey Spillane was dead set against the drugs racket." His eyes darted around the room again. "Unlike some other guys we could name." He mouthed the words "Jimmy Coonan." The branch of the Irish mob that was at war with Spillane's crowd.

"How do we get to talk to Whelan?" Shay asked. "How far is Montreal from here?"

"Five-and-a-half, six-hour drive."

"*What?* Driving for that long, you'd get from the southern tip of Ireland to the northern tip, the length of the entire country! And if you ever did it all at once, you'd be shattered!"

Brennan laughed. "Seamus Rynne, have you never looked at a map? The distance from New York to Montreal is actually a bit longer than the length of Ireland, and it represents nothing but a little boreen" — a small road — "in the context of the entire continent."

"No need for you guys to hit the road," Davey said. "Just make a long-distance call to Magnan's Tavern in Montreal."

"He takes calls at the tavern?"

"That's probably the only place he takes calls, Shay. He's there every night. Like me; I'm *here* every night! In fact, I'm gonna make a call right now, to another guy I know, and get the number for you." And so he did. A few minutes later he was back at the table and handed Shay a slip of paper with "Magnan's Tavern, Pointe Saint Charles, Montreal" on it, and the phone number.

Shay and Brennan thanked him, and he returned to his other companions. That's when Brennan filled Shay in on his conversation with his father about Deena. "Declan wants to know 'What is his name and where can he be found?'"

"Jaysus, Brennan! What's he going to do? Declan, I mean. He can't go up to the fucker and, well, what?"

"I think my oul fella's wiser than that."

317

"Hope to God he is."

"If we get the name from Deena, I'll insist on going with Declan if he thinks he's going to . . . take care of the situation."

"I have her number. Should I ring her from here?"

"Sure."

So Shay went off to use the telephone and came back, not with the pimp's name and address, but the address of Deena's flat. "She wouldn't say anything over the phone."

"She's home now, so."

"Let's go."

They drove to Deena's place, an apartment building with crumbling brick and rusting fire escape stairs, in midtown Manhattan. Shay said, "I'll go inside. You wait in the getaway car!"

He joined Brennan again a few minutes later, and handed him a slip of paper with the name and address of the man who thought he owned Deena Breathnach. Brennan pulled out into the street. Traffic was light, and he was able to make good time along the city streets. He heard a sudden squeal of tires and looked in the rear-view mirror. Glaring lights appeared in the mirror; an enormous car had roared past the little Volkswagen that had been behind him and the big boat of a car was now on Brennan's tail. "Mother of God!" he muttered.

Shay turned in his seat. "What the fuck is that?"

Brennan looked in the mirror again. He could make out the insignia of a Cadillac, souped up with a bright, metallic-red paint job, a huge aggressive-looking grille, and big, round glass covers over the headlights. "Pimpmobile," he said.

"What? You think that's Deena's pimp?"

"Hers or somebody else's who didn't like us being in the neighbourhood."

"So, pull over and let's have it out with the fucker!"

"No, he may be armed. Whoever he is. Or he may have some pals in the back seat. Can't tell from here."

"Christ! Speed up then, Brennan, and lose him."

"We're not going to have a car chase here, Shay. This isn't the films."

"But . . ."

Brennan decided to foil the man's expectations. He slowed down. This brought on several blasts of the horn from the Cadillac, and then from a line of other impatient New York drivers who had come up the street behind them. This must have been more attention than the Caddy jockey wanted; he made a sudden U-turn and was gone in another squeal of rubber on road.

Shay turned to watch the giant vehicle disappear. "I can't see him! Can't see in the windows of that thing."

"Tinted windows," Brennan said.

"If that was Deena's pimp, and he wanted to send a message to *us*, what's he going to —"

Brennan cut him off with a raised hand. Both of them knew that, whatever point the man thought he had made to the visitors to Deena's apartment, he'd be making a much more pointed statement to Deena herself. Brennan then indicated the piece of paper in his shirt pocket. "This tells us who he is and where he lives. I'll be handing it over to Declan."

Handing it over? Brennan could not quite imagine what Declan Burke would do with the information.

They made their way to Brooklyn. Brennan dropped Shay off with the assurance that he would keep him informed, and he drove to the house in Sunnyside. His mother greeted him at the door. "Are you stopping here for the night, Brennan?"

"No, I've an early Mass in the morning, and my other parish work. Just in to see Da for a minute."

She gave him a quick hug and a kiss on the cheek, and said, "He's downstairs."

Brennan went down to the family room and found his father watching a television documentary on the Second World War. He had a glass of whiskey in his hand. "Evening, Da."

"Ah, Brennan. Are you here for the night?"

"No, I'll be heading back to Saint Kieran's. Now I've something for you here, and you're going to promise you'll do nothing about it without speaking to me first."

"Are you the Pope now?"

"For now, and for our purposes here, I am. This is the name and address you asked for. The fucker followed us in his tarted-up boat of a car. I'll keep this until we come up with a plan."

"Give it over." He snatched the paper from Brennan's hand. Brennan reached for it, and Declan held it back. "Leave it with me."

"What are you going to do, Da?"

"I said leave it with me. Now, be off with you." There was no more conversation, and Brennan could read nothing in his father's cold-blue eyes.

CHAPTER XXIII

Brennan collected Shay at his hotel the next evening and headed for Sunnyside. "What did your father say?"

"All he said was, 'Leave it with me.' I don't know what he had in mind." Brennan turned his head to Shay. "I'll have a word with him after we fill him in on Davey's information about Montreal."

"Grand, so."

Declan was alone in the house when Brennan and Shay arrived. "Lads," he said, nodding to them. "Your mother is out seeing a play with a couple of her friends. *Man of La Mancha*." He said no more and waited for the news.

"We spoke to Davey at the Landmark," Brennan told him, "and he thinks there's a man in Montreal who can help us. Fella by the name of Whelan. Sounds as if he's a member of the, em, community there, which is similar to the community of Hell's Kitchen."

There was no reply from Declan Burke.

"Shay is going to see what Whelan can tell him about Jem O'Daly's hasty departure from here, and his arrival in Montreal."

"I see."

"So, we'll leave you a few bucks for the long-distance charges."

"Don't ring him from here."

"Why ever not, Da?"

Declan made no answer. What was the story here? Did he think someone was listening in on his calls? Who? Gangsters? The FBI? Did he not want a call to Magnan's Tavern in Montreal on his phone records in case of — in case of what? Well, Brennan was not going to pester him about it, with Shay in the room.

"No worries," Shay said then. "I'll ring him from my hotel."

"I'll come with you," Brennan told him. "Wait for me outside, would you, Shay? I'll be there in a minute." He gave Shay a wink of the eye when he said it.

"See you outside." And Shay left father and son alone.

Brennan faced Declan and said, "What are we going to do about Victor the pimp?"

Declan spoke in a broad New York accent. "Victah ain't gonna botha nobody no more."

"What? What do you mean? What happened?"

"I mean Deena has nothing more to fear from that quarter."

"What did you do, Dec, give him two in the head? Throw him from a fifth-storey window?" Brennan said it lightly, but there was a dark image forming in his mind.

"No, Brennan. I didn't shoot him. Didn't have him whacked. I put a word in a certain ear that Deena Breathnach should be protected, and that Victor the pimp should have the frighteners put on him in no uncertain terms. Victor is still alive and well, but he's had the fear of God put into him. And nobody is going to touch Deena Breathnach."

Brennan stood there, poleaxed. "Who . . . How in the hell did you manage that, Dec?"

"I'm thinking Victor is now a firm believer in those rumours about us Irish in New York. That some of us — not me, not you — some of the Irish here are so dangerous that even the Five Families are wary of us. It can be a useful reputation to have. Now, off with you and don't be annoying me anymore about it. Deena is safe. And I've found an apartment for her. Case closed."

Brennan left the family home with an image of his father walking into the White House Bar in Hell's Kitchen and sitting down to have a word with the Gentleman Gangster, Mickey Spillane.

ፙ

Shay and Brennan sat on the edge of Shay's bed in his Brooklyn hotel room, and Shay reached over to the phone and made a long-distance call to Magnan's Tavern in Montreal. Buckley "the Boxcar" Whelan, as advertised, was on the premises and was called to the phone.

Shay introduced himself and told Whelan that Davey had given him the number.

"Yeah," said Whelan, speaking loudly over the roar of conversation around him. "Davey called me. Told me you were looking for information."

"That's right. I'm a researcher with the RTÉ broadcasting service back home. And there's a lot of political turmoil going on there now. One of the men rumoured to be in the running in the next election is Jem O'Daly. And O'Daly is a suspect in a murder over in Dublin. Murder of his brother-in-law."

"That's what I was told, yeah."

"We've all heard the story about O'Daly bolting from here and going north to Montreal, but nobody knows how much is true about his sudden departure."

"You're a reporter. Or researcher. And you've been talking to a friend of Nicky the Shirt."

Right. Shay had forgotten that part. "Yes," he said.

"Are you going to write a story about the guys here in Montreal?"

"No, that's not what I have in mind at all. And I never reveal anybody's name if they don't want it revealed."

"I sure as fuck don't want my name revealed."

"It won't be, I guarantee it. So you've no worries on that score." Shay had no interest in Whelan, beyond what he could tell him about O'Daly. And, of course, unbeknownst to Whelan, Shay wasn't a researcher with RTÉ.

"Well, Rynne, I'm not going to get into this over the phone. But if you're ever in Montreal —"

"I won't be in Montreal, Mr. Whelan. I'm heading back to Ireland in a few days."

"Okay, listen. I can put you on to a guy who'll talk to you. He loves to talk about this stuff, as long as whoever he's talking to has information to make it worth his while. His name is Dermot Linehan, and he's a reporter with a shitty little newspaper here. He writes about, well, guys I know here in Pointe Saint Charles. That's his beat. Says he's gonna write a book; he's been saying that for years. But Dermot's an okay guy. He's always been good to me, so I try to be good to him."

This Dermot must have kept Whelan's name out of his stories, Shay concluded, used him as a source.

"Hold on. I'll give you his home number. And you can say you got it from me. But just remember: if you use anything he gives you, he'll want credit for it."

"I understand."

Shay could hear Whelan fidgeting around, maybe getting Linehan's number out of his wallet. Whatever the case, he was back on the line with the number. Shay thanked him and hung up.

"Could you hear any of that, Brennan?"

"I could."

"So, I guess I'll try Linehan. Wish Des Creaghan, RTÉ News, was here for this."

Shay dialled the number and reached Linehan's wife. Dermot was out but should be back soon. Shay asked her to have him ring the hotel and reverse the charges, and she said that was fine. Shay went down to the desk and told the man at reception that Shay would cover the cost of the phone calls. Then he went upstairs, poured a whiskey for himself and for Brennan, and waited for the phone to ring. It rang just under an hour later. Shay answered and held the receiver at an angle, so Brennan could hear.

Once again, Shay trotted out his claim to be a researcher for RTÉ; he was working for the well-known journalist Desmond Creaghan on a story about Jem O'Daly. He didn't feel he was being entirely dishonest; he would indeed be passing along all his information to Desmond. He promised that Linehan's name would be used if the Montreal story made it to air. There was a bit of back and forth about that, and Shay gave Linehan a couple of entertaining tales from O'Daly's criminal career, which had the reporter exclaiming "Wow!" and going for his notebook. Then Shay asked about O'Daly's arrival in Montreal.

"He had to get out of New York on the double," Linehan said. "He'd made a big mistake."

"Oh?"

"Yeah. He was playing both ends of the ice, and he got caught. Everybody thought of him as one of Mickey Spillane's boys. I mean, he was new. It was not as if he'd grown up on the West Side of New York, but he was at least on the fringe of Spillane's gang. Somewhere along the line, though, O'Daly got friendly with one of the Families. The Five Families. You know what I mean."

Shay knew: La Cosa Nostra.

"Don't ask me how O'Daly got linked up with them. I haven't got a clue. But you know one of the ways the Spillane boys used to make money? Spillane didn't go in for drugs, so he was missing out on shitloads of money that way. But one of the things he was doing — and you have to give him credit for having the balls to do this; I wouldn't have them, I can tell you. It's one thing to go into a bank and rob the place blind, fair enough. Nothing personal about it. But kidnapping guys associated with the Mafia in New York?! That's what he'd do. Spillane. Kidnap them and hold them for ransom. And the guys paid up. Ransom was paid, ten or fifteen thousand bucks, and the guy was let go."

"Jaysus! You'd have to be bold and fearless to try that."

"Oh, yeah. Well, Spillane's crew had one of these kidnappings planned. Somebody with connections to one of the mob families. And O'Daly got wind of it. He must have been trusted in Hell's Kitchen. But they shouldn't have trusted him, because he went to his Mafia contacts and tipped them off. So the plan was screwed, and some heat came Spillane's way because of it, because of those guys knowing about it. The revenge, of course, was an Irish guy kidnapped in return. Who knows what kind of rough treatment he suffered at their hands? And I don't know whether it was the details that O'Daly knew, or what it was, but Spillane caught on that it must have been O'Daly that leaked the information about the kidnap plan. So O'Daly was a marked man."

"No wonder he left!" Shay said.

"But he didn't just leave. How would he have known to come here to the Point? He had help. Now, we have an Italian mob here in Montreal, and they have ties with some of the mob guys in New York. They were running rackets here long before the Irish got into it. Gambling, brothels, loan-sharking. Christ, they were bringing in heroin years ago. I remember hearing somewhere that more than half the heroin in the U.S. came from France through Montreal, and that was in the 1950s. Well, you've heard of the French connection, right?

"Anyway, because of what O'Daly did, betraying Mickey Spillane, and causing one of the Irish boys to get snatched, O'Daly had a target on his back. So somebody arranged to get him up here to Montreal. Mafia guys who I think were in cahoots with the other Irish gang in New York. Who's the guy? Cooney?"

"Jimmy Coonan."

"Right. I never heard from whoever it was that arranged it, but I knew they sent O'Daly across the border and here to Montreal with a bodyguard. The plan was that he'd fly from here back to Dublin."

"So that's what he did? Caught a flight from Montreal?"

Linehan laughed. "Eventually."

"There was a delay?"

"What I heard was that he felt pretty safe once he got here, and he liked the look of the place. The city. And the clubs. And maybe the girls, too. Who wouldn't, eh? I heard that he stayed on for a while to enjoy — what is it you guys say over in Ireland, enjoyed the craic?"

"That's right."

"Sounded to me as if he got a bit cocky once he was safe here. Really went out on the town. And one story I heard came from a guy who'd met the bodyguard. The bodyguard was getting pissed off, with O'Daly going out to the bars, gabbing with all kinds of people. Bodyguard finally gave up on him, went back to New York. The last straw, I guess, was when O'Daly wanted to bring his family over instead of just getting the hell back to Ireland. O'Daly apparently put the money up for his wife to fly over here and join him for a couple of days. She didn't come."

"Didn't want a trip to Montreal?" Afraid Jem was in league again with men who have gorillas as bodyguards?

"Guess not. The way I heard it, O'Daly's brother came instead. Danny, or Derrick, or whatever his name was."

Shay heard the intake of breath by Brennan beside him. Had Jem's brother come to Montreal? Or his brother-in-law?

"Could it have been Darragh?" Shay asked.

"Yeah, I think that was it. I don't know any more about it. The guy was here for a couple of days, a weekend, whatever it was, and then they went home to Ireland. I hope this will add some interesting colour to your story, Shay. And, as I say, I wouldn't mind having my name associated with it somehow."

"Sure thing, Dermot. I very much appreciate your help here."

"You're welcome. Anytime."

When he had ended the call, Shay turned to Brennan and asked if he'd been able to hear.

"I heard."

"So, Brennan, Jem O'Daly betrayed Mickey Spillane's gang by tipping off the Mafia that one of their lads was going to be kidnapped."

"I wouldn't want to be the fella who did that."

"Right. So what do you think Spillane's boys would do in response? Would their reach extend all the way across the Atlantic?"

"I can't imagine they'd think of having him *whacked*, him being that far away. But he might worry about it anyway. Who wouldn't? Or now, with him cleaning up his act and going into politics, he sure as hell wouldn't want the story to get out, that story and the other stuff he got up to in New York. When was it he turned over the new leaf in Ireland? When did he start saying he'd gone legit?"

"Not long after he returned home to Dublin."

"So, Seamus, somebody could hold all this over his head. Even if he wasn't in fear for his life, he would be in fear of his hard-earned clean reputation taking a hit. And the somebody holding it over his head may have stood to gain from it." Brennan rubbed his thumb and finger together in a gesture that everybody knew meant money.

"Yeah, somebody may have been blackmailing him," said Shay. "But how could the fella from New York be sure of getting his payments once O'Daly was on the other side of the ocean? Sounds like a stretch to me."

Brennan said, "It is a stretch. Unless the fella wasn't in New York, but a little closer to home. Fella who'd seen O'Daly in Montreal."

☙

Shay spent his last few days enjoying more of New York's bars and restaurants, walking around the city, taking in the sights, catching a few films. Brennan had joined him on a couple of occasions; otherwise, he was a tourist on his own. Wouldn't have missed it for the world. He had heard a slew of stories about O'Daly, but whether any of that could be related to the murder — whether any of it would serve to clear Shay's father of suspicion — remained to be seen. And none of it could be passed along to his fellow gardaí, at least not yet, because he had kept his "mission" a secret from them.

Brennan drove him out to JFK airport, and Shay thanked him over and over for everything he had done for him and Des and Deena. Was Deena safe now? From what Brennan had told him, it sounded as if Declan Burke had worked his connections with the New York Irish mob. The mob that was feared even by the Mafia. Had the Irish fellas so terrified the man who "owned" Deena that he would never go near her again? Declan seemed to think so.

And Brennan said he'd be sure to get hold of some Irish newspapers to follow the story of Jemser O'Daly and the McLogan murder.

"I'll see you next time I'm over in Dublin. And you'll have to come to N'Yawk again some time. Set it up so Paddy Healey and Colly O'Grady can come with you. Imagine the craic, all of us together."

Shay could imagine, and he wouldn't want to miss it. "Good plan. That's what we'll do." And he said goodbye and headed into the terminal, his head filled with plans for his next visit to New York, with Healey and O'Grady, and maybe Des along for the ride again, too. The craic would be ninety on the isle of Manhattan.

∞

But there were good times to be had at home in Dublin, joyful times. When he arrived back home, he found a big envelope that had come for him in the post. It showed a return address in Drumcondra. When he opened it, he was gobsmacked to see what it contained: a *Young Romance* comic book! There was a bookmark inserted in the middle, and he turned to that page. And it was just like old times. Black curls had been scribbled onto the man, and the woman's hair was ginger. The woman had her back turned to the fella, and there was an agonized look on her face. The original lines of dialogue were left as they were: "I've been such a FOOL, a BLIND FOOL!!! — *Sob!* — It was YOU I loved all along!" Then, written in blue ink at the bottom of the page: "I was an arsehole, I was wrong. I'm sorry. You probably won't forgive me, but I wanted you to know. Le grá, Allie." With love, Allie.

Jesus Murphy! Now he could go and see her; she had made the first move. He wouldn't make a sudden appearance at the theatre box office; he had her address in Drumcondra. He didn't know the hours she worked, so it took a couple of tries, and one awkward conversation on the doorstep with her roommate, Carol. But then it happened. Allie herself opened the door to him, and they stood facing each other for the first time in more than two years. She was lovelier than ever. Her red hair looked stylish: shorter, just above her shoulders, and wavy. Her hazel eyes had the same look of mischief they'd had before. He didn't know what to do. He knew what he wanted to do, put his arms around her and clasp her to him, but he was afraid that would be too much like the love comic. So he stood there like a fella too thick to think of anything to say, and him from a race of people who were never at a loss for words.

She rescued him. "Shay, it's so good to see you. I didn't know if you'd come, didn't know what your reaction would be to the comic book. Come inside. It's just the two of us. Carol is out."

And so he went inside. She offered him tea and then laughed. "I've turned into my ma, I guess."

"You could do worse."

"I could, and I have. Let me explain it all to you."

And she told him that the man she had taken up with was an archaeologist, no real surprise there. He was a few years older than Allie. Shay didn't ask if he was a golden-haired Norse god. The point was, he had turned out to be less than godlike, and she'd been planning for nearly a year to come home to Ireland as soon as she finished her studies. And once she had soured on the archaeologist, she realized how much she missed old Shay back in Dublin. Shay filled her in on the eventful life he'd been living since she left. And then there was a scene right off the pages of *Young Romance*. And they were together again.

As summer turned to autumn, Shay and Allie spent as much time as they could in each other's company. And the Rynne family was delighted to welcome her back.

CHAPTER XXIV

Late in the month of November, Shay was sitting at his kitchen table, relaxing with a can of beer. He was thinking of Allie, and he had a plan: he intended to make a proposal of marriage. He formed an image of himself on his knees like a gom in one of those foolish love comics, begging her to be his wife. There was always Christmas Eve, and the old *Ah, look at that little velvet box under the tree; who's that for, I wonder.* She'd be in bits laughing, no doubt. And then he remembered something, and he was the one laughing. Years earlier, before they split up, Allie had been telling him about a friend of hers who got engaged to be married. The man slipped the ring on her finger and then, leaning in close, said to her, "Now, what do I get in return to seal the bargain?" And she said, "I've got it here in my pocket: a positive pregnancy test!" Well, he would think of some memorable way to make his proposal. The main thing was that he and Allie would be together, always. There was an old Irish blessing: May I see you grey and combing your grandchildren's hair. He knew he'd be as happy with Allie as a grey-haired gran as he was with her now.

But the good times were fleeting.

It was a chilly Friday evening, the first of December, and Shay was in Sheriff Street carrying out a pointless task, an investigation that was destined to go nowhere. He was questioning the neighbours about a street fight between two groups of young men, which had gone far out of control and resulted in serious injury to two of the combatants. As Shay expected from his own youth in Fenian Street, residents of the Corpo flats weren't about to give the peelers a *Hi howiyeh, cool oul day, isn't it?*, let alone details of who escalated the tensions by cracking an empty bottle of Paddy whiskey over somebody's head during the fracas. He and a uniformed guard, Allan McCarthy, were no wiser when they left than when they had arrived.

But the racket in Sheriff Street was forgotten in an instant when Shay heard a resounding boom. He knew immediately that it wasn't thunder. He couldn't quite locate the sound, but it seemed to have come from the river. He and McCarthy looked at each other. "Station, or —?" McCarthy started to ask, but Shay pointed to the river, only a couple of minutes away, and they rushed off in that direction. Shay was in no mood to engage in banter or argument with the urchins who ran along beside them, making faces and scurrilous remarks. One of them said, "Sounds like they blew up Store Street, peeler!" Shay ignored him and kept running.

Shay couldn't believe his eyes when he got there. Several cars were piled on top of one another with flames shooting out of them, in front of the Liffey Bar and the tall glass tower of Liberty Hall. Thick black smoke billowed out of the holes where car windows had been. Shay heard the cracking and clinking of broken glass as it crunched beneath his boots. Liberty Hall was Ireland's tallest building, the headquarters of the Irish Transport and General Workers' Union. Windows had been shattered in the union building, and dozens of white venetian blinds flapped back and forth in the wind. Windows had been splintered in the Liffey Bar, and in buildings along Burgh Quay as well, on the south side of the river.

But it was the sight of the people that had Shay nearly immobilized by the shock — people lying on the ground sobbing, some screaming in pain, some unconscious, many covered in blood. A man in a torn shirt was walking back and forth along the quay, dazed and shocked, muttering to himself. Some of the punters from the bar were standing out in front of it, stunned, drinks still in hand, slivers of glass in their hair and clothing. Someone was talking about a red wall of flame. And what Shay kept hearing was "Car bomb!" The fire brigades and the ambulances came screaming in, and Shay watched as severely injured people were attended to before being transported to hospital.

It wasn't lost on Shay that the Liffey Bar was known to be a Shinners bar, frequented by members of Sinn Féin. And the party often held meetings in Liberty Hall. Were they the targets of this attack?

He started to assist the other gardaí in diverting cars and pedestrians away from the scene. But no sooner had he begun this work than two other guards came running, and shouted to them, "We got a warning! Gonna be another bomb!" They turned and ran, and Shay and McCarthy ran after them. One of the guards turned his head and shouted again, "Behind Clerys! Have to evacuate!"

Shay kept on running, but all the while he was thinking the obvious: he was running into danger. There was a bomb, and he had no idea when it was set to go off. Would he arrive in time to get the people safely out of the way, or would the thing explode and blast him to the sky? The image of his mother came into his head. Deirdre Rynne at times had the eyes and the voice of a much older woman. She seemed like an oracle when she'd say, "Life is short. Do not be taking it for granted." But this was the work he had signed up for. He halted when he got to Sackville Place, a short street between Marlborough and O'Connell, alongside Clerys department store. He bent over and took a couple of deep breaths. He looked around and saw guards peering into cars parked along the street. Others were shepherding people out of nearby buildings. He set out to join in that effort. He started towards the CIE — bus company — staff canteen and saw a guard leading a number of men out of the building. He called over to the guard, "Anyone else inside?"

The next thing he knew, he was up in the air. He was aware of a thundering boom and a brilliant flash of light. And then he felt himself crash down on the pavement. He lay there on his back, stunned, staring at the smoke rising before him. He felt a sharp pain in the back of his head and in his left heel. Gradually, he tried moving his arms and legs. Everything was working, so he rolled over and shoved himself upright. He rubbed his head and saw blood on his hand. He looked around him. People were screaming and stampeding off in every direction. There were cars on fire, and there was a strong stench of explosives. Soon he could hear the sirens of ambulances all around him, the fire brigades roaring in, and guards with loud hailers urging people to clear the bomb sites. Shay did his best to bring order to the chaos and to assist those who were able, to get away. He saw two civilians carrying a man, his body contorted and covered with blood, to a space in front of a shop, which had been wrecked in the blast. They gently laid the man down and, soon after, by the light of a cigarette lighter, a priest from the nearby Pro-Cathedral gave the man the last rites.

With the ambulance and fire services doing their work, there was nothing he could do to assist for the moment, and he caught sight of a call box. He ran over to ring Allie. He knew she was working a shift at the theatre. Someone else answered the phone and said she'd go and fetch Allie. Shay's head was throbbing and he was vibrating with impatience waiting for her. Life is short and I've seen the proof of that today in our own city, he thought. Finally, she came on the phone.

"Allie!"

"Shay, are yeh all right? We heard —"

"Marry me!"

"What?"

"Ah, I'm sorry, I —" No, he wasn't sorry. "People are terribly injured here. I think a couple are dead. We have to live, so, well, I want us to be married."

God bless her, she didn't laugh at his words or his timing. There were no Dubs laughing that day. "Of course, I'll marry you, Shay. Why would I not?"

"That's brilliant, Allie! I can't stay talking now. I have to get back to the . . . the scene here in Sackville Place. Don't come anywhere near here, Allie."

"Are yeh sure yeh're all right, love?"

"I am, but I have to get back."

So they ended the call. He wished he could run about, leaping with joy over his engagement. But he returned to the wreckage of Dublin city centre.

☙

He soon learned that a warning had been phoned in to a newspaper in Belfast. The threat was known first in Belfast, not in Dublin. And the man on the phone spoke with a "Belfast-English accent." The warning was relayed to the Royal Ulster Constabulary and from there to the Garda Síochána in Dublin. But by the time the Dublin police got the warning, the first bomb had already gone off. Many believed the lateness of the warning was deliberate. It was also foreseen, some said, that buildings around Sackville Place would be evacuated and that people would be running around, many right into the area where that second car bomb was to go off. Which is exactly what happened. Two men, a bus driver and a conductor, died in the second explosion. More than a hundred others were injured in the two attacks. Shay knew all too well how fortunate he was to have got away with a bit of minor pain. The investigation was put into the hands of gardaí specially trained in these matters, for all the good it did. There were no celebratory gatherings in Garda HQ. No arrests.

The timing of the December 1972 attacks was interesting. Or was it more than that? The bombings coincided with measures being taken by the government of the Irish Republic to toughen the laws relating to terrorism. Putting aside its republican history,

Fianna Fáil was now, and not for the first time, more concerned with cracking down on militant republicans than celebrating them. Now, in addition to juryless courts, the government had written up a bill that would allow a man to be convicted of IRA membership merely on the word of a high-ranking garda. Convicted on the word of one man without any other evidence. The bill was opposed by civil liberties groups, the press, the trade unions, and some members of the opposition parties, concerned about the erosion of people's rights. Even some members of the government itself were against it. On the evening of December 1, 1972, it looked as if the bill wouldn't pass.

But that was before the elected members sitting in the Dáil that night heard the two explosions on the north side of the River Liffey. The governing party had its way. And, perhaps not coincidentally, British Intelligence had its way as well; they thought the draconian measures were a jolly good idea. The bill was passed. Southern-based republican subversives could be put away with much less bother now.

℘

Three days after the bombings, and the passing of the bombshell legislation, Shay and Des Creaghan were sitting up at the bar in Walsh's in the Stoneybatter area of the city.

"How's your head?" Des asked.

"It's fine. Bit of a scab, that's all."

"Sweet suffering Jesus, Shay, do you realize how close you came? We nearly lost you."

Shay gave a shrug, and they were both silent until Des asked, "Any chance you'll be involved in the investigation?"

"Not likely. Something like this is the preserve of the Special Detective Unit. State security, subversives, all that."

"Ah. Special Branch." It wasn't uncommon to hear the SDU called by its old name, the Special Branch.

"And there's all the technical stuff. Ballistics, prints, all that. I gave my statement about what I saw and what happened to me, and that's all they needed from me."

"Right." Des then offered his congratulations on Shay's engagement to Allie. And he didn't even laugh when Shay told him how he'd blurted out his proposal with the smoke of the bombs rising behind him.

"Proper thing, Shay." He clinked his glass against Shay's. "Carpe diem. Seize the day. And when do you think the big day will be?"

"Not for a while yet. You know how close she's always been to her cousin Patricia. Well, Patricia is married and living in Australia, but they plan a visit home. But they're talking about the autumn of 1974! That's when her husband finishes his course at the university."

"Nearly two years from now."

"Yeah, we may decide not to wait. But, then again, it's not as if we're going to change our minds!" And it was not as if they would be apart until the vows were exchanged; she was spending half her time at Shay's place now.

They drank in silence for a moment, then they turned to the subject that was uppermost in everyone's mind: the deaths of two men and the injuries suffered by more than a hundred other people in the car bomb attacks.

Shay brought up the new provisions that were now the law of the land. "How does all this get the government any further ahead if they manage to arrest the shower of shites that set off the car bombs? If they find them, they've got them for setting off the explosives, for murdering and maiming those people. What's the point of adding, 'And oh, yes, your Lordship, I think these men are also running with a bad crowd'?"

"You're missing something here, Shay."

"Yeah? What am I missing?"

Des lowered his voice. "All those members of the Dáil huddled in Leinster House that night, Fianna Fáil and Fine Gael, some of them anyway, they think it was the IRA that did the bombings."

"Why in the fuck would the 'RA blow up that bar, a Sinn Féin drinking spot? Why would they set off explosives here in Dublin instead of in the North, or in England?"

"Doesn't make a lot of sense, does it? But you know yourself, there's a powerful element in both parties that wants to crack down on the IRA." Des got up and ordered two more pints. When he came back, he said, "Won't the Brits be patting our politicians on the back now? 'Congratulations on all that cracking down, old chaps. Splendid fellows, all of you.'"

"Probably set those bombs off themselves, the Brits." Shay laughed and took a good long sip of Guinness.

But Des wasn't laughing. "That's exactly what some people are saying, that the Brits were behind it, or were in league with the people who did it. Think about the warning that was phoned in. The *late* warning. Not an Irishman ringing a Dublin paper. No, a Brit or a Belfast Englishman ringing a Belfast paper to warn of two bombs in Dublin."

☙

Three weeks after those two attacks, Sackville Place was targeted by bombers again. Saturday afternoons were always busy times in the city centre, and the streets were even more crowded on January 20, 1973, because Ireland was playing the All Blacks in a rugby match. The car bomb blew up near a pub and a betting shop. One young man was killed and more than a dozen people injured. A man with an English accent phoned in a warning, minutes before the car exploded. Not in time for the area to be cleared.

In the wake of all this, Shay could not believe his ears when DS McCreevy called him over and gave him the day's assignment. "You and Hannaway, get over to Connolly Station. There's a fella trying to sell fake train tickets, trying to defraud people heading for —"

Shay interrupted him. "That fella's been there for years. He picks up old ticket stubs off the pavement and tries to sell them. Nobody believes him, nobody buys them. Everyone's used to seeing him and they pass him by without stopping."

"So, Garda Rynne, you've known about this for years, and you haven't seen fit —"

Shay interrupted again. "The man is away in the head. He's a well-known character. There's no harm in him at all."

"Get the fuck over to Connolly, Rynne. Do as you're told."

"Our city is being blown up, our people being slaughtered, and you want me wasting my time on *this*?"

"Well, Rynne, I suppose I could lend you to the army, to the Explosives Ordnance Disposal team, to dismantle some of those bombs. Would that fit in better with your image of yourself? Or" — McCreevy put his finger beside his nose and put on a phony expression of thoughtfulness — "how about another sort of weapon, guns, for instance, if you're concerned about people being killed? If you could find some guns and put them out of circulation, that will save lives. How about that, Rynne?"

Shay lost the rag at that. "What kind of a peeler are you, McCreevy, that you laugh about people being murdered in our country? You use those victims to make a point for yourself!" He leaned over the detective's desk. "Or maybe those deaths and horrific injuries in Sackville Place were just *accidents*, eh, McCreevy?"

McCreevy's face turned a flaming red. "I could, I c-could —"

"You could what, McCreevy? Take me out to a bar and get me drunk and hope maybe I fall down a flight of stairs?"

McCreevy's reaction was strange. For a moment there, he looked not angry or aggressive but frightened. His lower lip quivered. Vulnerable, that was the look. Was his failure in the Goss's Hotel case much more painful for him than he usually let on? Was he still stinging from the way he was treated in Longford after his failure there? Suddenly Shay lost his taste for confrontation; let the poor, pathetic bastard sit here stewing by himself. Shay turned and walked away. He didn't bother his arse to go to Connolly Station.

He returned to his notes on an armed robbery case he'd been working on, and a theft from a tobacconist's shop. He wished he was working on the bombing investigations, rather than working these common, everyday criminal cases, but state security was not his beat. And he sure as hell wished he could do more than merely shadow the murder inquiry in which his own father was a suspect.

Talkie wasn't rearrested as 1973 rolled on, but neither was he cleared. There was not enough evidence to bring charges against him; how could there be, if he hadn't committed the murder? But the entire family was kept on edge by the fear that, at any moment, there could be a knock on the door at midnight, and Talkie taken away again in handcuffs. The tension was showing on him; he must have lost a stone in weight and his face was more lined than ever. And if what Shay saw a couple of days ago was any indication, he was heavily into the drink. Was he turning up for work like that? Would Burke Transport have to turf him from his job?

꽃

The year was an eventful one for the Garda. Early in February, the Gardaí received confidential information that the UVF, the Ulster Volunteer Force, was responsible for the car bombs in 1972 and 1973. The UVF were a Northern Irish loyalist group opposed to anything that might threaten the North's British identity and bring those six counties into a closer relationship with the twenty-six counties of the South. The UVF and another loyalist crowd, the Ulster Defence Association, had been planning more attacks on Dublin.

Shay knew that there were eyewitness descriptions of the man who had hired the bomb cars in the North. Other witnesses saw the cars and the men inside them. The investigators could have obtained photos of known subversives — possible suspects — and shown the photos to the witnesses in an effort to identify the bombers. But it wasn't done. The authorities in the South had made no arrangements with the authorities in the North to hunt down the suspects and make them available for trial in the Republic of Ireland.

At the end of that same month came vindication for everyone who had been dismissed as cracked and paranoid for thinking there was a spy with close ties to the Garda Síochána, and a Brit taking the secrets home to England. The spy was actually a garda himself, working in one of the most sensitive areas of police work: security and intelligence. This detective sergeant had been passing secret information from the Garda files to his British handler, a man who went by several different names.

The Fianna Fáil government was defeated in the election of February 28, 1973. The Fine Gael party formed a coalition with Labour and so were able to form the government. The former Taoiseach, Jack Lynch, said something of great interest later in the year: he suspected that many of the unexplained attacks in Ireland could be related to British Intelligence. Even the new minister for foreign affairs, Garret FitzGerald — and he was no anti-British radical — suspected the same. And not without reason: the same year, two brothers named Littlejohn were extradited from England to Ireland to be charged for a bank robbery in Dublin. But the earth-shattering news from this pair was that they had been working for British Intelligence, and their purpose was to commit robberies and other acts of violence that would be blamed on the IRA, in order to provoke the Irish government into cracking down on republican subversives!

Fianna Fáil may have lost the election, but they gained one new member in the person of Jem O'Daly. O'Daly wouldn't be getting a seat in cabinet this time round, but Shay could imagine him being perfectly content to bide his time on the opposition bench. Content? The man looked positively gleeful when Shay saw him on the telly, all puffed up with himself in his flashy clothes. Big effin' grin on his face. But Shay had another image in mind for the telly: O'Daly scowling and tripping and falling over his feet as he was hauled away in cuffs.

CHAPTER XXV

A storm over the Atlantic Ocean in the middle of January 1974 delayed several transatlantic flights. That resulted in Shay Rynne, Paddy Healey, and Colly O'Grady socializing not in Christy Burke's but in a bar at Dublin Airport. Brennan Burke had made good on his ambition to go to Rome for studies in theology and philosophy. He had completed his first year there and was now in his second. He had spent Christmas with his family in New York and, for his return, he had been offered a choice of flying via Dublin or Frankfurt. He had chosen the circuitous route, coming to Dublin for a short stopover. He would have about five hours, and the plan was to come into the city and meet his mates at Christy's for a couple of pints before returning to the airport. So Shay was at the pub, along with Colly and Paddy. But the arse fell out of the plan. The winter storm delayed the New York flight, and it was nearly three hours late arriving in Dublin. Brennan rang Finn at Christy's, and Finn passed the word along to the three pals. It didn't take long for them to decide to drive out to the airport and see Brennan there.

"Ragazzi," he said in greeting.

"What's that now, Brennan?" Paddy asked.

"I just said 'lads' the way we say it in Rome."

"You're a grand Roman now, are you, Father?"

"Amn't I grand wheresoever I tread, Paddy?"

"You are, Father. And it's grand altogether to see you. We didn't have you here in Dublin last year at all, or the year before."

"Duties of my calling, and studies in Rome. Hoped to get here, but it didn't happen. I'll make up for it on my next visit."

"Right, so," Paddy acknowledged. "How's the family in New York?"

"They're grand." He nodded in the direction of the bar, and they headed there, obtained their drinks of choice, and sat down at a table.

"Good thing they have seatbelts in those planes," Brennan said, "or we'd all have been smashing our heads on the ceiling. Food was flying, drinks spilling —"

"Drinks spilling!" Colly exclaimed. "They'll have to remake that film, what was it?"

"*Airport*, you mean?" Shay asked. "The one based on the book?"

"Yeah, that's it. They'll have to remake it, or do a sequel. *Airport Two: I'm Losing My Whiskey!* I'll write the movie script. 'Control tower, we're losing —' 'Repeat, please. You're losing altitude?' 'No, we're losing uisce beatha.'" The Irish for whiskey was "water of life."

"That will make millions for you, Col," Paddy said, "at least here in Ireland."

Drink formed the basis of another tale that was told round the table, this one from their past, the shared childhood of Brennan, Colly, and Paddy.

Colly got it started. "Well, I may be accused of being an informer if I tell this tale." He made a comical show of looking all around. "Wouldn't want anything to happen to my knees or I'd not be able to kneel in the confessional and tell this holy man my sins."

"Ach, your sins are well known in this city, O'Grady," Father Burke said. "People have been shouting your deeds from the rooftops for years. So say whatever it is you intend to say, slanderous though it may be."

Colly took a long swallow of his stout and leaned towards the others at the table. "Here it is, Shay. We were in school and we were all in love with Sister Theresa Marie who taught my sister's class. We were what? Eight years old? Anyway, we'd just had our Christmas pageant. Correct me if I'm wrong, Father Burke, but I don't believe you had a starring role. What part did you play? The ass, was it?"

"You don't know yer arse from a wise man, O'Grady," Paddy challenged him. "Burke here was one of the wise men."

"Well? Isn't anybody going to say it?" Brennan demanded, lighting up a smoke and offering the pack to the others. Paddy took him up on it.

"Say what?" asked Colly.

"I was kind of hoping you'd say it was typecasting."

"Ah. So it was, but here's the story, Shay. We all gathered in the gymnasium afterwards for a little reception put on by the parents. Cake, glasses of milk, that class of a thing. Except when it came Paddy and Brennan's turn to impress Sister. And what could be more impressive to a crowd of nuns and priests than a little boy with a vocation. Right, Paddy?"

"If you make a right bollix of something, but you had the best of intentions, it's not a sin, is it, Father?"

"Remind me of the details, and I'll let you know whether heaven or hell awaits you, young Patrick."

"All right, so," said the chronicler, Colly O'Grady. "Paddy had his altar boy kit, cassock and surplice, because he and Brennan were both altar boys at the magnificent church on the Rathmines Road, which says what on the front of it? Remind us, Brennan?"

"D.O.M., Deo Optimo Maximo, sub invoc Mariae Immaculatae Refugii Peccatorum, which, as we all know, means 'To God, the best and greatest, under the invocation of Mary Immaculate, Refuge of Sinners.' And I'm sure we're all thankful for that refuge."

"Amen," said Paddy.

Shay knew that Brennan's family had moved from the north side to Rathmines when Brennan was a little boy.

"Right. So Paddy has his altar boy clothes hidden in the jacks, and he goes in and puts those on. He sticks a little square of white at the collar, so now he's Father Paddy Healey. Brennan emerges as Paddy's altar boy. Their intention is to treat Sister Theresa Marie to a pleasant surprise. They are going to give her Holy Communion."

"And she's going to give us holy hell!" Brennan muttered.

"Communion. Paddy goes to the table and asks nicely for a piece of the white cake Mrs. Gillespie has made. She made brilliant cakes and sandwiches!"

"Only fitting," Brennan said. "Did yis know that the name Gillespie comes from the words for 'servant of the bishop'?"

"Quite so," said Colly, and he continued with his story. "So everybody's smiling at the dear little lads in their vestments. Even Father Kearns was smiling. Paddy gets his cake, hives off a piece, and forms it into a disc like the Communion wafer. Then he goes for the grape juice. Everything's going like a proper sacrament so far, righ'?"

"Mmmm," said Paddy.

"But there's nothing sacramental about grape juice, is there, I ask the good Catholics at this table?"

All agreed that grape juice was not sacramental. Not even close.

"No worries. Our boys were prepared for that. Weren't yis, Brennan?"

"We were."

"All was fine and good until the Communion wafer — piece of cake — had been consumed, and it was time for the chalice. The contents of the chalice *had the appearance* of grape juice. But it wasn't *only* grape juice in the chalice, was it, Brennan?"

"It was not."

"And Sister, looking down into the silver goblet and thinking it was grape juice, took a big feckin' gulp of it. And didn't she go choking and spewing it out all over her habit!"

Everybody laughed, and Shay asked, "What the hell did you give her?"

"I'll tell you this much," said Paddy, "it wasn't water turned to wine. I knew that wine was an alcoholic beverage of some kind, like whiskey and porter and, well, distilled spirit. My da had a fair collection of bottles in the press at home, including a bottle of poitín. Sister Theresa Marie was apparently unaccustomed to what the Yanks call moonshine, hadn't yet acquired a taste for it."

Colly put on a face meant to convey that he had lived the Seven Sorrows and said, "I understand that as a result of this blasphemous fiasco, young Paddy Healey was forever banned from taking Holy Orders. Amn't I right? Some said there was even a papal decree to this effect."

"Perhaps so," said Brennan. "I've always suspected papal involvement. How else to explain why Paddy never joined me as a living representative of Christ on Earth?"

Christ's representative took a look at his wristwatch and announced that it was time for him to go. So they drank up and walked out of the bar. The three friends wished Brennan well in Rome, and said he should be prepared for a visit, which could come at any time. The boys might appear while Brennan was having an audience with the Pope. You just never knew. "We will come like a thief in the night," said Paddy. "But bye for now."

"Mind how you go, lads," Brennan said.

Paddy and Colly waved back at him and headed for the exit, but something in Brennan's tone made Shay turn around. Brennan was standing there, not smiling but staring intently at his three friends. Shay heard the Rome flight being called, but Brennan was as still as a statue. "Your flight, Brennan," Shay called to him, then turned and walked away. But he caught sight of Brennan reflected in a mirrored panel ahead of him. And what he saw was Brennan raising his hand and making the sign of the cross in the direction of his departing friends.

When the three of them got into Colly's car for the drive back to the city, Paddy immediately starting planning an excursion for the three of them, a pilgrimage to Rome. So he and Colly began fantasizing about what they'd eat and what they'd drink, and it wouldn't be Communion wine and it wouldn't be poitín. But Shay kept picturing Brennan standing immobile in the airport. Was he nervous about the flight? Shay would have been, he was sure, after the kind of turbulence Brennan had experienced on the flight from New York. But he knew from their past conversations that Brennan loved flying; he was the furthest thing from a nervous passenger.

Shay remembered Finn on more than one occasion slagging Brennan about having "the sight," about being a Druid. Well, Shay wasn't going to dwell on it. He joined in the banter about him and Colly and Paddy taking Rome by storm, about all the Roman beauties who would admire their ivory Irish skin and their brilliance on the football pitch, and codology like that. And Shay brought up Brennan's invitation to visit him in New York, so that led to wild speculation about the craic they'd enjoy there.

They returned to the city and to Christy's. When their pints had been poured, and the other two fellas headed to their table, Shay stayed back and told Finn about Brennan's stormy flight to Dublin and his odd behaviour before he departed for Rome. Shay was relieved that Finn dismissed that with a little shrug. "Nothing unusual about a priest giving a parting blessing," he said, "any more than it's unusual for any of us to have a parting glass." And so Shay put it out of his mind and joined the other two at the table. And they made a night of it. There was a session on, and they all tapped their feet and sang along with the music. Just before the musicians returned from their last break of the evening, Finn came over to the table. He leaned towards Shay and said, "Bren's flight landed at Rome on time and without any trouble."

Shay looked up at him. "You rang him?"

"I rang the airline. All is well, buíochas le Dia." Thank God.

Shay gave him a nod, and Finn went back to his place behind the bar. Shay felt relieved. He was glad he hadn't said anything to Colly and Paddy. And he would not dwell on the fact that Finn had seen fit to ring the airline for reassurance.

☙

"Meet me down at the quays." It was the day after the airport send-off, and Shay was at work, and out of cigarettes. So he had ducked out of the Store Street Station to go and buy a pack. The city was shrouded in fog, and he could barely see across the street. He turned to see who had emerged out of the mist and appeared at his side. Vince Foley.

"What?" Shay asked him.

"North Wall Quay, fifteen minutes." Vince walked away.

What was this? Vince didn't want to talk in the station, or over at Reade's? Shay went into the closest shop, bought his pack of fags, and then headed to the river and walked east to North Wall Quay. Vince was standing there, smoking, peering through the fog at the ferry crossing the river.

"Vince, the only thing missing is a cloak on your back and a dagger in your hand!"

"It's about McCreevy," Vince said in a whisper, as if there might be an unseen listener lurking in the gloom.

"Fuck. What about him now?"

"It's been a long wait for DI Hennessy, but the talk now is that one of the superintendents will be retiring before too long, and Hennessy is in line for his job."

"Right."

"So he must be putting a little history together for himself, to present to the higher powers. He asked me to gather up some files for him to look over, investigations over the last few years that ended the way they should — in an arrest and, better still, a conviction. Murder inquiries, major crimes solved and sorted. That kind of thing." Vince looked Shay in the eye and said, "Including the Rosaleen McGinn case."

"Oh, yeah?"

"Oh, yeah. And there are parts of the record you'd not recognize, Garda Rynne."

"What do you mean?"

"I was shuffling through the papers, to see what DI Hennessy would want to read. And, Shay, the file has been altered."

"What? Altered how?"

"Tell me if this is the way you remember the murder inquiry getting started. I'm quoting from DS McCreevy's report now. 'I was never satisfied with the "accident" conclusion after the first look into the case, and I wanted more done. I wanted to look at it again.'"

"*He* wasn't satisfied? He's the one who wrote it off as a fucking accident!"

"You'd never know it from the way the file reads now, Shay. McCreevy goes on to make another claim. He writes, 'And I saw my opportunity when young Shay Rynne joined us at Store Street.'"

"*His* opportunity?!"

"Ah now, you're in for a bit of praise here, Seamus. McCreevy wrote something like this: 'I knew that Garda Rynne, with his background, would have sources the rest of us didn't have. So I put it to him, suggested some avenues to explore. The lad seemed willing.'"

"*Seemed willing*?!" Shay sputtered. "You know yourself, Vince, the last thing he wanted was the case opened up again! And you well remember how he treated me when I wanted to look into it. I had to do it myself, on the sly, and —"

"I know, Shay, I know. I just wanted to tell you what the oul begrudger is up to. And now I have to run. See you at the station. And you never heard any of this from me."

"Of course not, Vince. Thanks for telling me."

"And setting your blood boiling."

"Yeah, that, too."

Vince disappeared into the vapour, and Shay was left fuming. He lit up a smoke and cursed himself for being so soft on McCreevy after learning of his incompetence in Longford, and his weeping over his failures there. Well, Shay would have no pity after this. If McCreevy ever again hinted that he knew about the guns, Shay would retaliate. This time around he'd be taking no prisoners.

CHAPTER XXVI

S hay was off duty when the city blew up on May 17, 1974.
He was sitting in a bar in Capel Street, enjoying an early pub supper, when he heard a blast. Heard it and felt it like a kick in the head. For a moment he was reliving the blast that sent him flying up in the air and crashing down to earth. But he couldn't let that hold him back. He leapt up from his chair as his fellow punters reacted with "What the fuck?" and "Not again!" and he headed out the door. Didn't even think about waiting to pay his tab. Outside the bar he looked around but saw nothing, his view restricted by the buildings along the street. He decided to head for the bank of the Liffey where he'd have a line of sight in the directions of east, west, and south. He ran down the street to Ormond Quay and joined a crowd of people who were standing, confused, looking all about them. Remembering the scene last time when people milled about, not knowing when or if — and, oh Christ, here it was. Another blast. The sound seemed to have come from the northeast of Shay, and he set off in that direction. Some in the crowd started to follow, and he turned and raised his hands to

them. "I'm a guard. Stay back." There was no call for anyone else to run into the gap of danger, but Garda Rynne had no choice.

He ran along the quay to O'Connell Street and gazed about him. And saw a pall of smoke rising from behind Clerys department store. It seemed to be coming from Talbot Street, so he made that his destination. There were throngs of people in O'Connell Street. It was just around five thirty, rush hour on a sunny spring afternoon. He thought he heard another boom, a third explosion, but wondered whether this was his fear working on him. He kept on to Talbot Street, where his eyes were met by a scene of utter devastation. Billowing smoke, the acrid stink of explosives, mangled cars, shattered windowpanes, the ground level of Guineys shop now a gaping hole. Terrified people were screaming, crying, running off in all directions. And as he moved forward, he saw the carnage on the ground. Bodies with limbs torn off, bodies burnt beyond recognition, a woman decapitated. There was another woman with what appeared to be part of a car engine sticking out of her back. Could this possibly be real? It was all Shay could do to stop himself from being sick in the street.

He had a moment of indecision: stay here and begin assisting immediately, or cover the short distance to the Store Street Garda Station where he would receive direction for the most appropriate use of his time. He decided to stay, and bent over the injured, trying to determine who could be moved, who should get the first assistance when the ambulances arrived. In short order, the emergency services were on the scene: guards, firefighters, ambulances, medical and first aid people, priests and ministers. The hospitals were all on standby. A sergeant from Store Street came up beside him and said, "First bomb was in Parnell Street, this was the second, and I don't know yet where that third blast came from."

The sergeant ordered Shay to go to Parnell Street and direct people and cars away from the area. When he got there, he found the Welcome Inn pub aflame, and glass shattered all around it. Other businesses, too, were gutted. And the same scene of carnage on the ground. A man with half his head blasted off and a leg missing. And children destroyed as well. He saw a little baby, like a ragdoll torn to bits. He knew he would never get over the sight, not as long as he lived. He was as gentle as he could be, assisting the shocked and the wounded away from the scene, and wishing someone would come and carry him far from the slaughterhouse that had once been a city street.

Officers with expertise in fingerprints, mapping, photography, and ballistics conducted their investigations, and the Garda called in the army's Explosives Ordnance Disposal officers to examine the blast areas for clues as to the type and quantity of explosives used. Cordons were set up to prevent the bombers from crossing the border into Northern Ireland. Gardaí were sent to the train and bus stations, the airport, ferry and boat terminals to head off any suspects trying to get away. Shay was deployed to the airport, but nothing came of that.

He later learned that ten people had been killed in Parnell Street, including a young couple with their two baby girls, both under the age of two years. Another woman's baby was stillborn three months later. Fourteen people lost their lives in Talbot Street, including a woman who was nine months pregnant. Two were killed in the third explosion on the other side of the river, in South Leinster Street. And that wasn't the end of it. Just before seven that evening, a bomb went off in Monaghan, a town in the border county of the same name, killing six people immediately; another died later. In addition to the dead, in all the attacks something like three hundred people were injured.

The year before this, the governments of Ireland and the United Kingdom had begun working on a plan for a new elected assembly in the North of Ireland. Power was to be shared by those who were loyal to Britain and those who wanted Ireland reunited as one country and the Brits sent packing. The loyalists were enraged. As bad as it would be to share power with Irish nationalists, there was something that galled the loyalists even more: the fact that the Republic of Ireland would have a say in the administration of Northern Ireland. The fire-brand preacher from the North, the Reverend Ian Paisley, thundered against the agreement and famously said, "I say to the Dublin government: Mr. Faulkner says it's hands across the border to Dublin; I say, if they don't behave themselves in the South, it will be *shots* across the border!"

It was bombs across the border. Sent by people who didn't give a moment's thought to the children, women, and men whose lives would be destroyed.

℀

Brennan Burke left Rome with a busload of pilgrims in the early morning of May eighteenth. He had volunteered to escort the group to various holy sites around Italy. *Don* Burke — Father Burke — was not the tour guide or, better phrased, the spiritual guide, for the tour, because he was not an expert in the saints whose shrines were on the itinerary. But Don Valardo needed an assistant to help with the logistics, carrying luggage in and out of the lodgings, arranging meals, and all those necessary details. Brennan had become fluent in the Italian language over the past year and was more than happy to assist, because he wanted to see these towns and cities and the saintly relics and sites for which they were renowned.

The tour headed first to Tuscany, and the magnificent city of Siena, one of Brennan's favourite places in the world. The following afternoon, they were in the ancient city of Lucca, which rivalled Siena in its beauty. Many of the buildings were of varying shades of yellow, from a pale to a brilliant golden colour — yellow ochre, perhaps? Brennan reminded himself that this was a tour of holy sites, not an architectural tour.

Don Valardo led the group to the white marble interior of the Basilica di San Frediano, where the group prayed over the body of Saint Zita, a thirteenth-century saint whose body had been found incorrupt after three hundred years and who now lay mummified in the basilica. There was someone else of interest there as well, Saint Fridianus, for whom the basilica was named. He was an Irishman who had travelled to Italy in the sixth century and was made the bishop of Lucca. This was during the Dark Ages, when Irish monks set out across Europe to restore faith and learning to a continent where books and culture

353

had been destroyed by the barbarian invaders. Brennan remarked, of course, on the Irish saints once the present-day pilgrims had ended their prayers and were standing outside in the blazing sun. Even Saint Thomas Aquinas was taught by an Irishman, Brennan boasted, fella by the name of Peter. That's when a woman in the group stepped forward and said to him in Italian, "You are Irish yourself, Father?"

"I am."

"I am very sorry for what happened to your people."

"We've had a difficult history, to be sure."

"No, I mean what happened in Ireland this week."

Brennan was not a man for television, so he hadn't been the least inconvenienced by the absence of televisions in the monasteries where they had stayed for the past two nights. Usually, though, he was an avid reader of the newspapers. Even that had been neglected since the trip began. What had he missed? What had befallen Ireland now?

"I haven't seen the news. What's happened?"

The woman reached over and put her hand on his arm. "There were bombs in the capital city. Many people were killed. Children, a pregnant lady. I saw the paper this morning."

Oh, God! He excused himself, and took off at a clip to find a news agent and a copy of the *Corriere della Sera*. His heart nearly stopped beating when he saw what had been done to his city two days earlier, and to Monaghan town. The deaths, the destruction, the horrific injuries. He was desperate to hop on a plane that instant to go and try to offer comfort to the families and residents of Dublin and Monaghan. But he could not leave the tour group; his services were needed, and he had committed himself to the trip. He already had a flight booked for Dublin in the middle of June. He would change it. The pilgrimage would be winding up on the last day of May. As soon as he was free, he rang Finn Burke at Christy's.

"Ah, Brennan. I rang your number in Rome, but no answer."

Brennan explained the situation, and Finn gave him the terrible news. More than thirty people killed, nearly three hundred injured, many severely. And no, there had been no arrests as yet.

"Who did it?" As if he didn't know.

"Who do you think?"

"Right." Some crowd of Ulster loyalists taking the civil war across the border to the South.

"And, em, Brennan . . ."

Brennan didn't like the sound of his uncle's voice. It brought back the feeling of foreboding that had come over him at the airport in January, as he watched his friends walk away.

"Bren, I'm so sorry, but one of the people killed in Talbot Street was Paddy Healey."

This was so dreadful that Brennan was stunned into silence, lost for words. The silence stretched for a long moment. Then, "God in Heaven! Paddy! Those vicious, murdering . . . This is . . . I can't . . . I'll ring the family." But Brennan was so flummoxed he could not recall the Healey family's number in Rathmines. Finn looked it up for him, and he made the call. Paddy's mother answered the phone and heard Brennan's name but was unable to speak for the weeping. Brennan wasn't much better. But he managed to tell her that he would see her in a couple of weeks' time.

Somehow, he got through the day. That evening he was on his knees before Fridianus, the Irish saint, racked by grief. Grief and anger. He prayed for the soul of Paddy Healey, prayed for his grieving family, and for all the other victims and families. He knew what else he was supposed to pray for: forgiveness for the enemy, for the hate-filled butchers who had killed Paddy and so many others. It was right there in the Lord's Prayer: "forgive us our trespasses as we forgive those who trespass against us." It was right there on the cross. Jesus Christ in his agony saying, "Father, forgive them for they know not what they do." And Brennan was supposed to take the same tack, but he couldn't. Just could not. They know not what they do? They knew exactly what they were doing.

A priest was supposed to be a stand-in for the Son of God. Not many were worthy of that designation, God knows, and Brennan counted himself among the unworthy. He was more a son of Declan Burke than of God the Father. Declan, the IRA man who would never let something like this go unavenged. And that's what Brennan wanted to see; he couldn't help himself. He wanted revenge.

He continued with the pilgrimage and did his best to devote his attention to the people in his charge. He prayed at the shrines and reliquaries, and said Masses for the victims of the attacks. Finally, the bus was back in Rome, and he received gracious thanks from the people he had escorted around Italy. Then, on the morning of June first, he flew into the fractured city of Dublin. He had missed the funeral for his dear friend Paddy, and the Requiem Mass for several of the other victims, a Mass that drew thousands of people to the Pro-Cathedral and the streets outside.

Finn collected him at the airport. In a tone of cold fury, Finn gave Brennan the facts about the dead and the maimed, the ruin of the three Dublin streets, the destruction in Monaghan. Everyone knew someone who had been killed or injured. They stopped in at Auntie Cliona's place, so Brennan could console her and drop off his travel bag and have a quick wash. Then they resumed driving through the north side of the city, where Brennan saw the devastation with his own eyes. They drove south and crossed the Liffey and the Grand Canal and arrived in Rathmines. Brennan thanked Finn and told him he would find his own way home. Then he walked up to the brick Georgian house with a demi-lune fanlight over the yellow door. It was identical to the house three doors away, where the Burkes had lived after their move from the north side when Brennan was a very young child. Now, standing on the doorstep of Margaret and Jackie Healey, he steeled himself for the encounter with the parents of his lifelong friend.

He had never seen such desolation in anyone's face as he saw in the face of Margaret Healey. Brennan knew there was no greater pain than the loss of a child, and that was so whether the child was an infant or a grown man. Paddy's father, Jackie, was trying to hold himself together but couldn't manage it. If Brennan had imagined he could keep his own emotions in check, that illusion vanished in an instant. He was selfishly grateful that Paddy's siblings weren't on hand for the visit, not to mention Paddy's young wife and their three little children. Images came to Brennan's mind of himself and Paddy running joyfully down the football pitch, Paddy the fair-haired right-half forward, Brennan his dark counterpart on the left. And Paddy of the banjaxed Communion offering, plying Sister Theresa Marie, not with Communion wine or harmless grape juice but with a mouthful of poitín, ninety percent alcohol. And the laughs they had recently shared over that incident. The laughs they had shared over a lifetime. And now he was in tears as he held Paddy's mother in his arms.

CHAPTER XXVII

Walking home after Mass on Sunday, Brennan tried to think of something to take his mind off the bombings, the death of his lifelong friend, the deaths and terrible injuries, and the suffering of the other victims of the attacks. *What?* What was he thinking? What was wrong with him? Take his mind off it? There would be something wrong with a man who could take his mind off this catastrophe even for an instant.

So Brennan chastised himself for even thinking it. But was there some way he could make himself useful? To somebody? He remembered hearing of a program set up by a couple of church groups, and they used one of the north Dublin schools for their activities. Saint Laurence O'Toole's, was it? No, it was farther north in the city. Fairview, that's where it was. Saint Joseph's Secondary School for boys. The program was set up to help the local poor, and also some of the people who had resettled in Dublin after escaping the violence North of the border. Brennan could hardly imagine their reaction to the car bomb attacks in the city they now wanted to call home. Shay had told him about the program, and there was a connection to the murder inquiry. Jem O'Daly's wife, that was it. Shay said she was, or had been, one of the regular volunteers. Brennan had seen her at the Gormanston refugee camp on a few of his visits there over the years. He got into his latest Burke Transport loaner and drove across the Royal Canal and then across the River Tolka, in the direction of the school.

He arrived at the expansive brick building, went inside, and walked the corridors until he found the room where the relief program held its activities. A middle-aged woman sat at a desk with papers piled in front of her and looked up at him. "Welcome to Joey's," she said. He introduced himself and asked how he could assist the group. She told him that the people from the North were home in their various new lodgings, but that they gathered here three times a week for supper. The next meal would be tomorrow night, Monday, beginning at half six.

Brennan commiserated with her about the bombings, and the woman — her name was Dolores — told him how the program's volunteers were doing their best to assist the injured and the families of the wounded and the dead. Brennan said he would be joining them for the refugees' regular supper, and what could he bring to the table? Any kind of a treat would be welcome. Would beer or stout be appropriate, or perhaps not? Sure, a can or two for each of the guests would do no harm. So that's what he would do.

And he did. On Monday afternoon he bought several boxes of Butlers' rich, glorious dark chocolates. Then he stopped at an off-licence and picked up a couple of slabs of beer. He pulled in at Saint Joseph's just after six, and he helped the church ladies set the meals out on the tables. He lifted the beer onto the counter and put heaps of chocolates in little bowls. People started coming in, and he recognized a couple of the faces from his visits to Gormanston. There were just over thirty for supper, and a number of volunteers served the food. A young priest said grace, and the diners joined in. A young girl and two lads came in with a fiddle, guitar, and tin whistle and started up a session. They were good, and the guests appreciated the music, the distraction. Brennan sat at one of the tables, and he got into conversations and heard about new lives in County Dublin, and old extinguished lives in Belfast. And, of course, he heard about the people's fears that they had merely jumped from the pan into the fire by coming to Dublin.

Partway through his meal of meat pie and champ, he saw Etty O'Daly coming in with another woman. Etty had lost some of her weight since Brennan had seen her last, which seemed to accentuate her height. She went to one of the volunteers and apologized for being late. "I'll help with the dishes and the cleanup, Meg, and I'll not be late again."

Meg was peering at Etty with a look of concern. "No need for apologies at all, Etty. Sure, aren't you one of our most faithful volunteers? But what happened to you?"

"Ah, it's a story and a half. This poor man . . . I'll tell it to you another time. Right now, I'll fix myself a plate of supper." When she turned to go into the kitchen, Brennan saw her face. There was a cut on her left cheekbone and bruising around the eye. She herself looked like a refugee. He started to get up, but she disappeared behind the kitchen door.

The woman who had come in with her also declared her willingness to clean up after the meal but right now, "Me belly thinks me throat's been cut!"

Brennan took the opportunity to offer her a seat at his table, and she took it. Her meal arrived with the offer of a mineral or a glass of beer, and she enthusiastically opted for the beer. Brennan smiled at her and introduced himself, and she said, "I am pleased to meet you, Father. My name is Dervla. I live over in Ballybough, not far from here, as you'd know." Ballybough: the name came from the Irish An Baile Bocht. The poor town. Why, when they transcribed names from Irish into English, did they use "ough," which can be pronounced at least seven different ways? Brennan turned his mind back to Dervla, who appeared to be in her sixties, with a lined face, heavy eyeglasses, and crimped grey hair. She began to chat about some repairs that were being done to her parish church. Brennan smiled and nodded, but he had something else on his mind. Etty emerged from the kitchen with her plate and her beer, looked across at him and Dervla. Her face registered surprise at seeing him, and she nodded at him in recognition and then turned her head. She spoke to someone at the other end of the room and went off in that direction.

Brennan leaned in close to Dervla and said, "What happened to Mrs. O'Daly?"

"Oh! It was terrible! She arrived at my door two days ago. She looked awful! Her cheek was bleeding, and she had other marks on her face. She was leaning on the rail on my front steps, so weak was she. I took hold of her arm and helped her come inside and I said to her, 'In the name of God, Etty, what happened to you?' And she said, 'It was that poor man Doolin, you know who I mean.' But sure, I'd no idea who she meant, and she said, 'Ah, he's not right in the head. The good sisters take care of him, but he was out and I startled him.' Said she'd scared the bejesus out of him. Oh, I'm sorry for the language, Father. I'm all in a flap here. Anyway, this fella, startled as he was, took his fists to poor Etty. And God love her, she doesn't hold it against him at all. Him being a poor man who's only off his head. She's an angel, is Etty."

Brennan looked across the room and caught Etty looking back. She quickly turned to the person beside her and started talking. Why was she turning away? It was almost a guilty look he was seeing in her face.

Dervla hadn't seen Etty's eyes on them, and she continued her story. "And she told me, Etty did, that her daughter and her little one, the grandchild, were coming for a visit, in from County Carlow, and Etty didn't want them to see her looking like that. It might frighten her, the little girl. So she asked if she could stop with me for a night or two. And apologized over and over for asking! As if I'd mind, and me all alone in the house ever since my Fergus died, God rest him. So I told her she was welcome to stop with me as long as she liked, but shouldn't we be getting the doctor for her? No, she was having none of that at all. She'd be fine. Had she called the guards about the attack? No, no, the poor man was never right in his head. He was blameless. No, she would be fine with a bit of rest and quiet."

After supper, when some of the volunteers, including Etty and Dervla, were cleaning up, Brennan went around asking the newcomers from the North how they were settling in. There was nothing he could say to reassure them now that the war seemed to have followed them across the border. Everyone spoke of how shaken they were by the bombings, and he told them he had lost a very close friend. Also, a cousin on his mother's side had walked away from Parnell Street with minor injuries, and he could not imagine the psychological effects that would linger for her. His uncle Finn had known three of the people killed in Talbot and Parnell streets. Everyone commented on the tragedy of an entire family being killed, the mother, father, and two little girls. So the conversation turned into a bit of a counselling session, not that Brennan had much to offer that would provide healing or reassurance. Above and beyond his grief for Paddy and the Healey family, and all the others, was an overpowering sense of outrage at the slaughter of inno-cent women, children, and men in his city and in Monaghan.

The gathering started to break up, with people saying, "See you next time. Thank you again." And Etty came out of the kitchen, carrying a tray, and she began picking up dishes, cups, and glasses. "Here, Mrs. O'Daly, I'll hold that for you," he said, and took the tray in his hands. She looked up at him, and he saw apprehension in her battered face.

"Oh, hello. It's so good of you to come and help us, Father."

"Brennan," he said, smiling at her. Then he got right to the point. "Who did that to you, Etty?"

She stared into his eyes without blinking. He had always taken that as a sign of someone wanting to be believed, wanting to look sin-cere. Like a politician lying about where the brown envelope stuffed with cash had come from. "Ah now, Father. Brennan. There's no one to blame for this."

"Oh? How's that?"

"There's a man who lives near me. Well, not exactly near, but . . ." Not the owner of a pricey house in Sandymount. "I sometimes see him walking along the seafront, and he's a sad, poor soul. He's a little 'God help us,' if you know what I mean. Not right in his head. I've seen him countless times. But this time I came up behind him, didn't realize he hadn't heard me, and I startled the poor man, and he whipped round and he lashed out and hit me. A couple of times. And well, this is the result!" She pointed at the injuries to her face.

Maybe that's what happened. But Brennan thought back to the first time he had seen her, at Gormanston, and his impression that she had leaped at the chance to stay at the camp. And that it had come as a surprise to her husband, who had looked none too pleased about it. Was there a conflict between the two of them? Or was Brennan letting his imagination run away with him? Wait, though, there was something else. That story of her taking a punch in a late-night encounter in New York. Did that story have an element of the fable about it? And now, here she was with a bruised face and a guilty look. Why, if the culprit was some poor man with mental problems, would she be turning away now? Looking evasive? Brennan rested the tray on the nearest table, and reached out and put his right hand on her arm. "Etty. Tell me the truth."

Meeting his gaze again, she said, "I am telling you the truth, Father! I am. Now I've work to do here, seeing as I came late to the supper!" She tried to smile but she couldn't quite pull it off.

A couple of the other volunteers came by then, and Etty O'Daly got on with her work.

Brennan helped pick things up, and he stacked the chairs against the walls and then said his goodbyes and left.

On the way back to his aunt's flat in Brunswick Street, his mind was assailed by images of burnt-out cars smouldering in the Dublin streets, bodies lying broken. And an angry man beating the lovely Etty O'Daly about the face. Brennan pictured Jem O'Daly in this role. Why had he come to that conclusion? Wasn't it always the husband? And didn't the wife often come up with a story to exonerate him? If Brennan was right, what accounted for Jem O'Daly's violence towards his wife? How long had it been going on? What, if anything, could Brennan do about it?

∽

Early on Monday afternoon, Shay was in Store Street gabbing with some of the other young guards when Vince Foley approached him and gestured with his head towards the door of the station. *Meet me outside* was the message. So Shay walked outside a couple of minutes later and Vince was there. He had information for Shay again. "There's a witness coming in. Fella from the solicitor's office. Jem O'Daly's solicitors, I mean."

Oh, God, the papers Shay's father had claimed to have taken off Darragh McLogan. The papers the solicitor's clerk said never existed. Lorcan was the clerk's name.

"Lorcan?" he asked.

"No. Somebody else. He's coming in to talk to Griffith. I don't know anything more than that."

An hour or so later, who should appear but DS McCreevy. He walked into the workroom and said to one of the other guards, "Some of the lads are going over to Reade's for a few after work. Care to join us?" And then, oh so casually, "Oh, how about you, Rynne? Or, sorry, maybe you'll have other things on your mind today. Some other time, perhaps." This said with a creepy McCreevy smirk on his face.

That fucker. He knew about the witness coming in. A witness who might finally seal the fate of Shay's father. Well, Shay knew something, too. And it was past time to use it. "Thank you, sir. But not today. I've some more Xeroxing to do. I've been copying parts of my files, investigations I did well on. In case I try for a promotion someday. Handy rig to have, that new Xerox, so much faster than the one we used to have, when I first started making my copies."

The face on McCreevy was a sight to behold: his lips did a kind of spasm and his eyes jerked away. There was no mistaking the fact that he had got the message. Shay's records, Shay's successes, McCreevy's alteration of the Rosie McGinn file. And the threat of a Xerox copy somewhere, like a ticking time bomb. Or like a stolen handgun with the safety disengaged. Shay lowered his own face, got back to work, as if McCreevy had ceased to exist.

Shay heard nothing more about the new witness, and that made for another sleepless night. What new information did Colm Griffith have? What would this mean for Talkie Rynne?

At seven o'clock the next morning, Shay's phone rang. It was his mother, and he could hear the panic in her voice as soon as she spoke his name. "Shay! Get over here. The guards just rang. They're on their way over!"

"Ma, what did they say? I'll be —"

"Come now!"

Shay pulled on his clothes, gave his teeth a quick brushing, jumped into his car, and drove across the city as if the furies were after him. But it was his father they were after. Why would they ring first and tip off Talkie that they were coming? Didn't they think he might scarper as soon as he hung up the phone? Go on the run and find a hiding place to escape them? But they'd find him; they'd not be in any doubt about that.

He pulled up in Fenian Street, wrenched the car door open, and ran up to the flat. His mother and father were sitting there, petrified. Talkie's hands grasped his knees, and he was trembling. He hadn't tried to escape after all; even as agitated as he was, he knew they'd get him. Shay could hear Francie in the bedroom with little Kevin, jollying him into some kind of game. Even through the closed door, Shay could hear the desperation in her voice.

And then it came. The knock on the door. Shay signalled to his parents to stay put; he would handle this. He took a deep breath, told himself to stay calm, and opened the door. And it was Detective Sergeant Colm Griffith standing there. Alone. He showed no surprise at seeing Shay in the flat. Just nodded at him and walked in.

"Mr. Rynne," he said, standing in front of the sofa where Talkie and Deirdre sat, their eyes riveted on the detective. "I've welcome news for you. You are no longer under any suspicion."

Talkie's eyes didn't leave Griffith's face; he looked like a man whose life had taught him that welcome news came so rarely that there was always a catch, always bad news in its wake.

"You are in the clear."

Talkie finally found words. "D'yeh mean you've found the man that did it?"

"No, we haven't. Not yet. But your version of events the night of the McLogan party has been confirmed. The solicitor's clerk, Lorcan, who brought the papers to McLogan, papers relating to the restructuring of O'Daly's companies, and then denied it . . . A colleague of Lorcan's discovered that he had done exactly that: taken highly confidential documents from the office and passed them to McLogan."

"Thank you, thank you!" Talkie was sobbing with relief, as was Deirdre. Shay struggled to avoid breaking down himself.

Griffith turned to Shay then, smiled, and said, "Garda Rynne, why don't you take the day off, enjoy some time with your family here. And we'll see you tomorrow."

There was conversation after that, but Shay was barely aware of it, so overwhelming was the relief that his father would never be prosecuted for the murder of Darragh McLogan.

ᴄ⁄ᴐ

Brennan, like all the Burkes, was unaccustomed to calling on the police. He almost felt as if he should be sneaking in under cover of darkness. But if it was a battered wife he had seen, the consequences should rightly befall the husband who did the battering. And what if the husband, in this case, had done more? What if his guilt and tension over another deed, and fear that his wife harboured suspicions about him, had boiled over and been visited upon her?

So, the day after his conversation with Etty, Brennan walked across the north side of Dublin, walked along Talbot Street with its shattered shopfronts, its eerie calm after the bombing, walked amid the ghosts of Paddy Healey and the others who had died in these streets. Against his will, he pictured the pregnant woman, the people with their limbs blown off, the two babies and their parents, and so many others. The images brought on sorrow, created a fury within him. He stopped, made the sign of the cross, and said prayers for the victims. Once again, he could not bring himself to follow the creed of his faith and pray for forgiveness for the perpetrators. And what about a man who beats up his wife? A man who kicks to death his brother-in-law?

Forgiveness for him? Apparently not, in Brennan's mind; he kept walking to the Store Street Garda Station.

Garda Rynne was not in today. Could anyone else be of assistance? No, he said with thanks. He walked home and dialled Shay's number in Emmet Street. No answer; he'd try again after a while. So he headed to the family bar. And when he arrived at Christy's, Finn had good tidings for him. "Talkie Rynne's been cleared of the McLogan killing. Detective Sergeant Griffith delivered the news in person early this morning. Talkie rang me to let me know; never have I heard a man so joyful! Shay's there with him; Griffith gave him today as a holiday."

"Ah, that's brilliant news, Finn. What a relief for them all."

So he knew where to find Shay, got the phone number from Finn, and rang the Rynnes in Fenian Street. And when Deirdre Rynne put her son on the phone, he sounded as if he was filled with the joy of the Resurrection. "It's all over for him, Brennan. He's been cleared!"

"What a relief for all of you, Shay. Give him my congratulations."

"Give them to him yourself, why don't yeh? Come over. We're having a bit of a celebration here, as you might imagine. We've had very little to celebrate in this city, God knows. When did you arrive?"

"Got news of the bombings, and came here as soon as I finished up with my obligations in Italy. Landed here on Saturday. Went to the Healeys' place in Rathmines. It was excruciating."

"Ah, Brennan, it must have been. I was heart-scalded when I heard about Paddy. He was a wonderful fella."

"He was."

"But, em, if you feel like stopping by here . . ."

"I do. See you soon."

Brennan walked to his aunt's place to get his car. When he arrived at the Rynnes' flat, he found Talkie happily blitzed and everyone around him jubilant at the reprieve. Shay introduced him to a lovely, red-haired young woman named Allie.

"Allie, this is Father Burke, visiting here from the Vatican."

"The Vatican!"

"That's a bit of an exaggeration, Allie. Lovely to meet you."

"And lovely to meet you, Father."

"Call me Brennan."

"Brennan, it is."

Shay put his arm around her, pulled her close, and said, "We're going to be married!"

"Congratulations to you both! When's the big occasion?"

"Not till the autumn," Allie said, "but I wish it could be sooner! What I want is for us, the people in Dublin, to have as many happy events as we can, to show those fuckers . . . Oh, sorry, Father."

"No need to apologize, Allie. I regard those fuckers the same way you do."

"Right. No need to be polite about the kind of men who would come into our cities and murder all those innocent people. I want to show them that our lives will go on, that we won't be kept down out of fear of the likes of them. Shay and I want to start rebuilding the population of Dublin!"

Shay leaned towards Brennan and whispered, "Thought a few months ago that the repopulation was underway, but it turned out to be a false alarm."

Allie gave him a playful punch on the arm. "What did yeh tell him?"

"Nothing, dearest."

"Anyway," she said, "we're getting married. We've got all the paperwork done, for church and state. But we've a few months to wait. Seems like forever!"

Brennan said to them, "Why wait?"

The bridal couple looked at one another, said something about waiting for a cousin to come home from Australia, but that was no longer a sure thing. Once the idea took hold, the Rynne family were celebrating not only the father's reprieve but the son's imminent marriage. Why wait indeed?

Brennan would leave it to Allie and Shay to make whatever arrangements they had to make with the civic authorities, if any, and Brennan would handle the sacramental side of things. Before he left the flat, though, he wanted to speak to Shay about the supper in Fairview. "I want to fill you in on something I saw and heard yesterday evening."

"What is it, Brennan?"

"It's about Mr. and Mrs. O'Daly."

"Oh, Christ. Let's go outside."

"We can sit in my car."

When they were seated in the car, Brennan said, "Here's the story. I was helping out at Saint Joseph's school, you know, the group that's assisting some of the people from the North who have resettled here. They have suppers for them three times a week. There'll be one tomorrow. So I attended the supper yesterday, tried to help out a bit. One of the volunteers is Etty O'Daly. She arrived late, full of apologies. And her face was cut and bruised."

"Fuck!"

"Yeah. She saw me looking at her and avoided my eyes. I cornered her friend, a woman by the name of Dervla, and asked her what happened. And she told me what Etty had told her: that this man who's mental in some way, not right in the head, had hit her. Said she had come up behind him, surprised him, and threw a fright into him, and he reacted."

The man may have reacted, but Shay Rynne did not. Just sat there, looking intently at Brennan as the tale unfolded.

"I managed to get Etty alone at the end of the supper, and I asked her point-blank, 'Who did that to you?' And she gave me the big-eyed, unblinking stare."

"Right, the one that's supposed to say, *I'm not avoiding your eyes, I'm not blinking, I'm innocent, and I'm honest. Honest, I am.*"

"And she gave me the story of this poor, unfortunate man, sure, there's no harm in him at all."

"Except that he pounds women who get in his way. If he exists at all."

"Exactly. I wasn't buying that any more than you are. I said to her, 'Tell me the truth,' and there was no mistaking the look of fear in those eyes." Brennan paused and lit up a smoke. He offered the pack to Shay, and he took one. "So, Garda Rynne, what are we going to do about this?"

"About Jemser O'Daly."

369

Brennan nodded. "About Jemser O'Daly."

"Well, if Etty doesn't want to report him . . ."

"They never want to admit it, the wives. Don't want to inform on their husbands, don't want to admit that their family life is a shambles, don't want the *shame* of their friends and neighbours knowing about it. *They* are ashamed, the women, the victims, while the real shame, the guilt, lies solely with the husbands. Jesus the Christ, who suffered and died on the cross, could you do that, Shay? Could you strike a woman? I know I couldn't. Never even been tempted, even at times when I've been in a row with a woman; it never occurred to me to raise my hand."

"Same with me, Brennan. I remember when I was just a little lad, and my sister did something to annoy me. She was in a wax and wrenched the wheels off a toy lorry I had, one of the rare toys Da had been able to . . . get for us. And I reached out and punched her in the shoulder. And I felt like a nasty brute then, at the age of nine or ten, knew it was wrong. Sure you could hit your brother, but . . ."

Brennan smiled. "Nobody's saying a lad can't hit his brother."

"How about a brother-in-law? A man who gets into a temper and beats his wife might well do the same to her brother." Shay returned to the injured wife. "You remember what we heard when we were in New York."

"Yeah, I was thinking about that. Jem took her along to a meeting with some character who sounded more than a little dodgy, and he had a bodyguard —"

"And the bodyguard, a gorilla, as Jemser described him, made a lunge for Jemser."

"Though why he'd have done that remains an unanswered question."

"And Etty stepped into the breach."

"And took the punch that was coming for her husband. And that's how she ended up bruised on that occasion."

"Bit of a legend, perhaps, Brennan? They concocted a tale far more fanciful than the old 'She walked into a door,' which we'd likely have dismissed, having heard it so often."

370

"And maybe we'd think the New York story was so preposterous they wouldn't have made it up."

They were quiet for a moment, then Brennan said, "So, Guard, what are we going to do about this, if our speculations are correct? We have a man, an elected member of the Dáil, beating his wife."

"But we don't even have her, herself, giving evidence against him. I've been on calls for cases like this, Brennan, and the wife won't say a word against the man. She'll say she fell or, yeah, walked into a door. And you can be sure that's exactly what I'll face if I try to go after him for it. Evidence of violence, no evidence of who did it."

"Let's give it a try."

"Give what a try, Brennan?"

"Let's talk to her. She'll be at the supper at Joey's tomorrow evening. We'll come in near the end of it, and try to get her alone."

CHAPTER XXVIII

O n Wednesday evening, Shay came to collect Brennan for the
drive to Joey's, the school in Fairview. When they were on their
way, Shay said to him, "It means a great deal to me and Allie to have
you, my pal Brennan, officiating at our wedding."

"I'm delighted to be doing it."

"Thanks, Brennan."

They talked a bit about the plan — the wedding would take place
on Saturday — and then they arrived at the school and entered the
room where the supper guests were enjoying their pudding. Etty
O'Daly was among those pouring the final cups of tea and coffee
before things would wind up, and the clearing would begin. She saw
Shay and Brennan and faltered in her step towards a woman holding
out a teacup. Etty looked like a woman who was not only serving but
had been served; there was drink on her, if Brennan's observation was
correct. Her eyes were bloodshot and her gait unsteady. He doubted
that he'd been the only one to notice. She avoided the eyes of the priest
and the peeler, and carried on her duties. So they moved about the
room, chatting with people, asking how things were going. But they

had no intention of letting Mrs. O'Daly leave the hall without coming clean about the facial injuries that her makeup could not conceal.

As the volunteers cleared the tables of plates and cups and silverware, the guests filed out. But Brennan and Shay stood their ground. Etty peered out from the kitchen a couple of times until, finally, she gave in. There was no point trying to evade her inquisitors, so she came towards the two men. "Father, Garda Rynne, you're here to see me."

"We are," Brennan replied. He could smell something alcoholic on her breath.

"I explained to you the other night, Father, how I got hurt."

"You did. Could we go someplace and talk, Etty?"

"I don't see what there is to talk about."

"Yes, you do," Brennan said, in his most gentle voice.

And something about it worked on her; he saw tears springing to her eyes. "All right," she said, though she could hardly be heard.

"A snug?" Brennan whispered to Shay, who nodded in agreement. Many of Dublin's drinking spots had snugs, separate little rooms, some of them with doors. A place for private conversations.

"We'll go over to Kehoes," Shay decided, so they got into Shay's car and drove across the river and through the city centre to Kehoes on South Anne Street. Shay and Brennan each ordered a Guinness, Mrs. O'Daly a glass of red wine.

Brennan decided it was best to ease into things, even if she knew exactly what would be coming, eventually, as the night wore on. "How is life as a politician's wife now, Mrs. O'Daly? Do wives of TDs have a social role they have to play? Dressing in their finery and hosting the other wives when they'd rather be left alone in peace?" Brennan smiled as he said it.

She knew what he was up to, but she played along and told him about lunches and events that were de rigueur for the spouse of a Teachta Dála. It was not always what she wanted to do; she might want to spend time with her own family and friends, or go for a walk, read a book, or watch a program on the telly. But it was worth it, because of all the good her husband would be able to do for his people. Nobody knew and understood the poor people of Dublin better than Jem O'Daly. Oh, yes, everybody knew his history, but he had put that behind him, and he would be a great representative of his constituency.

"You and Jem have been married a good many years now, amn't I right?"

"You are. We married young. We began walking out together in our teen years and married when I was barely twenty years of age. We had to, er — well, I found I was . . ."

"Children are a gift," he assured her, with a fatuous piety that did not come naturally to him, even in his role as a priest of God.

"It's a good thing, because we have three of them!"

"All the better."

"Had them when we were very young. Of course, it was difficult to keep them fed, put shoes on their feet, especially in those early years. Jemser took on a number of jobs. Labourer, delivery man, you know."

"Right."

"But it still wasn't enough!" Her voice rose a notch. "Why do the men who own the shops and build the houses, why do they think they don't have to pay a living wage for a young man and his growing family?"

"Why indeed? It seems they're just looking out for themselves at times, doesn't it?"

"It does, so. And that's why Jem . . ."

Brennan stayed silent and waited for her to continue. She took a long swallow of her wine and darted a look at Garda Rynne. She said, "He owned up to all that stuff he did, owned up to it publicly when he announced that he'd be running in the election."

"And people appreciated that, I'm sure," Brennan said. "Him being honest about, well, about his past."

"They did. I . . . I knew what he was about, him and the sacks of things he came home with and hid in the house." Again, a look at Shay. "He's already been punished for all that. I knew it was wrong. He was committing crimes, but how else were people like us supposed to have anything at all? And he spread it around, did Jem. The oul wans on our street, they loved him! 'Have a nice ham for your Sunday tea, Mrs.

Mooney.' And the other young families. 'Here's a few quid for books for the little lad starting school, Mrs. Finnegan.' And like that."

Brennan looked at her near-empty glass. "Would you have another?"

"I would."

So he got up and ordered another glass of wine, and Guinness for himself and Shay.

She took a good, hearty swallow of the wine and said, "He'd not be happy, seeing me like this."

"Like what?"

"Drinking all this wine."

"Why would Mr. O'Daly not be pleased with you enjoying a glass or two?"

Her large grey eyes shifted from one side of the room to the other. "He'd be afraid I'd be talkative with it, so."

"What would be so wrong with that?"

She seemed to catch herself on then and said, "Fellas elected to the Dáil, you know. They want their families on their best behaviour!"

"As you are today, Etty. No worries there."

Brennan looked at the poor old woman sitting across from him. But he shouldn't have thought "old." Older than Brennan, but she wouldn't have been past her mid-forties. She looked tired and worn, no more meat on her now than on Brennan's plate on Good Friday, and her brown hair was turning grey. Clean it was, but hanging slack along the sides of her face.

And the drink wasn't doing her any good. Brennan was troubled in his conscience. He hadn't forced the wine on her; she'd been into it before he saw her at the supper, but still he knew he was using her intoxication to overcome her defences. Saint Thomas Aquinas tells us we are not to use an unjust means to achieve a just end, because the justice of the end is undermined by the injustice of the means employed. Though some moral philosophers maintain that it is permissible to use an evil means to prevent a greater evil. The old "lesser of two evils" distinction . . . He shook off his philosophizing and pursued his means to an end.

He got to the point. "Etty, I sit in the confessional every week, in my parish in New York City, and occasionally when I come home here to Dublin." She gave a wary nod; she didn't know where this was going. "And do you know what I hear?"

"Some terrible things, I'm sure, Father. Brennan." Her speech was beginning to slur.

"Some terrible things. Some very minor things that I couldn't remotely consider sinful." He smiled when he said it. "But, yes, some awful things, too. And I get women coming in, wives."

She didn't respond; it was as if she had no curiosity whatsoever about what a wife might say in the confession box.

"Once in a while, a wife will think she's confessing a mortal sin by admitting she has come to hate her husband and wants to leave him. When I hear this, and I probe her a bit for more information, it often comes out that the husband has been hitting, beating, abusing his wife." He could see Etty O'Daly steeling herself not to react. "But she doesn't want to break up the family, and she can't afford to live and bring up her children without their father's wages coming in. Sometimes, God help them, these poor women even claim it's their own fault that the husbands hit them. 'I deserved it, Father. I drove him to it. I'll not do it again.' Can you imagine a victim of violence taking the guilt upon herself?

"But, as I say, the women don't know how they and their children can survive without the husband and father, the wage earner. And they also feel shame and embarrassment, even though, of course, they have done nothing to be ashamed of. Now I know there are some priests, especially in the past but some still now, who give the woman a talk about the sanctity of marriage, and how she and the husband ought to make more of an effort to sort out their differences. Well, I never, ever tell an abused wife to stick with the man who is hurting her."

In a voice he could barely hear, Etty said, "What do you tell them?"

"My first reaction, in my earliest years as a priest, was to tell them to go to the police. But then I backed off away from that. Don't get me wrong: I fully believe the husbands should be charged with assault. But I know how daunting, and how dangerous, this would be to a vulnerable woman. So, instead, I offer to set them up with social workers or other professionals who are experts in the field of violence within families. If criminal charges come out of this eventually, so be it, but the wife has social workers or others in the field to support and protect her and her children."

"You two got me . . ." She started again and tried not to slur. "You got me here to tell me this."

"We did, yes. We *know*, Etty." He did not mention that the punching story from New York, recalled in the light of her more recent injuries, reinforced the suspicion that it was the usual suspect — the husband — who was guilty. "Now you say it's some poor man who's off his head and lashed out at you. But it's Jem. And if he's under stress about something he's done, something he thinks you know about, you are in more danger than ever."

She picked up her wine glass, which was nearly empty, but her hand was shaking so badly, she replaced the glass on the table.

"Is there something he's done, Etty, that's got him wound up? And the tension comes out in the form of violence against the person closest to him?"

Her hand shot out as if to slap her interrogators away, and the wine glass went flying. Brennan caught it and held it. "No!" she cried out, "he didn't do anything!"

"What do you think accounts for his . . . his behaviour now?"

"It isn't now! It was him being in America, him and his swanky clothes! How dear that must have been, all that clobber on him. The money for that. And him thinking he was one of them, one of those New York gangsters. Them with their . . ."

Her face was flushed, with drunkenness and resentment. The dam was about to burst.

"Their fancy women! The gangsters with their cashmere overcoats and their fedora hats, and their big whacks of money, and their fashion models! Actresses off the telly, or whatever they were. That's probably what they told them, the girls told the fellas. Girls all tarted up and dressed like showgirls. Or prostitutes! Oh, Jem swore to me on his mother's grave he never had anything to do with them over there. Well, I'll bet his poor mother is spinning circles in her grave, because I didn't believe a word out of his mouth."

And she was right, Brennan knew. He remembered what he had heard in New York about the actress or showgirl Jem had been squiring around.

"Jem would never have been able to resist all that," Etty said. "If he went along with them, the gangsters, on their bank robberies, or whatever all they did, and him all dressed up like them, do you think he didn't go whoring around while he was at it? Of course, he did. And that's why . . ."

"Why what, Etty?"

"The likes of me wasn't good enough for him anymore. But he tried to bring me up — or down! — to that level. Shoved a packet of pound notes at me one day after he came home from New York, put me in the brand-new Jaguar car he had then, and dropped me off at the shops in Grafton Street, and told me to buy some *sexy* clothes and makeup. And I'm such a sad, pathetic article of a wife that I tried to buy the things that would please him. So I kitted myself out in a slinky, shiny red dress and put all this makeup on my face. Rouge and eyeshadow and bright-red lipstick, and I felt like a right gobshite. And I presented myself in front of him. And I was all nerved up, scared that he wouldn't . . . he wouldn't rush into my arms in a fit of passion. He'd only laugh at me. As anyone would, who had any sense. But he . . ."

And at this, the poor woman burst into tears. And Brennan felt like a heel, which he was, having brought her to this point, by using her weakness for the wine to batter down her resistance. He felt like a pervert, a voyeur into her intimate life with her husband. "What did he do?" asked Burke the voyeur.

"His face turned to disgust at the sight of me. Even when I tried, I couldn't measure up. Couldn't be the fancy woman he wanted. Well, look at me! And then his disgust turned to rage! And he came at me and . . ."

Oh, God.

Brennan saw Shay sit forward in his chair. Brennan almost expected him to take out a notebook, but he merely sat and readied himself for what was to come.

"He drew back his fist and smashed it into my face. He fucking — he beat me till I was howling in pain! That's what my own husband did to me! I couldn't show my face outside the house for days on account of it!"

"Oh my God, Etty, I am so very sorry." Sorry that it happened, sorry that he had wormed it out of her. And yet it had to be out in the open, what that gouger had done.

She was convulsed with the crying, and Brennan got up and went round to her side of the table. He drew her up as gently as he could and wrapped his arms around her. He couldn't come up with anything to say that would be equal to the situation except, again, "I'm so sorry."

After a few seconds, she seemed to pull herself up straight and she said — she claimed — "I'm all right, Father. Brennan. I'm grand." And she turned away and then sat down in her chair.

"You say you're all right, Etty, but how can you be? After being beaten up by your own husband. Did you . . ." He knew the answer to his question, so he changed it to a statement. "You didn't take him to law over it."

She gave him the kind of look he deserved. Of course she hadn't laid charges. The wives never did. "How could I have done that, Brennan?" The effects of the drink were even more noticeable now, in her face and in the slurring of her speech. "How could I make a show of us? Have us disgraced in front of our neighbours and the public, and the whole thing reported in the newspapers? And him setting his sights on politics?"

"It wouldn't have been you that was disgraced, Etty. Only him. And he fu— he surely deserved it."

"It doesn't work that way, Brennan." It was as if she were explaining the facts of life to a tender young child. "So any time he did it, I had to —"

"How often did he attack you like this?"

"It wasn't often, only once in a while. And he'd be full of remorse for it, and he'd apologize."

There was nothing unusual about that, Brennan knew.

"Months would go by and our lives would be almost normal. But then something would set him off. It was a rage in him. And it was me that brought it out in him, the wife that couldn't live up to his expectations. His standards. I shamed him. I was no longer good enough for him."

"*You* weren't good enough? *He* wasn't good enough to be in the same room with you, Etty. So, that was when it started, after he came home from New York?"

"The first time was in New York. I went over to visit him there. Darragh and Muriel, too. Jemser and I were out one night, with people he'd met there. A bunch of gangsters! I think they were the Mafia! And their women. They had some name for them, a word in Italian, I can't remember now. But they weren't their wives. And all Jem had was me! And I didn't measure up, and he started talking about me going to a hairdresser, losing weight, buying new clothes and all that, and I laughed. He got into a furious temper and he hit me, bruised my face. Then he was shocked at himself. And he was all apologetic. And he told me to hit him back. 'Thump me as hard as you can, love. I deserve it.' So I did. And then he made up a foolish story to tell Darragh and Muriel, a tale about one of the gangsters and his bodyguard, and he pretended that I stepped into the middle of a fight and got hit. I don't think they believed a word of it!"

Brennan exchanged a glance with Shay. So much for the fabled fight with the gorilla. Then Shay seemed to be telegraphing a message to him. If Brennan was reading him correctly, it was time to get to the other point of the exercise.

"Etty, did your brother know what Jem was doing to you?"

"Darragh?" Her voice caught when she uttered the name of her murdered brother. "I . . . I think he pretended to believe me when he spotted the odd bruise on me. I never let him or anyone else see me after the most ferocious times. He pretended to believe my excuses. What he might have said to Jem about it, I've no idea."

380

Brennan avoided Shay's eye as he contemplated what Darragh McLogan might have said to the man who'd been brutalizing his sister. If the guards could get Jem for the assaults on his wife, could this lead them to somehow make a case that he had killed McLogan to keep the abuse from becoming public?

"He can't be allowed to get away with this crime, Etty."

Shay spoke up then. "I'll go in and remove him from your house, Etty. I'll arrest him and have him charged."

Her eyes were wide with fear. "No! You can't do that! He'll kill me!"

"Etty, we'll have him out of the house. He'll be under arrest."

This had the poor woman on the verge of hysteria. Weeping, shaking, putting her hands up as if to ward off Shay and Brennan and their threatening — threatening to her — talk of arrest. "He'll get out sooner, or he'll get out later. And he will kill me." She lurched towards them and nearly knocked Brennan's glass off the table. She managed to steady it with a shaking hand. "I should have killed *him*." She reached around and tried to get a grip on her handbag, but the hand got tangled in the strap. Brennan leaned over and untangled it and placed it on the table in front of her. "I want to go. I have to go. Take me to Dervla's."

So Brennan and Shay split their bar tab, and they supported the sobbing, drunken woman out of the bar. They got her into Shay's car, waited patiently for comprehensible directions to Dervla's place in Ballybough, and pulled up in front of the house. Etty insisted on walking to the door under her own steam, and they waited until she was safely inside.

Shay looked across at Brennan, and Brennan nodded. They both knew they wanted a calming drink or two at Christy Burke's. They drove to the bar, went inside, greeted Finn, and got their drinks.

When they were seated at a table, Brennan said, "So, is there anything you can work with? Do we have a motive here — McLogan confronts O'Daly about the abuse visited upon his sister, and O'Daly loses it and kicks him to death? Kills him in a fit of anger coupled with fear that the dirty secret will get out?"

"We might be able to suggest that as a motive. We wouldn't get far without some evidence of O'Daly's involvement, but we have that in the form of the construction rubble on his one sock. And we have him lying; he said there was no argument between him and McLogan at the party. But we don't have McLogan to tell us what he knew!"

"Right. Problem solved, from the point of view of O'Daly. And meanwhile, the poor woman lives in fear. She thinks he'd kill her if she reported him for the abuse."

"She's probably right, Brennan. Little wonder she said she should have killed him, rather than living with the constant fear that some night he's going to kill *her*."

Brennan played her words back in his mind: "I should have killed *him*." Yes, instead of living in fear of him killing *her*. He listened to the playback in his mind again. There was another way to interpret it, but it didn't make any sense unless . . . He looked at Shay and said, "Should have killed *him* instead of —"

"Instead of somebody else. Fucking hell! Do you think?"

"Why would she?"

"What was it she said when you asked her about him, about her brother? He pretended to believe her?"

"That's what she said. But did he perhaps know perfectly well that her injuries were the result of O'Daly beating her? The pair of us sussed it out. How could he not?" Brennan sank his whiskey in two swallows and put down his glass. "There are two possible motives here, Shay. One, McLogan confronted O'Daly about the abuse, and O'Daly knocked him down and kicked him to death."

"And even in this storm of emotion," said Shay, "he had the presence of mind to take off his own shoes and put on McLogan's, so there was — difficult to say premeditation, given such a very short time frame — but he knew what he was going to do."

"Yes. And the second motive is that of a woman who may have been looking to her brother for support and protection."

"That's what her sister said at McLogan's funeral, that Darragh was the big brother who always protected his little sisters. Had he failed in that duty, or that role, later in life? Did he pretend to believe that

Jem hadn't laid a hand on her? Did he know the truth and not do anything about it? Afraid of Jem himself, maybe? I've heard of more than one instance of Darragh trying to placate Jemser. 'Yes, Jem, sure, Jem,' sort of thing. Placate him, please him, suck up to him."

And she had come to despise him for it.

CHAPTER XXIX

Shay's sleep that night was disrupted over and over again by images, or dreams, of a man and a woman, and sometimes a boy and a girl, standing face to face and shouting at each other. He could not hear the words, but the facial expressions were clear; they ranged from bitterness to fear to grief. He knew somehow that the two figures were not Etty O'Daly and her husband, but Etty and her brother. And he knew he had to talk to Etty.

At half seven in the morning, he was standing on the doorstep of the house where Etty was staying in Ballybough. He knocked and waited, and the other woman came to the door. Dervla, the owner of the house. She was wearing a faded pink housedress and a white wool cardigan; her hair was in curlers. What should he say to her?

"Dervla?"

"Yes?"

"I'm Garda Rynne. I'm sorry to be disturbing you so early in the day, but it's important that I speak to Mrs. O'Daly."

The woman's left hand flew up to her heart; she stared at Shay in alarm. "Is something wrong? Has something happened?"

"No, nothing's happened, but I must speak to Etty."

"She's still in bed. But I'll go and wake her. You come inside now. Have a seat in there." She pointed to the sitting room. "Would you like a cup of tea?"

"Thank you, Dervla, but no, I won't have tea right now."

She nodded and headed for the staircase. Shay entered the sitting room and sat in an armchair. The room was clean yet cluttered with mementos, family photos, and little porcelain figurines of dogs and cats. And, like so many others of her generation, she had an image of the Sacred Heart behind a red candle holder on her mantelpiece. He smiled when he saw a racing form on a side table; Dervla must be following the horses.

He sat for a few minutes, and then he heard footsteps on the stairs. Dervla came down followed by Etty. Etty looked as if she had spent the same kind of night Shay had. Her face was puffy and her eyes red, but she had tried to dress for the visit, in a dark-brown trouser suit. He could smell lavender and mint as she came up to him — soap and toothpaste. She looked over at Dervla, who said, "I've a program I listen to on the radio. It's downstairs. I've some cleaning to do down there. The two of yis have your conversation. Take your time. I'll be downstairs." Her nervous chatter continued as she left the room.

Etty's voice came out as a harsh whisper. "Why are you here, Garda Rynne?"

He stayed silent until, a few seconds later, he heard the sound of the radio. Then he had to make a decision. How quickly, and how forcefully, should he get onto the subject? He nodded to the chair beside him, and she sat down. "Etty, you look as if you didn't sleep a wink."

"Is it any wonder, after the questions you and Father Burke were firing at me? That's all I could think of all night, and the drink didn't help matters at all."

His conscience was fairly clear on that point. He and Brennan hadn't discouraged her from consuming the wine, to be sure, but she had been into it before they saw her. She was a willing participant in the night's drinking. "I'm sorry you had a sleepless night, Etty. I didn't sleep well myself."

"And why would you be going without sleep?"

"Because I kept picturing what happened. You and your husband. You and your brother."

"My brother!" It came out as a squeak.

"Why did you do it, Etty?"

"Do what? You don't think I . . ."

"I don't think it. I *know*." He sounded more confident than he felt. But he hoped to leave her little room to manoeuvre if she really had killed Darragh McLogan. "I'm here by myself, Etty. This is not an official interview." If he failed to — deliberately chose not to — follow the proper procedures for taking a statement and obtaining a confession, then whatever she told him would almost certainly not be admitted as evidence in a court. He did not spell this out for her.

"Not an official interview. That's supposed to comfort me?"

"There's not much comfort to be had, I know. Your husband should be arrested and charged with the assaults he committed against you."

"No! I told you! He wouldn't be in jail forever and when he gets out . . . You know what he'd do."

She was quaking, trying to hold her hands still. But not succeeding. She was fearful and weakened by a night without sleep. A night filled, no doubt, with images much worse than those haunting Shay's own late-night hours.

"My own fear in this, Etty, is that if we arrest him and he knows what you did to Darragh, *that* will be dangerous for you." He leaned in close to her, and she tried to shrink away. "Does Jem know about Darragh?"

"No! He can't understand who would have . . . Sometimes he thinks it was someone in the party, in Fianna Fáil, somebody who got into a row with Darragh at the Ard Fheis. He's never even . . . never even considered that it, that I . . ."

"Darragh must have hurt you very badly. I don't mean physically —" Shay halted in mid-sentence. Or was there a physical aspect to it?

But Etty cut into his thoughts. "No, Darragh never touched me in any way, hit me. Never. But . . ." She looked around the room, as if someone might have crept in. The radio was still playing downstairs in the kitchen. Then she broke down, wracked with sobbing. "He was my brother. My older brother, and he didn't do a fu— didn't do a thing! He tried —"

Her voice failed her, and it took a moment before she spoke again. "He tried to follow after Jem that night at the party, but Jem didn't notice him. Everyone else had left the house. Muriel had gone up to bed. I started into the sitting room to turn off the music; Jem had a record album going in there. But I saw him and Darragh still talking, and I don't know how Darragh was able to carry on a conversation, he'd had so much to drink. As I did myself; I was way over my usual limit of, you know, three or four glasses. Anyway, I didn't go in when I saw them there.

"Darragh was saying something about a photo being taken for the newspaper the next day, that he had arranged with a news photographer to take photos of Jem and Darragh out at the track with the horse Jem had bought a couple of months ago. The picture would show Jem's fun side; it would be a 'grand thing for the campaign.' They were looking ahead to whenever there would be an election, and Jem would put himself on the ballot. I said to myself, Sure, he doesn't want any photos taken at home. Why? In case Jem pounds me again and gives me another black eye and a bloody mouth between now and picture time? But Jem wasn't paying him any mind, started walking to the back of the house.

"And I looked at my brother trying to trot along behind the great man, staggering and tripping and not being able to keep up. And Jem not even aware that he was there. He'd already forgotten about Darragh. And they went out the back door; I don't know why. Not long afterwards, Jem came back inside and went up to get ready for bed. Then Darragh fell over his own feet and landed on the ground, in the midst of all the mess caused by the construction next door. I looked out the window and saw him, lying there moaning and trying to say something."

The talk was coming out of her so fast and furious Shay could hardly keep up with it. But he knew better than to interrupt.

"I saw my brother lying out there, and out I went. There were some bottles and glasses out there; guests had wandered out with their drinks. And there was a broken bottle and a plate of food spilt. So I wanted to clean it all up, help Muriel out a bit. They have the young one who cleans for them, but I thought about it being summer, and midges being attracted to the mess. I was still in my high-heeled shoes; they were new and white, and I didn't want to get them dirty out there. I noticed that one of Darragh's shoes had come off him, and that gave me the idea to wear his shoes — comfortable, flat loafers — while I tidied up. They were a bit big for me, but then so were my high-heeled shoes. I'd had to glue insoles into them for the party. The glue kept seeping around the insoles and sticking to my feet. It's a wonder I could even get them off me."

There was a look of confusion about her then. "Where was I? What was I saying?"

"You were telling me about putting Darragh's shoes on your feet for your cleaning up outside."

"Right, right. I'm so . . . The memory of it . . . Darragh was lying there, scuttered with drink, and he was whinging about Jem. 'Etty, go get Jem for me. He didn't even listen, and me after helping him.' Or something like that. I thought to ignore him and I started to pick up the broken glass. But then I thought how pathetic he sounded, how pathetic he was, and I turned back and stood over him and said what I'd been wanting to say for years but never did."

She stopped and took a deep breath, slashed her hand against her eyes to wipe away her tears. But she resumed speaking. "I said to Darragh, 'Look at the state of you. You're a sad excuse for a man. You following after Jemser like a poodle and you knowing full well what he's been doing to me!'

"'Ah, now,' he starts to say to me. And it was one 'ah, now' too many. Sure, when it all started, I pretended I'd got injured in other ways, and he believed me. Or pretended to believe me. But eventually I had told him the truth: that it was Jemser hurting me. That night, I turned on Darragh and said, 'You told me you'd confront him and you'd straighten him out and you never did! You, my brother, and you not protecting me. Instead, you trail around after Jem, boosting his career and your own future at his side. Or seven steps behind him, but still your future tied to his! Him being the husband who beats me senseless, and you don't have the bottle to stand up against him and stand up for me!'

"Oh, I was raging. And I realized he wasn't hearing me. He'd gone to sleep, passed out with the drink. And here was me with the anger that had been building up all this time, and I drew off and brought my fist down on his face, and he whimpered like a little child, and he tried to grab my hand. But he was so drunk, he was incapable. He looked up at me with almost terror in his eyes. And I realized something then: that he should be afraid of me, that I should have taken him in hand years ago. And I lost the run of myself entirely then.

"I pulled my foot back and gave him a terrific kick in the ribs. And he let out a yelp. But there was nobody around to hear him. Muriel was upstairs in their bedroom at the front of the house. Me and Jemser had the room next to it. And the neighbours next door were out of their place because of the construction. Nobody heard us. And I couldn't stop myself. He put out his arm to stop me, tried to raise himself up. I drew off and kicked him with all my might, kicked him in the head! God forgive me! He fell back. And I did it again. I was kicking out at him, and at Jem, for all the beatings Jem had done to me and Darragh had ignored and let happen. It was as if I was kicking the life out of the two of them. And then I copped on to myself and went into the house and left him out there."

She was shaking. She covered her face with her hands and sobbed, "And he died of the injury to his brain. I did that! Oh God, oh God!"

Shay wanted to put his arms around her, comfort her, but he stayed in place, immobile. Questions kept coming into his head, things he should ask her. He thought of the evidence, the debris found on her husband's sock. What was the explanation for that? He ventured a question. "Etty, there was evidence — dust and stuff from the construction site — found on one of Jem's socks. How did that happen?"

She stared at him as if it was difficult even to process his question. But eventually she spoke, and he had to strain to hear her. "When

I, when I left him there, Darragh, I took his shoes off me, and I picked up my own, and started to walk back into the house with just my stockings on. Nylon stockings. And I looked down and saw that some of the dirt was on my feet. There was a bucket of rainwater out by the back door. Muriel uses it to water their flowerpots. So I washed the dirt off my feet so I wouldn't track it into the house. I went up to the room where we were staying and changed into my nightdress. And I threw my shoes into our travel bag. We'd just brought the one. But I remembered that my shoes were dirty from being out there, so I took them out and washed them in the bathtub."

After this recitation, she looked at Shay as if she had no idea who he was. As if she had been back in her brother's house all over again and had forgotten her surroundings in Dervla's place.

After a long moment of silence, she said, "What did you ask me?"

"I asked how the dirt would have got onto Jemser's sock. Were his socks in the bag?"

"They were. He was . . . He was there snoring in the bed, sound asleep."

So the dirt from her shoes had been transferred to her husband's sock before she thought to wash the shoes. The sock was the main piece of evidence against him. Dirt on the soles of his shoes was unremarkable; it was known that he'd been outside. But not in his sock feet.

Shay had no idea what to do next. He had a confession of murder; the case was solved. But he could not bring himself to do the obvious.

"You're going to put me in jail!" she whispered. "My life is over!"

He wanted time to think. If he put her under arrest now, or took her to Store Street for a cautioned statement, the wheels would start turning and would not stop until Etty O'Daly had been crushed beneath them. He had to think.

"Etty, I'm leaving now."

"What are you going to do?" It was almost a scream.

"Nothing now. Does anyone else know this?"

"Of course not!"

"Keep it that way." He didn't know how to make his exit, so he called down the stairs. "Dervla! I'm on my way now." He had to say it twice, before he heard the radio switched off, and the woman saying she'd be up in a jiffy.

"What are you going to do?" Etty said again, this time her voice barely audible.

"I'm not going to do anything without talking to you first. This conversation was between you and me, nobody else."

"But —"

They were saved by Dervla appearing at the top of the stairs. "Etty, are yeh all right? What's happened?"

"Just the same thing again, Dervla. My brother's death and all that."

Dervla nodded her head. Shay slipped out the door.

CHAPTER XXX

O n Saturday morning, Father Burke was standing at the altar of Dublin's magnificent Pro-Cathedral, backed by a semicircle of Doric columns. The bride and groom stood before him, and golden light shone down on them from the high windows of the domed cathedral. Shay and Allie were dressed in suits. His was grey, hers pale green with a matching cap, which brought to Brennan's mind the elegant style of Jacqueline Kennedy. Shay's little nephew, Kevin, was bouncing with excitement as the ring bearer, and he was togged out in a Dublin blue football jersey. Finn Burke was on hand, and there was a good turnout, given the short notice, from family, friends, and fellow gardaí. Brennan found the event particularly poignant and he imagined everyone else did, too, given that the cathedral was situated between two of the bombed-out streets, Parnell and Talbot, and had held funerals for several of the victims, with large crowds bearing witness outside the building. Now, the church was the site of a life-affirming — perhaps defiant — event, as the young couple embarked on their shared future.

Shay and Allie were elated after their rush-to-the-altar wedding (though the rush was not for the usual reason). Everyone gathered for a reception afterwards at a modest little hotel not far from the church, and then the bride and groom set off on Saturday afternoon for their two-day honeymoon in Killiney. One of the actors Allie knew through the Gate Theatre had a house there and was away for the weekend, so he offered the house to Allie and her new husband. Killiney was famed for its lovely strand, its spectacular view of the Irish Sea, and for the beautiful houses high on the hill overlooking the water. The Irish Sea was not quite warm enough for swimming in early June, but the sand felt lovely on their feet as they walked the strand. The honeymoon was brief but heavenly, and they savoured every moment before returning to the workday world on Monday.

When they were back at the house in Emmet Street, Shay had the television on and watched the news. Near the end of the broadcast was a story about Jem O'Daly and a couple of other politicians bringing boxes of clothing, toys, and other items to Saint Joseph's school for the people who had fled the North and for other poor people in the Fairview area. Shay noticed Des Creaghan standing in a crowd of reporters with their microphones and notebooks. Des whispered something to the woman standing next to him, and they shared a laugh. The other pols had their wives with them, and when it was Jemser's turn to speak, he gave his spiel and said, "Mrs. O'Daly would love to be here with us today. As you know, she has a long history of involvement with the refugees, at the camp at Gormanston and here at Joey's. But her sister in England isn't well. She took a bad turn and, of course, Etty was immediately off away on the boat to be at her sister's side in Bristol." Shay didn't listen to the rest of the blather.

On Tuesday morning he was once again at the door of Etty's friend Dervla.

"Ah, Garda Rynne!"

"I'm sorry to be bothering you, Dervla. But I'm wondering about Etty."

"Such a shame about her sister. You know she's gone over to England? Etty has. She's years younger, the sister is, younger than Etty, so she is, but her health has never been good, God bless her."

"When did Etty leave for England?"

"Oh, she left right away when she heard. That was Saturday. She barely had time to say goodbye to her husband, I don't think. Off she was."

"I know you've been very good to her, Dervla."

"Ach, anyone would help out . . .'"

"Etty had been staying here for a while. How long was she here?"

"It would have been a week, a week and a half, I suppose it was. Those injuries, you know, from that man. That poor soul along the seafront. She didn't want her family seeing that, and upsetting themselves."

"I wonder what she told them about coming to stay with you. Did they know about the injuries?"

"Oh, she'd have given them a nice story. Spare them knowing about all the bruises, sure. I think she told them she was coming here to help *me* out. I told her I might be moving house, this place being too big for me now. She did help me to pack some things away."

Was that what she told Jem? Or did she tell him to eff off with himself, and she was going to stay with her friend? Well, nobody but the two of them would know how that conversation had gone.

"Right," he said to the woman standing in her doorway, "so, any idea how long she'll be in England?"

Dervla fingered a holy medal hanging round her neck. "Only God knows, doesn't He? If her sister is poorly, I'm sure Etty will stay at her side. If she gets better, please God, we'll have Etty back with us again."

"Thank you, Dervla. I'll not keep you any longer."

"Sure, it's not a bother."

He said goodbye and left, his mind in turmoil.

The killer had fled the jurisdiction. Here was the biggest success in Shay's career, and the suspect had absconded.

But part of him was glad of it, happy to hear that Etty had got away. She had suffered bouts of abuse at the hands of her husband, spread over several years. Shay understood all too well why she had not been able to bring herself to have Jemser O'Daly charged with the crimes. Then the person she expected to help and support her, protect her from her husband's assaults, turned out to be useless. Darragh

McLogan had been more interested in being supported by O'Daly than in protecting his own sister. And all this finally erupted the night of the McLogan party. Etty lost control, and in her fury, she punished her brother. Kicked him over and over in her hurt and anger. As much as Shay would like to close the file on the murder, a case in which his own father had been a suspect, he could not bear the image of Etty standing trial, being convicted, spending perhaps the rest of her life in a prison cell. Let her stay across the sea in England. Fair play to her.

CHAPTER XXXI

All was good for Shay on the home front. He and Allie were bliss-fully happy as a married couple. But the long summer days of 1974 went past without any sign of an arrest for the bombings in Monaghan and Dublin. By the second week of July, the members of the Garda unit conducting the investigation had "returned to their stations," according to the chief superintendent's report. By the second week of August, the Dublin investigation report was completed, with nobody on the books for the killings.

Shay was stewing about this as he sat smoking and sinking pints in Christy Burke's pub on a night in early September. Allie was working her shift at the theatre. She had gently dismissed his suggestion that he escort her to and from the theatre, rather than have her walk by herself. "As much as I'd be chuffed to have a Garda escort, Shay my love, how would that protect me from a car bomb?" She knew it made no sense, and, of course, so did he. He knew he couldn't protect Allie or the other members of his family.

But, like everybody else in the city, he was on edge. He'd been blown into the air by one of the bombs, had seen the bodies torn apart, and then there were more bombs. When would the terrorists strike again? Shay was well on his way to being langered, and that was a far better state to be in than sober. Or was it? All the whiskey and porter in the Republic of Ireland was not going to wash away the knowledge of what was happening in his city, in his police force. He felt not a twinge of remorse for being indiscreet, for sitting at a table at the back of Christy's with Finn Burke and telling Finn exactly what he thought of An Garda Síochána's, and the government's, failures in the previous month, August of 1974.

"I'm not codding you, Finn, they've wound up the investigation. Three car bombs here in Dublin and one in Monaghan, thirty-four deaths including that full-term baby, and nearly three hundred of our people injured. An atrocity like this, committed against us, and our investigation is over three months later. Over and done. And not one of those northern loyalist murderers brought to justice!

"This in spite of so many leads that weren't followed up. I've heard that the British authorities and security forces in the North have scads of information about the bombers. Eyewitnesses were able to pick out suspects after being shown photographs; some of the witnesses connected the men in the photos to the bomb cars, or recognized them from behaving suspiciously in the context of what happened. Was this crucial evidence followed up? Nah."

Finn sat glowering across the table, a cigarette forgotten in his ashtray.

"Our government had solid information about this. They knew the Brits even had the *names* of some of the men believed to have been involved. Members of loyalist paramilitary groups. Yet this information was never followed up, no arrangements made with the authorities in the North to get those murdering bastards down here to face trial. Those of us at the bottom of the Garda hierarchy are wondering what the fuck the higher-ups are doing. Or, should I say, not doing! And where are the members of our government? Sitting on their arses, doing nothing. It has to be said that the government of this state has shown very little interest in solving this war crime against our country!"

It was a fierce look on the face of Finn Burke. He didn't have his dark glasses on, and his grey-blue eyes were narrowed and his lips clamped shut. Then he said, "The men who govern these twenty-six counties are obsessed with one thing above all others, and that is the Irish Republican Army. They're afraid of the Officials, that they're going to overthrow the government and turn this into a communist state. And they're in fear of our lads, too." There was no question of who "our lads" were — Finn and the other members of the Provisional IRA. The Officials wanted a political solution, a socialist-Marxist solution. The Provos knew that would go nowhere. As far as they were concerned, the Brits and their toadies in the North never responded to anything less than the violence they themselves perpetrated up there.

"All those repressive new laws here," Finn continued, "I'm not alone in thinking part of the motive for that is to bring joy to the Brits! Remember how everybody laughed when some of us suspected that the Brits not only had spies here in this part of the country, but had a man in the Garda itself? Everyone thought we were . . . What's the word for nutters who think everybody is out to get them?"

"Paranoid."

"Paranoid, right. Well, they *are* out to get us, always have been, and that detective sergeant, that spy, was helping them out with secret documents from the Garda Síochána."

"You'd wonder if they have more spies inside the Garda, inside the government!"

"Our government, right. Wouldn't doubt it. Do you know what was keeping the members of our government up in the night, Shay? What had them panic-stricken? Their big fear was 'Brits out'! Our government was terrified that the Brits really would pull out of the North."

"Leaving a civil war in their wake," Shay replied, "and it might spill over into the South."

"It already has done. I suspect that's what motivated the Dublin and Monaghan bombings. The loyalists want to bring the war to us. And I have it on good authority that the Brits aren't just standing by and doing nothing; they're colluding with the loyalist paramilitaries and their bomb makers and assassination squads. Sure, it sounds barmy, but I'm telling you I have good authority for saying it."

Finn signalled his barman for two more pints of Guinness, and when they arrived, Shay took a big mouthful. "I feel like walking out, Finn. Quitting the Garda, heading up North, and joining a force that will try to put those loyalist fuckers in their place. Leave the Garda behind, leave Fenian Street behind, and go North."

"Ah, you'd not be leaving Fenian Street behind. We're all on Fenian Street in our own way, Seamus!" But then Finn gave him a long look, a serious look. What he said came as a surprise. "Don't do it, Shay. As much as I'd like to see you go active" — go active, meaning join the Provos — "we need good peelers. I'm not talking here about peelers sympathetic to the republican cause." He smiled then. "Though that's a fine thing in itself. But no, there's many a good man, and woman, too, in the Garda. Now more than ever, this state needs good coppers. And you're a good copper."

Later, lying in bed, with his head pounding from the drink and the worry, Shay's thoughts returned to his day-to-day concerns as a guard. He longed to confide his secret, the secret of Etty O'Daly's confession, to someone and hear someone else's perspective. He had seen a photo in the paper a few weeks earlier, showing Etty and Jem together in Dublin; her summer break in England was over. It was grand talking to Finn about the state's scandalous inaction over the bombings. But he couldn't tell Finn what he knew about Etty. He hadn't even told Allie, didn't want her burdened with it.

There was, though, one person he could talk to in confidence. Father Brennan Burke was used to keeping secrets; his job, his vocation, demanded it. On pain of excommunication, Shay knew. Shay would not be making a confession to Brennan, of course; he would be revealing someone else's confession — a non-sacramental confession — and he knew the secret would be safe with Brennan. But Brennan was in Rome. What time was it there? Shay looked at his clock. Half one in the morning in Dublin, an hour later in Rome. He made up his mind to ring him early in the workday.

Brennan was bathed and shaved, cool and refreshed, but he knew the feeling would not last for ten minutes in the searing heat of Rome, even in September. His plan was to do some research in the library at the Pontifical Lateran University. And he knew how cool it was inside the Lateran basilica. Another advantage, if any more were needed, of the great architecture of Rome. But he'd have to endure the scorching sun to get there. He would put it off for a bit, say his morning Mass here in his room and do some reading before heading out. He meant to read some scriptural commentaries, but he returned to a book he'd begun the day before, by a Jesuit scientist, all about the moon and the craters named in honour of some of those Jebbie scientists and mathematicians. He was admiring a photo of the full moon rising over Dubrovnik when his phone rang.

"Brennan, how are yeh?"

"I'm grand, Shay, and yourself?"

There wasn't much in the way of small talk before Shay got to the point. "Brennan, I went to see Etty O'Daly after you and I talked to her in Kehoes. The morning after."

"Yes?"

"Yes." And then it came. Shay recounted the conversation he'd had with Etty, her admission that she had killed her brother in a burst of disappointment and rage. It hadn't been planned; it hadn't been foreseen. She just lost the head and went at him.

"She lashed out," Shay said, "after years of abuse, years of being a battered wife."

"But it wasn't her husband she killed."

"If only! I'd be tempted to overlook it, Brennan, pretend I didn't know, if it had been Jemser himself she kicked to death. Even if she was taken to trial for it, she might get a short sentence from a merciful judge — a battered woman finally driven to end it. But she didn't kill the husband. She killed her brother."

"He'd always been the big brother, protector of the younger kids. But when his sister was being brutalized, he didn't have the balls to stand up to Jemser O'Daly. He'd turned into O'Daly's lapdog, trailing after him and begging his pardon."

"I know, I know. But that wouldn't stand up as a justification for killing the brother. And, of course, there's something else."

"Oh?"

"Brennan, how can I justify bringing charges against this poor woman who lashed out and killed a man, while those men who murdered dozens of our people and injured hundreds more go free?"

"I know, Shay, you're in a cleft stick here, and I want to help you. Let me think about this. And you can be sure I'll be thinking. How about if I ring you tonight?"

"Good, Brennan. Talk tonight."

Brennan went out into the scorching sun of day and waited for the bus to take him from his place near the Greg — the Pontifical Gregorian University — to the Lateran university and basilica. He was almost sick in his stomach as he considered the moral quandary Shay Rynne was facing. And it was a moral quandary for Brennan himself: What was the right thing to do here? What advice should he be giving to Shay?

When he got to the Lateran, he headed straight for the basilica, which was originally founded in the time of the Emperor Constantine in the fourth century. It had undergone much rebuilding since then. With its grey stone classical exterior, many commentators had noted over the years that it looked like the front of a palace rather than a church. But it was in fact the church of the Bishop of Rome. In other words, the Pope was its parish priest. The interior was dazzling with its soaring columns, statues, mosaics, and frescoes. And the thick walls, bless them, kept it cool inside.

He genuflected and blessed himself, and beseeched the Almighty to grant him wisdom. He slipped into a pew and thought about Etty O'Daly, pictured her in the dock for murder. Her, a battered wife. But it wasn't the abusive husband she had killed; Brennan wouldn't suffer a qualm about letting that go. The victim was her brother, who had never laid a hand on her. Nor had he stood by and held Jemser O'Daly's coat while he battered his wife; Darragh hadn't aided his brother-in-law in that way. But he had failed to protest, failed to step in and protect his sister. With women's liberation these days, something Brennan understood and welcomed, perhaps there would be some who would sneer at the notion of a girl or a woman looking to the men of the family, the brothers, for protection.

But, no, surely people would see this as a situation where someone — in this case, a man, but the reasoning applied equally to a woman — close to the victim knew of the abuse and made no effort to stop it. Brennan was a strong opponent of the death penalty, judicial executions anywhere in the world, and that's what had been meted out to Darragh McLogan. It hadn't been planned, premeditated; it was a result of Etty once again seeing her brother fawning upon Jem O'Daly instead of standing up to him in the name of the McLogan family.

Brennan's mind turned then to Shay himself. Everybody knew how important promotion is to a policeman, and Shay Rynne was a good policeman. Coming from a poor area of Dublin, growing up in a Corporation flat, he had been dismissed by his fellow guards as a corner boy, a lad from the tenements who, sooner or later, would show his true colours and revert to criminal or low behaviour. He had proven them wrong. Brennan knew how Shay's determination and skill had solved the murder of his childhood friend. Sure, he had taken a step backwards with the gun incident, which Shay had revealed to him one night when they were out together in New York. Brennan believed him when he said he had taken the guns for use in the North, to defend the people under siege. He hadn't told Brennan how the guns were to get to the North, but Brennan had a fairly good idea who the Dublin connection might have been. In the wake of that incident, as Brennan understood it, there was a superior officer who had it in for Shay, who apparently knew what Shay had done. The man had held this over Shay's head for years, hinting that he would reveal it, portraying it as all the proof anyone needed that Shay Rynne was a low character and always would be.

But Shay had defied the begrudgers and had done excellent work on the cases that came his way. Now he had solved the murder of a prominent politician. Brennan, on his knees in this ancient place of worship, tried to clear his mind about the dilemma facing Shay. Surely, he would have to identify poor Etty O'Daly as the killer. Brennan knew his own conscience would forever trouble him if the woman was sent to prison for the rest of her life. Even if she was convicted of manslaughter, she would likely spend years in a cell. Her family would be devastated. But what of the McLogans? They deserved to know, at long last, who was responsible for Darragh's death and to know that justice would be done.

When Brennan was back in his apartment, he rang Shay, and they got themselves agitated about it all again. Shay again brought up the bombings of this year and the years previous, and the indications that nobody was ever going to be held to account. And Etty O'Daly would be prosecuted and jailed for the unplanned killing of her brother.

What Brennan said next offered Shay no comfort, but it would go a long way towards offering justification for an arrest. "Think of it as seeing justice done for Muriel McLogan and her family, even if there is no justice for the victims and survivors of the bombings."

"I know," Shay agreed. "As a guard, that should be my first obligation. My duty to the McLogans."

Neither of them spoke for several seconds, and then Shay said, "If I do it, if I go for Etty, I'd be spoiling for the chance to go for Jem as well, for all the beatings he inflicted on her. But that would bring out in the open her motive for killing Darragh, so I can't go after the fucker."

"Unless worse comes to worst . . ."

"And she gets convicted. If that happens, God forbid, but if that happens, I'll have TD Jemser O'Daly behind bars in the Joy." Mountjoy Prison.

"And if that's how things go, and that history can come out, the court may show some leniency in sentencing, given what she suffered. Let's hope so, anyway."

"Let's hope so," Shay echoed. But he sounded far from hopeful as he bade goodbye to his friend and counsellor.

CHAPTER XXXII

"**I**'ve been hoping for a place like this to call home, Shay."

By "this" Allie meant Dalkey Castle. They both had the day off; it felt like summer in mid-September, so they had taken a day trip to the little coastal town of Dalkey with its big, imposing Norman castle and lovely harbour.

"Someday I'll present you with the keys to a place just like this, Allie, I promise you."

"'Someday' sounds a little too far away, love. I'd like it for April."

"April?"

"Lots of space for the three of us."

He looked at her. "The three . . ."

She couldn't hold it in. She moved to Shay, threw her arms around him, and made her announcement. "Our first little Rynne is due in April!"

Shay greeted this news with a joy he could never have imagined; he clasped her to him, kissed her, and then twirled her about in a dance of celebration. Their day in Dalkey passed in a blur of happiness. He was over the moon about becoming a father. He had an unnerving moment when they drove back into Dublin: he thought of the pregnant woman who had been killed in the recent bombings, and another woman's baby who was stillborn a few months later. How could Shay ever hope to protect his family from an attack like that? But he did his best to blank that out. They called in on Allie's and Shay's families, and they were all euphoric. There was a celebration in their local pub, Moroney's in Pearse Street, and everyone was on the drink except the expectant mother. And she was every bit as merry as the rest of them.

But in the workaday world, Shay knew there could be no more faffing about; he had to make a decision about Etty O'Daly. More than three years had passed since the death of Darragh McLogan. Shay wondered whether there was anything in the murder inquiry files that pointed to Etty's guilt, even if the connection had not been clear at the time. If the only evidence was her statement to Shay, a judge would almost certainly exclude it from any trial. It was not a cautioned statement; it had been made without the protections the law affords to those accused of a crime. And nobody apart from Shay and Brennan knew she had made it. So, as far as the guards and the courts were concerned, it didn't exist.

Now that his father had been cleared, Shay felt entitled to look at the files relating to the case. But still he would prefer to do that without DS Griffith or, God forbid, McCreevy, looking on. So on Tuesday, he delayed his departure from Store Street until his superior officers had left for the day. Then he pulled out the files.

He skimmed over the witness statements from the party and found nothing that would have raised suspicion about Etty. He turned to the forensics reports and saw the reference to construction debris and other material on Jem O'Daly's sock, the blood of Darragh McLogan on Darragh's own right shoe. And then he saw something he had glossed over on earlier readings of the documents. Apparently, others had glossed over it as well. But now it could be crucial.

Inside McLogan's shoes were traces of a glue that was used by shoemakers and shoe shops. This finding had not raised any alarms; it was just a type of glue that would be found in shoes, and it was found in McLogan's loafers. But Shay knew from his painful conversation with

Etty that this glue had come from her own high-heeled shoes and had been transferred to McLogan's shoes. Physical evidence linking her to the killing. But if this glue was a common item found in other people's homes, it would not necessarily implicate Etty.

Shay was loath to upset Muriel McLogan again, but he was determined to follow the trail, especially if it led to the innocuous finding of the product on the shelves of the McLogan household. So there he was once again at the house on Amiens Street. Muriel answered the door, and the expression on her face left little doubt that she was indeed upset to see him. The widow was gaunt, pale, haunted-looking. She and her family had spent three years grieving for Darragh, three years not knowing who had taken him from them. So it was not just courtesy on Shay's part when he said how sorry he was to be bothering her again. "But we review our unsolved cases from time to time, as you might imagine," he babbled, "and I wanted to ask you something."

"Yes?"

"There was a trace of something found out in the back garden and, em, here is my question: did anyone here at the time of your husband's death have a kind of glue that is used for shoes? Not regular household glue, but —"

"No, I don't remember ever seeing anything like that. I've never heard of it. We have the regular glue for papers and that, but not the kind you're asking about."

What Shay felt was disappointment; he had not been presented with an innocent explanation for the stuff found inside Darragh's shoes. He also had a feeling of shame; here he was, hoping for something that would help acquit the person who had killed the McLogan family's husband and father. But he knew his course was set; he was going to carry through with his plan. If he arrested Etty, that would meet his obligation to Muriel and her family. If Etty was acquitted, well, he had done his duty as best he could. He said a hasty thanks and goodbye, and made his retreat from the widow's door.

As he walked back to Store Street Station, he went over the witness statements in his mind. Nobody had said anything that would have implicated Etty O'Daly; there was nothing about an argument or tension between her and Darragh. With the exception of Etty and Jem, and Muriel, of course, everyone had left the party while Darragh was still up and walking. Most of the guests had known, or been able to estimate, what time they had departed. One man, Rooney, had not been very precise, but given his reputation as a cadger of free drinks, he may have been incapable of remembering when he stumbled out into the night. Shay had not been present for the interview with Rooney; the man had been on the other team's list. His statement showed that he had in fact said very little about his time at the house, but he "thought" it was fairly early when he left. And, Shay now recalled, of all the witnesses who had mentioned Rooney, none had said they had seen him leave. But then again, none had seen him have any contact at all with Darragh McLogan; the impression left with the guests was that Rooney had wormed his way in to wet his throat, and he'd had little to do with the events of the evening, political or criminal.

Should Shay go and speak to the man? What was he hoping for? Was he hoping that a conversation with the cadger would somehow throw up enough dust to obscure the trail leading to Etty O'Daly? As in, *Here's a man who can't account for his whereabouts after midnight, so the inquiry remains open until such time as concrete evidence can be produced against a suspect.* Well, whatever his motive, Shay decided to pay him a visit.

He got the witness's full name, Clary Rooney, and his address from the file, and he set out on foot, alone, to his home on Summerhill. He figured that the tried-and-true method of loosening someone's tongue with drink would be especially effective with a man like Rooney. But he had reckoned without the fact, soon apparent, that Rooney lived with his mother, was caring for her in her old age, and did not drink at home. Shay learned all this when he arrived at the Rooneys' tiny rundown terraced house, introduced himself, and was shown into the cramped little sitting room. The old lady was reclining in a chair, wrapped in a blanket, and Rooney was standing there sober as a Belfast Presbyterian on a Sunday afternoon. But Shay would have a go at him anyway. When Rooney heard that Garda Rynne's visit was related to the McLogan murder, he suggested that they go into the kitchen and Rooney would boil the kettle for his guest and his mother.

Shay mustered as much patience as he could while Rooney fussed with the tea things, and then he gave his spiel about a periodic review of the file and asked his questions as the two of them stood facing each other.

"How well did you know Mr. McLogan?"

"Ah, not well at all, but I knew some of the other fellas who were there."

"Were you invited to the party?"

His face coloured at that. "Well, not exactly."

"What do you mean by that?"

"I was walking by and heard the music, saw people on the front step, and some of the fellas waved me in."

"Who did that?"

"I don't remember now. Long time ago."

"Did you have a conversation of any kind with Mr. McLogan?"

"Well, no, except for nodding and saying hello. He was busy with the party men, you know, the political men."

"What time did you leave the house?" Rooney's reaction was surprising. He looked down and his face flushed again. "Mr. Rooney? Nobody seems to know when you left."

The man gripped the countertop and then made his admission. "It was very late when I left."

Late? He had told the other guards he thought he'd left early.

Rooney choked his next words out. "It wasn't until after . . ."

Christ, what was this? "After what?"

"I had a load of drink in me, and I needed to have a slash. I went looking for the toilet. There was one upstairs and one on the ground floor, but there was somebody in each of them. So I headed down to the basement, and there was a laundry room and it had a sink and, well, I had a slash in the sink. And I was so fluthered with the drink that I passed out in that room without even . . ." More embarrassment here. "Without even zipping myself up. I fell unconscious. And by the time I came round, I looked out . . ." Rooney picked up the teakettle, but his hands were unsteady, and he set it down with a clatter.

His mother called out then. "Clary! My tea!"

"You'll have it in a jiffy, Mam."

"What did you see, Mr. Rooney?" Shay demanded. "A man was murdered, and nobody's been brought to law over it. You have to tell me."

"That room, it's the basement. There's a window. You can see the back garden, and I looked out and saw a man's legs. They weren't moving at all. I . . . I very quietly walked up the cellar stairs and outside. And . . ."

"And?"

"I saw him. Darragh."

"Yeah, you saw him. So, what did you do? About the man lying there, mortally injured. Or was he dead by then?"

Rooney lifted his hands and covered his face. He choked and began to sob. Then his mother called out again, and Shay cursed the timing. "I'd better —"

"Yes, go and see to her."

So Shay waited, his left leg shaking as it often did when he was impatient, waiting for something to happen. When Rooney came back, Shay asked again, "What did you do? Anything at all for the man lying there?"

"I didn't . . . I couldn't . . ."

"Why couldn't you?"

"Because of Jem."

"What about him?"

Rooney looked away, and his voice was barely audible. "I knew he'd been there. Out there with Darragh."

What? What was he saying? "What do you mean, he was out there? When was he out there?"

"His scarf was there. I'd heard the lads slagging him about it at the party. A scarf that said 'New York Police' on it."

This sounded vaguely familiar. Hadn't Shay heard or read something about a scarf? He couldn't recall the details. All he said was, "Go on. Tell me."

"It was lying there beside Darragh. Beside his hand, or maybe he even had hold of it. I can't remember. But I — The problem was I didn't see it until I, well, I stepped on it."

"It was beside Darragh's hand and you were so close to him — his body — that you stepped on it?"

Rooney nodded his head. Tears were spilling from his eyes.

"Why did you go so close to him?"

"I . . . didn't know if he was, if he was still alive."

"And was he?"

Now it was a shake of the head. "I don't think so. I panicked! There I was, stepping on that scarf, my shoe on it, and my shoes were dirty with mud and, I don't know, stuff from all the construction next door. And I . . . This will sound foolish to yeh." How could it sound any worse than what he'd already admitted to? "I like to read, you know, those detective stories. And it's always about fingerprints or the sole of somebody's boot or shoe, and the mark it makes. And I . . . I fuckin' panicked that the peelers would find my footprint, the shape of my shoe, and they'd find out and come for me!"

Shay couldn't resist. "And here I am."

"I didn't do it! It wasn't me. It was . . . It was Jem's scarf out there. Maybe Darragh grabbed it off him!"

"We didn't find a scarf."

"No. I told you I panicked. I took it and then I was scared someone would see me with it, so I stuffed it away."

"Stuffed it away? Where?" Shay knew there had been no scarf found during the search of the back garden. But could this be evidence that Shay could use to direct suspicion away from Etty? Away from Etty to her abusive husband? No, that was out of the question. Taking guns for the defence of the persecuted people in the North was one thing, but trying to fit up someone for a murder that his wife had admitted was just not on.

"There was a pile of earth and grass in the garden next door. It looked as if it had been dug up or disturbed, and then patted down again. I ran over there and shoved the scarf under the dirt and patted everything down again, and then I fucked off home."

"Well, first thing tomorrow morning, you're going to fuck off to Store Street, and you're going to give us a statement."

Rooney had the look of a man who knew he could no longer avoid his fate.

ꙮ

Back at Store Street, Shay tried to recall what he had heard or read about a scarf. He couldn't remember, so he retrieved the file and began to read. Ah, there it was: Stacy Magee had said Jem O'Daly was wearing a New York Police Department scarf he had been given in New York, and there were a lot of comical remarks about it over the course of the evening. As the evening grew cool, and Stacy was serving drinks out in the garden, she mentioned the cooler temperature, and Jem had offered her the scarf. She declined, and he then put it on Etty, and she apparently kept it on. The piece of evidence that Clary Rooney thought pointed to Jem O'Daly pointed instead to his wife. Had it fallen off during her attack on McLogan? Had he pulled it off her? Either way, there was physical evidence linking her to the murder.

When Shay got home that evening, he was on the phone to Brennan Burke in Rome. "I'm sorry to be pestering you again, Brennan. But you're the only one I can talk to about this."

"No bother at all, Shay. And no apology required. What's on your mind?"

"I now have evidence I cannot in good conscience ignore." Shay told him the story and gave him a phone number.

ꙮ

Brennan wanted desperately to go to Dublin, but there wasn't time. So he had to use the telephone to offer whatever advice and comfort he could. "Etty, what I have to tell you is . . ." This was one of the most difficult, most agonizing, conversations he had ever begun. "You are going to be arrested, Etty."

411

"Oh, God!" she cried out. "Oh, God!"

"I know, I'm so sorry. But Shay Rynne asked me to speak to you, give you a warning of what is to come."

"I . . . I don't think I can . . . I won't survive this!"

"You will, Etty." He had no certainty that she would, but he repeated it. "You'll survive it, and I have some things to tell you to help you through this. I'll be on my knees praying for you; I'll be saying Masses for you. But what you need right now is some practical, secular advice. First of all, whatever you do, don't give the guards any information. Don't make a statement; don't answer any of their questions, no matter how harmless the questions may seem. The only thing you say is that you want your solicitor. And you must hire a very good, very experienced defence solicitor."

"I can't believe this conversation, Father Burke. I just can't believe I've got myself into such a fix!"

"I know, Etty, I know. Now, about solicitors?"

"I don't . . . Jem has . . ."

"Don't use one of your husband's lawyers, Etty. Get one of your own. I can get names for you."

"I know of some good ones who do, God help us, criminal work!"

"Now, as you know, I myself am not a lawyer. But I know this much: whatever you told Shay Rynne —"

"No! He's going to tell them everything! He told you!"

"No, he isn't. And I myself never told a soul, and never will. Shay confided in me because he wanted my guidance, my support, because this is so upsetting for him. He doesn't want to do this, Etty, but he has to. Now, here's what is vitally important: what you told him was not a proper statement, was not done according to proper procedures. He did not give you a caution, did not recite the lines about 'You are not obliged to say anything, but anything you say may be used,' or however it is worded. Because of that, it is highly unlikely that whatever you told him would be admitted into evidence by a judge. And nobody else knows about it. In other words, as far as the guards and the courts are concerned, there has been no statement. And you'll not be giving one. So whatever evidence they may have will be much weaker than any admission by you. And there has been no admission."

"This will kill me!" Her voice was shrill with terror. "I'll be in prison. I'll never survive that! And my family, they'll disown me. And Darragh's family! Muriel, the children . . . And it's all my fault!"

If only there was a defence of "She has suffered enough." This woman's anguish over facing her family would be punishment enough, a sure means of deterrence. *Your Lordship, she will never offend again.* She broke down weeping.

In the face of all this, Brennan was not about to bring up the subject of Jem and the crimes he had committed against her. Shay had said, and he was right, that the situation with Jem would open the door to the question of motive in Etty's trial. Jem's abuse and Darragh's failures to confront him were the cause of her attack on Darragh. Any word of this in court would bolster the case against her. And who knew what Jem would do in retaliation if she made her accusations public? That would have to wait.

The phone conversation ended with Brennan seeking assurance that she had understood the importance of his advice: to remain silent and call a solicitor. All he heard was the sound of a woman wailing the end of her life, and then the phone went dead, severing the connection between herself and Father Burke.

CHAPTER XXXIII

The day after Shay's visit to Clary Rooney, Shay and DS Griffith brought their jittery, nerve-racked witness into the Garda station and took his statement. Rooney stuttered through his recollections, wide-eyed and shaky. As if he was the one facing arrest. Or perhaps facing the wrath of Jem O'Daly. Then, later that day, Shay and Griffith were standing in the McLogans' back garden in Amiens Street while a Garda team began digging in the garden next door, looking for a scarf that had been buried there more than three years before. Shay caught a glimpse of Muriel McLogan peering out her window, and the pity he felt for her went a long way in easing his conscience about having Etty charged with the killing.

In the neighbouring garden, there were flagstones, piles of household goods that had been pitched out back, and small patches of grass and weeds. So it was no easy task for the guards. But after a couple of hours, they called over to Griffith. "We have it. This must be it." Griffith and Shay walked over to take a look. Shay said, "That's it." The cloth was filthy with dirt but it had been white, and there was a New York Police Department symbol visible on it.

Etty was the only one home when Shay and DS Griffith arrived at her Sandymount house to make the arrest. Shay knew that Father Burke had spoken to her, warned her, counselled her. If the truth be told, Shay had been hoping she had fled the jurisdiction, gone off to England again. But no, here she was. She burst into tears and collapsed at their feet, and they had to lift her and help her to stand. Shay and Griffith took her in their car to Store Street Station and gave her the required caution: "You are not obliged to say anything unless you wish to do so, but anything you say will be taken down in writing and may be given in evidence." Shay sent up a prayer of thanks that she was savvy enough, following Burke's persuasion perhaps, to ask for her solicitor. And she said nothing before the solicitor arrived and nothing after that.

She was released on bail, and Shay was not privy to whatever excruciating conversations must have occurred in the following months, between her and her family, her and the McLogans.

The jury trial got underway in the Central Criminal Court on March 10, 1975. The courtroom was located in the great, imposing Four Courts building overlooking the River Liffey. Columns lined the front of the courthouse and encircled the building's high central dome. Etty O'Daly stood charged with the murder of her brother Darragh McLogan. Representing her were a senior counsel and a junior counsel — the defence barristers — and her solicitor. Mrs. O'Daly wore a plain brown suit, no jewellery. She was thin, her face haggard, eyes haunted. There she was, in view of her husband, TD Jem O'Daly, who looked positively murderous himself. And in view of Muriel McLogan and her sons and daughters, their wives and husbands. The judge and barristers in their dark gowns and grey wigs imparted a sense of gravitas to the scene.

Shay told himself it was highly unlikely that the jury would come back with a verdict of murder, which would require proof that the accused intended to kill or cause serious injury to the person and that the person died as a result. The lesser offence of manslaughter was appropriate where the intent required for murder was absent. Manslaughter often involved a criminal act that carried the risk of bodily harm — for example, an assault resulting in an unintended death. There was often an element of uncontrolled emotion or provocation in manslaughter cases, which erupted into violence. Sentences had ranged from no imprisonment at all to life. Usually, of course, something in between.

The trial began with prosecuting counsel's opening statement. And then it was DS Griffith in the witness box, followed by some of the other guards. When it was Garda Rynne's turn, he testified about his role in the murder inquiry, his evidence of the shoes, and his interviews with witnesses, including Clary Rooney. Shay breathed not a word of any incriminating admissions by Mrs. O'Daly. Senior counsel for the defence, Damien McMurtry, SC, was a tall imposing figure of a man. He asked a few perfunctory questions, but Shay was not grilled while in the box.

The state pathologist was called to testify about the injuries and cause of death, and a forensics officer told the court that the kicking had been done with Mr. McLogan's own shoes. The forensics officer then spoke of the glue found among Mrs. O'Daly's belongings at home and the traces in Darragh McLogan's shoes. Again, McMurtry did not spend much time cross-examining the expert witnesses. Shay figured McMurtry would later make the point — likely call a witness to testify — that the shoemaker's glue was a common product and might be found in any number of homes, in the shoes of any number of suspects. If today's witnesses had not been cross-examined at length, Shay knew it would be a quite a different scene the next day with Clary Rooney in the box.

Shay avoided Etty O'Daly's eyes as everyone filed out of the courtroom at the end of day one of the trial.

The trial resumed in the morning, and the first witness was Stacy Magee, who testified about finding McLogan's body and alerting Mrs. McLogan. Prosecuting counsel then asked her about a scarf she had seen on someone at the party. She told the story of seeing the white New York Police Department scarf on Mr. O'Daly, who later put it on his wife. The scarf was entered into evidence. Damien McMurtry, on cross-examination, asked whether she had seen Mrs. O'Daly out in the back garden with the scarf on, and she said no.

Clary Rooney was sworn in as the prosecution's final witness. The man was nervy, agitated — clearly not a willing participant in the trial. When it was time for cross-examination, McMurtry went all out to discredit Rooney's evidence because of the amount he'd had to drink, and because he was the only one who claimed to have seen the NYPD scarf near the body. McMurtry made much of the fact that Rooney had not come forward with his story until confronted by the Gardaí three years after Mr. McLogan's death. When Rooney was finished, counsel for the prosecution wrapped up the state's case.

And then came the big moment of suspense for the court, the jury, the onlookers: would the accused woman take the stand in her own defence? Shay knew the age-old question would have bedevilled the defence team: an accused person faces grave peril if he or she gets up to testify. Prosecuting counsel can be dangerous on cross-examination, can elicit a fateful slip of the tongue or a damning admission. But a jury will always wonder: if the accused is innocent, why not get up and say what happened? What is she hiding? In this case, the defence team decided to put the client in the witness box. And Shay trembled for her.

She began weeping as soon as Damien McMurtry asked her to identify herself. Tears streamed from her eyes, and she made no effort to wipe them away as she whispered her name. She could barely be heard, but McMurtry did not make her repeat her name. He addressed her in a gentle, quiet voice. Shay knew what to expect: Etty would testify that she had put on Darragh's shoes to be more comfortable while cleaning around the back garden after the party. She would deny having the scarf on her when she was out in the garden; she had no idea what Clary Rooney — the gatecrasher who had passed out drunk in the laundry room — was on about.

But that is not what she said. She turned her ravaged face to Muriel McLogan. "I can't do this! I just can't!" Her voice now was loud and shrill. "Prison will be no worse for me than facing you, Muriel, you and all the family!"

Etty's lawyer shouted at her to be quiet, then pleaded, "Your Lordship, may I —"

But Etty talked over him. Her testimony would be for Muriel and the McLogan family. "I am so sorry. I have regretted it every moment of the past three and a half years. I didn't mean for it to happen! Darragh knew Jem had been beating me, many times over the years."

"*What?!*" That was Jem, bolting forward in his seat.

"Mrs. O'Daly!" This time it was the judge imploring her to stop.

But to no avail. Etty leaned forward and declaimed to the gallery. "Darragh did nothing to protect me, to help me. He was more concerned with Jem and the politics than he was about me being beaten black and blue! Prison will kill me!" Now she could barely choke out the words. "But I am so sorry! I don't deserve to live!"

Finally the judge put an end to it. The court was adjourned, the jury released. Etty was escorted from the courtroom. To the cells? Shay wondered. But he knew what would be going on behind the scenes, her defence team telling her exactly what to expect once she was convicted, urging her to rethink the decision to admit to the killing. There would be discussions between the prosecution and defence about the plea, about sentencing, and then there would be a discussion with the judge. It was nearly two hours later when Etty O'Daly was brought back to court to be rearraigned on the lesser charge of manslaughter. The jury had been dismissed. Etty was bent and sick-looking, like a woman who had been given a glimpse of hell. But this was only purgatory; hell was yet to come.

The judge addressed her and outlined what it would mean for her to change her plea, the risk she was taking, the rights she would be giving up. Did she understand? She stood before him and gave him a weak "Yes, Your . . . Your Lordship."

Then she was asked for her plea.

She answered in a whisper. "G—" and Shay saw Damien McMurtry take hold of her arm. She tried again and finally recited her lines. "Not guilty . . . of murder but guilty of manslaughter."

The judge asked her again whether she was making the guilty plea of her own free will, without promise or duress. She answered yes. The judge accepted the plea, and McMurtry eased the defeated woman down to her seat. The prosecuting counsel announced that he accepted the guilty plea for manslaughter and would not be offering any more evidence. The case was then set down for sentencing, when Etty O'Daly would learn her fate, would learn how many years of her life would be lost behind bars.

With a last, furious look at his wife, Jem O'Daly fled the courtroom.

Shay ran after him, ordered him to stop, and commandeered another guard to assist. They placed the raging man under arrest.

CHAPTER XXXIV

The rain battered the windows of the Rynnes' flat in Fenian Street as Shay's family and friends huddled inside, gathered for a celebration. It was the middle of April, and Shay's success in the Darragh McLogan murder inquiry and the arrest of Jem O'Daly for multiple assaults had earned Garda Rynne a promotion to sergeant. He wasn't a detective, not yet. He would do a spell as a uniformed sergeant and then he would go through the interviews for promotion to the rank of *detective* sergeant. He was on his way.

Here he was now with Allie and their beloved week-old baby boy. Everybody oohed and aahed as a joyful Talkie Rynne rocked the contented little black-haired, blue-eyed baby in his arms, and Granny Deirdre sang him a lullaby. Here was Shay, basking in the pride of his da Talkie, his ma Deirdre, his family and friends. Detective Sergeant Colm Griffith and Finn Burke were there, raising their glasses to him. Even little nephew Kevin had been permitted a small glass of porter. In the child's other hand was a toy Garda car, which he waved about with the requisite sounds of a motor. Also present, of course, was Des Creaghan, that other boy from the flats, now with Ireland's national broadcaster, and his wife, Fiona. All of them were here to celebrate the triumph of Garda Sergeant Shay Rynne.

Des had a story ready to go on RTÉ. He had cleared it with Shay, and Shay was all for it. The story would open with the exemplary police work and promotion of Shay Rynne, the boy from the Fenian Street flats who had confounded his critics and shown that he was no mere corner boy. Shay was the peeler who had solved the Rosaleen McGinn and Darragh McLogan murder cases. He had arrested TD Jem O'Daly for his long history of battering his wife. Creaghan would make it clear that Etty O'Daly had not intended to cause her brother's death, but had lashed out in a fit of rage and despair over what she saw as his failure to protect her from Jem. Mrs. O'Daly had been sentenced to five years for manslaughter; she would almost certainly be released early for good behaviour.

Creaghan's story would continue:

> Garda Rynne makes no effort to hide his sympathy for Mrs. O'Daly and what she endured, but he knows that justice had to be done for the McLogan family. Now the question must be asked: When will we see justice meted out to those terrorists, many of them known to the authorities on both sides of the border, those men who came into our cities a year ago and deliberately murdered more than thirty of our citizens, and left hundreds more maimed and injured? And how about the men who set off the bombs in 1972 and 1973? When are they going to be arrested and tried?

The story would be on the radio tomorrow, but Shay wanted to bask in the joy of today. Late in the afternoon, he made a call to Rome, and Father Brennan Burke offered his blessings and congratulations.

"Thank you, Brennan, and thank you for all your help with . . . my work. You know how much it meant to me. And now I've a question for you, a theological question. Is it permissible for a man to be named godfather to a baby if the man is more than a thousand miles from the christening? Would there be an exception if the man is in the holy city of Rome? Or would the man have to be present for the christening of little Brennan Thomas Rynne?"

"I . . ." Brennan began, and then there was silence. Was this Brennan Burke at a loss for words? Not for long. "I'll be honoured. I'll be there. For you, for Allie, for Brennan Thomas Rynne."

AUTHOR'S NOTE

The following characters were real, not fictional: Jack Lynch, Charlie Haughey, Frank Sherwin, Father Flash Kavanagh, Father Bartholomew Cavanagh, Ian Paisley, Mickey Spillane, Maureen McManus Spillane, Eugene McManus, Jimmy Coonan, Owney Madden, Joey Gallo, Garret FitzGerald, and Brian Faulkner. All other characters, including Paddy Healey as victim of the Talbot Street bombing, are fictional. The Arms Crisis and related trials were real events, as were the bombings and the burning of the British Embassy. And there really was a spy in the Garda, a detective sergeant arrested in December 1972 for passing secret information to his British handler. There was evidence that he was not the first such spy to be recruited.

At the time of writing, no one has ever been charged for the 1972, 1973, or 1974 bombings. This despite the fact that, in 1993, the Ulster Volunteer Force (UVF) claimed responsibility for the 1974 bombings in Dublin and Monaghan and boasted of the "successful conclusion" of the operation.

ACKNOWLEDGEMENTS

I would like to thank the following people for their kind assistance in researching and writing this book: Retired Garda Detective Liam Browne, Joe McGuinness, Ronan Holland, Colm Wallace, Kevin O'Callaghan / Ordnance Survey Ireland, Frankie Quinn / Belfast Archive Project, Joan Butcher, Joe A. Cameron, Rhea McGarva. And Myra Donnelly, Brideen Morgan, and Nollaig Bonar, the Dublin members of our ciorcal comhrá. Thanks as well to a shady character, who shall remain nameless, who shared her expertise in phone-tapping in Dublin. And to my daughter Pauline: thanks for introducing me to the Landmark Tavern in New York! As always, I am grateful to my very astute editors, Cat London and Crissy Calhoun.

The people I have thanked here helped me at various stages of the research and writing, or with various points of fact, procedure, or law. That should not be taken to mean they necessarily share the perspectives or opinions of my characters.

Any liberties taken in the interests of fiction, or any errors committed, are mine alone.

℘

The following books and publications proved invaluable in the writing of *Fenian Street:*

Barron Reports, and reports of the Houses of the Oireachtas, Joint Committee on Justice, Equality, Defence, and Women's Rights, on the 1972, 1973, and 1974 bombings. Several reports, 2003 to 2005.

Brady, Conor. *The Guarding of Ireland: The Garda Síochána & The Irish State 1960–2014.* Dublin: Gill & Macmillan, 2014.

Cadwallader, Anne. *Lethal Allies: British Collusion in Ireland.* Cork: Mercier Press, 2013.

Conway, Kieran. *Southside Provisional: From Freedom Fighter to the Four Courts.* Dublin: Orpen Press, 2014.

Dillon, Martin. *The Dirty War.* New York: Random House, Cornerstone Digital, 2012.

English, T.J. *Paddy Whacked: The Untold Story of the Irish American Gangster.* New York: Harper Collins, William Morrow Paperbacks, 2006.

English, T.J. *The Westies: Inside New York's Irish Mob.* New York: G.P. Putnam's Sons, 1990; St. Martin's Paperbacks, 1991.

Keane, Daithí. *The Irish Mob.* Documentary TV series, shown on Netflix, 2016.

Kearns, Kevin C. *Dublin Tenement Life: An Oral History.* Dublin: Gill & Macmillan, 2006.

Kearns, Kevin C. *Dublin Voices: An Oral Folk History.* Dublin: Gill & Macmillan, 1998, 2001.

Madden, Lyn and June Levine. *A Story of Prostitution.* Cork: Attic Press, 1987.

Mulroe, Patrick. *Bombs, Bullets and the Border: Policing Ireland's Frontier: Irish Security Policy, 1969–1978.* Newbridge: Irish Academic Press, 2017.

O'Connor, D'Arcy and Miranda. *Montreal's Irish Mafia: The True Story of the Infamous West End Gang.* Toronto: HarperCollins, 2014.

Ó Faoleán, Gearóid. *A Broad Church: The Provisional IRA in the Republic of Ireland 1969–1980*. Newbridge: Merrion Press, 2019.

Tiernan, Joe. *The Dublin and Monaghan Bombings (and The Murder Triangle)*. Cork: Mercier Press, 2000.

Wallace, Colm. *The Fallen: Gardaí Killed in Service, 1922–49*. Dublin: The History Press Ireland, 2017.

Leabharlanna Poiblí Chathair Baile Átha Cliath
Dublin City Public Libraries

This book is also available as a Global Certified Accessible™ (GCA) ebook. ECW Press's ebooks are screen reader friendly and are built to meet the needs of those who are unable to read standard print due to blindness, low vision, dyslexia, or a physical disability.

Get the ebook free!
details inside

At ECW Press, we want you to enjoy our books in whatever format you like. If you've bought a print copy just send an email to ebook@ecwpress.com and include:

- the book title
- the name of the store where you purchased it
- a screenshot or picture of your order/receipt number and your name
- your preference of file type: PDF (for desktop reading), ePub (for a phone/tablet, Kobo, or Nook), mobi (for Kindle)

A real person will respond to your email with your ebook attached. Please note this offer is only for copies bought for personal use and does not apply to school or library copies.

Thank you for supporting an independently owned Canadian publisher with your purchase!

Printed on Rolland Enviro®.
This paper contains 100% sustainable recycled fiber, is manufactured using renewable energy - Biogas and processed chlorine free.

100%

PCF

BIO GAS®
ENERGY

PERMANENT